DEADLY ACCOUNT

DEADLY ACCOUNT

JERE G. MICHELSON

Michelson Publishing
Printed in the United States of America

First Edition: Fall 2018

www.michelsonpublishing.com
The publisher is not responsible for websites (or their content) that are not owned by publisher.

Library of Congress Cataloging-in-Publication Data
Michelson, Jere G.
Deadly Account / Jere G. Michelson – First Edition

ISBN 978-0-9980282-0-0 (hardcover)
ISBN 978-0-9980282-1-7 (softcover)
ISBN 978-0-9980282-2-4 (e-book)

For my dear family,

Jennifer

Ian and Sydney

IanSydious

1

*H*indsight is 20/20. I never liked that phrase, and today I like it even less. I remember the first time I heard it many moons ago, and I asked my father what it meant. In his 'Dad' voice he said something like, 'well Jon … it means if you have the benefit of knowing what will happen before it happens, then you'd be able to anticipate and change what happens.' I think I said to him his explanation doesn't help me at all. He just laughed and said he could see why. To him it sounded a lot like a politician's excuse for a broken promise.

I can't help but obsess over that old proverb now. How in God's creation could I have known that in just a few moments from a chance interaction with a total stranger, fifteen people will die? Countless others won't make it home after work tonight, either. Their workday will end prematurely, stressing the resources of our local hospitals and urgent care centers. Maybe I could have made a difference if I had some reasonable mindfulness of my surroundings – and possibly a crystal ball to see into the future. I possess neither.

It's just that there was something about his face and his pancake nose that struck me familiar and anxious and I felt like something wasn't right. It was the kind of nose Rocky Balboa wound up with after he lost his first fight with Clubber Lang; the tip pressed in, nearly touching his upper lip with a wide nostril flare. It looked as though he went toe-to-toe with a clothes iron – and lost. This guy had all of that and what looked like a marginally successful cleft lip repair. The briefcase he carried was out of place with the rest of his get-up. He might have been as tall as I am, maybe even taller than six-foot two, but he had what appeared to be a pretty rock-solid physique, much unlike my waspish frame. His faded jeans and tight black t-shirt clashed against the over-sized black leather briefcase more suitable for an accountant or lawyer than the main antagonist from Rocky III.

I guess I should feel lucky. By that point, there would have been nothing I could do to stop the bomb that destroyed literally half of the Portland Bank & Trust building even if I acted on my gut. I can tell you first-hand; Survivor's Guilt is a real syndrome. It all unfolded incredibly quickly.

When I went into the bank that morning, I needed only to stop and withdraw cash for my March Madness college basketball tournament picks in the office pool our firm hosts. I work for Harding-Williams; auditor extraordinaire and soon-to-be certified public accountant, Jonathan Kirouac Williams, at your service.

When I finished with my withdrawal, I exited the bank through a maze of fabric-roped tension barriers, not unlike moving through an airport TSA security checkpoint. Before I went back to the office though, I needed to make a stop for doughnuts and a coffee from Dunkin' Donuts across the street. I passed him just as I went through the door and when I saw him, I momentarily lost my balance. As I steadied myself, the briefcase he carried landed against my thigh with an audible 'thud,' followed by the delayed onset of pain. Exactly the same as when you stub your toe and initially feel nothing, but you know by the count of three: one, two, three … the pain train enters the station. I angrily cursed myself for being chronically clumsy. After immediately processing the event, I dismissed the entire episode just as rapidly. I had a coffee with my name on it and an audit meeting to get back to. If I was lucky, my co-worker and best bud Santa saved a chair for me somewhere in the vicinity of Alison.

Dunkin' is located about a one-minute walk from my office, and it's a straight shot. I breeze in and out quickly, and with a to-go order in hand, turn back to cross the Union and Middle Streets intersection. There he goes. I see Rocky III exit the bank and disappear around the corner – without his briefcase. This is where my 'Hindsight is 20/20' experience begins, and the existence of the Harding-Williams office building ends.

I'm down to the wire for arriving at our office meeting on time, and I stand perched at the crosswalk waiting impatiently for the 'walk' signal. The traffic lights finally turn red, and the moment my foot reaches pavement, I'm physically staggered by an ear-shattering blast followed almost instantaneously by the southern base of the building blowing out in a fine mist. Two concussion pulsations smash into those of us nearby in successive waves, causing everyone in the vicinity to reel backwards. I immediately jam my fingers into my ears, attempting to relieve the tremendous high-pitched hissing pressure hammering me, as does a young woman standing to my left. Cars coming up the south-side street skid to a halt, buried under a coating of pulverized concrete. The initial destruction is surreal, almost dreamlike, and it's not finished yet.

Traffic lights detached from a snapped support pole nearest the building barrel-roll across the street toward a few of us frozen in place. I vaguely recall thinking that close up they're a lot larger than I expected. Miniature trees jutting out of city planters imbedded within the concrete sidewalks burn like candles on a birthday cake. Downed electrical lines sizzle, with some shooting sparks like Morning Glories on the Fourth of July. I struggle to take in the whole of what unfolds in front of me; and frankly, a part of me feels as though my mind has made this all up.

Fire burns from the southern side at every floor of the building. Molten material, in what I can only describe as 'fire blobs' about the size of tennis balls, systematically rains down to the courtyard below. Black smoke billows from ruptured openings where walls existed just seconds ago. The choking smell of the smoke reaches us rapidly; it has a pungent, oily feel to it that undeniably can't be good to breathe in. I can see people on the third floor dangling from window ledges by their arms and drop-ping down below. They don't go far; rubble and wreckage reaches well above the second floor. Panicked and injured people climb down and flee the area, dodging debris and each other. The woman beside me screams in horror and disbelief, and I turn away in heartbreak as we bear witness to someone jumping from the fifth floor – my office floor.

It doesn't take much longer for the heavily damaged southern face of the five-story building to eventually succumb to gravity and slide down to Earth, burying the hopefully now-vacant vehicles jammed up on the street from the initial explosion. I can only watch in shocked silence. The pandemonium of surrounding external stimuli overwhelms all of us.

It isn't until the dust settles that the rest of nearby traffic stops, and the city screeches to a halt. In stark contrast, the northern side of the building appears untouched and what remains of the south side looks like television reports of the Alfred P. Murrah Federal Building following the Oklahoma City bombing.

Like some giant demon came up and took a massive bite out of one whole side.

2

Fifteen short minutes ago I was sitting upstairs from the bank in my over-sized, wall-less, window-less workspace in 'The Bull-pen' at Harding-Williams; the leading certified public accounting firm in the Greater Portland, Maine area.

We occupy floors three through five of the five-story Portland Bank & Trust building. The bank occupies the lobby and second floor. Harding-Williams resulted from two of the former Big Eight accounting firms whose local offices opted to pull out of Portland, essentially giving up on the unappealing and idiosyncratic Maine business climate. Add to that the monumental collapses of shady-run companies like Enron and WorldCom, and all of the regulatory challenges coming into play for Big Business, and the decision was easy. Some partners had no stomach for picking up stakes and relocating to Boston, and others had no stomach for standing in the unemployment line, so they merged practices and Harding-Williams resulted.

The Bullpen exists for the newer associates who have next-to-no seniority in the firm and are not yet viewed as marketable assets, or competent accountants some would argue. We're more akin to a herd of cattle in a feedlot; ten first- and second-year associates seated around an over-sized table more suited for a Thanksgiving gathering than auditing. When all of the staff are in the office, it looks like an absurd version of the Last Supper.

Fortunately, I've managed to squeak by the certified public accountant exam. Once I finish two years in public accounting, I will have satisfied the requirements for becoming a CPA. That alone will earn me a private cubicle and rid me of my 'Bullpenner' status. Honestly though, I'm not sure how I got through the exam, and I suspect more than a few partners at the firm wonder the same thing.

We each have a laptop, land-line telephone extension, and zero privacy. I'm especially disadvantaged, as this lack of privacy cuts deeply into my internet browsing time. My fantasy league standings suffer immeasurably.

When I finished college, I had no honest expectation of working in public accounting, let alone slog through a second year of busy season. I would have been just as happy, probably more so, bartending or maybe getting into beer-making. Without a doubt, I had plenty of practice with quality control and taste-testing in our college fraternity house. I was a marginal student, but I could crank it up when I had to. I think the only reason I got hired at Harding-Williams is because I commented during my job interview, at great risk, that my name is already on the building. It might save them on business cards somewhere down the road.

Good thing there aren't as many accounting students these days to compete with. The one hundred-fifty credit-hour rule, essentially requiring a master's degree to obtain a CPA license, steers a lot of students away from accounting and into business or finance majors requiring less credits. Four years of college classes is plenty for most. I stuck it out only because I was trying to prolong my time with my Sigma Epsilon brothers for as long as I could before having to actually work.

"Let's head down, Jon."

When I hear this, I instinctively lean over, look past the Bullpen wall, and take in the sight. It's Alison Brigham. She smells as captivating as she looks. I enjoy it when she says, 'let's head down' – her signature expression, as she breezes past the Bullpen. Alison is two years ahead of me in tenure; a second-year senior and on the threshold of becoming a manager. She's my direct supervisor on several engagements, and as far as I'm concerned, she is welcome to participate in any engagement with me – in or outside of work. I go out of my way to insert myself into as many client relationships as I can that she manages.

I am more than delighted to routinely trail her to the fifth-floor conference room for our weekly audit department training and planning sessions. It affords me the opportunity to continue eye-balling her rear-view at a leisurely pace until I catch up. I'm not customarily attracted to shorter women, but Alison's an exception. Five-foot two never looked so good except when enveloped in long, chestnut hair leading to breasts so eloquently, albeit immaturely, described by my fellow Bullpenner Ben Crindle as 'racktacular.'

"Hold up, Jon." Ben says, fiddling with a file folder.

Big Ben Crindle is an ex-jock nicknamed 'Santa,' who occupies the workspace next to mine. Most think he's referred to as Santa because 'Crindle' sounds a lot like 'Kringle.' It's a reasonable assumption; however, his nickname didn't come to pass until he entered into a long-term relationship with a girl whose name is Merri Moss – and her middle name is Kris. If two people were ever meant to find each other, this would be them.

Santa is light years ahead of me in audit process knowledge but cannot for whatever reason pass the CPA exam. Exam anxiety, maybe. For this reason, he can't be promoted to manager, let alone partner, not that he cares. Santa isn't long for the public accounting world, and I can't blame him. He once confided in me he would swallow a few happy pills before starting the exam process just to ease his anxiety. I suggested he may want to try something a little stronger instead.

Santa played college football, anchoring the offensive line for the perennially underachieving Dartmouth Big Green. He's a midwestern, cornfed-type with no neck, making him look like his round face is too little, and his brown eyes are too close together. But he's a heck of a nice guy and would do anything for anyone.

"Wait up." He says as he catches up to me.

"Hey bud, I've only got about a fifteen-minute buffer before the meeting." I reply in a hurried voice while breaking away from my covert stalking of Alison. "I need to go downstairs and get some cash for Andy and then I'm going for a coffee. If anyone asks, tell them you saw me on the phone with a client … and save me a seat."

"No problem. I'll get one next to Alison. Hey," he calls out as I'm hustling to the stairwell, "bring me back a doughnut, will ya? One with frosting."

"You pull off the seat next to Alison and I'll bring you two."

But first, hit the bank for cash. I'm in no mood to listen to Andy dress me down for a late payment. He's our administrator of the March Madness pool; a partner in the tax department, and a real pain in the ass if you don't get your picks in on time or honor your other sports-related gambling deadlines.

3

The hum of emergency sirens steadily intensifies from seemingly every direction. My heart sinks as I race to the courtyard with no real idea of what I can accomplish. I make it as far as the sidewalk some fifty feet from the building before my open path disappears. People covered in dust and ash scurry about frantically; some wander directionless, and others simply stand and stare. It looks eerily similar to the footage of the World Trade Center attack, though on a smaller scale.

Shredded, charred paper wafts down from the sky, reminiscent of a bizarre ticker-tape parade celebrating a world champion sports team. Ash and debris roll low, rumbling along the cobblestone searching for an escape route. I know immediately where the bulk of the 'confetti' stems from – our file room occupied the fourth floor on the south side and the library sat directly above it on the fifth floor, opposite from our conference room. Both appear to be *simply gone*.

Most likely as a result of endlessly watching the September 11th footage of the collapse of the North and South Towers in New York City, it seems no one has any expectation the building will stand indefinitely. There is no orderly filing of tenants exiting the building; people stream outside from every which way, and oddly, at that moment I'm reminded of smashing open my ceramic piggy bank when I was ten years old and watching the chaos of coins scatter randomly as they hit the floor.

I'm beginning to see through pockets of haze and smoke as air particles settle out. I'm constantly rubbing my eyes, though; my contact lenses feel like sandpaper scraping against my eyelids each time I blink. Activity around me undoubtedly happens much more quickly than I'm processing – time appears to move in slow motion. Rescue personnel – police, firefighters, and EMTs, dart throughout the crowd attempting to triage the wounded and bring about some degree of order to the area. Intermittent crackles emerge from walkie-talkies, interspersed with the shouting of instructions.

My thoughts shift to Harding-Williams employees. I continue forward, and then pause when I feel my cellphone vibrate in my pocket. I reach down, and almost without thought, look at the number expecting, hoping, to see Santa's number. It's my mother. How in the hell could she have heard about this so quickly? As usual, I reject her call and continue my push against the human wave flowing against me.

People continue spilling from exits and I begin to see familiar faces from co-workers. Panic rises in me steadily as my senses become clearer and the shock fades somewhat. Police cordon off the area as first-responders enter the building amid the chop of helicopters arriving over-head.

HW employees stream out; some of them battered and bruised, some bloodied. We have roughly two hundred total employees, and Lord only knows how many were in the building this morning. I feel a glim-mer of hope and relief realizing the majority of people would have been in the fifth-floor conference room opposite the blast area getting ready for the audit meeting.

No sooner do I think this when I see Alison standing on the back side of the building in an open-air parking lot frantically waving an arm as she yells into a phone. I can't really tell if she's injured, but one side of her body droops considerably lower than the other. At least she's able to talk on the phone – that's a good sign.

As I step closer to her, I realize she looks relatively unscathed. Her clothing is immaculate, and her hair as fine as always. When I look down to her feet, I see one heel has broken off of her shoe causing her body to sag.

"Alison, are you okay??" She appears at first not to recognize me.

"Wha … huh?" She cuts off her phone conversation. "Holy shit, Jon! Holyshiiiiit!"

"Alison, where's Ben?" I shout, though she's only two feet from me.

"He's gone!" She bawls in a warbled pitch, tears streaming.

"What?? What?? How do you know that?! … Tell me!" I'm in a full-on panic and feel like I've been kicked square in the gut.

"Because I saw him in the stairwell. He got out ahead of me and I haven't been able to find him outside anywhere!"

"Jesus Christ. I thought you meant he didn't make it out alive."

Alison takes off her undamaged shoe and we shuffle with the flow of people at the direction of police. I can see up ahead where we're relocating to. A crowd funnels into a barricaded area, preventing anyone from backtracking toward the building. Most talk breathlessly into their phones.

I hear another crackle of a city police officer's radio indicating a full mobilization of law enforcement, including FBI and Immigration and Customs, to find and apprehend the attempted robbery suspect or suspects. I think back to the guy I bumped into earlier. This doesn't strike me as a robbery. If Rocky III went into the bank with a black briefcase and came out without one, I'm thinking they need an FBI anti-terrorism squad.

Santa sees us as we approach the mass of people. He's jumping up and down to get our attention and we wiggle through to get over to him.

"WHAT THE FUCK HAPPENED??" Santa gurgles, like he has a Dixie-cup of mouthwash in his throat. "Jon, are you okay? We didn't know if you had made it back into the building or not." He says with a face so red I think he may pass out.

"No ... no." I trail off almost incoherently as I re-live the image of the building erupting in front of me. "I, I hadn't made it back yet. I was on my way when I saw the whole thing happen from out here."

It might be better not to rehash the event too deeply until I have a chance to process it myself. I want to know what happened to my co-workers, my firm, and my livelihood.

My phone rings again. It's my mother. You couldn't script this any better. Reluctantly, I bring the phone to my ear ... "Hey."

4

"JK, thank God you picked up! I worried myself sick when you didn't answer my first call. Are you hurt, are you alright?" She prattles on a little too breathlessly.

She calls me 'JK' like it has a magical meaning to it for us. It's 'Our Special Name.' Really it began when I was a kid just to differentiate me from my father – also Jonathan. We have different middle names, so using 'Senior' and 'Junior' didn't quite work. Even though my father has passed, she continues to use it much to my dislike.

"I'm okay, Ma, I wasn't in the building."

I can't bring myself to call her 'Mom.' Saying 'Ma' is detached. Using 'Mom' has a bit too much emotional closeness to it for me.

Rewind a dozen years back, and the former Sabrina Williams, now Sabrina Garibaldi, decided on a lovely summer day in July she no longer loved my father, nor did she have any desire to be a mother – at least an involved one. My last memory that day was of watching the back of her head disappear as she left the house and listening to the side door slam shut with a resonating 'clang.' Undoubtedly, she was acting upon a decision she had made some time ago, because she did not leave alone.

Lorenzo Garibaldi held the door open for her, though I didn't know who he was at the time. I vaguely remembered seeing him behind the counter at the laundromat we used in town. My twelve-year-old self didn't readily put it together they were a couple. Is he here for our dry cleaning?

Enzo, as he is called, wears a lot of gold. I was advised in grade school, and with a child's conviction, that Italians wear a lot of gold and they are the only ones who look good in it. Like the old television show says – kids say the darndest things!

My father was heartbroken. We heard the car backing out of the driveway, and when we were finally able to look away from the door and then look to each other and talk, I asked him if he wanted to go bowling. I don't really know why – in retrospect to break the ice, I suppose. He said he wasn't really up for it right now if that was okay with me.

He died just four short years later when I was only sixteen. His cause of death was listed as a heart attack. He surely did die of a broken heart.

"I'm watching the news and I see a bank robbery or something going on …"

As she shifts into verbal overdrive, my mind drifts a thousand miles away while the meaningless buzz of my mother echoes in my ear. The color of the scene playing out before me slowly drains into a grayish blur not unlike the sweeping motions of a charcoal pencil drawing. If you've ever watched 'VH1 Classics' and seen the music video *Take On Me* from *a-ha*, circa 1986, then you know exactly what I'm talking about.

"… thank God you were outside and not in the building!"

That strikes me back to reality. "How did you know that?"

There's a perceptible hitch in the connection and a slightly too-long pause.

"I, I just assumed you'd be nearby on a work day and if you answered your phone you'd be outside."

An officer addressing the crowd of people abruptly announces through a bullhorn he and his crew will be collecting names and contact information from everyone for follow-up questioning. Santa and Alison are required to have a medical evaluation as well, because they were in the building, though I guess they could refuse. I suppose a psychological evaluation may be part of the protocol as well.

"Ma, I gotta go; it's crazy out here and I have a lot to do." The 'crazy' part is true, though I don't really know what I need to do at the moment or where to begin. I'm kind of playing this all by ear, but I know I have to get out of here and head to my apartment to try and regroup.

"Please call me later, JK, okay?"

We both know it won't happen. It's way too late for her to try and be a mom now – the best either of us can hope for is to be friends. That may happen someday, but not now.

I refocus on the scene, noticing Alison and Santa drifted away from the perimeter of the triage area and stand up front in hastily-formed lines. Uniformed officers with clipboards take down contact information, so I cut into line with them.

"After we get finished here, can we meet later for drinks?" I'm hoping this isn't too casual a statement to make given the current state of affairs, but really, I don't want to be alone tonight.

Alison chimes in first. "Absolutely, I don't want to be by myself tonight."

Serendipity! That's music to my ears. This is a great opportunity to connect – when emotions are running high.

For a moment, I kind of feel a little badly, but quickly it passes. Who am I to reject a beautiful woman in her time of need?

We make plans to connect later on tonight, so I'm hopeful their medical evaluations will be perfunctory. Santa jabbers with a 'clipboard cop' but I have no doubt he'll come out and bring Merri along, too. I like Merri; she's easy on the eyes and can almost keep up with Santa drink for drink and she can easily kick my ass.

5

It takes me a few tries to get the key into the opening of the lock. The doorknob on my apartment could use a healthy dose of rust-buster lubricant to free it up, but today that isn't the cause of my difficulty.

My hand trembles somewhat as I try to line up the key with the keyhole. A sobering reminder of what just happened across town and its effect on me. I live on the west side of Portland in an old gray Captain's house that has what would now be deemed a sub-standard in-law apartment. It's a dingy, one-bedroom walk-up, but the price is right and I have unlimited heat and hot water. I also spliced into the owner's cable, so all things considered, it's a good deal. He lives on the first floor and I don't see him much; he keeps to himself which is fine by me.

Inside, I keep reminders of my father visible everywhere. Pictures of us together over the years hang on the walls, though there aren't many – pictures or years. I have an old telephone of his in the shape of Snoopy, with his dog-arm extended to cradle the receiver. I don't have a land-line telephone number; it sits out only for decoration. Every piece of furniture I have comes from him save the *Ladies' Man* waterbed carryover from the early nineties my uncle gave to me. My father's brother was my keeper growing up. Without him I don't know what I would have done, or where I would be. He gained custody of me at sixteen when my father died. My mother pretended to fight it, but it was clear it was for show. He was around eleven or twelve years younger than my dad, and a bachelor – still is – so to me he was as much an older brother as a father figure. Man, I had independence. He wasn't around much, and I had no curfew – not that I abused it. He's a life-time merchant mariner for an oil company, so he's usually at sea for months at a time.

I turn the television on and move into the kitchen to get the first of many beers I will consume tonight. The flat screen flickers to life on News12, my standard morning channel, with not-unexpected mid-report coverage of the event in Portland.

Man, this is big. Big like nothing we've ever seen before in our city.

> "… confirmed by Federal agents and state law en-
> forcement officials to News12 this past hour in Port-
> land, Maine as what was first described as a bank
> robbery attempt gone awry, but later confirmed that
> it appears to have been aimed at a specific target lo-
> cated within the bank …"

Huh, they're right, and they got there quicker than I thought. I need to tell someone what I saw at the bank this morning. I'm supposed to get a call from Portland police for an interview tomorrow, so maybe I'll wait until then. Black Briefcase Guy should be on twenty different surveillance cameras in and around the bank. Police, FBI, whoever; will key in on him quickly.

I move over to the couch to watch the coverage with one hand reaching for my phone and one hand on my Pabst Blue Ribbon. Nothing beats a cold PBR.

> "… possible ties to terrorist cells in remote areas of the
> U.S. …"

As the reporter drones on, the news camera pans throughout the damaged building complex, open plaza, and roped-off gawkers looking for their fifteen minutes of fame. Some position themselves to be as visible as possible, not unlike those posturing for the outdoor camera at the *Today Show* in Rockefeller Plaza.

I'm not sure who to call first, not that I have a lot of choices. I start dialing Santa's number when the phone drops from my hand. In the backdrop of the reporter and among the people at the scene, I also see … *Enzo*?? God damn and my mother's with him. What the fuck is she doing over there?

At that moment, I receive a text chime from Santa, pulling my attention away from the television:

'A's' is Asbury's, a kind of hipster bar but with cheaper drinks and plenty of PBR on tap. Most of the younger office worker crowd make their way to Asbury's at some point for happy hour during the week as well as hang out on weekends. I've managed to hook up a few times there (though Pam was a psycho – but that's a story for another time), so I'm pretty much a regular now. Still, my hookup-to-attempt batting average is so low I'd be riding pine on a junior varsity high school baseball team.

Asbury's is crosstown, so either I have a long walk, or an Uber call ahead of me. Our typical short bro conversation continues:

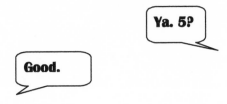

I let him know I'll connect with Alison, and he ought to make sure Merri comes. Santa saves me the Uber call and says he and Merri will pick me up at four-thirty.

That's perfect. I can hardly wait for four-thirty to arrive. In the meantime, I see a quick nap in my future. As my adrenaline rush fades, I'm feeling wiped out. I need to rest and recharge for tonight.

6

F ive o'clock couldn't come fast enough. I had to shut the television off – not because I couldn't fall asleep with it on; I just couldn't bear to listen to the reports any longer. Names of the victims were starting to come out. I'm on a new text thread from co-workers indicating Roger Contreras and Sarah Jarowicz from our office were killed in the blast up to now. Some are still missing and many more are wounded. I'm tormented by the thought it more than likely may be Sarah I witnessed jumping from the building. News reports indicate the bank has suffered the majority of casualties which is exactly what I hoped for and expected, understanding our all-office audit meeting was taking place on the opposite side of the building.

Sarah was our file room manager. Despite advanced technology and the world's imminent migration to electronic records; accountants, especially the Old Guard, still are comforted by their fair share of paper shuffling. Sarah made certain all of the paper in need of shuffling was in perfect order. She was a fifty-something woman who was undeniably the sweetest person I've ever met. I'm resolute in my conviction to spill everything to the FBI and police in my morning interview.

Santa arrives precisely at four-thirty. He drives up next to the base of the side-entry staircase and rolls his passenger-side front window down.

"Hey, get in shotgun." He calls out as I'm making my way down the stairs.

He is the most punctual dude I've ever met. Not so with me. No doubt the reason why I was outside during the blast instead of preparing for the meeting.

I get in the car and right away I hear, "Hi, Jon." It's Merri.

"Hey Merri … Why are you sitting in back?" I say, leaning over my shoulder to look at her. She's a bit on the chunky side, but the curves are absolutely in the right places and I'm okay with that.

"I spoke with Alison earlier. We're picking her up at her mom's house. I thought you two bromance buddies would enjoy the front seat."

Apparently, Alison didn't go back to her apartment, but rather to her mom's house which I discover isn't far at all from my place. Nice, this is seriously turning into a double date. Again, for a split second, I feel a pang of guilt for attempting to capitalize on a tragedy, but just as rapidly as the first time, maybe even quicker, it passes.

We arrive at a well-preserved, brick center-chimney home sited within immaculate grounds, with Alison crossing the front yard before we can even come to a full stop. Sweet Jesus. She wears tight faded jeans with a number of trendy 'accidental' rips on the thighs. She complements them with an ultra-tight, faux-worn out J. Geils almost-sleeveless white concert t-shirt. She couldn't get in the vehicle fast enough; it looked as though she might jump in the backseat *Dukes of Hazzard*-style through an open window.

"Get me the hell out of here and to a bar." She declares.

Ahhh … from the lips of an angel. My boner, which took notice of her outfit immediately, wholeheartedly agrees.

Asbury's is active tonight, but decidedly somber. Our building complex isn't very far away; maybe a mile or two. As Tiger's latest arrest dominates the wide-screen televisions surrounding us, we start the ball rolling with cocktails and PBR for me, but it quickly regresses into shots and a drowning of sorrows of sorts. I'm actually impressed with Alison's ability to handle her business. No training wheels on the tequila shots – straight up – no lime, no salt.

We spend a great deal of time talking about and toasting Roger, Sarah, and our wounded colleagues as well. Earlier, Alison contacted two of the nearby hospitals; they won't let visitors in outside of immediate family. I recall my story of witnessing a jumper from the top floor and my educated guess as to who it was. We sit for a long while in devastated silence.

Alison thumps her now-empty shot glass onto the table startling us, winces a bit, and asks if anyone saw Bob this morning. Bob is Bob Roberts; whose full name is Robert Roberts. Bob is a long-standing audit partner in the firm, focusing on manufacturing and industrial companies. Alison does the majority of her work for Bob as the Partner-In-Charge. I've often wondered; who the hell names their kid with the same first and last name?

Bob is probably fifty, has two ex-wives that I'm aware of, and subscribes to the *I'm Newly Divorced And Need To Lose My Gut To Attract A Girlfriend* method of fitness. He rides his bike to work on occasion and tries to talk cool with the younger staff; all in a losing effort. He still has an over-sized belly, balding pate, and the nastiest breath of anyone I've ever met – bar none. I cringe on the rare occasions he needs to come into the Bullpen to talk to one of the associates. I just sit there thinking, can't he smell that? Once, at a company outing, we had a Tug 'O War contest whereby Bob was unluckily positioned directly behind me. As he strained in a full-on, face-reddened, teeth-clenched exertion, I swear I could smell the stank permeating through his cheeks.

As I consider Alison's question, I'm looking at her, and I realize something isn't right. A tear streams down her face and before I can say a word, she breaks down into a heaving, drunken mess.

"I've been sleeping with Bob!" She blurts.

I don't know that I heard that right.

"Really?" Santa chirps in an unusually high-pitched tone, completely astounded.

"Yes ... I, I really don't remember how it started, or why, but, but ..."

Ugh. She begins to run off her whole relationship timeline with him half-coherently, half-not, and all I can think of is *Good Lord, how can you stand that breath?*

Alison abruptly gets up and heads to the bathroom with Merri following closely in tow.

"Can you fucking believe that?" Santa says.

I have nothing really to say but I slightly shake my head, mouthing 'no.' I have no idea why, but at this moment I'm strangely more attracted to her than I have ever been.

After a few minutes, the girls return to the table and an awkward silence hangs over the booth. I begin to try and break the ice, but Alison cuts me off.

"I have to tell you and Ben something."

She always calls him 'Ben'; never 'Santa.' Come to think of it, I've never heard Merri refer to him as anything. Santa and I exchange a quick glance. He has a stupid look on his face and at that moment I think he looks a little cross-eyed.

"I hope neither of you judge me about Bob." No one at the table utters a peep. She continues on. "I knew it was wrong when we started, but I was lonely, bored, whatever; and I didn't know how to get out of it. What I'm going to say doesn't leave the table ..."

Alison is clearly in charge now. She pulls herself together and is back to, or almost back to, her old self despite being drunk.

"Bob called me last night. I think he might have been drunk or possibly on something, because he was super difficult to understand. He told me he's made some bad choices and his life had fallen apart."

I can see that despite Alison's hard veneer, cracks are starting to show. Her bottom lip begins to quiver slightly, and clearly it's bothering her because she's trying in vain to rub it out.

"He was crying and saying to me he's done some inappropriate things with General Defense and he's in trouble. I tried to calm him down and have him tell me what's wrong. The nearest I can tell is he may have colluded with them on inventory valuation issues ... or something like that ... asset misappropriation or manipulation, but it was hazy."

"Seems a bit dramatic for a late-night call and a breakdown." I say.

She dismisses my comment with a trace of annoyance. "You're right, it's more than that."

"That's your client." Santa injects. "You've audited their financials. What'd you see?"

"That's the thing." Alison blusters. "Bob always did the inventory attestation. He said there were idiosyncrasies surrounding inventory and it was easier for him to deal with it; plus, the client preferred it that way. I never really thought twice about it. It's always been done that way even before I was on the engagement."

Everyone's silent. Merri's the first to talk.

"I'm not getting the significance here, but there's a spooky vibe going on. What's the deal with General Defense?"

I want to hear more about the Bob affair, but Santa responds to Merri.

"They're one of our largest, if not the largest client of ours. They run a billion-dollar weapons defense company providing weaponry, munitions, and other really cool shit to the U.S. government and other law enforcement."

Alison follows up with a more detailed explanation:

"Their marquee product is what's called a *suppressed weapon system* for the U.S. military – Army, Navy, Air Force, and Marine Corps. They also supply Special Forces and Counter-Terrorism units throughout Europe, Central America, Asia, and the Middle East. They hold a patent on a specific 'suppressor' design which is like a high-grade silencer for automatic weapons."

"Holy shit, that's badass." Merri says.

"Yeah … it's badass." Alison agrees. She goes on, "I told Bob I would see him this morning at work and help him sort through whatever mess he thinks he may have gotten himself into, but he hadn't come in before the explosion. I've tried to call him a bunch of times today, but there's no answer."

"I wouldn't worry much about it given what's happened today." Santa says at virtually the same time I mutter, "Don't worry about it."

We order another round of drinks and I tell Alison to just catch up with him in the morning. With all the mess happening in our complex today, it's not a stretch that she couldn't connect with him.

"Well, now it's my turn." I begin. That gets me the attention I'm looking for. I'm not sure where to begin, or how much of my morning to disclose, so I just go with a stream of consciousness. The trip to the bank

… the Rocky III encounter … coffee at DD … the departure of Rocky III without the briefcase … the destruction.

I finish my story with downing my beer in one take for dramatic effect. When I begin speaking again, a foamy belch comes chugging out of me like a runaway freight train. We all start laughing, which triggers beer suds to shoot out of my nose. This makes us laugh even harder and sets off the beginning of the end to our night at Asbury's.

Alison says, half-laughing, "Are you really serious about what happened to you this morning?"

"Yeah, for real."

"Man, you gotta tell somebody, bro." Santa adds.

"I know, I know." I say softly. "I needed to process what the hell happened today, and I also wanted to talk to you guys about it before I did anything. When I'm in my police interview tomorrow, I'll tell them everything."

The night is still fairly early, but we're pretty much wiped out. What started out as a crazy, sad day morphed into a bizarre evening to say the least. Santa calls for the bill and I reach for my phone to call an Uber. Santa says he'll take us all back using Homerunners. They're a car service that comes to get you with two drivers. One person to drive you home in your own vehicle; another to follow and pick up the first driver. Twenty dollars plus one dollar per mile. Not a bad deal. I note Santa has the phone number on speed dial.

Homerunners shows up at A's, and Alison goes straight back to the third-row seating in Santa's ride.

"Jon, come back here with me."

I glance at Santa, try to keep my cool, and then join Alison while Santa and Merri climb into the second row. As we ride across town to the West End, I feel Alison's hand brush up against mine, and very naturally, we begin holding hands. It feels like a jolt of electricity coursing through me. We make the short ride back to my apartment pretty quickly, and as we approach my driveway, I look at Alison and silently mouth, *come up?* I think I'm being smooth, but it probably looks more like Will Ferrell in *Old School* after he accidently shoots himself in the neck with the animal tranquilizer dart. She simply nods, 'yes.' We both exit the car right away and thank Santa and Merri for coming out tonight, not pausing to allow time for any questions they may want to ask.

7

W e clomp noisily up the rickety staircase, giggling and partially using each other for support. I imagine my landlord listens to us wondering what the hell is going on, but I don't let it sidetrack me from the important task at hand.

I struggle between fumbling with the lock and keeping Alison squeezed between me and the door out of fear for her falling backwards down the steep stairs. It's no easy assignment with the both of us buzzing this hard, and I worry she may feel I'm being overly aggressive with how I'm positioned. I needn't have worried though; upon entering my apartment, Alison happily announces she has to pee and makes a beeline for the facilities. My apartment isn't all that big, so she doesn't seem to have a problem finding it. I'm doing a rapid processing of the state of affairs of my apartment – dishes are passable, trash is taken out, I can't remember what my bedroom looks like; but I know the bed isn't made, and I'm sure I left the toilet seat up.

Oh well. I go over to the kitchen and grab a bottle of vodka from the freezer and club soda and cranberry from the fridge. I mix a couple of drinks, still waiting for Alison to come out. Either she's taking humankind's longest pee, or maybe, just maybe, she's 'getting ready.'

Alison eventually finishes and joins me on the couch. She plops down, letting out an audible sigh.

"I feel as though I could sleep for a week." She says as she shifts sideways, putting her feet in my lap. I take the opportunity to slip off one of her shoes and begin to rub her foot.

"Ahhh … that feels nice. Thanks, Jon."

We're relaxed and feeling good, talking about her family, where she grew up, college and such; all the while I alternate the rubdown between her feet. Her parents divorced when she was in college (Mom got the house, I note), but up until then she had a fairly idyllic upbringing. I'm not much interested in discussing my family tree, so I casually redirect the conversation back to her each time it comes up.

Eventually the night gets long, and I thought the evening was drawing to a close as Alison finishes her drink, but instead she rolls off of the couch and walks to the kitchen, returning with the bottle of vodka. I watch in amazement as she pops the cap, takes a gulp, and passes me the bottle. I take one. Periodically over the next hour we alternate with the vodka shots. I'm getting pretty shit-faced, so I need to find a way to slow the roll, but Alison beats me to it. Abruptly she stands up, wobbles slightly, and without a word reaches back for my hand to encourage me to stand up as well. With her entire hand squeezing just my index finger, she leads me to my bedroom while looking at me with a sensual look I swear I can taste. She turns the light on as she enters the room.

"I want to see everything." She purrs.

Meow. I don't respond – I'm mesmerized. She stops at the bed, puts her hands on my shoulders and gently spins me around so the back sides of my knees are leaning up against the railing, and pushes me backwards. I flop down, then shimmy to the center of the bed and she immediately crawls on top of me. The weight of her body resting on mine feels so good. Like it belongs. We belong. I don't think I've ever kissed some-one so deeply or passionately; I didn't want the moment to end.

Alison props herself up onto her elbows so she can look at me.

"This waterbed is funky." She says playfully.

I wrap my arms around her, snaking up the back of her too-tight t-shirt, to meet a three-row clasp bra. She kisses me wildly as I pop them one at a time. When I get them all, she presses herself up to her knees and begins to grind herself into me, riding hard.

Still lying on my back, I rapidly take my shirt off and throw it to the floor. Alison reaches for her shirt, and with crossed arms in one swift motion, slips her shirt and bra over her head and heaves it to the floor.

I can hear the angels singing from the happy choir of Heaven.

She has the body of a goddess – good Lord, please let this not be a dream. As I reach for her breasts, she begins to mouth something to me.

"What?" I whisper. "I can't hear you."

Alison sways considerably. Shit … oh shit, is she … is she gag-ging??

My voice rises quickly. "Hey, are you okay?? Are you gonna pu …"

The volume and velocity of puke is as impressive as I've ever seen. Perhaps more impressive are the retching sounds coming from this tantalizing picture of perfection. I employ a Navy SEAL-worthy escape maneuver from underneath her and pop off of the bed as the first wave of vomit splashes onto me. Alison flops face first into the pillow, passed-out cold. God damn it. I roll her onto her side, clearing blankets from her face so she won't pull a Jimi Hendrix and choke on her throw-up.

Alright, now what? I need to get a bucket. On second thought, it would probably be better for me to move her to the couch and position a mop bucket on the floor to the side of her head. That way I can keep a close eye on her and clean up in here.

Picking her up is no walk in the park, however. She's essentially motionless, dead weight, and Christ she smells foul. I reach underneath her shoulder closest to me and attempt to slide her to the edge. This is no easy task in a waterbed. Her boobs are staring me in the face and I feel a brief pang of remorse for what will not happen tonight. I pause, go to my dresser and pull out a t-shirt, then clumsily tug it over her head and arms.

Attempting to move her again proves just as difficult. I slide her as close to the edge as I can to attempt to 'forklift' her like I'm going to carry her over the threshold on our wedding night. Her upper body slips out of the crook of my arm and she lands on her back with a resounding 'thud.'

I instinctively freeze like a deer caught in the headlights.

Alison grunts, but otherwise doesn't seem fazed. I interpret this as a positive sign and pick her up from her underarms and back-walk her toward the couch, legs dragging behind her. This feels like a scene out of a Three Stooges episode, minus one of the Stooges.

After hoisting her up onto the couch and fetching a pillow and blanket for her, I spend the rest of my night alternating between making sure Alison's airway is vomit-free and performing a hospital-grade de-contamination of my bedroom.

8

Morning comes exceedingly quick. Mainly for me because I was up nearly until dawn. Sunlight blazes through the double-hung window, illuminating a galaxy of dust suspended in its beam. Alison is still passed out on the couch, but I'm reasonably confident she's through the danger zone and I don't need to watch over her any longer. I cleaned her up as best as I could; I washed her face and tried to swab her hair to at least get the chunks out. Coffee's going – I'm pretty hung-over myself, so I'm preparing for the worst for her.

I'm not sure what the heck we're supposed to do today relative to work. Clearly, we can't go back to the office – there is no office. I have my police interview scheduled in a couple of hours at eleven o'clock, but other than that, I don't know what to do. In one of our periodic office training sessions, I vaguely recall going over a Continuity of Operations Plan, or CO-OP, awhile back; its intention to protect the firm and recover and preserve information and resources in the event of a catastrophe. If this doesn't qualify as a catastrophe, I'm not sure anything would. I think there's some sort of off-site work and data recovery action plan if disaster strikes. I suspect clients must be attempting to bombard us with questions and concerns.

I drop into an armchair with my coffee and phone. I have two messages from Santa already:

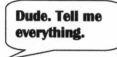

Dude. Tell me everything.

Wakey, Wakey. C'mon...

I respond that I'll fill him in next time I see him. Normally, I'd be psyched to give him the details, but under the circumstances I think this is an in-person update.

While I text back to him, another country is heard from. Alison slowly moves on the couch, and I look up from my phone. She gradually rolls off and without saying a word, trudges directly to the bathroom. I hear the water from the sink running and no bodily noises. That's a good sign. After a minute or two, she comes out and back over to the couch; riding gravity downward more than intentionally sitting.

"Hey." I say.

Her response is somewhat predictable. "Wow, it smells in here. I'm sorry, Jon."

"No worries. It's not a big deal." I lie through a fake smile. "I spent the better part of the night cleaning up and keeping an eye on you. How're you feeling?"

"Not bad, all things considered, but most likely I'm still drunk. I have to confess I don't remember much after getting here. Oh, and by the way I used your toothbrush."

That's fairly incredible considering how much we put down last night; and note to self – get a new toothbrush.

I fill her in on pretty much everything that happened last night, skipping the part about her award-winning *Flashdance* shirt removal sequence and subsequent boobage staring me in the face as I tried to move her from the bed. She picks up on it pretty quickly, though.

"This is your t-shirt?" She says shyly.

Her profile is concealed from me by perfectly placed tendrils of hair and I think that is exactly as she wants it.

"Yeah, don't worry about it. I gave it to you when your shirt … well, uhh …"

"Was soaked in throw-up?" She finishes.

"Um, well yeah, exactly. Uh, do you want coffee?"

"No, but if you have a Coke or Diet Coke that would be great."

I get up and head to the kitchen. Soda's a staple for me and Diet Coke is on the menu. Before I make it to the fridge, Alison calls out, "I got a text from Julie." Julie's our human resources director.

"There's a firm-wide meeting happening today at three o'clock at the University's Portland campus. It's in the Grayson Auditorium. It says to text everyone you have contact information for to spread the word as well."

"I've been wondering what we're supposed to do." I say, setting her drink on the side table next to her. She takes a chug. I continue on, "I have my interview at the police station soon."

Alison takes another drink and places her can down on a nearby coaster. "I'm going to walk over to my mom's house and clean up. I need to check up on Bob and I have my police interview at one-thirty. I'll see you tonight at the firm meeting."

She gets up, moves over to me, and bends over giving me a kiss on my forehead.

"Thanks for babysitting me last night."

I don't say a word. She turns, picks up her soiled shirt and walks out through the door. I can't stop thinking about her. I'm still re-living the moment long after the echo of her footsteps thudding down the stairs disappears.

I have about an hour before I need to leave for the police station. I finish my text to Santa and collapse on the couch in total exhaustion.

9

The police station is a beehive of activity. I'm in a sarcastic, less-than-tolerant mood and it doesn't help that my head pounds like a bass drum during the Macy's Thanksgiving Day parade. People seemingly interview everywhere. A uniformed woman with a clipboard stands near the entrance portico intercepting everyone entering the station. She resembles an officious Walmart greeter. I want to ask if they're violating the maximum occupancy standard for the building but think the better of it.

"Name." She says authoritatively and without the slightest lilt in her voice indicative of asking a question.

"Jon Williams." I reply languidly.

After flipping through what seems like every page, she reaches for a different clipboard. She looks me up and down and in an intrusive tone says, "Through the double doors and take your first left. Room A-32. Second door on the right."

That seems odd to me. People sit at open desks all around me and I'm going to a different area?

I don't have the patience to ask for an explanation as to why I'm re-directed to another location and she clearly has no interest in offering a reason. She's already moved on to the next lucky contestant.

I make my way to the double doors, extending my arm out as I approach to push them open. The doors are unexpectedly locked when I make contact, snapping my elbow awkwardly and jamming my shoulder into the socket from the resistance.

"Christ." I mutter as the sound of a buzzer goes off signaling the doors are now unlocked. They begin to swing open automatically, so I proceed to walk through while attempting to rub out the pins-and-needles feeling in my arm.

I have no trouble locating room A-32. Someone stands in the hallway signaling for me to come down. What the hell's going on, I think as I approach.

"Jon Williams?"

"Yes."

"Agent Scott Brown, Federal Bureau of Investigation."

Brown is straight out of Central Casting. He's completely bald, appears to be in his late thirties and skinny-fit, with the prototypical solid black suit and red power tie.

He attempts to flash his identification badge and quickly put it away, but I intercept it for a closer look. It seems real to me, but what do I know? I can't imagine he would be allowed back here without proper credentialing. I hand it back.

"FBI? What do you want with me? Why am I back here?" I try to sound calm, but I'm fairly sure I'm not successful. There's a distinct uneasiness in my voice matching my disposition.

"Relax Jon, we're back here for a little privacy. Come on in and let's talk."

Agent Brown opens the door and motions for me to enter. As I pass through the entryway I see the room is fairly dim. When my eyes ultimately adjust, I see someone else. I can't take my eyes off of the man with the pressed-in nose and scarred lip. Rocky III – the man with the black briefcase.

10

"Ahhh, I see you recognize this gentleman." Agent Brown declares, with what appears to be a macabre touch of amusement. "We thought you may have based upon the interaction you had with him as you were leaving the bank."

"How did you kn ..." I begin to say, but Agent Brown cuts me off.

"Because we noticed and identified you the morning of the explosion through our video surveillance cameras, Jon."

This makes no sense. The FBI staged a bungled bank robbery? They killed and maimed how many people? As I attempt to process this, Rocky steps forward to me with hand extended.

"Mr. Williams, I'm Agent James Reyes; pleasure to meet you. Have a seat and we'll walk you through what took place inside Portland Bank & Trust yesterday. It's important you understand what it was you saw and the confidential nature thereon."

Agent Reyes pumps my hand with enough force to slightly bob my head. He's clearly as strong as he looks. He's wearing much the same suit as Agent Brown, though he fills it out and appears much more the part of an FBI agent. His slight accent betrays a Brooklyn or Bronx-ish tone; one he attempts to mask but hasn't quite succeeded.

Agent Brown begins the discussion. "Jon – you're here because you observed Agent Reyes entering the bank yesterday morning. Agent Reyes reported to us, and we confirmed on video surveillance, you had a fleeting yet impactful interaction with him as you collided with one another. Furthermore, subsequent to Agent Reyes' exit from the bank, our cameras captured you observing him as he crossed the intersection. Then, shortly following Agent Reyes' exit from the bank, the explosion occurred."

Jesus, Big Brother really is watching.

He continues, "We can only imagine how this must look to you Jon; we need to make certain you understand what took place. We don't want to cause panic and alarm within the greater community. We were receiving intelligence from the bank president and senior staff that they believed the bank was under some sort of surveillance. It is unclear to us at the moment what precipitated the suspicion, though we do know the banking industry uses a range of software designed to monitor customary human behavior within the banks' clientele and determine anomalies utilizing intricate algorithms. We consistently work with the local banking community under the Patriot Act to weed out organizations that attempt to manipulate the public through the banking process and engage in serious crimes like human trafficking, elder abuse, fraud, and identity theft. This particular bank however, reported anomalies within physical cash deliveries."

I suspect I have a blank stare on my face, but no matter, Agent Brown is determined to forge ahead.

"As part of our investigation, we charged Agent Reyes with positioning an EMF – Electromagnetic Field – detector in the lobby. The EMF detector was inside the black case agent Reyes was carrying."

His prolonged, undoubtedly-scripted diatribe continues.

"It's kind of a 'black box' similar to what one would find on an airplane. It sweeps the physical area, searching for electromagnetic fields and devices, as well as records data. It can also scan for GPS sources that may track whereabouts of cash deliveries, detect bait money, and in some instances, perhaps disable security features within the bank. But we were too late. We didn't expect an imminent attack to the building. It was sheer luck Agent Reyes didn't get caught up in the explosion."

Yeah, right.

"Why are you telling me all of this?" I ask.

"Because we would like you to understand what transpired, so you don't lead law enforcement in a direction they should not be going in." He replies. "The FBI is in charge of this investigation and we don't want aggravation or involvement with local law enforcement to saddle us in any way, nor do we want to risk public panic."

As I see it, I have two choices: one, I can pretend like I believe them, smile and politely walk away; or two, I call bullshit and ask what really happened. The safe move says I'll go with the former and then get the hell out of here.

"This is sickening on so many levels," I begin, "we lost – I don't even know how many people yesterday – from what appears to be a bank robbery gone awry. Absolutely tragic."

I slowly shake my head side-to-side as I stare reflectively at the floor trying to sell the effect. It seems to work.

"Truly tragic." Agent Brown says, followed with Agent Reyes adding, "Indeed, I'm lucky to be sitting here today."

Agent Brown proffers, "There are fifteen total dead. Two from your office and thirteen from the bank – including their president. Our latest information indicates those wounded are presently in stable physical condition."

"So, I'm guessing we're about done here?"

I wince a bit as I realize I may have oversold the lilt in my voice. Before either answers, I press on, "You all have my contact info if you need anything else from me."

I flash a toothy smile and start to back away hoping they won't re-engage in conversation.

"Thank you for your time, Mr. Williams." Agent Brown states without any discernible emotion.

"Thank you." Agent Reyes chimes in.

I quickly make my way back to the lobby and see numbers have dwindled, but still a great deal of activity takes place. I head toward the front vestibule, and as I reach for the door, I receive a brusque tap on my shoulder. Startled, I wheel around and stand face-to-face with a dude in street clothes.

"May I have a word with you outside?" He says with firmness in his voice. It was less of a question and more of a certainty as he ushers me out ahead of him. When we hit the street, I shake loose of his grasp, albeit a light one.

"What the hell do you want?" I have a healthy dose of irritation in my voice.

"I'm sorry for the urgency. I'm Detective Mike Bond with the Portland police department." He says while handing me a business card. "Listen, I don't have much time to talk. Can we discuss what you saw yesterday?"

"I already explained what I know to the FBI."

"And what did they tell you?" He seems pretty irritated, and I think I know where this is going.

"That they were investigating some unusual activity at the bank and before they could set up monitoring devices, a bomb planted in the lobby detonated in some sort of botched robbery attempt."

"A botched robbery attempt?" He questions with disdain while smoothing back the hair matting to his forehead. "A botched robbery attempt? Do you think an explosive in the lobby could cause that amount of damage? Not a chance. The upper floors blew out more forcefully than the lobby! There was a much bigger target there with a significantly more complex device or system!"

Christ, he sounds more reasonable than the FBI and it seems as though he knows the details.

"Can we keep this between us?" He asks.

"Sure," I reply, "I don't know anything else, anyway." I tuck the business card in my pocket and begin to turn away.

"Good luck." I say as I head out, and I mean it.

11

Dude, can you pick me up for the meeting?

I seriously need to buy a car or at least get a bike. Relying on Santa for rides as much as I do must be getting old for him. It certainly is for me. The walk back to my apartment from the police station area ordinarily wouldn't bother me much, especially if the weather cooperates, but today it's annoyingly cold out.

Before I begin to wallow in self-pity, Santa texts me back:

Ya, be ready at 2:30

Man, I'm not sure what I'd do without him. He sends a follow up text:

Using a phallic eggplant emoji is a nice touch. I have a couple of hours to kill before Santa picks me up for the firm meeting at University Campus, so I stop at Market Deli on my way back home for a bite. I send a message to Alison asking how she's doing, and she responds back that she's functional. Honestly, I'm drag-assing from last night; I'm not sure how she's able to stay upright.

As I begin to text her back, my phone vibrates in my hand. She's calling me.

"Hey. What's happening?" I try to act casual.

"Ugh, I've pretty much slept all morning at my mom's. I'm feeling shitty, but I'm pulling out of it."

She sounds a little raspy, but not bad. She's got game. I'm even more impressed.

"Listen, I'm calling to let you know I'll probably be late to the meeting. I've got a bunch of stuff to do and then I'm going to go by Bob's beforehand. I've been texting him periodically throughout the morning and I'm getting no response. I'm a little worried."

I feel a pang of jealousy at hearing that, but what can I do? I'm certainly not going to say anything right now.

"Got it." I say. "Santa and I will sit out back. Meet us when you get in and if I see Bob when we get there I'll let you know."

"Perfect – thanks. I'll try to slip in unnoticed."

I disconnect the call and walk into the deli where they make my usual chicken salad wrap without me having to order it, and then head for home.

Santa picks me up at two-thirty on the dot. I could set my watch by it if I wore one. No sooner do I open the car door when I hear, "Get in. Did you fuck her?"

"Hey dude, thanks for picking me up." I say, trying to steer the conversation away knowing full well I will fail miserably.

He knows exactly what I'm attempting to do. "Ah, you didn't. Loser."

"Actually, I could lie and tell you I did, but the truth is a hell of a lot more interesting."

I don't think I've ever heard Santa laugh as much or as hard as he did when I finished last evening's narrative.

When we pull up to the parking garage, I let Santa know Alison will be late and meet us in the back of the auditorium. The foyer to Grayson Hall connects to the parking garage, so it doesn't take us long to walk in.

As we enter the building, you can feel the emotion hanging in the air. Sadness permeates everywhere as our co-workers begin ambling into the auditorium. We take seats in the back. A panel of people sits in chairs on the stage including Calvin Harding, the managing principal of the firm. Julie, our human resources director, sits next to him as does our chief operating officer. Muted conversation drifts throughout the room with no real intelligibility; just the indistinct murmur of a crowd.

Calvin stands up and slowly approaches the lectern, generating a sweeping hush over the room.

"Everyone," he begins slowly and softly, "thank you for coming here today. My intent is to pay tribute to those we so senselessly lost and those still suffering. Not only those from our family, but also those within our building – our larger community. We are all suffering."

I can see two large portraits propped up on easels. They are of Roger and Sarah; Harding-Williams' dead.

Calvin reminds me of William Shatner as James T. Kirk from *Star Trek*. He uses gel product in his hair giving him the late 60's slicked-back 'wet look' and has an eerily similar stunted cadence to his speech pattern. I'm struggling to remain focused on the substance of his tribute to Roger and Sarah. I find myself wanting to hear him press Scotty for more power only to learn he's *giving it all she's got, Captain.*

I smile at the thought only to be brought back to the moment by the booming voice of our chief operating officer, Harold Osterman. Apparently, I drifted off on my *Star Trek* voyage where no man has gone before for a smidge too long. Calvin had completed his tribute and turned the meeting over to Harold for the operations portion.

Harold's stature does not reflect the commanding nature of his voice. He has thinning brown hair coupled with wispy baby hairs that are propped up and seemingly defy gravity. It's as though someone rubbed a helium balloon alongside his head and the generation of static electricity caused a follicle free-for-all. Harold's been around the block on this kind of stuff; he knows the ins and outs of this company probably better than anyone.

"Everyone, this is such a difficult time to contemplate moving ahead with operations, but I need to give you an overview of how we are to move forward."

Harold commands the room. "Most of you, if not all, are aware we have a Continuity of Operations Plan, or CO-OP. We intend to set up temporary operations at the Portland Convention Center until such time as we locate appropriate space to lease. In fact, that process is currently underway."

I'm feeling a little guilty because I'm only half-listening to him and fidgeting in my seat. Nevertheless, Harold continues on:

"Concurrent to facilities relocation, we are working on the data recovery process as well. Everyone is aware that our file room was completely destroyed in the incident. For some time now, the firm has been in the process of digitizing our data files and converting our manual filing process into a cloud-based format. As you've no doubt been aware, HW has been systematically moving our working files to the basement and subsequently converting them to digital format with the goal of leaving only permanent documents in the file room. Fortunately, the majority of current work papers in the file room were superfluous. They had previously been converted to digital files that were already preserved prior to the attack. Those paper files were slated to be destroyed once we finished the conversion project. What's left of the paper files in the basement represents about twenty-five percent of our clients' working files – much of which remains intact; the other seventy-five percent had already been safeguarded. Our IT group is in the process of inventorying the client master list for affected files and will circulate information to you as soon as it's available. With that introduction, I'll ask Peabo to walk you through his group's plan on the IT side."

"Wow, that's some serious advanced planning. It doesn't seem as though we'll be out of business for very long." Santa whispers to me.

"Agreed. You think we'll get paid during the transition?" I ask kind of distantly, not really needing or expecting an answer.

My thoughts drift, as they have been periodically, to Alison. I wonder how her police interview went and if she saw the same FBI people that I did. I also wonder if I'll get the opportunity to go out with her again. I make a mental note to slough off any awkward tensions that may linger when she gets to the meeting.

My daydreaming evaporates when my phone begins vibrating in my pocket; I pull it out and see its Alison. I quickly sweep out of my seat and answer "Hello?" in a hushed voice as I exit the back of the auditorium. Santa's looking at me like, 'What?'

"Jon, I'm on my way to get you and Ben." She's clearly in distress.

I'm standing in the auditorium foyer. "What's wrong?" I feel an instinctual protective temperament wash over me.

"I got a package from Fed Ex delivered to my apartment from Bob. It's … it's some kind of a rambling manuscript … I'm not sure …"

"Have you spoken to him yet? I haven't seen him here."

"No. I tried calling in the time between my mother's house and going to the police station, but he didn't answer. Then I went to my apartment before the work meeting and found the package. I'm scared, Jon; I want to go to his house, but I want you to come with me, and Ben too, if he can."

"Yeah, of course. Absolutely. I'll go get him and you can pick us up out front."

I disconnect the call and head back to the meeting.

"Hey, we gotta go." I say a bit too loudly, unfortunately. Heads swing around our way, and I proceed to slink down into my seat.

"What the fuck are you talking about?" He whispers to me with annoyance.

"Alison's coming to pick us up. I'll tell you about it out front."

I relay the general gist of my conversation with Alison to Santa as we wait. He's now as alarmed as I am, and I look less of an idiot and more the part of a caring advocate.

I spot Alison's white Fiat coming up the hill pretty damn fast. She pulls an impressive Tokyo Drift curbside stop, and we quickly make our way down to her.

As we approach the car, it becomes obvious Santa will have an issue getting into the Fiat. I'm riding shotgun for sure, so he needs to get into the back. I'm finding this amusing. The car is a two-door, so Santa alternates between squeezing and wiggling his way into place. As I push the front seat back, his knees jam up to his chin.

"Should take my car." He grumbles.

After I get in, I get my first opportunity to look at Alison and I see clearly she's been crying.

"Hey you." I say, trying to lighten the mood as she speeds off. "Tell us more about Bob's package."

An awkward silence washes over the car.

"Not funny, Jon." Alison is irritated at the remark. I rapidly look to recover.

"C'mon. That's not at all what I meant." It sincerely wasn't. "I was talking about the Fed Ex from Bob. Where is it?"

"Shit. God damn it! I left it back at my apartment! I was in such a rush I forgot to grab it on my way out." Alison sputters.

"That's okay. Just tell us about it." I'm actually really interested in what it says.

"At the bar," Alison begins, "at A's do you both remember when I told you about Bob's mini-breakdown?"

"Yes." We both say in unison.

"It's a confession. The document Bob sent me is a confession. He's tangled up in illegal activity! You've got to read this!"

Alison is on the verge of a mini-breakdown herself it seems.

She goes on, "I haven't read all of it yet; I was too upset, and I want to just talk to him in person. He's involved in a scheme with General Defense and the government!"

"Holy shit!" Santa says.

"Nah, c'mon. This is friggin' Maine for Christ's sake. Who does shit like that?" I say insistently.

We must be getting close to Bob's house. Alison's taken a series of turns guiding us to a fairly high-end neighborhood.

"He's at the end down on the right, gray saltbox, and his Volvo's in the driveway. He's got to be home!"

As we pull up to the curb, I'm trying to process the upcoming conversation with Bob.

> *Well, hello there Robert Roberts. Just two no-bodies from your firm along with your illicit lover at your service for a wellness check.*

I smile to myself at the ludicrous thought as I get out of the car. Alison's way ahead of us; almost to the door, in fact. It's evident she has no intention of knocking; she's fumbling with a key with the clear intent of steamrolling her way in.

I wait for Santa to spring himself from the jack-in-the-Fiat-box before walking up the driveway. Alison's already gone in to look around for Bob, as evidenced by the sequence of lights brightening the interior as she makes her way through the house.

Approaching the entranceway, Santa scowls, "What the hell?"

I look at him and before I can respond, it hits me in the face like an invisible wrecking ball.

"What the fuck is that smell??" I squawk, trying not to breathe out of my nose.

We're assaulted by the foulest of garbage smells that best guess says must have been rotting for days. Dude must've bailed out and left food behind – or his dog or cat died.

Before either of us can pinpoint the horrific source of stench, a gurgling, pitiful squeal cuts through the house. Santa's gone. I barely see him dash up the stairway taking the steps at least three at a time. I briefly think, *hey, that Dartmouth football background comes in handy.* I'm clumsily chugging right behind him, and when I make it to the top of the staircase and to the nearest bedroom, it all falls into place. Bob's home all right. He's been home for quite some time it seems. Alison's on her knees sobbing intensely while Santa stands with mouth agape, looking at him. Bob dangles; dead as dead can be, by a cord suspended from the center of the fashionable tray ceiling of his master bedroom.

12

I unconsciously move the open collar of my shirt over my nose to cut down the stench, never losing sight of Bob. His eyes are blood-shot and swollen; bulging out almost as though they could burst at any moment. The cord around his neck is nearly invisible; the fat folds of his chin wrap around it as gravity buries it deeper into his flesh. He's twirling ever so slightly, reminiscent of a yo-yo fully drawn-out as it dangles from a child's finger trying to get the last portion of the string unraveled.

I'm brought back to reality by the retching sounds now coming out of Alison. She's dropped to her hands and knees. It instantly brings me back to my bedroom and the sensory reminder of her vomit from last night.

"We've got to get you out of here." I say as I bend down to help her up.

"Dude, give me a hand here." I grunt as I struggle to lift her.

I feel like I'm having some sort of bizarre déjà vu. I look up to Santa for a little assistance. God damn, he looks like he's seen a frigging ghost (maybe he has) and now *he* begins vomiting in some nasty, visceral sympathy reaction to Alison.

"What the fuck." I mumble to myself while prodding Alison toward the door. At least she's half-helping me now.

"Let's go." I grumble forcefully to jolt Santa into following us.

After the three of us stumble into the hallway, I quickly shut the door and we collapse to the floor.

"We've got to call somebody." I squawk.

Talk about stating the obvious. No one objects when I pull my phone out to dial 9-1-1. I uncaringly see I have several missed calls from my mother. Now's not a good time, Ma, I have a dead dude I need to deal with at the moment.

Before I begin to dial, Alison finally chimes in.

"I, I think we should w-wait to call anyone." She sobs, near hyperventilation.

"What? Why?" I pause while waiting for her response.

"Are you kidding, Alison?? Bob's hanging from the ceiling for Christ's sake." Santa barks. He's finally come back to his senses as well.

Before she has an opportunity to clarify, we hear the front door softly open and then shut. Instinctively, the three of us freeze, gaping at each other. Muted footsteps begin padding through the downstairs with lights systematically shutting off virtually in the same order as we turned them on.

I look at Alison and she motions to us with one finger over her lips in the 'shhhh' gesture. I make a mental note of how damn sexy she looks doing that. She rises to her feet, waving to Santa and me to follow her down the hallway.

Alison whispers, "We're going to the spare bedroom." She gestures down the hall. "There's a back stairwell to the living room we can go down if someone comes up here."

"What? Why does that matter? Why are we whispering?" Santa breathes back. "Let's go downstairs and tell whoever's here what we've discovered."

Alison throws him a harsh look and motions for us to trail her. When we get to the back room, she turns to us, and very softly she answers Santa questions.

"I read enough of Bob's manuscript to know he was in trouble. This may not be a suicide. What if he was murdered and they're coming back to clean up evidence?"

Her voice cracks hard on that last part.

"Jesus, isn't that even more of a reason to call police?" I answer. Holy shit, you've got to be kidding me. This is fucking surreal.

Before either of us responds further to Alison, we abruptly hear someone lumbering up the stairs carrying what I can only picture in my mind as a vacuum cleaner clattering off of the railing spindles, sounding like a toy xylophone. I envision whoever it is doesn't expect anyone to be here with all the noise echoing throughout the house.

It doesn't last long; seemingly just long enough to walk up and down the hallway and then footfalls resonate as someone descends the stairs. My heart beats in my throat. We hear the front door shut and for a moment all is quiet.

No one says a word. Alison pads over to the door and opens it up just enough to peer through a crack.

"I think we're good." She says quietly, visibly shaken up. "Let's get the hell out of here."

I'm of the same mind. I've had enough of this shit show. Santa and I walk over to the doorway where Alison has already swung it wide open.

"Hold up. Now what's *that* smell? Jon, you smell that?" Santa barks.

"Oh shit! Yes!" I holler. "It's gas! Those ... those were gas cans coming up the stairs! We're in trouble; we've got to get out!"

As if right on cue, the fire trail comes roaring up the staircase; charging down the hallway like a devil-snake escaping purgatory. Alison instinctively slams the door shut and grips each of us by the shirt to encourage us in the right direction toward the back staircase leading down to the living room.

We take the staircase minimum two steps at a time. The base of the staircase opens up on the opposite side of the house furthest from the main entrance. Clearly there was gas sprayed throughout the first floor. Flames crawl all over the interior walls, floors, and ceilings. Acrid, black smoke hangs in the air, making breathing virtually impossible. Again, I pull my shirt over my nose as Alison guides us through the kitchen and out the slider onto the back deck.

"We need to leave before police and fire crews get here." I gasp between hacking coughs. "We can't be found here."

We race around the side of the house. Fortunately, the sun began to set when we arrived, so we have cover in the darkness and there is an abundance of trees and shrubbery to hide behind. We quickly sprint to the car in record time and I dive into the back seat head first for ease of escape. There's no time for Santa to try and squeeze in.

"Hey, go slowly – don't draw attention to us as we leave." Santa instructs Alison as she slams the car in gear.

I manage to prop myself up and look out through the back window as we speed off, witnessing the warm glow of orange just becoming visible from Bob's house.

13

"Oh my God! What the hell just happened?!" Alison trembles as she speaks, causing her Fiat to shimmy side-to-side just to the edge of losing control.

"Deep breaths, Alison, deep breaths." Santa encourages. "Whoever set that fire knew someone else was in the house."

"I doubt it. Did you hear the racket they made coming up the stairs? They expected it empty and most probably knew Bob was hanging in the bedroom." I reply.

Alison groans at that. "What if they saw my car? What if they can trace it back to me?"

Alison has a legit concern there. No one says anything, leaving her questions momentarily unanswered.

"Could be," I finally say, "but at least we parked on the road. It wouldn't be as obvious to someone as parking in the driveway would."

Silence floats down over the car as we all contemplate the drive to Alison's apartment to pick up the manuscript. I am now hugely interested in learning what Bob has been up to.

The drive home gives me some time to process. Should we call police? They're no doubt on scene right now. Would it do any good to disclose we were there? I don't know the answer, but my inclination is to wait to look at Bob's Fed Ex to Alison. I don't see why anyone would murder Bob by hanging and then subsequently set the house on fire. Why wouldn't they just take him somewhere and make him disappear? This whole thing is nuts.

My phone begins vibrating in my pocket, breaking my stream of consciousness. I look at it; shit, it's my mother. I don't answer. I scroll through my contacts list, find my mother's profile and activate the 'block calls' function. Not interested in connecting with her.

We get back to the city, pass by my place and make our way to Alison's apartment. It's a well-lit, newer apartment complex with both outdoor and under-building parking. I contemplate how she can afford this place and then imagine her mom or dad, or perhaps both, probably help her out. We get out of the car quietly and walk up to the elevator.

Santa breaks the silence. "Hey guys, how about taking me back to my car and I can connect with you guys tomorrow? I'm not doing well with all of this and I don't think I'm gonna be much help tonight. I can catch up with you guys later. I also need to connect with Merri. I have about thirty texts from her and she's wondering where the hell I am. I'd rather just talk to her."

Alison starts back to the car, but I interject. "Why don't we get the letter and take it with us? I'd like to look it over on the way."

"Yeah, fine." Alison says.

We head upstairs and Alison quickly retrieves Bob's letter from the kitchen bar counter and turns back to leave. Santa and I don't enter past the doorway.

Giving it to me, she says timidly, "Happy reading."

I roll it up into a scroll and tuck it under my arm as the three of us go back to the elevator and down to her car. Santa and I switch seats again. I ride shotgun and he squeezes into the back positioned like he's ready for the final push in childbirth. I smile at the visual and unroll the letter.

My first thought is it's less a 'manuscript' as Alison describes it and more like a rambling 'I'm sorry' letter to her coupled with a declaration of the misdeeds he's committed.

"Bob has indeed hung himself," I announce, "or was forced into hanging himself."

I watch a lot of crime drama shows, so I can't help but offer the scenario.

"He begins by saying he cannot continue any longer doing what he's doing, and he's worried he's about to be caught. Jesus Christ. I'm only skimming through this, but it appears he was knuckles deep in illegal shit just like you said."

Alison glances sideways at me with despondent eyes but says nothing.

We're getting close to University Campus, and Santa's drop off, so I set the letter down for now. We arrive, pull into the parking garage, and Santa directs Alison to his spot. I get out of the car to make room for Santa to get out.

"See you, big man." I say, giving him a bro hug.

"Okay, catch up with you tomorrow. Can I let Merri in on this?" He asks, looking at Alison. She doesn't shift in her seat; she simply nods slightly. She follows with a pathetic, "Bye, Ben."

I get back in the front seat while Santa disappears into his beast of a ride. Alison stares into her lap with both hands still on the wheel.

"Are you okay?" I ask lamely.

"No, Jon, I'm not okay," she says with no trace of anger, "but I'm glad you're here."

I feel a warm flutter in my stomach hearing her say that.

"Do you want to go back to your apartment and read this over?"

After all that has happened over the last couple of days, particularly today, I wasn't looking to get laid, though I wouldn't have turned it down either.

"How about we go to A's? I'd like to get something to eat and I could use a drink."

That actually sounds like a better idea than mine, so off we go to A's.

14

It doesn't take long to get over to A's from the University, and it's not very busy, which is fine with me. We both go to the bathroom to wash up as soon as we get inside, giving me the opportunity to check myself in the mirror. It looks like I've been in a street fight. My hair is crazy messy, and I have a scratch running the length of my right cheek to my jawline. I have no idea how it happened, nor did I feel it. My best guess is it happened as we ran past the shrubbery planted around the side of the house.

I can see across the back bar as I leave the men's room and notice Alison made it back to the booth already. As I approach, she motions me to her side.

"Come sit next to me on this side, that way we can both read at the same time."

"Good idea." I reply and plunk down next to her. Even with the faint smell of smoke on her, she stills smells breathtaking.

"I took the liberty of ordering you a PBR when the server came over. You were still in the bathroom, so I hope that's okay."

"Yeah … no, that's perfect, thanks." I stammer. She's perfect, I think to myself.

Our server brings over the drinks; Alison's having wine and I'm delivered a sixteen-ounce PBR. I would have ordered the twenty-two-ounce 'Goliath' size, but hey, nobody's perfect. We each take a slug, mine considerably larger, and situate the document between us.

It opens:

Dear Alison, I don't know where to begin, so I'll just start from the start. I'm so sorry you are reading this. You've been a light in my life that I was missing for a long time and I never wanted to hurt you.

Tears stream down her face. Bob's opening volley is essentially an ode to Alison and more of a love letter than anything. I knew this was coming because it was the part I had read in the car on the way to dropping Santa off at his car. Alison reads intently.

I don't want to live with what I've done, and frankly I don't think the people I'm dealing with are going to let me live much longer anyway. I've been trying to extricate myself from this and I see no way out. Please don't reveal this to anyone. I don't want my children to know what a failure and terrible person their dad was.

Man, that last part actually got to me as well. We had to take a break and let Alison compose herself to continue on to the cause of Bob's misdeeds. We finish our drinks and have another round on the way.

"Just reading this part," I say, "it looks like Bob killed himself before anyone else could."

Alison challenges my theory. "Then why not check to see if he was home before they burned it? Someone wouldn't have known if he was there or not when they set the fire."

She's got a point. "Unless they've been watching the house and knew he was home." I reason.

We look at each other at almost exactly the same time.

"Then they probably knew we were there." We both whisper.

We continue to look at each other for what seems like a minute but was probably only ten seconds or so.

"Let's read through this damn thing." Alison snaps. I discover I like it when she gets feisty.

The letter goes on:

My financial situation was very tight after my first divorce. Alimony and child support for two kids strained my marriage with my second wife, and after the second divorce with an additional child, I was unable to have any sort of life for myself. I was falling further and further behind with spouse and child support payments. At the time, I had spent time bird hunting with the guys from General Defense and, after getting trashed after a day's hunt, we got to talking about personal stuff. I pretty much spilled my guts and thought that was that.

This is totally mesmerizing. Straight from the mouth of a dead man. Alison never looks up. I decide I better get reading before she turns the page on me.

Sometime soon after, I was leaving work one night, and when I opened my car door there was a brown bag sitting on the seat. I was thinking, 'what the fuck?' and then I opened it. There was $20,000 cash in it and a note with a phone number on it. I was scared shitless, but part of me was also excited. I wish I could go back in time and take a different course, but I can't. I called the number all the while wondering how in the hell anyone made it into my car, and the person on the other end simply asked me to *meet him that evening. I was directed to the back of a small building on the waterfront down by the fish exchange. When I arrived, it was difficult to find, and I nearly turned around. But before I did, a gentleman appeared through the back door and asked for me to come in. I had never seen him before; he was dressed sharply, and he was quite friendly. He told me to come inside and asked me to sit. He said he wouldn't take up much of my time but understood from some clients of mine I was having some financial difficulties and he was here to help. Would I be interested in doing some outside work for our client? This guy was sent by General Defense! I really wasn't too interested, and I told him so – nothing good can come from it, but he asked me to go home and think about it and meet him tomorrow. He went on to say if I had no interest in learning more, simply return the $20,000 and I can be on my way. I spent the better part of that night looking at the money. I decided I wanted no part of it, and when I went back the next day, I had the bag in hand with every intention of returning it. Nevertheless, when I met with the mystery man, I found myself asking for more detail of what they wanted me to do.*

God damn! Bob was taking dirty money from General Defense, for what??

I look at Alison and tentatively interrupt her reading.

"Jesus Christ, General Defense is into illegal shit!"

"It appears so." She says cautiously. "It also means they likely know who I am and probably you too, for that matter. You've spent time on the engagement."

"Maybe, but we've done nothing wrong."

"Ya, but they may not know that." She is absolutely right.

"I knew something wasn't right." Alison whimpers. "I knew it wasn't right with Bob breaking protocol with the audits."

"Hey, don't beat yourself up; it's his name on the audit reports."

That's my lame effort at comforting her, and to no surprise, it's wholly ineffective.

Alison turns to me with a drained look and asks, "Can we finish reading this back at my apartment? I feel like someone could be watching us or something. Totally paranoid, I get it. I also want to check the news to see if the fire is being reported."

I'm all on board, so we ask for the bill and make our way back to the Fiat, and within ten minutes we're back at the underground parking garage. There were around two dozen televisions at A's where we could watch the news, so now I'm running about two dozen different scenarios through my head as to how the rest of the evening could unfold. I decide it's best not to process too hard and just let what happens happen.

15

W e hop on the elevator and ride up to her floor. We're really not saying much; I'm letting her take the lead on this. When we come to the door, Alison pulls out her apartment key and attempts to unlock it.

"What the hell, I can't get the key in." She says while trying to jam it into the hole.

After a few more failed attempts, I ask her if I can try. She hands me a bulky keychain with about fifteen 'non-key' trinkets attached – and very slowly and gently I try to insert it into the hole. I alternate each try between a push and a wiggle; this seems to be effective.

After a good deal of effort, I eventually force through the blockage and hear the 'click' signifying success. I push the door open for Alison to enter first and I follow behind. She hits the light switch, illuminating the apartment. We stare silently in disbelief. The apartment is in complete disarray; the floor littered with everything not nailed down. Couch cushions, dishes, eating utensils, cupboard contents; you name it. Alison darts ahead, but doesn't get far before I reach out, clasping her wrist.

"Let me go first." I insist, holding her back. "Stay by the door, I'll be right back."

To my surprise, she listens to me and takes a step back. I start a walk-about, carefully, to see if anyone's still here. I have one eye on an escape route back to the front door while I look at the mess strewn about. Christ, it looks like everything has been touched. After searching through every space within the apartment, including closets, I come back out to the living room.

"No one's here. Whoever did this is gone."

"Look at this!" Alison cries. "Look around ... nothing's broken! It's as if stuff was placed chaotically, *but there isn't a thing broken.*"

I gently shut the front door. It makes sense now why we had so much trouble getting in. Someone damaged the lock when breaking in.

I turn to her. "You're right. I don't see anything broken. It's like somebody's sending you a message."

"Why ... whyyyyy ... WHY IS THIS ALL HAPPENING?!" She blubbers.

I sit down on the carpet next to her, wrapping my arm around her. She naturally falls into the crook of my arm and I simply hold her quietly.

Alison raises Bob's letter. "They were looking for this, weren't they." She says softly as more of a conviction than a question.

I hadn't thought about it, but it does make sense.

"We're not safe, Jon. If they know about this document, they're going to want to hurt us, too."

"I agree. We need to leave here. It's not safe to stay."

"Should we call the police? We should call the police." Alison answers her own question. "We didn't do anything wrong! We need to blow the cover on this for safety's sake! We need to whistle blow against General Defense!" She's nearly out of breath when she finishes.

I think back to my meeting with the FBI about the building explosion and subsequent meeting with Mike Bond. As I re-live the moment, I keep processing Detective Bond's statement: *There was a bigger target there.* I apprise Alison on my two-part interview at the Portland police station.

"The guy that brought the briefcase into the bank was an FBI agent? Does that make sense to you? Who does that?"

I didn't understand her last part about 'who does that?', but nevertheless, the skepticism in Alison's questions are valid.

"Yeah … no, it doesn't make sense to me. I didn't feel comfortable with the FBI, but Bond seemed like the real deal."

"We should call Bond and get his help. We need protection. I also need to call my mom. I'm going to stay with her."

"I'll call Bond. If this is related, then we just need to tell him everything. Like you said, we've done nothing wrong. On your mom, do you think it's a good idea to bring her in right now? I'm worried you may put her in danger."

"Oh, God … I didn't even think of that."

"Look," I interrupt before she completely falls off the deep end, "my Uncle Danny lives in town. He raised me after my father died; he's like a brother to me. He's a merchant mariner, so he stays out to sea for months at a time, and when he's here portside, he lives at his girlfriend's house, mostly. If you're all right with it, I can call him and you can stay there – if you're all right with it." I stress.

After a moment of processing, Alison says, "Okay, call him. I'll stay there on the condition you stay, too."

"Absolutely."

I'm caught off-guard with her offer and somewhat surprised at myself that trying to score is least on my mind. I'm genuinely concerned with both of our well-being.

After hearing my response, Alison seems to lift up a bit.

"Okay, I don't have it in me to clean anything right now. I'm just going to pack some things and I'll be out."

Despite having said that, I notice she's detouring at every turn picking up things and organizing while she goes. I try to find a bar chair, dodging the heap of shit in the way.

Sitting down, I pull my phone out to call up Danny's number. I don't call him uncle, we're too close in age for that; and besides, I think he'd give me a solid beat-down if I tried to. Danny's a tough bastard. He fought Golden Gloves all through high school, into the Navy, and then for the National Guard when he finished active duty. Now he's out to sea for half of every year. You have to be a tough son-of-a-bitch to work on those freighters for a living.

My uncle answers his phone. "Yeah, what's up."

"Hey Danny, it's Jon."

"No shit, Jonny Boy, what's up?"

"You local?"

"Yeah, why?"

"I need a place to crash. My apartment's getting painted and I need to split for a little while." I don't want to bring him in on this mess if I don't have to.

"No problem. I'm at Jennifer's, anyway. The key's in the usual spot."

"Thanks man, I really appreciate it. Just one other thing … you mind if I bring my girlfriend over, too?" I take some liberty in describing Alison as my girlfriend. It rolls off of my tongue nicely.

"Ech. Yeah, I guess. Don't be a fucking pig over there, though." Uncle Danny has a way with words.

"Heh – no worries – best behavior."

"Yeah right, Jonny." He counters. "Hey, beers sometime."

"Definitely. Thanks Danny, I really appreciate it."

"No problem." He clicks the line dead before I can say goodbye.

Man, I love that guy. I shift in my seat to put my phone back in my pocket when I hear Alison moan loudly from the bedroom.

"Jonnnnnnn!"

I'm out of my bar chair and on the fly towards her room. She's standing just past the doorway with her back to me, looking at the far wall. Hanging on it is a picture of her and her mother; and in the middle of the frame, directly below Alison's beautiful face, sits a large kitchen knife plunged straight into her chest.

"Move!" I bark. "Grab your stuff, we're going. Now!" I snap.

This has the intended effect. Alison shakes her head back to reality and starts hustling. In under five minutes, we're out the door, down the stairwell, and at her car.

"Just go." I tell her. "I'll give you directions."

16

"I'm so scared!" Alison sobs.

"We're good." I reply, trying to console her. "Nothing to worry about."

I was scared too, but there's no use in letting her know that. It will only exacerbate her anxiety.

"Where are we going, Jon?"

"My Uncle Danny's. I'll explain on the way."

I walk Alison through the truncated version of my dysfunctional family, though I don't address still having infrequent interaction with my mother, nor does she ask. I spend most of the time talking about my dad, and of course Uncle Danny, seeing as how we're going to his place.

"I want you to go through the West End, but circle back down-town." I instruct.

"W-why? What's wrong?"

"Look. Bob's dead. Probably hanged himself, but possibly not. His house has been burned down and we may have been spotted in the process. Your apartment has been rummaged through. I hesitate to call it ransacked; I'm sure whoever did this was worried about neighbors and noise. When you put it all together, it tells me someone might know Bob left you a package and they're trying to clean up loose ends. If I'm right, and I sure as shit hope I'm not, we may have someone following us."

"Jesus Christ." Alison moans.

We make our way back downtown passing by A's in the process and I ask her to pull over to the curb. I direct her to park on this particular side street because it's only one block from the police station.

"Alright, let's just sit here for a moment. I want to see if anyone looks out of place or anything's suspicious."

I scan our surroundings as best as I can. What a mess. Maine in March is not welcoming. Thoughts inevitably turn to spring, but winter continues its icy hold with a tight grasp and won't easily let go. It gets dark early and though much of the snow has melted; slushy, dirty snowbanks still guard every street corner.

Christ, everything and everyone appears suspicious. A custom-wrapped box truck sits near a shop. A black Mercedes SUV is parked in front of a corner deli. A white delivery van with the back doors propped open services a retail outlet. This is probably a useless effort, but Alison needs some reassurance right now.

"Okay, I don't see anything shady here and I've been looking at all the cars we've passed. I'm not spotting anybody tailing us."

What the hell do I know, though.

"Let's move around the corner and pull into the Portland police parking garage. If anyone followed us, they're not gonna follow us in." I reason.

"Ya ... ya, that's a good idea." Alison brightens just a little.

After we enter the second level of the garage, we drive over to an isolated area out back and shut the engine off. We both sit in silence for a moment before Alison turns to me.

"Hey, while we're here, why don't we go in and find the detective you were talking about earlier and tell him what's happening?"

I consider her idea. "That's not a bad suggestion."

We enter the police station lobby where a wall-mounted television broadcasts the evening news. No surprise – Bob's charred house is the 'Breaking Alert' story. I reach for Alison's hand and squeeze tightly. First responders are still on site, though I can see the fire is out.

We watch for a while to learn what's being reported. A sanguine newscaster reports there's a casualty; though no identification will be released pending next-of-kin notification. She makes no mention of arson, but without question, investigators will discover it quickly. Accelerants are not difficult to detect, particularly in the manner in which it was applied in this case. In all likelihood, no information will be released so as not to taint the investigation. Bob's cause of death will be discovered, no doubt. Remnants of the cord Bob dangled from will remain and a forensics review will not detect smoke in his lungs, providing there's anything left of him to autopsy; proving he was dead prior to burning.

"Can I help you?" A female voice rings out through a speaker behind us.

We whirl around to see a uniformed police officer with a pleasant expression standing over a long, thin microphone more suitable for Bob Barker on the *Price Is Right* than the Portland police department.

"Yes, thank you," I respond as we move toward the safety glass separating the officer work space from the lobby, "we're hoping to catch up with Detective Bond. Is he available?"

"One moment." She replies and vanishes from sight through a side door barely visible to us.

Alison tugs lightly on my arm and I turn to look at her.

"Are we going to tell him about the letter?" She says with doe eyes I cannot resist.

I almost-imperceptibly shake my head, indicating 'no.' "We're being video-recorded right now." I whisper. "Probably listening devices as well."

We turn back to the booth in time to see a man in street clothes come into view with the uniformed woman trailing behind.

"Can I help you?" He has to lean over quite far to speak into the stick microphone.

"Hi." I offer. "We're looking for Detective Bond."

"Mike Bond no longer works here." I detect some vitriol in his voice.

"Since when?"

It probably isn't a good idea to be so gruff. He's not interested in filling me in.

"Not your concern. What is your issue?" This isn't posed as a question insomuch as it is a command.

"Oh ... nothing really. It's personal; we're friends of the family just in town for a little while." Not bad for having to think on the fly.

"Sorry. Can't help you."

I'm getting the sense he couldn't give a damn about Bond and perhaps it's personal. Well, it's not my battle. I walk away back toward the television with Alison following closely behind.

"Now what?" She asks with concern bordering on a plea.

"Let's get out of here. Bond gave me his card – it has his number on it. We can call him when we get to my uncle's."

I glance at the television and notice the nightly news has been replaced with *Wheel Of Fortune*. Why do they still need Vanna White, anyway? She doesn't turn the letters anymore; she just touches them and they 'mysteriously' reveal themselves. Seems pretty useless to me. The marketing and brand value of an icon, I guess. I finish my internal debate of the pros and cons of Vanna White's skill set while peering out of the bank of windows and onto the street below. A light snow falls now, looking picturesque as it passes through the streetlight beam, notwithstanding spring is just around the corner or so says the calendar.

Before I turn for the exit, something catches my eye. There's a Mercedes SUV – black – parked on the corner with its back to us, just a few hundred feet away. I can't tell if anyone's in it, but I don't see any exhaust coming from the tailpipe and there's a light film of snow coating the vehicle. Seems to me no one is likely in it. It strongly resembles the one that was a block or so away when we stopped to check our surroundings earlier.

I pull out my phone and dial Santa.

"Who're you calling?" Alison asks.

I raise one finger in a gesture for her to wait a minute. My conversation with Santa will fill her in even though she'll only hear one side of it.

"Hey, Jon. How you doing?"

"Good, man. Listen, I need a favor. Can you pick up Alison and me at the Portland police station?"

"What? Why?" Santa says with anxiety in his voice.

"No worries – we're fine. We came to the police department to meet with the detective that 'sort of' interviewed me yesterday, but he's not here. All along, we've been watching for cars that may have followed us, and it's probably nothing, but there's one car out front I think we may have seen a couple of times hanging around. I was hoping we could slip out unnoticed and you could bring us to Danny's."

"Danny's? Why Danny's?" His question is legit.

"Somebody's been in Alison's apartment. The place is trashed. We thought it would be safer to go to Danny's place; he's letting us crash there for a while. I'll explain it when I see you."

"Jesus Christ, did you tell him what's going on?"

"No, I made up an excuse for now."

"I'm on my way. Merri's with me."

"Thanks, bud." I say. "Meet us on the second floor of the parking garage. We'll slip out unnoticed." Hopefully slip out unnoticed.

I disconnect the call and walk over to Alison. She's moved over to the window bank and now she's looking at the SUV. It hasn't moved.

"Are we leaving my car here?" She asks, but already knows the answer.

"I think it's probably safer that way." I reason. "We can get it in the morning."

Alison and I wait on the second-floor deck of the parking garage when Santa and Merri drive in. We hop in the second row and keep pretty low even though the windows have a dark tint and are virtually impossible to see into.

"We're heading to Danny's, right?" Santa confirms.

"Yeah. We need a break," I say while looking at Alison, "and I want to read the rest of Bob's letter."

Alison stares at the floor and says nothing.

Merri speaks up. "Can we hang out with you guys? Ben doesn't want to ask but I don't mind asking."

So she does call him 'Ben' after all, I note and chuckle. Merri's good people.

"Of course." Alison responds.

Good, Alison's talking now. Her silence began to worry me.

We circle down to the garage exit and turn onto the arterial. Alison and I continue to stay low trying to keep out of sight, but we discover there is no need. The Mercedes is gone.

17

U ncle Danny's house is near enough to the water, but not directly on it. It's a nondescript, two-bedroom cape situated on a dead-end road in a secluded Portland neighborhood. There's no garage and virtually no land; the yard consists of alternate patches of wispy dune grass poking through hardpan and scrubby coastal bushes that make it seem small. The house comes across as pretty rundown; the gray exterior could use a good scraping and some fresh paint.

We drive down the private road and turn into his dirt driveway. Santa's enormous vehicle fills the entire width of the parking area. We all get out and I walk to the center of the front yard and hunt for the house key. It's usually hidden under a curl of large chain links connected to a massive, rusty anchor 'decorating' my uncle's property. I make a mental note to cut a copy of the key. I have no idea where my old key went to.

Alison stays very close to me wherever I go. I'm enjoying the protector role ... or maybe I'm just embracing it. I'm determined to get us through whatever the hell is going on.

For as neglected as the outside of the house is, the interior is in complete contrast. Hardwood floors dominate throughout. In the kitchen, cherry cabinets and granite countertops frame spotless stainless-steel appliances. My favorite room, the finished basement, includes a world class man cave complete with a pool table and wet bar. Every tastefully-decorated room in the house displays a slightly different nautical theme.

Alison and I give Santa and Merri the rundown of our events since we parted and predictably, they're just as worried as us.

"It's time to bring the police in." Santa insists, but I sense he's at the same time reasoning it in his mind.

"Yeah, we're just about there, too, but we want to finish reading Bob's letter and connect with Detective Bond." I reply.

Alison adds for emphasis, "And we'd like to learn more about Bob's situation." Surprisingly, Alison holds it together pretty well when speaking of Bob's 'situation.'

"I get it." Santa supposes. "You said Danny doesn't know?"

I contemplate his question for a moment walking through in my mind Danny's probable reaction if he finds out what's happening.

"Right, but I'll bring him in if I need to. He'll go bat-shit crazy the minute I tell him. If the building explosion and Bob's demise aren't related, then I probably won't."

Alison objects. "Do you really think it matters? Even if they're not related, we're in trouble because of our General Defense audits and what we know from Bob."

"Eh, you're right." I backpedal. "Well … let's see what we're up against."

Alison goes out to the car and returns with two large overnight bags. She takes the letter from one of them, then tosses it onto the kitchen table. We all stare stupidly at it.

"Well, it's not going to read itself." Merri says with a wry smile, lightening the mood considerably.

We all pull up chairs and mostly sit gathered around one side of the table, leaning over so we're propped up above the letter. Alison's in charge of possession, so we wait for her to open up to where we left off:

> *He never mentioned exactly what he wanted me to do. He simply repeated that his client was interested in my services. I pressed him somewhat, but he was evasive. He asked if I would like to earn what I was holding in the bag every month. I just about shit myself. He knew he didn't need to tell me it was untraceable. I just sat there like a dumb ass. He never pressured me. Eventually, I looked at him and said I'd do it. I was scared to death, but equally exhilarated. Even though I agreed, he still didn't tell me what I was expected to do. He told me if I wanted to accept the deal and the money involved in exchange for my services, I needed to tell him exactly that. It was at that moment I realized I was being recorded. No doubt an insurance policy to protect them in case of a rat. I said yes almost without realizing it. I was explicit to him I would accept money in exchange for my accounting services. There was no turning back now.*

Dang, Bob was a stone-cold player. An unintentional player, but a player nonetheless. I have sort of a perverse new-found respect for him.

"This isn't real. How can this be real?" Alison says in disbelief. Everyone is in disbelief.

"Totally mind-blowing. You had no idea of any of this?" Santa asks incredulously.

"No idea." Alison replies. "Except I thought it was weird when he paid in cash all the time. He always carried a stack of bills with him. Whenever I would mention it, he would say he'd rather leave the high-tech payment methods to the Millennials."

I continue her thought process: "He was trying to find ways to put the cash to work."

We all reflect on it for a moment. There's still quite a bit more to read, so we settle back in to finish.

After I verbally committed to the arrangement, he finally opened up. I never caught his name, and I wasn't going to ask. I just thought of him as 'My Handler.' He looked connected. He looked powerful. I did learn he wasn't employed by General Defense – he claimed he was an 'independent contractor.' He's a hired gun. After I accepted the offer, his attitude changed pretty quickly. He wasn't as nice as he was at first. He wasn't violent; more business-intense, but the threat of physical harm was always there.

They wanted me to help them with weapons diversions from the U.S government to terrorist cells in Pakistan, Afghanistan, and God only knows where else. I didn't get much detail on the back end of it, nor did I really want to know. I was charged with manipulating shipments of weapons to U.S. Defense Agency through falsified documents and concealing it with fraudulent annual attestation engagements.

And there you have it.

Merri asks a question the rest of us already know. "What's U.S. Defense Agency?"

Alison fields this one. "They're a clearing house for the various military branches that acts as the purchasing agent. The Army, Navy, and all the others, don't purchase weapons for their branches independently. For best pricing, ease of traceability, and to satisfy regulatory conditions, U.S. Defense; a pseudo-government agency, does all of the buying. Then the military branches bulk 'buy' their weapons from USD. They're General Defense's biggest customer. GD never has to deal with all the separate military divisions directly."

I've already started to read ahead.

The idea in concept was pretty simple, really. General Defense would bill U.S. Defense for 100% of a shipment and get paid for 100% of that shipment. However, they would only deliver roughly half of the weapons. The rest would be diverted to other locations – I think terrorist cells and such, but maybe other groups – and get paid again for that piece from them. Who the fuck really knows where it went. Bills of lading, purchase orders, shipment receipts all needed to be falsified. On top of that, at year-end there was always a discrepancy with inventory counts and valuations I had to clean up. What I thought was a simple idea, in reality was more difficult than I expected to execute. I never wanted you to be a part of it, Alison. That's why I always did the inventory piece of the audit.

I think back to our conversation at A's and now it makes perfect sense. Everything Alison described regarding the audit engagement was legitimate except for inventory. Revenue accounts would reconcile fine. U.S. Defense was paying in full, so General Defense's cash and income accounts would reconcile as well. GD's receivables would work out for the same reason. U.S. Defense wasn't receiving everything they expected to receive, though. Or were they? Why wasn't that a red flag for discovery? Maybe they had someone on the inside? Or maybe what they were receiving was exactly as expected and the finance department wasn't in sync with operations. You can't really tell. It seems like this was all about somebody pocketing the cash for the diverted weapons. GD got paid in full, and then someone at GD got paid again.

"God damn."

Remarkably, this comes from Alison.

"So, let's follow this through." Santa says. "GD would prepare a shipment of … pick a number, say, a thousand assault rifles; then deliver maybe half to U.S. Defense and half to wherever, but bill U.S Defense for all of it. Sound about right?"

"Does to me." Alison concedes.

"And then someone at GD was collecting again on the diverted weapons with Bob getting paid to cover the tracks." He adds.

Ding, ding, ding; we have a winner folks, get that boy a stuffed animal from the top row. We all let out a collective breath and keep on reading Bob's pièce-de-résistance.

> As far as how I managed my part of the scheme, it was centered on falsified records. Purchase orders were entered into GD's system by USD electronically. Shipments were assembled, and the trucks were packed as usual. Rather than have all of the trucks go to USD, typically some would go to USD with something less than the amount indicated on the purchase order, with the remainder sent to the Middle East, mostly. I would prepare a phony bill of lading showing the same quantity of weaponry on the paperwork as was loaded onto the truck headed just to USD. When the shipment arrived at USD, the bill of lading and the physical count always matched up. The only thing we needed to deal with was make sure the purchase orders matched up as well.

"I think I know what a purchase order is," Merri interrupts, "but what is a bill of lading?"

"A bill of lading is really just a document showing the quantity of goods being transported, so you can be sure you didn't lose anything to theft or error along the way. If the bill of lading says you should have a hundred widgets onboard, then you should be able to count a hundred widgets on the truck." Man, I actually sound like an accountant.

"But it also interacts with a purchase order." Alison points out. "If someone at a company orders a hundred fifty widgets through a purchase order, and the bill of lading and physical count only show a hundred widgets, then where did the other fifty widgets go? It could be an honest mistake or something bigger."

"Oh, I get it." Merri says. "Then the buyer will either pay only for the hundred widgets they received or demand another fifty before full payment is made."

"Exactly." Alison responds. "In Bob's part of the fraud, he has the bill of lading and physical count match up, but not the purchase order. GD wants to deliver something less than what was ordered but collect the full amount per the purchase order."

Again, I'm reading ahead.

The only way we could figure out how to make everything match was to engage someone at USD; a counterpart to me that could alter the purchase orders. That wasn't my area of expertise. That was left to My Handler. He was charged with finding the right guy in purchasing or IT at USD, or maybe both for that matter. It took some time, but he pulled it off and we were in business. I overheard people talking that in my four and a half years, the scam had netted some $150 million. No shit.

We never had any trouble with GD. The problem began with USD. It started out last year with their leadership unable to figure out why the military branches were consistently complaining about a lack of weapons in the field despite steady increases in quantities ordered. They were continually increasing order requisitions, yet service personnel were still lacking arms. It was explained to me that since all the records matched up: purchase orders, inventory records and counts, etc., USD and the government thought either the military branches were under-ordering, or thefts were happening with transactions between USD and the military branches. The USD guys were able to forge requisition documents explaining away differences and creating confusion with timing inconsistencies of weapons still owned by USD but stored at the various branches until title passed and was reflected in the accounting records. This was merely a Ponzi Scheme fix, though. It was destined to ultimately collapse. USD's auditors requested a wholesale change in internal control procedures to reflect transfers earlier. When this year came, and discrepancies continued, they dug deeper. They wanted to meet with us at HW. They wanted to go over my audit work papers of GD's inventory and revenue recognition methods. I wasn't about to turn over my work papers voluntarily, but as with any government agency, USD went under a forensics audit. It was just a matter of time before my records were subpoenaed. My audit work papers would match up with GD's accounting records, but not from GD's records to USD's. It will be traced directly back to me. My Handler was pressuring me to falsify or alter documents, but I could see the house of cards falling down around me. I tried to extricate myself knowing I would fail miserably.

"How exactly would a storage argument prevent USD from being discovered by their auditors?" Merri asks.

"I'm pretty sure USD would have argued they moved weapons to the branches just for off-site storage space concerns and they hadn't technically 'sold' anything to the branch yet." Alison responds. "It would muddy the picture relative to inventory valuations, but as Bob writes, it's not a sustainable solution. The minute our audit records were compared with USD's accounting records, it would be exposed."

We're getting close to the end of Bob's confession. I can't wait to read the rest.

I didn't see a way to alter or destroy all of our records. We have years of paper files. We have electronic records in off-site data storage houses and now we're migrating to a cloud-based storage process. Records are everywhere. I told them I couldn't possibly trace it all back. My Handler beat me hard on my legs and back; all places not easily visible. Alison, I'm done. I'm being watched. My house is bugged. My kids are in danger. You may be in danger. They won't let me out alive.

"Do you know what this means?" I say, looking around at everyone in an 'Aha!' moment. "The bombing wasn't a bank robbery attempt! It was General Defense trying to destroy our accounting records and throw off ... well ... throw off everyone! Bond was right! There *was* a bigger target there! The FBI guys ..."

I pause. I'm in a full-on frigging tizzy now. I need to see Bond and see him quickly. This whole god damn thing is tied together, I'm sure of it.

"All right, slow down, dude." Santa urges to try and get me to cool out, but it doesn't work.

Alison openly weeps now and focuses on the remainder of the document.

And finally Alison, after four and a half years of heinous, illegal wrong-doing on my part, I've amassed a fair amount of dirty money. You know the financial reporting rules in the banking industry as well as anyone. I couldn't easily fold the money into the banking system without it triggering regulatory watchdogs, nor could I simply deliver cash to my exe's in any meaningful amount without causing suspicion. I spent what I could – a lot of it on stuff for us. That answers your question as to why I always paid in cash. Funny thing is, I would have rather used a debit card.

My kids should be OK. They will get my retirement account and the proceeds from my house sale. For you, I left the money I couldn't spend. There is $500,000 cash in Big Billy's self-storage facility near the mall. I hope you can find a way to use it and it is not a curse. It's in Pod A, unit 35. The keypad code to get in is the month and day of our first date. You said I wouldn't remember, but I did. Best day of my life.

I love you.

> *Bob*

18

Alison gets up and walks to the sink, proceeding to blow her nose with a paper towel. I half-heartedly point to a box of tissues on a nearby side table. She doesn't see me.

I didn't realize their relationship was as significant as Bob intimates; she didn't let on in her conversations with us. It makes sense, I guess. The emotional display at A's, having a key to his house (or former house – good luck on the sale proceeds going to your kids), the constant worrying about not having contact with him for even one day.

Santa catches up to us reading the document. "Holy shit! He left you a half-million dollars?!" He exclaims with his mouth frozen agape.

Merri slaps him hard. "Shut up, asshole." She then hugs Alison tightly. "It's okay, hon." She says soothingly.

With anyone else I'd be disturbed, but this is standard operating procedure with them.

"I didn't know he felt so strongly." Alison burbles pitifully.

"Do you know what the code is he's talking about?" I cautiously offer, hoping it doesn't set anyone off; particularly Merri. Thankfully she doesn't react, and after a moment I refocus in on Alison.

"Yes," she says distantly, her thoughts seemingly far away, "our first date was November 13th. We laughed about it because it was a Friday – Friday the 13th – as unlucky as it gets."

Oh man, you said it sister.

"So the code …" Merri begins.

"… Is one, one, one, three." Alison finishes.

We're all silent and looking at Alison. Her nose is red and crinkled up – she's processing.

"This doesn't make a lot of sense; it can't go all the way to the top leadership at General Defense." She reasons. "They have shareholders and a board of directors. Someone's got to be managing this from the inside at a lower level and hiding it."

I'm not interested in analyzing what's going on at General Defense right now. Bob's message from the grave rings in my ear: *My kids are in danger. You may be in danger.*

"Alison, listen to me. Right now, our first priority is safety. Bob was warning you. This letter is his confession. We can take it with us to Bond and then figure out how we report this, and our next move to clear our names."

"Okay, right … you're right." She whines. "I just want to close my eyes and have this all go away!"

"Except for the half-million!" Santa pipes up. Merri follows by smacking him upside the back of his head.

As Santa rubs out the stinger from Merri, she gets up from the table and announces it's time for them to head out. He follows her looking like a bad dog that piddled on the carpet.

Merri gives Alison a big hug and whispers something in her ear. She comes over to me next and gives me a hug.

I whisper, "Bye Merri, take it easy on the big guy, eh?"

She whispers back, "No worries, Jon, that's just our foreplay for later." She follows with a kiss on my cheek and a wink.

Gulp.

"Call me tomorrow, dude. I'll come get you guys and bring you to your car." Santa offers.

"Thanks, bud. Talk to you later."

After they leave, we sit in silence for some time. Neither of us knows what to say, so I break the ice by simply reaching for her hand.

"Can we go over how we're approaching tomorrow?" She asks, peering up at me.

"Well, it's up for discussion, but I think we should contact Bond first thing. We can tell him what we know and get his advice and go from there."

Alison mulls it over for a moment. "Okay. What should we do about Ben and Merri? They're expecting to pick us up to go after my car. I don't think we ought to involve them any further."

"Hmmm. I hadn't thought of that. You're probably right, and if they pick us up, there's a decent chance they'll want to come along. I'll call an Uber tomorrow morning to come get us and then when we get to your car I'll text him that we're all set."

"Good idea. I'm not sure how an Uber would actually find us though, but whatever."

Alison gets up and walks to the bathroom. She looks defeated. I pick up a few empty glasses and bring them to the sink. I'm pretty tired; I trudge down the hall to the spare bedroom. I may have some old sweats or something still hanging around I can change into. While rummaging through the closet, I hear a soft knock on the door frame. Alison stands in the doorway in cute Dalmatian pajamas.

"Whatcha doing?" She asks.

"Just looking for some of my old clothes. I didn't get a chance to go by my apartment to get anything. I thought if you're okay with it, you can sleep in the master bedroom. I'll crash in here. It's my old room." I say half-laughing.

"Can I stay in here with you?"

"Uh, yeah … sure." I say in an insecure tone that I fail to hide. Under normal circumstances I would have had some liquid courage to bolster my nerve. "I'd like that."

She walks over to give me a warm embrace I can only describe as sort of *sliding* into me. With one hand behind my head, running her fingers through my hair, she kisses me deeply. Wasting no time, her other hand softly snakes its way down the front of my pants massaging gently. Quickly, it becomes pure animal lust. I'm not certain who removes their clothes faster, but we wind up naked at pretty much the same time, shattering the Olympic record for tandem undressing along the way.

Dropping to her knees, Alison stares at my not inconsiderable erection. "Well, hello Mr. Wonderful." She purrs.

I'm so hard, I could cut glass. I feather my fingers into her hair and squeeze tightly; every part of me in total ecstasy.

"C'mon." Alison rises up and encourages me to lie down in bed. She guides me into her with an audible sigh.

"Ahhhhh … yeeeeeesssss. That's perfect. Just like that, baby." She groans.

Oh man, I need to switch up thoughts or I'm in big trouble. The point-of-no-return kind of trouble.

"Faster, Jon; faster!" She demands.

I don't speed up the rhythm, though. I don't dare to. I don't want it to end. She encourages me, moaning, "Go for it, baby; do it, we can go again later."

That's all I need to hear. I shift into overdrive, and I indeed go for it. Fortunately, we're pretty secluded. With the amount of noise we made, I'm fairly certain we would have awoken the neighbors.

19

"**R**un, Jonny, run!" My dad shouts loudly with a huge smile on his face.

I can hear him through the earhole in my batting helmet. I grind my teeth with determination, pumping my arms as fast as I can. I round first base and then I'm on to second. Passing second base and on my way to third, I look right at my dad. He's the team manager and third base coach. He's wheeling his arm wildly in a circular motion, over and over, instructing me to go for home. I see my mother over his shoulder; she's in the concession shack, but she's excitedly watching me, too.

"You got this!!" He cries proudly. I'm already almost to home.

I cross home plate with my arms stretched skyward. My batting helmet flies through the air when I launch it off of my head in celebration. My teammates charge from the dugout, mobbing me. I plow straight through them to my dad and jump into his arms. It isn't everyday a nine-year-old hits a walk-off home run to clinch the victory in Little League. Well, maybe it is, but that doesn't make it any less special to me.

Then, as usual, it's at this moment I wake up. Do you ever have a recurring dream so pleasant, so precious; you just don't want to wake up? This one is mine.

Except my dad really wasn't a very good coach, and in actuality, this particular play resulted in me being tagged out at home plate by a mile. Wasn't even close. We went on to lose in extra innings, but no matter to me. It's one of my most cherished memories of him. Oftentimes, I wake up having to wipe a few tears away.

Not this time, though. Morning arrives and I'm in no hurry to get out of bed. Alison lays on my chest, still snoozing; my arm wrapped around her, trying not to move so as not to disturb her. This proves progressively more difficult by the minute because my arm has fallen asleep and become quite uncomfortable. I don't like the pins-and-needles feeling.

"Can we just lay here all day?" Alison says lazily while rubbing her eye.

Ah, she's awake. Perfect timing for me; my arm is about to fall off, so I take the opportunity to adjust. Rolling over, I wrap my other arm around her and very naturally we morph into a spooning position.

"Well yeah, actually we can."

Alison rolls out from beneath my arm, completely naked, then walks out of the room. I can hear her in the bathroom. She doesn't seem remotely self-conscious with how loudly she pees. I like that. When she comes back to the bed, she hovers over me; her magnificent boobs tantalizingly close to my face.

"Oops. My mistake." She says while smiling. "We need to get the day started. Let's call Bond."

She's so close to me, I can smell minty toothpaste on her breath. Again, it makes me wonder how she could withstand Bob's breath.

She lingers with a devious smile. "But first, I need a little something ..."

I squeeze her breasts and she lets out a soft moan. I need a little something, too.

All right, *now* I've got to get up. I've lounged in bed way too long. Alison's in the kitchen making coffee and the aroma has made its way throughout the house. I love that smell.

I can't imagine Uncle Danny has any real food in this place, at least anything with a valid expiration date on it. After getting dressed and finishing my toiletries, I join Alison at the kitchen bar.

"Look, PopTarts!" She says excitedly, pushing a box of pastries toward me. "I found them in the cupboard. I haven't had these since college."

"Good. They're the frosted ones. At least there's something here we can eat."

I have my phone in one hand and Bond's card in the other. I dial his cell number thinking there's no better time than the present.

"Hello." A voice grumbles on the other end. I don't recognize it as Bond's, but then again, I didn't talk to him for long.

"I'm looking for Detective Bond. This is Jon Williams." I choke down a bite of PopTart.

"Jon, I've been waiting for you to call. When can we meet?" He sputters.

Man, this guy goes right on the offensive. Before I can respond, he stammers on:

"Roberts is dead. Your work partner. This is definitely related. I told you that wasn't a bank robbery attempt."

"I know." I reply coolly. "We have some information."

I momentarily change the subject. "What's going on with you and the police department? We went by to talk to you and they said you didn't work there anymore."

"Partially correct. I'm on an administrative leave – unwillingly. We can discuss it when we meet and the sooner the better. I do not want to alarm you, but you may be in danger."

"Yeah, we're aware. We're being careful." I confirm.

"Let's convene at the food court; Three City Plaza at noon. Will that work?" He asks businesslike.

"Yes actually, we'll be in that area to pick up a vehicle, anyway. That works out well." Quite well.

He disconnects the call. Alison looks at me intently. Man, even with bed-head she is absolutely stunning. I fill her in on the meeting details, though she got most of it from my side of the conversation.

She hands me her cell phone. On it is a text message from Julie, informing those on her contacts list that Bob's name has been released for those who hadn't already heard or figured it out from the address of the fire.

Alison appears pretty strong right now in spite of the grisly reminder. I don't know what to say. I hand the phone back and breathe out a sigh. There's nothing really I can say.

She breaks the ice. "Well, let's get this ball rolling."

I activate the Uber app and punch in the meeting place for about a quarter-mile away. I don't want the driver getting too close to the house out of an abundance of caution. Same holds for the destination – I specify a drop-off spot a few blocks away from the police station. Alison gathers a few things, I pocket the letter and we head out the door. Other than just about everything else happening in our lives right now, it's a perfect day. The sun shines gloriously, forcing me to squint – I don't have sunglasses.

Alison pulls out Hollywood Ray-Bans and we walk hand-in-hand toward the pick-up spot.

Alison calmly turns to me. "You ready?"

"Ready, Freddy."

20

Bond isn't hard to spot. He's wearing the same red flannel shirt he had on when I first met him. Trying to get over to him though, is entirely another matter. Navigating the food court at noon on the weekend proves challenging. He sees us approaching, giving us a wave from his table.

"Over here." He says, beckoning as we walk up.

Files are assembled neatly on the table top. I see writing on the tabs, though I can't make it out. They look like personnel files.

"Please, sit." Bond says amicably while offering chairs. We do as instructed.

"Hi, I'm Mike Bond," he directs to Alison while extending his hand, "pleased to meet you, Ms. Brigham."

That throws me for a loop.

"Pleased to see you, too." Alison says, shaking hands. "How did you know my name?" She continues calmly; reading my mind.

"You are a part of my research into a financial crime case I've been pursuing. Also, Jon kept referring to 'we' when we talked on the phone. I expected you would be here. I'll get into it in greater detail, but first, do you all want to get food or something to drink?"

Bond's affect today is much different than it was when we first met. He seems friendly; more self-assured.

"Yes, I would actually. I need something more than a PopTart." I smile at Alison.

She follows me as we move away from the table. I also want a chance to talk to her alone before we talk to Bond.

Alison beats me to the punch. "That was a little creepy – that he knew my name."

"I know. I thought the same thing. You handled it well, though. No trace of surprise I could detect."

"Thanks." She says softly. "I was hoping my nervousness didn't show. Do you think I'm in trouble here? I'm not so sure this guy's going to be our advocate."

"Let's be honest with him." I reason. "With Bob's letter and our information from these last couple of days, we'll be fine. You'll be fine. If we detect any issue or concern, or if he can't do anything for us, we'll get up and leave. It's really busy here; there won't be a problem with a quick exit. Sound good?"

"Sounds good!" Alison links her arm with mine and we go to check out the food court offerings.

At this moment, I would do anything for her.

"We need to make some room." I say. We each carry a tray with food and fountain drinks. I'm not optimistic there's enough space.

Bond starts moving file folders to the floor. "No problem. I can move these. I wasn't planning on going through them, anyway."

Alison and I place our trays on the table and we each pull up a chair and sit.

"All right, here we are." I mumble through my first bite of chow mein.

"You called me, but I'm happy to take the wheel if you'd like." He responds.

Bond gets right to the point. The friendly demeanor he first portrayed has all but disappeared and the Bond I was exposed to at the police station returns.

"I received a tip recently – anonymously, indicating an individual at Harding-Williams may be involved in a financial scheme affecting the U.S. government."

He lowers his voice considerably.

"Bob Roberts." He continues on, while reaching for a file folder and waggling it in front of us. "I've been gathering research on him."

"What exactly constitutes 'research?' What do you know about Bob?" Alison interrupts. As I expected, it didn't take her long to find her voice.

"Not much." He admits. "I've found mostly readily accessible stuff … public database information … Google searches. The tip only said Bob Roberts was involved in a federal manipulation scheme, so I began surveillance on his house to see who was coming and going. That's when I became familiar with you, Ms. Brigham. You work at Harding-Williams, correct?"

Alison doesn't respond. No need to.

"I didn't have much to go on, frankly," he carries on, "but then the building explosion happened. I told you it wasn't a bank robbery attempt. Law enforcement knows that for sure even if they're letting the public continue to believe it is. It has to be related. The subsequent house fire confirms it in my mind."

Something's not right here.

"Then why aren't the police, FBI, whoever, all over this? Who else knows about the tip?" I ask.

Bond looks down at his hands. "As far as I know, no one actually. Just me."

"No one else knows about the tip? Then most likely they can't link this together." I ponder this for a moment. "This is because of your administrative suspension, isn't it? You can't, or don't want to share this with anyone. Why?"

Bond sighs and pauses; he's battling an internal war.

"Look, I have twenty-five years as a detective and I need to get to thirty for my full pension. I've put my entire life into police work. I need to bring this in and clear my record." He asserts with determination.

Christ, he's holding back information from law enforcement for his own benefit.

"Do you think we're in danger?" Alison asks.

Bond glares intently at her. "Prior to the discovery of Roberts' body in his burned-down house, I would've said probably not. Are you aware he was dead before the fire reached him; probably before the house was set on fire?"

Quickly I interject before Alison inadvertently reveals anything we've discovered. "Really?? He was killed first? Was the house burned to destroy evidence?"

"Yes and no." Bond replies. "Or, rather no and yes. I have contacts at the medical examiner's office. Looks like he asphyxiated, though it's difficult to say for sure. The damage to the body was extensive. There are indicators it may have been self-inflicted. I'm guessing the arson was a follow-up attempt by someone or some ones to destroy any evidence he may have left behind."

Alison's lower lip begins to quiver. No doubt she's hurting right now. I put my hand on her knee under the table to console her.

"Bob committed suicide? Someone came in to clean up? This is crazy, it sounds like something straight out of a movie. If this went down the way you think it did, Bob must've played a role in *something*. A big role." I posit.

"A starring role." Bond agrees.

Man, we know a heck of a lot more than he knows right now, but his intuition is spot on.

Again, Bond faces directly to Alison. "Do you have any information to share with me about what Roberts may have been in to?"

"Well, I ..." She starts to say while reaching for her bag, but I quickly squeeze her knee under the table. "I, I did notice him behaving a little odd lately, but with everything he had going on; the divorces, work schedule, his children's schedules, I didn't think anything of it."

Nice recovery, Alison. Now isn't the time to disclose the letter, if ever.

"He didn't talk to you about any wrongdoing ... any personal issues?" Bond presses.

"Ya, he bitched about his last wife all of the time. She was making his life miserable."

"What about at the office? Did you work on any common clients together?" Bond delves deeper.

Oh man, I'm crossing my fingers. C'mon Alison, don't be specific, but don't lie either. He may already know.

"Yes, quite a few actually." She replies coolly. "Look, I want to help you, but I didn't pry very far into his personal life. We weren't much more than friends."

That stings a little. I'd say they were slightly more than friends. No matter. I pause to finish eating and Alison follows suit. This gives us an opportunity to put a halt to a conversation transforming into an interrogation.

I try to change up the subject. "Why are you under suspension?"

He looks at me calculatingly; seemingly sizing me up.

"Let's just say sometimes I don't know when to quit and occasionally it pisses people off."

That I can believe.

"Do you know those two FBI agents you met with; Brown and Reyes?" He asks.

"Yeah, what about them?"

"You were the only person they interviewed that I witnessed. Odd, right? Why do you think that's the case?" He sounds genuinely perplexed.

"What? I'm the only one they met with?" Now I'm genuinely perplexed as well.

Bond nods in response.

"Uh ... I don't really know. They said they saw me on the surveillance video and knew I had an interaction with Reyes on his way into the bank the morning of the explosion."

This gets Bond's attention.

Sitting bolt upright, he says, "What? A surveillance tape? Reyes went into the bank that morning? Tell me what you know!" He follows up with a sheepish, "Please."

This is the part of the investigation I'd like to know more about. I rehash my morning from the point of leaving the bank's ATM, bumping into Reyes, crossing the street and returning in time to see Reyes exit the bank, to the subsequent blast. I also relate my interview with Brown and Reyes as best as I can remember.

"I highly doubt there was a surveillance tape. I think Brown was more likely watching the event and noticed you." Bond exclaims excitedly. "That EMF story? Total bullshit. That was likely an incendiary device helping facilitate a detonation. They've gotta be part of this; I don't know how yet, but I can feel it."

He carries on, "I never trusted either of them. They're renegades butting into local law enforcement every opportunity they get, constantly flashing their badges. They're mainly the ones I was talking about when I said I sometimes piss people off."

"Going back to your previous question, Ms. Brigham," he says earnestly, "yes, now I do think you both may be in danger."

That's all I need to hear. This meeting is over. My next task is contacting Uncle Danny. He'll know what our next move is.

I rise from the table with Alison right behind me. "Thank you, Detective Bond." I say, offering my hand. He stands up and firmly shakes my hand.

"I'm going to get to work on this immediately. Can we keep an open dialogue?" Bond requests.

"Yes, we'll let you know if we discover anything further. Please let us know if you do as well."

"I will. And I need to tell you this – I think there may be dirty cops in the station. I'm getting pushed out because I don't play like they do." Looking at us anxiously he urges, "Take care of yourselves. Both of you."

"Let's get to the car." I'm encouraging us to walk faster.

Alison picks up her pace. "Jon, I'm scared."

"No worries, when we get to the car I'll call my Uncle Danny. We'll meet up with him and bring him in on everything. He'll know our next move. We've been super-careful with keeping out of sight going to and from his house – we're safe there."

"I need to call my mom. She'll worry if I don't check in."

I see her point. "Yeah, good idea. We don't want her to worry. We should also do some housekeeping about work. We ought to both take some vacation time and stay out of the office this upcoming week. They'll be expecting us at the temp site on Monday, otherwise."

"I can do that." She says, then looks at me wonderingly. "When we were at the table, you squeezed my knee fairly firmly. You didn't want me to disclose Bob's letter, did you?"

"Yeah, that's right. I'm glad you caught on."

"You don't want him to know?"

"Not right now, but maybe later as he learns more." I explain. "We have to be careful what information we filter to him. I don't want to put either of us in his crosshairs. Also, I don't want him to find out about the money in storage."

"Jesus Christ, I forgot about the money." She says softly.

Bob's worry rings in my head. *I hope you can find a way to use it, and it is not a curse.*

We make our way to the car and I call Uncle Danny.

"Jonny Boy, what's up? How's the house working out?"

"Good Danny, it's fine. Thanks again."

"No problem, what can I do for you?"

"Hey, do you remember when I said the reason I needed to stay at your house was because my apartment was being painted?"

"Yeah."

"Well, it's something bigger than that. I need your help. Can we meet at the house?"

"On my way." He says. "You okay?"

It would be better to lay this out for him in person. "Yeah, I'm okay. I can explain it to you there. Danny –"

"What?"

I take a deep breath. "Thanks for all you do for me. I love you."

"Shut the hell up, asshole." He snaps. "Ehh … love you, too."

21

I t's chilly inside the car. The Fiat's been sitting idle for a fair amount of time and has to run some before the heat starts to crank up. I need to let Santa know we Uber'd into Portland for Alison's car, so I pull my phone out to text him.

"Who're you calling?"

"Texting. I'm letting Santa know we're good on a ride." I try to compose a text, but my fingers are cold and aren't working as well as I'd like them to.

"Are you going to tell him about our meeting with Bond?"

I'm feeling like a contestant on a quiz show, but she's nervous and chatty, and I get it.

"At some point, either on the phone or when we see him again. I'm not going to text him the story."

We ride the remainder of the short trip mostly in silence. Uncle Danny's probably already at his house right now waiting for us, no doubt wondering what's wrong. I imagine my relationship with Danny to be a lot like his must have been with my dad. His parents, my grandparents, died before their time; one in a car wreck and the other from cigarettes – the old coffin nails. Dad was twenty-seven at the time his last parent died when he gained custody of Danny, who was only around fifteen. Danny couldn't wait to get out of the house after high school graduation. Dad said he was a fighter; always in a scrape or two. He frequently got into more trouble than his opponents did because of his boxing training. After graduation he went into the Navy for two reasons – one, he loves the sea; and two, he was told by the recruiter he could box in the service and kick as much ass as he wanted to without getting in trouble for it. He's calmed down a lot since then, but I still wouldn't cross him.

Alison breaks me out of my zone-out. "Do you think we should drive all the way to the house? I mean, we didn't want the Uber coming all the way down the road. Maybe we should park on a side street near where we were picked up and walk the rest of the way?"

"That's not a bad idea." I consider. "Especially if someone follows us."

"After we see Danny, we ought to go to Big Billy's and check out the money." I'm a little excited to see if it's really there.

"Okay." She says dejectedly.

My phone vibrates. A text from Santa lights up the home screen responding to my earlier Uber text:

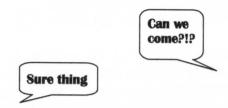

I guess he wants to see the half-million in cash as well. I'll be surprised if Alison wants to keep the money. She'd be right in turning it in, too. Probably go a long way to clearing her name.

The walk from the car to the house helps clear my head. Alison reached out for my hand early on, significantly buoying my spirits. We take a roundabout route down to the public beach; walking about a half mile or so, then come up from the dunes and enter the road further down from the house. Finally, we backtrack a considerable distance. We see no one on the beach, so I think we're good.

Danny's Jeep sits out front, more on the yard than the driveway, and as we approach we can hear Led Zeppelin loudly singing about wanting a *Whole Lotta Love.*

I open the storm door and the music goes quiet.

"Jonny, get in here." Danny shouts.

"Hey, Danny." I respond. "Thanks for meeting with us. Let me introduce you to Alison."

I move aside, and Alison steps up to greet him. She reaches her hand out to shake his, and he snatches it and pulls her in for a warm hug and kiss on her cheek. Danny wears a huge smile on his face causing his eyes to squint with exuberance. He has shag-curly black hair with just a few flecks of gray sprinkled about. Danny's one of those guys just below average height; probably around five-nine or so, but he's built like a brick shit-house. The gray sweatshirt he's wearing looks like it's caked in sea salt and maybe some grease. He was more than likely out pulling lobster traps this morning just for fun. This guy's never met a stranger. He looks like he smiles out of every pore in his body.

"Holy! You are totally stunning!" He says uninhibitedly, over-enunciating every word. "Seriously, you guys are dating?" He looks at me incredulously and then back to Alison. He doesn't give either of us any time to respond and goes right on jabbering, probing Alison to admit if she's my girlfriend.

"Thank you, and yes, Jon is my boyfriend." Alison answers as she looks at me and smiles. "At least I think I'm his girlfriend."

She says it inquisitorially, and I don't miss a beat. "Of course. From my wildest dreams to reality."

"Ha! Don't blow it, dork." Danny injects sarcastically but light-heartedly and we all laugh. "Alright, tell me what's going on. By the way, I bought some food and drinks and stuff – booze too, to stock the house for you. Feel free to help yourself to whatever you want."

"Thanks, Danny." I reply as Alison says, "Thank you."

"Well, I don't know where to start." I announce while walking to the refrigerator to get a beer. I bring one back for everyone. I'll have whatever anyone doesn't want.

"I think we might be in some trouble." At hearing this, Danny goes quiet. The transformation is startling. "You know about the building explosion in Portland?"

"Yeah. Crazy scene down there." He says.

Alison nods in agreement.

"That's where Alison and I work … where we used to work." I backpedal.

"Jesus Christ, Jon I didn't even think of that. Are you okay? You guys okay?" He's sitting on the edge of his seat, focused on us intently.

"Yeah, we're good. Alison was inside the building, opposite the blast and didn't get hurt – she walked out totally fine." I'm looking at her when I say this; she seems to be re-living the moment.

"I was outside when it happened, but this is where it gets crazy."

I move pretty quickly through the events of the day prior to and following the blast, skipping the events of the evening back at my apartment, though. I'll leave that for story time after this is all over and Uncle Danny and I are out for beers. Conversely, I do recount everything I can remember about the next day with my time at the police department with Agents Brown and Reyes and the follow-up interaction with Bond.

Uncle Danny interrupts. "Brown and Reyes are full of shit."

"Absolutely! Bond thinks so too, but it's more than that. He said I was the only person he saw them interview! We met with Bond again earlier today and he told us some things that have us nervous. I'll get to that in a minute, but I'm gonna let Alison pick up from here."

"Well," she begins, "this is awkward for me to talk about, but I was in a short-term relationship with one of the partners in the firm."

Uncle Danny looks at me.

Alison quickly pipes up, "Jon and I weren't together then."

"It's cool." I say. "Go on, Alison."

"After Jon had his FBI interview, we were expected to attend a firm-wide meeting later in the afternoon to figure out what we were supposed to do about work in the wake of the bombing. I hadn't heard from Bob – his name was Bob – since before the blast. He didn't come to work that day and I couldn't get in touch with him. I was worried for his well-being, so I asked Jon and another friend of ours to come with me to his house to check on him."

"You said 'was'." Danny interjects, and I just nod my head. Alison isn't able to talk about it any further, so I recount our experience in Bob's torched house.

"God damn, that was the house over in Fairview Hill?" Danny asks. "Is this all related?"

"Exactly and yes." I respond. "We almost didn't get out."

I assume control of the story and finish up while Alison goes to the bathroom to regroup. I take the opportunity to talk to Danny privately. "Let's wait for her to come back so she doesn't miss anything, but Danny this is fucked up. There's more to it and ultimately, we don't know what to do. I'm pretty fucking nervous, but I'm trying not to let on to her that I am."

"You haven't gone to police yet, beyond Bond?"

"No. That might not be safe either. Bond told us more."

Danny has trouble remaining patient and waiting for Alison to come back. "How do you know this is all related?"

Alison catches the question as she's walking back and answers before I can.

"I'll show you."

22

D anny quietly puts down Bob's letter. I had taken the opportunity to mix drinks for us while he was reading and I'm just returning to the table.

After I sit down, he says, "Definitely related. Did he kill himself or did somebody set it up to look like he did?"

"Eh, we're not sure. His letter seems to support that he did himself in. Bond doesn't know about the letter, but he knows Bob was dead before the house was torched. He has contacts in the medical examiner's office and he told us the autopsy report indicates there wasn't any smoke damage to his lungs, and they found remnants of the cord. Obviously, we already knew it. We saw him swinging from the ceiling. We think the fire was set only to destroy any evidence that may have been left behind."

Alison becomes noticeably uncomfortable with the casualness of my response. "I'm sorry, babe." I reach out, placing my hand on hers. It's trembling slightly.

I focus my attention back to Danny. "I'll tell you about the rest of our meeting with Bond, but first I want to tell you why we're here and why we may be in danger."

I detail the trip from Bob's house to Alison's apartment, and its subsequent condition, including the knife imbedded in the picture. I follow that up with our pop-in attempt to see Bond at the police station, our discovery of his administrative leave, and finally, our encounter with the Black Mercedes SUV.

"We didn't think it was safe to stay in either of our apartments, and I didn't think it was smart to go to the police, so we called you. We figured you would know the next move."

"Good plan, I'm happy you did. Anybody catch sight of you at Bob's house?"

"Not that we're aware of, but we can't be sure." I reply.

Alison adds, "No one from law enforcement at least."

I recount the follow-up meeting with Bond. "We just got here from talking with Bond. We parked at the end of your road and walked in through the beach inlet in case anyone followed us. Bond knows some of what's going on with Bob's role in the weapons scheme and he's been working on the case. Says he received an 'anonymous tip.' His motivation, in part, is because of his administrative suspension from the police force that he believes is caused by 'pissing people off' at the station. He thinks Brown and Reyes are bad news and later on in the meeting he said he thought there may be dirty cops there as well. He's hoping that breaking this case will get him reinstated in good standing."

Danny's looking up at the ceiling, ruminating. "Neither of you had anything to do with the fraud, correct?"

"Correct." I reply.

"But both of you know exactly how the fraud works from this guy's letter?" He asks rhetorically. "And you said you didn't show the letter to Bond?"

"Nope. Bond knew who Alison was from his own research into the case. It spooked us some. He knew she had worked on the account; I worked on it too, and we were afraid he might try to wrap us up in it. It was easier for us to keep the letter to ourselves than share it with him and risk having to try and un-ring the bell."

"Makes perfect sense." He opines.

"Which part?" Alison questions.

"Well, Bond's point of view, at any rate. He's investigating Bob and knows you guys are on the account as well. Bob turns up dead and Jon is the only person he's seen interviewed by the FBI's Bash Brothers."

"So where does that leave us?" I grouse.

"Look, I'm trying to get a lay of the land here. The part I'm not getting is the FBI thing. Someone else besides you has to know about … what's his name? … Reyes? … and his involvement in the bank and calls bullshit on their EMF explanation. Reyes sounds like more than just 'bad news' as Bond puts it. Since when do FBI guys wear street clothes when they're on duty?"

Good point. I hadn't thought of that until he mentioned it.

I want another drink, but I'm thinking it's probably a good idea to switch back to beer.

"Anyone?" I offer, shaking my empty glass, rattling ice cubes. No takers. On my way to the kitchen I divert over to the bathroom to take a leak. I pull my phone out and look at it while I'm peeing and see a text from Santa:

While I finish my business, I text back to him one-handed that we'll meet him and Merri at Big Billy's at five.

As I'm getting another beer out of the fridge, a fleeting thought crosses my mind that I 'broke the seal' but vanishes just as quickly when I get a return text from Santa saying, 'OK.'

"So, where does this leave us?" I ask once more, walking from the kitchen to the table. I start to feel a buzz coming on.

"Alison's apartment was ransacked. Bob's house was torched. You think you may have been followed when you were looking for Bond the first time." Danny recounts.

I get where he's going with this.

"Somebody knows that you guys know what's going on. They probably know Bob has mailed you something too, Alison, because they were looking for it at your apartment."

Exactly what I thought. We're both glaring at him intensely.

"What that says to me is even though you weren't in on it; they know you know about it, and they probably aren't gonna let up until they find you."

"So, where do we go from here?" He asks, with every intention of answering his own question.

"You're both safe here for now; it seems you took good precaution in the event you were initially followed. I have a buddy of mine who works for the Department of Homeland Security. I'm gonna connect with him on the down-low tomorrow and see what he recommends. We'll figure out how to handle this."

"So we just sit tight?" I'm anxious for a resolution.

Danny's right to the point. "Don't contact police or FBI. Except for Bond. He may have useful info. Don't tell him where you're staying or anything that could identify where you are."

He continues, "You guys can use my Jeep. Alison, I can relocate your car. I assume it's the white piss-cutter parked on the side street before my road that sticks out like a sore thumb? I noticed it as I was coming in. I got here about ten minutes before you did."

"Yes." She says glumly.

"Fine. I'll take it either to your apartment complex or a parking garage or wherever you want me to store it. Personally, I would take it to your apartment. If someone's looking for you, they already know where your apartment is, anyway."

"In the meantime," Danny says as if we weren't already hanging on his every word, "Jonny, when's the last time you handled a firearm?"

Alison glances at Danny and then over to me. Danny reassures her it's nothing to worry about and he's only being overly cautious.

"Last time I went to the range with you, I guess. I can't recollect another time since then, really. It must be at least five years."

"Alright, we're gonna run through it just for kicks and then I'll leave two handguns here for you. A sweet Glock Gen Four I bought last year and my old Ruger. I have plenty of others at Jennifer's."

Danny disappears towards his master bedroom.

"Jon, this is crazy! If we need guns to stay safe, we need to tell someone what's going on, right now!" Alison implores.

"I hear ya. Can we wait until Danny has a chance to talk to his guy? What if Bond is right? What if we tell the wrong people at the police station?"

Alison fidgets and doesn't like it, but I think she gets it.

"That's it then. After we hear from his guy, we go to the police or a news station or to somewhere we know we'll be okay." She counters.

Danny comes bouncing back carrying two black gun cases. He loves dealing with firearms.

"Check this out." He's animated as hell and opens up one of the two cases to reveal a shiny brand new-looking nine-millimeter semi-automatic handgun. She really is a beauty. I pick it up, open the action, peer inside the chamber to ensure it's empty, and then close it up. I do this in one swift motion and then proceed to aim it at an imaginary target before putting it down. Danny's frigging loving it; he's smiling from ear to ear. Alison is nervous, but I think deep down she may feel reassured with my familiarity with firearms. I have to admit it, I feel cool as a dog's nose in December right now.

"Ah, I'm not worried about you." Danny laughs. "You haven't lost anything."

I replace the Glock in its case and set it aside the Ruger. "Magazines? Ammo?" I ask.

"I'll load you up. No problem. Hey, once I get it together, why don't we go get rid of your car?" He directs to Alison. "And by the way, I'd love to check out that half-mil if it's okay with you?"

"Funny thing you ask." I say, grinning. "We would too. We're meeting someone there at five. The guy that was with us at Bob's. Let's get the car squared away and go."

23

W e're cutting it close to five o'clock on our foray to Big Billy's. Danny left the house before us and took the same backtrack route that we did coming in; walking down around the beach out of an abundance of caution. We left his house sometime thereafter, with Alison driving Danny's Jeep, so we would get to her car at the same time Danny does. He thinks I've had too much to drink to be safe behind the wheel and he's probably right. Danny trails us back to the apartment complex so he can drop off her car. We park a couple of blocks away and wait for him to walk back. Big Billy's Storage is in the opposite direction, out near the mall, so we pull a 180° and hightail it out.

Santa and Merri are already in the parking lot when we pull up. They get out of the Beast and stand next to the Jeep, waiting for us to get out.

"Hey, buddy." I say as I open the door. "Meet my Uncle Danny. Danny this is Ben, the guy who was with us at Bob's house. We call him Santa; I do anyway, and this is his girlfriend, Merri. She knows everything going on."

"Santa? What the fuck for … you a jolly old bastard?" Danny grouses. "Ahh … I'm just playing; nice to meet you and you too, Merri." His trademark smile returns. Dang, Danny threw me off there for a second.

Santa and Merri try to shake hands but predictably, hugs come out of Danny.

"Seriously though," he asks, "why Santa? That's a stupid fucking nickname."

"Some other time." Santa grins. I look over to Merri and see a wave of relief wash over her.

I give her a wink and change the subject. "Alright, who's ready to go in?"

The storage building is actually quite modern, unsophisticated name notwithstanding. It's a block-style, multi-tiered, climate-controlled facility with what appears to be impressive security and surveillance.

"How do we get in?" Danny asks.

"We have a keypad code. It was in Bob's letter." I respond.

Alison steps ahead to the access door and enters the code, 1-1-1-3. She pulls the handle and … nothing. Her hand wrenches off of the handle unexpectedly, jarring her fingers in the process.

"Damn it." She winces, waggling her hand.

"Let me try." I offer as I press forward. "One, one, one, three." I count off as I key it in. I tug on the door, and as before, it doesn't move.

"Look at the units inside." Santa observes through the window. "There are keypads next to each of them. There's a different code to get into the building than what's on the unit."

Great. What the hell's the code to get into the building?

"Alison, what's the code to get inside?" Merri asks, mind-reading me.

"I don't know." She mumbles while retrieving Bob's letter. "He only referred to our first date which was on Friday the 13th."

She paws through the letter seemingly for the better part of the next half-hour, and we see no other mention of a code.

"There's some serious security here." I say, pointing to cameras positioned intermittently throughout the property. "We can't stay here. We're gonna draw some unwanted attention at some point."

"Why don't we get dinner while we're out this way and figure out the next move." Santa suggests. "I'm hungry."

"You're always hungry." Merri counters.

"I'm in." Danny snaps.

That settles it. We're going to dinner.

We decide on Larson's for dinner. It's a mall-chain steakhouse, but the food is pretty good, and the beers are ice cold. Santa eats like a frigging horse and Merri rides him on it like a seasoned cowgirl.

"Christ, Ben. You're making me nauseous just watching you."

We must make an interesting picture to the rest of the patrons. Santa smiles with a mouthful of mashed potatoes while Merri chastises him. Alison is distant, presumably wracking her brain trying to see where she went wrong on the code. Danny's kind of quiet, pretty much minding his own business, and I'm doing my routine psycho-analytical judgment on everyone.

"We met with Detective Bond again." I direct to Santa. He looks up, but before he responds I give him the details. "He knows Bob was in a scam at HW and Alison worked on the account. He got an 'unsolicited anonymous tip.' Not sure how detailed the tip was but he's pretty intuitive as to what's happening. He knows Bob was dead before the house burned, but not if it was a suicide or homicide. He got access to the autopsy report. Added to that, he believes the bombing and Bob and all of us are related."

"All of us? What does he know about Merri and I?" Santa asks concernedly.

"Merri and me, dude. Object of the preposition. And not much."

I can't help but be a dick with the grammar thing and I'm tired of recounting the story. "We didn't share the letter with him. We weren't comfortable doing much of anything until we talked to Danny."

Santa responds indignantly. "Screw you and your object of the preposi …"

"I got it!" Alison suddenly roars, vaulting up from her seat. She jars the table hard enough to knock over her water glass and scare the living shit out of the rest of us.

"I got it." She repeats breathlessly. "We went on two first dates! When Bob asked me out, he asked me out on two first dates! He said the time between the first and second date was excruciating. Should I call? Should I text? Am I getting mixed messages? He thought people needed two dates to decide whether or not there's a connection worth continuing. He called them two first dates!"

"How could I have not pieced this together sooner?" She goes on. "He asked me out for Friday the 13th, one, one, one, three; but he also asked me out for that following Sunday at the same time. One, one, one, five! We need to go!"

We clear the bill, gather our stuff, and head for the door; all in record time. I have to stop and pee again because I've chugged a couple more beers since leaving Danny's. Alison is super-annoyed at having to wait for me, but what are you gonna do?

"One, one, one, five." Alison slowly verbalizes each number as she punches them into the keypad. The green light activates, and we hear a distinct 'click' sound indicating the door is unlocked. Alison opens it up and we all push feverishly in as if at any moment the door will change its mind and re-lock before we can enter.

There's no one around. The facility has twenty-four-hour access and at seven-thirty on a Saturday night, no one's here.

"We're looking for pod A, unit 35." Alison reminds us.

This place has the feel of a mini-airport. Departure from Concourse A, Gate 35.

It's easier finding the unit than I thought it would be. Each floor is designated a 'pod,' so pod A is simply the first floor. Ten units border each wall of every pod – forty per floor. We locate unit 35 and all stand silently looking at the door.

"Well ... ??" Danny squawks.

We watch Alison as she approaches the keypad. She types in the code and we subsequently hear the familiar 'click' indicating the door is unlocked. It resembles an overhead garage door. We wait for her to lift it up.

"Is there a light in here?" Alison asks.

I reach inside around the corner behind the keypad and my hand runs over a switch pad. I flick it up and the room lights up with a bright fluorescent haze.

"Get inside." Danny orders, and we follow. "Clear the opening so I can shut the door."

When we're closed in, we take a moment to look around. It's a large room, probably fifteen by fifteen feet, with much more space than Bob needed. On the floor, sits a bunch of brown bags spread about with no readily apparent regard, as if someone simply threw them out with the weekly trash.

Santa inspects the room. "There must be a couple dozen bags in here."

"I suspect there are twenty-five bags." Danny interjects. "His letter said he was receiving twenty thousand-dollar payments."

Danny's dead right. Twenty-five brown bags, each teeming with cold, hard cash. Oh man – big bills, little bills, all kinds of bills. They actually take up less room than I expected. In the back of the container sits probably a dozen empty bags scattered about.

"I don't want it." Alison states matter-of-factly. "I don't want it. Nothing good can come from this."

I'm not surprised by her position. "Let's just lock it back up." I suggest. "I think we ought to get out of here for now and chill out somewhere and figure this out."

No one counters my proposal, so I assume we're all in agreement. Everyone trickles out orderly; I flick the switch off and pull the door closed. I punch in the key code, hear a 'click,' and pull back on the door to ensure it's auto-locked. It doesn't move.

"So where does everyone want to go?" I ask. I don't really have a preference, but I do have to pee again before we leave.

24

We ultimately decide to call it an early night. I'm a little disappointed because I'm ready to go out, but it's probably a smart move to keep a low profile.

"You ought to think about moving the money." Danny says to us as we drive him back to his girlfriend's house. "If anyone has access to the letter, they'll know it's there. And they'll find a way to get in and get at it."

"I don't want it." Alison repeats.

I join in the dialogue. "Understood, but would you rather have those assholes get it? Illegal or not, Bob worked hard for that money; he paid for it with his life. He earned it, and he wanted you to have it."

So there.

Alison's eyes penetrate into me, but before she responds, I add meekly, "We don't want the police to get it either, do we?"

Alison smiles warmly. "We?"

I kind of wrinkle up my nose and mouth trying to look cute, but I imagine I more likely resemble Yoda.

"You're right, though. And Danny, let's figure out a safe place and move the cash tomorrow." She says straightforwardly.

Danny doesn't hesitate. "Perfect. I've got exactly the spot if it's okay with you. I have two firearm vaults in my basement. They're both large stand-up models for safely storing guns. I only use one of them; the other one is empty. They're fireproof and weighted so they can't be easily hauled off – in fact, it would be virtually impossible. I think all of the bags could fit in one safe; if not, we can stuff the rest into the other one."

"What could be better?" Alison responds, sounding somewhat relieved.

"Cool." Danny adds. "Let's deal with it first thing in the morning."

Nice. I'll get to spend some time with Alison alone on a Sunday afternoon. "Great. We'll figure it out in the morning and have the rest of the day free." I respond optimistically.

Alison and I drop Danny off at Jennifer's house and head back to his place. She looks tired tonight and with good reason. We could both use a full night's sleep. We pull into Danny's and head inside.

"I'm going to get into my pajamas." Alison says, disappearing down the hall.

I want to check out the two gun vaults. I don't recall ever having seen them. I walk down into the basement, remembering a door situated on the far side of the house. I open it, revealing an unfinished, smallish storage area housing the furnace and oil tank. Against the basement foundation, stand the vaults. They're taller than I expected, probably close to five feet each, and maybe three feet wide and deep. Both safes are black as night except for a shiny combination dial and three-spoke steel handle on each.

These are perfect, I think to myself.

"Hey." Her voice startles me. I spin around to see Alison standing in the doorway. "Do you see anything you like?" She purrs.

She's wearing a black, satiny baby-doll negligee draped open in the front exposing her taut stomach, and matching panties.

Those are perfect, I think to myself.

She gives me the 'come here' finger gesture while strategically placing the tip of her tongue over her front teeth. So damn sexy. She turns around and starts to walk away, revealing that the backside of her panties consists merely of a thin black string visible only when it escapes from her bum cheeks.

I follow her out of the room virtually in a trance, like a cartoon character physically raised off of the ground, floating to the source of a delicious aroma by the vapors of the scent.

She pauses at the pool table. Turning to me with an inquisitive look, she pats her hand on the green felt surface.

"Want to play?" She entices me with eyes piercing directly into my soul.

I nod my head and attempt to say 'yes,' though nothing comes out but a muffled squeak. She laughs at my struggle, but not in a condescending way. She's feeling like a woman; an erotic, sensual woman enjoying the effect she's having on me.

Alison pushes herself up onto the railing into a sitting position and I draw close to her. The pool table is high enough so when standing in front of her, we are nearly eye-to-eye. She wraps her legs around me, pulling me in tight, and begins unbuttoning my pants. I'm trying to remove my shirt at the same time in between deep kissing.

I swing up onto the table while reaching for her G-string. I tug on one side; it stretches out, but it's not coming down. It feels as though it might snap if I pull too hard. I abandon that side and move over to the other. I pull gently, but that side won't come down either. Christ, I didn't refer to the G-String Remover User's Manual in advance. I pull harder.

"Wait ... wait a minute, baby. You'll rip them like that. You have to pull both sides at the same time straight down, like this. They're a little tight."

Alison helps me out by taking it off herself and then places it in my hand. I look at it stupidly. I think it's contracted to the size of a small rubber band.

"Hey." Alison brings me back to the moment by lying back onto the table, pulling me into her.

This is happening. Holy shit, this is happening.

25

D anny stocked his place pretty well. There's something about a sunny morning, particularly on the weekend that energizes me, so I'm up making breakfast. I can hear Alison rustling around in the bedroom – good timing, I'm almost done.

"Good morning." She calls out.

Alison comes into view from the hallway and walks up to me at the stove. "Mmm, that looks yummy." She says while stretching her arms around me and delicately giving my crotch a wrap-around squeeze. "The eggs look yummy, too."

I turn to face her, then plant a kiss on her forehead. She's wearing her Dalmatian pajamas again and looking pretty damn adorable with her hair tied up in a messy bun.

"Well, hello there. Coffee's going and there's Diet Coke in the fridge. Pick your poison. You hungry?"

"Ya, starving. Hey, after we move the money out of the storage unit, can we stop by my apartment so I can get some more things? I need more clothes and personal items and stuff."

"I think so. How about we clean out the storage unit and bring it back here to lock up, and then we can go to both of our places? I need a bunch of stuff, too."

"That sounds perfect!"

"Great. Grab a plate. Everything's ready."

Breakfast is relaxing, but we need to plan for how we approach the day.

"Getting the money and bringing it here shouldn't be a problem. I'm gonna have Danny go with us. He needs to show us how to get into the safes." I also want Danny with us for protection in case we have any trouble.

"But," I continue, "we ought to be careful going to your apartment. Going to my place should be fine, but when we go to your building, we should park a ways away and walk over like we did with Danny when we brought your car back."

"Okay. Let's eat, then I'm going to shower and get ready."

"Perfect. And after I'm finished, I'll call Danny and get the ball rolling."

Ugh – and I'll have to clean this breakfast mess.

"Hey Danny, it's Jon."

"Jonny Boy, you ready to go?"

"Uh … no, not really, but we can be in about a half-hour."

"Step it up boy, the day's a-wasting."

"Christ man, it's eight-thirty."

"Exactly."

"How about meeting us at Big Billy's in an hour? By the way, I took a look at the gun vaults last night. You're totally right. They couldn't be more perfect."

The thought crosses my mind that his pool table is pretty damn awesome, as well.

"Yeah, I think so, too. Listen, go into my bedroom closet. In the back, on the right, I have a stack of old Navy stuff. In the pile, I have a folded-up, camouflage Navy duffel bag. Bring it with you; it should hold all of it."

"Will do. See you in a bit."

We disconnect the call and I look at the kitchen mess with loathing. I spend some time working through it, but eventually lose my mojo. "Ech, later." I mutter.

I head down the hall to Danny's room, passing Alison along the way. She's exiting the bathroom completely naked, save for a bath towel wrapped around her head like a turban.

"Oops." She feigns embarrassment as she vanishes into the bedroom, shutting the door behind her. I can't help but laugh.

Danny's closet is a heck of a lot bigger than I remember. It's not Imelda Marcos shoe storage-size, but it's definitely walk-in. It occurs to me it's been renovated sometime after I left. I flick the light switch and see why. He stores military boots seemingly of every style on neat racks lining the base of the wall. Dress shoes, camouflage boots, work boots, everyday boots, and sneakers. All of his old uniforms hang orderly from front to back, along with naval hats, shirts, and coats. He has a lot of stuff in here. Danny's punched through the old wall and incorporated the adjacent storage closet into the expansion. In the back righthand corner sits a pile of assorted bags and backpacks. The camouflage duffel is easy to find and I pull it out, revealing a sizeable photo album lying underneath. My heart skips a beat. I tuck it under my arm and leave with the duffel.

Finishing kitchen clean-up wasn't that bad, if I'm being truthful. In the interim, Alison got ready faster than I thought she would, helping us to get out with plenty of time to meet Danny. Big Billy's is just as deserted on a Sunday morning as it is on a Saturday night, and we handle our business efficiently and without incident.

Danny follows us back to his house, driving with the money in Jennifer's car. It didn't all fit into the duffel bag, but last minute prior to leaving his house, I went back into his closet and brought another smaller bag I had found.

Danny carries the bigger duffel bag into the house double-slung crisscrossed over his back and heads directly to the basement. I follow along with the smaller bag. There isn't much room to spare with the two of us and the bags crammed into the corner nook. No issue to him though, he proceeds to launch straight into his vault-opening infomercial.

"Alright. It's pretty simple. Spin the combination dial two full turns clockwise to reset. Then it's the usual stop on the first number, back counterclockwise to the next number, and then you turn clockwise to the final number. BUT –" Danny explains, "on the final number you have to go one full turn past it. So, you just skip it and land on it at your next pass. Got it?"

He's demonstrating with the actual combination while he's talking, and after he reaches his final number he begins to rotate the three-spoke handle like he's steering an old pirate ship.

"Wa-La." He says proudly, opening the door.

Voilà, but whatever. I'm not correcting him. Santa, yes; Danny, no.

"Let's pull these shelves out; we ought to be able to squeeze all the money in."

He's sort of right. We try jamming all of the money in while it's still in the brown bags and it becomes clear it's not going to work. Rather than place the remaining bags into the other safe that's already part-way full, we remove all of the bundles from the bags and stack them in neatly. This works out, and with a little room to spare.

We step back and gaze into the safe. Jesus Christ. There's a half-million dollars in there.

"Hey, Danny." I say when we get upstairs. "I found this photo album in your closet under the duffel bags this morning. I didn't open it; I wanted to make sure it was okay with you."

Danny looks at the book I'm holding.

"Yeah." He says softly. "Go ahead. You'll like it."

I sit on the couch with the album in my lap. Alison perches next to me and Danny's close by. I open up the first page to reveal a sleeve of old Polaroid Instamatic pictures. They're of my dad and Danny. Some together, some solo. My grandparents are in some of them as well. I page through the album and see they're all primarily of Dad and Danny. You can feel from the pictures that Dad was reserved and quiet and Danny was a handful – never sitting still. Man, I miss this guy. When I get to the last page, my emotions get the best of me: It's me, Dad, and Danny. Dad must be early thirties and Danny late teens. I'm around four years old and eating an ice cream cone on a sunny day. Almost certainly, I have more ice cream smeared on my face than what made it into my belly.

Danny's emotional as well. "Keep it."

"Thanks." I say, tucking the picture into my shirt pocket.

"I'll catch up with you guys later. I gotta get back to Jennifer's."

"Okay, thanks for the help today."

Danny heads out the door quickly, and I'm sure it's because he doesn't want us to see him sad. Alison and I are right behind him and on our way to each of our apartments.

26

It doesn't take me all that long at my apartment. I only need clothes, shoes, and some extra toiletries. Alison goes through my refrigerator and dumps everything that could possibly spoil. Great idea. I should also do something about the mail before it piles up too much, though it's mostly junk, anyhow. We finish up with emptying the trash into outdoor receptacles and quickly get out of Dodge.

I can sense Alison's reticence during the drive to her place. The condition of her apartment will trigger an immediate reminder of the encroachment upon her safety and security.

"You okay?" I ask.

"I can't go back to that apartment."

"No? How're we gonna get your stuff?"

"No, I mean I can't go back to living there."

"Yeah, I get it. Well, you can stay with me as long as you need to ... or want to."

I sneak a fleeting glance her way. She squeezes my thigh while continuing to stare out of the window.

This is the first reasonably warm day we've had in a long time. The short walk from the side street we parked on is actually quite comfortable, so we take our time. We're hand-in-hand, chattering about.

"Do you think anyone will find it odd we're both out of work this week?" I ask.

"Oh God, no. At least half of the office will be out if not more, I imagine. Anyway, the partners will have their hands full dealing with business issues; primarily client management. I suspect they'd rather not have us around adding to the mess."

She's right, of course. We're sailing in unchartered waters relative to work continuity; we're better off hanging tight and letting them sort out the best plan for moving ahead. Lord knows we have some emergency cash to tide us over if we need it in the meantime.

We arrive at her building complex, enter into the underground parking garage, and wait for the elevator to come down. This must be the slowest elevator in the history of human conveyance, so I begin to look around for her Fiat. It's the weekend, so the parking deck is packed with vehicles and I don't readily spot it. The elevator car arrives, and eventually, we make the ascension to her floor. Alison hands me the key.

"Will you open it up?"

"Of course." I respond as we stand in front of her door.

I deliberately work the key in a slow fashion through the damaged stick points. It feels a little easier this time than last, but I think the better of telling Alison this. I open the door slowly. Alison stands directly behind, affording me the opportunity to execute a rapid scan prior to her entering. It looks just as it did when we were here last.

"Do you want me to start picking up while you're packing your things?" I'm already beginning to clean while I wait for her response.

"If you want to. Don't knock yourself out, though."

My obsessive-compulsiveness will get the best of me if I don't start organizing. Alison rolls directly into her bedroom and I get to work. It's actually pretty quick-moving. Couch cushions reassembled, knick-knacks placed on side tables nearest to where they lay; undoubtedly some not correct, kitchen cabinet doors closed, magazines arranged orderly on the coffee table.

Alison pokes her head out of the bedroom doorway. "I feel so violated. There were people in my bedroom … in my bathroom. Pawing through my personal things."

I don't know how to respond to her, so I don't.

"Wow, that looks much better, thank you." She says appreciatively while zipping through the living room and dropping bags next to the front door. "I just need to pack some bathroom toiletries and we can get out."

"No worries. Take your time. I'm gonna check out some sports highlights, anyway."

The television remote control sits on the living room floor about as far away from the flat-screen as it could possibly be. I bend down to pick it up, then pause at the window when something outside catches my eye. It's a custom-wrapped seafood box truck. The same one we saw the night we stopped in to see if Bond was at the police station. I'm certain of it. The decorative wrap shows a faded, over-sized penguin wearing a chef's hat, holding up a fish in one hand and a whisk in the other.

That sends me over the edge. We need help, and we need it now. I snap my phone out and hit up Danny.

"Danny, it's Jon." Before he can respond I explain to him what I'm seeing out of Alison's window. "We can't do this alone any more. We have to get some help. I want to call Bond."

"Yeah, I agree with you. It's time. Where and when? I want to be there to meet him."

"Great. I was hoping you'd be on board."

"Who are you talking to?" Alison finished in the bathroom and now stands next to me, concerned.

I put my phone on speaker.

"Danny, Alison's with me. I'll call Bond right now and tell him what's going on, and that we received a letter from Bob and we want to show it to him. We'll bring it with us. When we get a meeting location, I'll let you know."

"Got it. How're you getting out?"

"We didn't park in the apartment complex; we can slip out."

"Okay. Call me if you can't. I'll be waiting."

"Thanks, Danny."

I disconnect, and before Alison can say anything, I point out the truck. "Same one from when we went to see Bond at the police station."

"I remember." She replies solemnly.

"Detective Bond, this is Jon Williams."

"Please, call me Mike."

"Mike, we need to meet. We know more about what's going on with Bob Roberts than we told you. A lot more."

I'm fast-talking to squeeze everything in as quickly as possible. "Alison received a letter from him recently, detailing his involvement in a weapons scam involving a client. We think we're being watched."

"General Defense – correct?"

I look at Alison. She knows we have to come clean.

"Yes. That's right." I admit.

"I figured as much. You very well could be under surveillance. As I said to you before, I'm convinced Reyes and Brown are involved. Both would have the capacity and means to pull it off. I'd like to see the letter if I could. Where can we meet?"

"Jesus Christ, how about the police station?" I shoot off while mimicking a 'what the fuck?' face to Alison.

"Umm, how about the parking garage next to the police station, say, on the third floor, back side? I can't exactly conduct business inside the police station just yet."

"Fine. Thirty minutes and we'll be there." I disconnect the call. "This guy's a piece of work."

"Agreed. What the hell did this guy do?"

I immediately call my uncle. "Danny? It's Jon. Thirty minutes on level three of the police station garage. Back side."

"Alright. See you there."

27

W e skip the elevator and take the stairs to the ground floor. I'm betting it's safer than going down to the underground garage. If the apartment is under surveillance, the Fiat most likely is as well. We exit from the side entrance nearest to a wooded line of trees for cover. I'm hauling one of the bigger duffel bags plus the smaller toiletry bag and Alison carries one big bag. Not exactly inconspicuous.

We jump into Danny's Jeep, backtracking through side streets, steering clear of any route remotely within the vicinity of the apartment building.

"Well, that worked out okay." I surmise.

"Ya, I didn't see anyone around. Let's just get to the police station; I'm so sick of this."

"Me too, babe."

My phone vibrates in my pocket. I reach in, then punch in my security code one-handed as I drive out of the neighboring development and onto the main thoroughfare. Santa sent me a text:

"We're on our way to see Bond." I dictate into my phone. I look at the screen to see how the translation came out:

I pass my phone to Alison. "Can you help me with this?"

"Sure." She snatches my phone. "Want me to swap out 'behind' with ... 'ass' or maybe 'bum'?"

"Hmm. 'We're on our way to see ass.' Strip club jokes. Funny."

She starts laughing at her corny joke and I can't help but laugh with her.

"Alright, I changed it to 'Bond' and sent it."

"Thanks."

"Hey, he's right back at you. He wants to know if we want to meet up afterward."

"I think it depends on how it goes with Bond."

"You mean 'behind'?" She teases.

"Yeah, something like that. It depends on how it goes with your behind. Wait, I know – ask him if he wants to meet us later at your behind … or ass … or bum."

"Jon! How dare you!" She slaps me on my forearm, pretending to be grossly insulted and embarrassed.

"You won't even get my bum." She sighs matter-of-factly.

Bam. Mic drop. #Gameover.

"Damn, baby that's cold. Well, uh, maybe you could just let him know I'll connect with him as soon as we're done?"

"Mmhmm."

It continues to warm up as the day progresses, truly turning into a magnificent day. The dirty, leftover winter snow piles that always seem to hang on well into spring are getting a solid jumpstart toward the melt-off.

"Hey, Danny's behind us." I note after looking in my rear-view mirror as we pull in. "Good timing."

We pass through the check gate at the parking garage and start the circular climb.

"He said third floor, right?"

"Ya, back side I think he said." Alison recalls. "And no butt-sex jokes!" She adds affectionately, waggling a warning finger at me.

"I would never joke about butt-sex … again."

We negotiate the corkscrew incline and enter into the third deck of the garage with Danny right behind us. Going slowly; presumably in the right direction, we start scanning side-to-side. It occurs to us we don't know what kind of vehicle Bond drives.

Against the wall bordering the elevator shaft and furthest from the deck entrance, we spot a single car. The back of it looks like a police-type vehicle with a Crown Victoria-style body or something close to it. Someone's in it; I can see the outline of a person sitting inside through the back window.

"That car over there. Gotta be him. I'll park here and walk over to the car and make sure it's him. If it isn't, I'll be right back. Stay here for now."

"I don't want to stay here by myself."

I can't say I blame her, and frankly, I love that she wants to be close to me. We exit the Jeep as Danny's walking over to us. He's parked nearby.

"You have the letter?" I ask Alison.

"Ya, it's in my bag."

Danny's looking at us.

"You ready?" I ask him.

"Ha. C'mon, man. I was born ready. Let's go."

I take the lead with Danny behind me and Alison closely in tow. The driver-side door tucks in tightly adjacent to the elevator wall so we approach from the passenger side. I notice a 'Police Interceptor' insignia on the rear bumper. Huh. Interesting he still drives an unmarked police vehicle while on suspension.

Damn, I can't tell for sure if it's him. The side windows have a dark tint, revealing only a silhouette. I rap my knuckles on the passenger window. No movement. Nothing. I look at Danny and he nods his head toward the door in a signal for me to try the door handle.

I pull the handle, open the door, and stick my head into the door-frame.

"Mike? What the fuuu …? Whoa, shit! Shiiit!"

I forcefully rear back into Danny, catching him completely by surprise, sending him into Alison.

"What the fuck, man?" Danny's rubbing his cheek on the spot where my elbow connected.

"It's him, it's him. He's gone. Oh shit! We gotta get out of here! We gotta go. Fuck, he's dead."

"What? Move." Danny directs.

I take Alison by the arm and motion her back to the car, walking part of the way with her. "Go back to the car, baby. He's gone. He's dead. He's been shot." She moves without delay and without objection.

I'm prattling on rapid-fire. Stopping to take a deep breath, I turn around and cruise back to the car. Danny's bent over; he's peering into the vehicle. As I reach him, he steps back then closes the door and wipes the handle and surrounding area clean with his shirtsleeve.

"Gunshot to the head. At least one. Firearm's by his side." His assessment is almost clinical. "We need to leave. Now."

"Let's go to the station!" I plead.

Danny grasps my shoulders as though to pull me back to reality and locks eyes with me. "Someone else must find him. You cannot create a link, or maybe another link to him or what he was working on. We must leave now."

Rational thought flows back into me and we cruise back to the vehicles.

"Meet me at my house. Don't stop, don't deviate. Go straight to my house. Got it?"

"Yes. Got it."

"Hey. Look at me." Danny says calmly. "You okay?"

"Yeah, I'm good. Right behind you."

"It looked like a self-inflicted gunshot wound entering the side of his head. His firearm was by his side; the same side as the entry point. He was still strapped in his seatbelt, allowing him to remain upright. File folders were visible; nothing else around that I could detect." Danny expounds soberly, describing the scene.

We're sitting around his kitchen table in a state of semi-shock.

"Doesn't make sense. The guy had no reason that we knew of. He said he needed to get back in good standing to finish his pension requirements. That doesn't sound much like someone who wanted to off himself." I'm trying to process what I saw with little success.

"Yeah, but nobody really knows what's going on in someone's personal life. It might not make any sense, but it sure as hell looks like a suicide." Danny says.

"Why would he have agreed to this meeting last minute if he was planning on killing himself?" Alison asks.

Danny and I glance at each other and leave her question unanswered.

"In any case," Danny offers, "you both need to stay far away. If forensics comes back asserting a homicide, you become prime suspects if law enforcement links you to his case. Your best scenario has the medical examiner's findings coming back as a suicide with no further review into Bond's work."

"So where does that leave us?" Alison appeals.

"We need to go to police, FBI, whoever." I chime in.

"Yes, but we don't know who we can trust. Was Bond working with anybody?" Danny asks.

"Don't think so, but he could have been." I say.

"Let's go right to the police chief. Does that make sense?" Alison inquires.

All three of us look at one another, slowly nodding heads.

"It does, pending the determination of Bond's death. We need to wait for that." Danny reminds us. "If it doesn't come back as a suicide, we need a Plan B. If it is ruled a suicide, we need to make sure we don't give them cause to re-open an investigation with whatever you choose to disclose to them, either."

"So," I begin, "if he didn't kill himself, and I don't think he did; who did it and how the hell did they know he would be there?"

"All good questions. My guess is the likely source came from a listening device. Someone has his house tapped." Danny turns and looks at Alison. "Or yours."

"We were there." Alison bemoans. "After we finished moving the money, we went to my apartment to pack clothes. Jon, you were talking to him on your phone. You discussed where and when we would meet him! You called Danny and said it out loud to him, too!"

Alison has tears streaming down her face realizing we may have played a role in Bond's death. An innocent role, but a role nonetheless.

"Well, if that's the case then it's all on me, not you. If someone wanted him dead, they would have found out where he was going to be regardless of our phone conversation."

"Exactly." Danny agrees.

Alison peers into her lap. Softly she whispers, "Does that go for us, too?"

"We got you." Danny assures her, placing his hand onto hers. "I'm gonna stay here tonight if that's okay with you two."

"Ya, of course." Alison replies.

"Absolutely." I throw in for good measure. "And Alison, I think the Plan B Danny says we need to prepare for includes contacting Peabo and having him access work papers, files, and anything else he can find on General Defense and your work associated with them. We need to see all of Bob's inventory attestations. We should document and catalogue everything you worked on, in addition to the extent of Bob's involvement – and your lack thereof. Let's see if we can catch up with him tomorrow. Our IT group has to be at the temp office trying to put everything back together. That, coupled with Bob's letter, will be your – our – prime defense. That also reminds me we should be thinking about lawyering up."

"Who the fuck's Peabo?" Danny says with a not-so-subtle hint of revulsion.

Alison fields this one. "Peter Bowen, our head IT guy. He goes by his nickname, Peabo. Kinda like J-Lo."

"No kidding? I didn't know that." I interject. "I thought Peabo was his last name."

Alison throws me a look of semi-disgust. "Dude, seriously??"

Danny adds, "Man, you guys know some people with the dumbest fucking nicknames."

Can't really argue with him there.

28

The sun hangs low in the early spring sky. We've just finished dinner with clean-up underway. We all participated in cooking the meal, relaxing us somewhat following the day's events. I've been checking online periodically for news on Bond's death. He's been found, though not identified. The report simply states a body has been found in a vehicle at the Portland police department parking garage.

We never connected with Santa after we left Bond, but I called him and let him know what happened. He's pretty much freaked out and nervous for everyone's safety, and rightfully so. At Danny's suggestion, I mentioned he may want to step back and distance himself from us for the short-term until we get this sorted out. Following a short protest, he agreed.

"Jon, you want to go downstairs and shoot some pool?" Danny asks.

"Sure, sounds good. Babe, you want to join us?"

"No, that's okay; you need a little alone time. I'll finish cleaning up. Go ahead."

"You sure?"

"Of course. Get out of here." She flashes me a smile looking to be genuine and free of apprehension with being upstairs alone. "I'm texting with Merri, anyway. We need girl time, too, ya know."

"Right on. Come on down whenever you're done."

Danny and I head downstairs to his well-appointed man cave.

"I still can't believe there's a half-mil in my gun vault." Danny says with a truncated laugh.

"I know. It's nuts how this whole thing unfolded so quickly." I respond while racking the pool balls. "I mean, I guess it's been going on for a long time with Bob, but we got swept up into it so damn fast."

Danny chalks his cue. "You know, somebody out there's upset this money pipeline is ending. I gotta believe they're trying to find a way to keep it going or to eliminate all ties to it."

"Eh, I think you're right. Maybe it's both. Bob's gone and now Bond's gone. We've got to cover our asses. That's why we're going out to see Peabo tomorrow and gather everything we can on the work files. I want to see what Bob's inventory valuation and documentation procedures look like."

"How's that gonna work?" Danny asks while breaking the rack.

"Well, I'm not totally sure. What we had in paper filing is probably destroyed from the bombing. It's definitely not accessible right now. We've been in the process of transferring all of our paper files to electronic form and that's what I need to find out about. I don't know if Peabo transferred all of GD's information yet and how accessible it is with all the shit going on at work."

"GD?"

"General Defense."

"Got it." He says, sinking his fifth consecutive ball.

Danny lines up the eight ball for the win. "By the way, I wanted to thank you for sleeping in your old room and not defiling my bed."

He proceeds to fire off the winning shot from a spot pretty damn close to where Alison and I had crazy jungle sex the night before.

"Yeah, no problem. Respect, right?"

"You ever talk to your mom?" Danny asks while waiting for me to re-rack.

"Nah. She tried to reach out a little while ago after the bombing to see if I was okay, but not much. I don't really have it in me to connect with her."

"Understandable." Danny knocks in two balls on the break.

"Hey, Minnesota Fats, gimme a chance will ya?"

He beams a 'Danny' smile. "Beginner's luck."

"Did Dad ever talk to you about his break up with my mother?"

"He did a little. I was pretty busy back in those days, though. I was out to sea a lot; still in the Navy. I feel really bad I wasn't able to be there for him more to help him through it. It might've saved him."

"C'mon, you can't take that on your shoulders."

"I know, I know. I never thought he and your mom were a good fit. He was a quiet, low-key guy. Your mom was the adventurous one. It seemed to me they were opposites from the start. I think he wanted to be more outgoing like her – and maybe like me. Honestly, it wasn't a big surprise to me when she left. What was a big surprise was how he pretty much gave up on everything after that – except you."

Danny pauses from the game. He's looking at me. "You've done well, Jon. You're actually a perfect mix of both of them. You have your dad's level-headedness and intelligence, but you also have your mom's adventurousness and street sense. A pretty strong combination."

Ironically, Danny proceeds to sink another ball off of a combination shot.

"You might be right," I say, "and speaking of a strong combination ..."

Alison glides down the stairs, picks up the remote control, and fires up the wide-screen.

"Hey guys, he's been found. You need to see this. A newscaster broke in on the show I was just watching." She's flipping through channels trying to find the right one. "They said news crews are on site where police are investigating a body found in a parking garage this afternoon. They said they're standing by for the police to issue a public statement. It's supposed to begin shortly."

We pause our game and join her on the couch. She lands on the right channel still running a commercial.

"Well, here it is." I say. "Let's see what they've come up with." I have a pit in my stomach and I'm starting to sweat.

"It's all good." Danny says. "You didn't do anything wrong in any of this. The truth will come out soon."

The commercials finally break and the reporter reappears. She's outside in front of the police station, an empty lectern visible in the background illuminated by portable construction flood lights.

"We're standing in front of the Portland police department where a body was discovered in a car earlier today. We understand the chief of police will be issuing a statement at any moment. Behind me sits ..."

"I always find it strange how newscasters can remain so upbeat no matter what the situation." Danny remarks.

"I know, right?" Alison replies. "It's like they don't really process the event, they just focus on their own appearance and delivery."

I couldn't care less, really. I've got to go to the bathroom pretty badly, but I'm trying to hold it so I don't miss anything. The newswoman continues to blather on, filling dead air space until the press conference begins, and I know the second I get up to leave, it'll come on.

Thankfully, people come into view and begin to assemble at the podium, triggering the jabbering news lady to kick it up a notch.

"Let me take you to the news conference by Portland police where Douglas Morelli, the chief of police, is now addressing reporters."

"Ladies and gentlemen, thank you for your time. Today, at approximately two-thirty pm, the Portland police department received word of a body discovered in a car situated within the adjacent parking garage by an employee of the property manager. Before we begin, the Major Crimes Unit continues to process the scene and I would like to remind the media that there are still a lot of unknowns and we will not disclose everything about the case, or what has been provided to us, for the integrity of this investigation as it is active and ongoing. This afternoon, a white male was found with a fatal gunshot wound. Preliminary forensics analysis indicates the injury was self-inflicted. This individual is known to police, and as you are aware, we cannot comment on the specifics of the case. We want to stress – the public is not in any danger. We are withholding information on the victim's identity pending next-of-kin notification."

"I'm surprised they're calling it a suicide. Seems like a rush to judgment to me." I say.

"Knowing what you know, that would be a natural conclusion." Danny replies. "But the general public doesn't know that, and I'm sure the police want to avoid creating a panicked and on-edge community."

"Makes sense." Alison adds. "And if there are crooked cops in Portland, they're gonna want to bury this."

As I head for the bathroom, I call out, "Yes. Well, tomorrow is a new day. We'll connect with Peabo and see what we can dig up."

29

Neither of us slept much, to no one's amazement. Nervous energy kept us awake far too long and roused us at sunrise. For the better part of the night, I ran through multiple scenarios of how the day could go, not sure if I was dreaming it or if I was awake. More than likely it was somewhere in the middle. Danny's up too, though he's not going to the office with us. He plans to catch up with us afterward. I don't think he wants us out of his sight.

"Did you bring your work laptop with you?" I ask Alison as she breezes into the kitchen fully dressed and ready to go.

"No. Mine was lost in the building. I have my personal laptop, though. I'm ready to rock and roll." She's eyeballing me lounging in my boxer shorts and a t-shirt.

"Perfect. That'll work. My laptop's gone, too." I say after taking a sip of coffee.

She continues to look at me stone-faced.

"Uhh, gimme five minutes and I'll be ready … want to come help me get dressed?" I'm entertaining myself by pushing her buttons and she knows it.

"Go help yourself. And hurry it up."

"Danny's Jeep kicks ass in the snow and mud." I proclaim with a pretend air of superiority as we leave the house and drive down his dirt road.

Spring in Maine is mud season; too warm to ski and snowmobile, and too damn cold for nearly everything else except the Frost Heave Long Jump Olympics – coming to a road near you.

"I have to agree with you on that one. Much better than my car in the snow."

"Aww, I like your Fiat. It's so adorable. Looks just like a giant white Tic-Tac."

"Boy, aren't you just full of it today." She jokes, smiling at me through her eyes. I'm slightly overwhelmed.

She points to the road ahead of us. "Eyes on the road, sweetie."

"Right. Hey, you think we ought to call in and give a heads-up to Peabo before we get to the convention center? I'm guessing he's pretty dang busy right now."

"No, not really." Alison replies. "We told work we weren't coming in this week. I don't want to give anyone advance notice we're going to be there today. Hopefully, he'll just direct us as to how to access the files and we can be on our own."

"Okay. No one's going to care that I show up, but some of the partners might want you to check in with them. I don't think we want them hanging around with us and Peabo inviting questions. Maybe you should go and check in with them when we get there, and I'll go see him myself?"

"Good idea, actually."

"I have them once in a while."

"When I get done making rounds, I'll meet up with you. It will actually look better with us visiting separately."

She's right on that point. No one aside from Santa has any idea we're dating and it's probably best to keep it that way – at least for now. And speaking of Santa, I need to check in with him when we're there, too.

A cluster of cars sits corralled in the furthest back corner of the convention center parking lot. I recognize a number of them, including Santa's SUV. We drive over to the Beast, and ease into an open spot next to his.

"Ready?" I inquire while turning the car off.

"Ready!" Alison responds, slapping both hands onto her thighs, confidently.

"Let's get 'em!"

I open my door with a little too much vigor, proceeding to ram it into the side of Santa's passenger door.

"Dang. I left a dent. Don't tell him it was me."

"Jesus Christ. Let's go."

We have a short walk from the parking lot to the building. HW put out informational signage directing us exactly where we need to go, and when we enter the building, our receptionist comes over to greet us from a makeshift welcome area.

Alison speaks first, though. "Hi, Sharon. How are you?"

"Hi guys, it's so good to see you both!" She looks drained but cheerful as always. "I'm okay. It's been hard as you know. We're trying to get things set up, but it looks like an emergency room triage area here."

"Hey, Sharon." I add.

"Hi Jon! You guys go look around. We have all the rooms along this side of the building," she points to the east side, "and all of the open floor space behind these doors here." She gestures behind herself like a *Price Is Right* hostess showing off a new car in the final showcase.

"Thanks Sharon. Where is the IT group? Out back?" I speculate.

"Exactly. They have the most space, actually. They're working so hard right now."

"Thank you, Sharon, and nice to see you too, Alison." I hope I played that off convincingly.

I open one of the doors positioned behind Sharon leading to the temporary work space. Massive dividers cordon off a section of the convention center floor where portable tables are set up. Each table accommodates a computer tower, monitor, a wide assortment of ancillary hardware, and an IT technician. Clearly, we've engaged consultants or temporary workers to help with the task, as there are some folks here I don't recognize. I do, however, recognize Peabo. He has about fifteen empty Coke cans strewn about his work space.

"Hey, Peabo." I call out as I approach him.

He scarcely acknowledges me before hunkering back down to his monitor. "Hi, Jon."

"How's it going?"

"Really?" He responds morosely, taking a moment to look up at me. I pull up a chair and sit beside him.

"Stupid question. Sorry."

"It's alright. Sorry I'm short. I've been up for way too long, and this is a complete shit show."

"That sucks. Hey, I was hoping to try to access some of my client files. You know, get a jump-start on organizing my client list."

"You and everyone else here."

"So, do we have access to anything yet?" I probe.

"It depends on the client. I'm in our digital information system right now working on it. We have an offsite recovery system process that in theory should allow us to replicate copies on a real-time basis. *In theory*." He expounds sarcastically.

"So … what you're saying is some of us may be screwed."

"Pretty much. I think most of you will be screwed to some degree. What I'm discovering is when I access client files, I'm getting information but there's a lot of stuff missing. The downloads are only replicating schema on specific files within the master client file; other files have disappeared, or I simply haven't been able to locate anything yet. I don't know which it is. I don't know if I ever will."

"Well, can I look for my files on the server?"

"There isn't a server anymore; at least one you're familiar with, but yes, you can."

Peabo continues to hammer away on his keyboard for the entire time he's carrying on a conversation with me. I'm not entirely sure he's accomplishing anything or if he's only pretending to work, hoping I give up and go away.

"What you used to access on the G: drive at the office no longer exists. If you can find an open work station out there," he gestures, but doesn't look up, "access the L: drive. I've mapped that drive to the public cloud, replicating our G: drive. It should mirror our site drive. If I, or any one of our consultants managed to find, download, and save files, they'll be there."

"Thanks, buddy. Can I tap into you later if I need some help?"

"No."

"Alrighty then. Thanks. Nice talking to ya."

There are a few work stations vacant, so I take the nearest one. All of these computers must be brand spanking new. I detect the 'new electronics' aroma coupled with the smell of packing Styrofoam found only in brand new devices. I grip the mouse, springing the home screen into life. This baby is super-fast. I'm used to a clunky old laptop. Then again, I'm still a Bullpenner getting the hand-me-down junk.

I access the available system drives from the drop-down menu and two network locations appear. One labeled 'old G: drive' and one called 'mirror L: drive.' Well, Peabo said go with L:, so L: it is.

Double-clicking the L: drive brings up our master client list exactly as I'm accustomed to seeing it. Alphabetically ordered, each client name contains a file folder icon preceding it. I quickly scroll down scanning for 'General Defense' and find it with no difficulty. Drilling into the client folder reveals a subset of folders each represented by a different year beginning with 2018 down to 2006.

"Bingo!" I announce to no one. I swivel around, checking out everyone around me. Nobody looked up.

As I set back to work, a chair thuds next to me.

"Bingo? You feeling lucky, boy?" Alison plonks down next to me, smiling.

"Hey. How's it going?" I ask in a voice barely above a whisper. "All set?"

"Ya, it's all good. I connected with most of my client engagement partners as well as Calvin and Harold. They're on the other side. I also saw Ben. He wants you to stop by before we leave. For the first time in a few days, I feel a little normal."

"Cool."

"Whatcha got here?"

"Well, I had a good conversation with Peabo a little while ago."

"Really?"

"Um, no, but that's not the story. He's not confident our disaster recovery plan is solid enough to recover everything. I just got into the reproduced server, accessed GD, and I'm about to look for the files."

"Sounds perfect." She examines the contents of the master file onscreen. "Let's start with 2018."

"Right on."

I double-click on the 2018 folder. Empty. 2017 … empty. 2016 … empty. Every one of them – empty.

I get up and walk over to Peabo.

"Hey, I have a master client file with folders for years 2006 to 2018. Every folder is empty. Have the files not been recovered yet or are they corrupt or is something else going on?"

Peabo says nothing in response and doesn't look up. After an extended silence, he finally answers.

"Could be any or all of that."

"Man, that's not helpful."

"Welcome to my world. Who's the client? I'll add them to the list."

"General Defense."

"Alright. I'll let you know what I find."

"Thanks."

I walk back to Alison and explain our predicament.

She's less concerned about it than I. "Well look, we have Bob's letter. I don't think we need the client files. They may not show anything, anyway. Any investigator worth their salt can take Bob's letter and tie it in with a forensic investigation and figure out what happened."

"Yeah, they can figure out the scam, but can they figure out only those responsible?"

"With Bob's letter, I think so."

"That's if they believe the word of a man who's no longer here to defend himself – or defend us."

Alison doesn't look as upbeat anymore. I feel bad for throwing shade on her, but we still need to be careful.

"Hopefully, Peabo can work his magic and find what we need and we put this whole mess behind us."

"Why don't you check in with Ben and we can get out of here and get some lunch."

"Yeah, sure."

I walk over by myself. I gave Alison the keys to the Jeep so she can wait outside without drawing attention to us.

"Hey, buddy." I plunk down in an open chair amidst a smattering of second-year staffers.

"Hey, I thought you guys were out this week?"

"We are. Just a quick trip in to try and find GD files and attempt to stitch Bob's mess back together."

"Right. I figured it was something like that. Any luck?"

"Not yet."

"So, what's your next move?"

"Well, we're not sure whether we'll be able to eventually locate anything helpful. We've kicked around the idea of going to the chief of police and telling him what we know along with showing him Bob's letter."

"Danny okay with that?"

"I think so. I'm going to connect with him now and hammer out the details."

Santa looks at me earnestly. "Good luck, dude. Seriously."

30

The light turns green and I hang a left onto the turnpike connector. I need to get out of the city for a while and I think it will do Alison some good as well. We can find some place to have lunch out in Southborough.

"So, where are you taking me?" Alison probes while fixing her hair in the sun-visor mirror.

I punch the gas pedal and merge onto the turnpike. Danny's Jeep has some growl in her.

"I'm thinking we go pub-style. Burgers and fries? What do you think?"

"Ya, I could go for that. I'll even pay."

"You have enough cash?"

She laughs. "Mmhmm. And I know where to get some more if I run low."

Alison proceeds to unbuckle her seatbelt and reposition herself closer to me. Much closer to me.

"Hey Jon," she breathes into my ear, "have you ever done it in a Jeep?"

Her hand rolls up the inside of my thigh coming to rest on my instantaneous erection. At the same time, she's kissing my neck.

Actually, I have. This isn't the first time I've borrowed Danny's Jeep.

"No, but I sure as hell would like to."

She unzips my jeans, springs me free, and repositions her head down to my lap. I can see nothing but the back of her head as we speed down the highway.

"Ahhhh. Oh my God. Yessss …"

In my rear-view mirror, I see a tractor-trailer closing the gap on us. I don't care. I don't give even the slightest of shits he's approaching. Eventually he overtakes us, and we hear the 'waaht … waaaahhht' approval of his air horn as he blows past us.

We're coming up to our exit, so I ease off of the gas pedal, letting the vehicle decelerate on its own in preparation for exiting the turnpike. Much to my disappointment, Alison rises up and moves back to her seat.

"To be continued."

Dang. Had I known she'd stop, I would have gone right past the exit.

I wasn't down for very long, though. When we pull into Bulldog Brewing Company, Alison instructs me to park at the far end of the lot furthest away from the building, along the wood line edge. I'm more than delighted to comply. Nobody's around on a Monday afternoon, not that I care right now, anyway. This time we move into the back seat and spend the better portion of the next half-hour 'christening' the Jeep, as Alison dubbed it.

The restaurant is bare, save for us. I'm sitting at our table when Alison returns from the bathroom.

"Our server's been over. I ordered us drinks. Hope that's okay." I say.

"Ya, of course. Are we all set with meeting Danny and going to the police station later?" She asks while sitting down.

"Yup. He's going to meet us there. I don't see why we can't go straight there after lunch. I told him three o'clock."

"Perfect."

Our server comes back with drinks and we place our burger orders. I'm going for the Delightful Double and Alison settles for a Simple Single. I don't want her to witness me slaying the Treacherous Triple yet. Too soon.

"How's your mom?" I ask.

"That's random. Fine, why?"

"Well, it seems to me you guys are close, and you haven't had much contact with her lately. I was wondering if she was worried about you, if she knows what's going on; you know, stuff like that, that's all."

"Yes and no on the part about being close. She's kind of a functioning alcoholic. She doesn't work. She's living off of what my dad split with her after the divorce plus she's riding the alimony pony. She won't remarry, so she has that gravy train coming in forever."

"If you don't want to go there, that's fine by me."

"No, it's okay. I'm fine with it. She can be a colossal pain in the ass sometimes when she thinks I could use some 'mothering.' It happens in spurts, so us not having communication for an extended period of time is not that unusual. She's half in the bag most days and she doesn't know about anything going on with us."

We continue our conversation revolving around Alison's child-hood and what she was into as a kid. She shows me some pictures from her smartphone of her when she was little. She was as adorable then as she is now. She had an older brother who passed away from cancer when she was eight. That marked the beginning of her mom's downward spi-ral. Her dad hung on until Alison was almost through high school before he drifted away; eventually divorcing her mother when she was in col-lege. She stays in contact with him, though visits get more infrequent as time passes.

Our food arrives, and we dig in like it's our last meal.

"Everyone's got a story." I say between bites. "The older I get, the more I'm convinced there is no 'normal.' We're all crazy to a degree. The people laying claim to being 'normal' are abnormal in my view."

"Well put."

We eat the rest of our lunch engaging in mindless banter to pass the time until we're ready to meet Danny at the police station.

"You sure you want to pay for this?" I ask as Alison slides her debit card into the bill folder.

"I have half a million dollars sitting at your uncle's house." She says in response.

"Right. You got this."

We square up with the server, grab our coats, and head for the exit. As we approach the door, I stop dead in my tracks, jutting my arm sideways to block Alison from walking any further.

I see them through the window. It's Brown and Reyes. They're standing next to a gray sedan, and parked directly next to them, a white box truck with an over-sized penguin and whisk emblazoned on the side.

"Oh shit." Alison squeaks as she sees what I'm looking at, and slowly retreats. "What do we do?" She's panicked, and with good reason.

"Damn it. The box truck is theirs. That's not good. Bond warned us they're bad news. I don't know what they want, but it can't be good. They know we're here; they didn't stumble upon us by accident. They're the ones who've been watching us in that truck."

Alison looks at me with pleading eyes.

"Okay. Here's what we do. We're going to walk right through the kitchen and out the back door. They saw us come in, but they don't have to see us come out. We'll break along the back side of the parking lot to the Jeep and take off. We're parked pretty far away, and we can hug the wood line. They may not see us. If they do, we're driving straight to the police station anyway. Let 'em follow us there."

"I'll text Danny when we get in the car and let him know what's happening." Alison offers.

"Great idea."

I gently place my hands on her cheeks and focus directly into her eyes. "Are you ready?"

"Yes. Let's go."

I take her hand in mine and we circle back toward the kitchen. We push through the double doors, quickly locate a back door and make a beeline for it. Two line cooks check us out from the food prep area, but with little interest. Alison and I manage our way out of the building and into a three-sided, fenced-in area containing a trash dumpster and a used deep-fryer oil receptacle.

"Okay, we're going to walk out of here and as soon as we reach the end of the building, we sprint straight to the car. Got it?"

"Yes. I got it."

"Good. Let's go."

As we exit the fenced-in area leading into the employee parking area, I see a hand appear out of my periphery and reach out for Alison.

"Hey! Get away from …" Agghhhh. I feel a sharp sting in my neck. "Whaaa?" I dizzily swing around while grasping at the spot on my neck. The fuzzy face looking back at me fades to a pinpoint and disappears.

31

My father and I sit on the same dock at a modest camp we rented some fifteen years ago. It's a warm summer morning; the sun feels so good on my face. Dad's health has worsened over the past couple of years; he's thin and ashen, though I haven't thought much of it, really. The stillness of the water evaporates when he flicks a pebble into the lake. We stare hypnotically at the ripples extending outward in concentric circles. He turns to me.

"You know … your Uncle Danny's right; you have done well, son. I'm proud of you. I've always been proud of you. I also think Alison is a sweetheart. You'll do well to keep with her."

"Thanks, Dad. I hope to stay with Alison, too. I really like her. But … wait, how do you know about Alison … how do you know what Uncle Danny said to me?"

My father gazes at me with pure love in his eyes. "JK, can you hear me?"

"Why did you call me JK? Only Mom calls me JK. I can't stand that."

"JK ... JK, can you hear me?"

I slowly open my eyes, struggling to focus. My vision sharpens enough to see my mother hovering over me.

"He's coming out of it." She turns to someone in the room. I'd like to see who it is, but my body feels like a massive stone. I can scarcely move.

She wipes my forehead with a damp facecloth. "Don't struggle, honey; it will wear off shortly."

"Where's Alison?" I struggle to sit upright, aided by an adrenaline jolt coursing through my body. "Where is ALISON?!"

"I'm right here, baby." She's on my left and appears perfectly fine.

"What the fuck's going on? Where are we?" I demand.

"Okay, okay, hear me out for just a minute and I'll answer any questions you have." My mother responds. "You're in a hotel suite – and safe I might add. We had some people pick you up at the restaurant this afternoon and bring you here."

"We? Who's we?"

"Your mother and me." A man's voice calls out from the bathroom, and I know who he is even before setting eyes on him. I have an instant post-traumatic flashback to that awful day my mother walked out on my father. I maintain an image of her soon-to-be husband holding the door open for her as they leave together seared into my memory.

Enzo walks into the room. "We had our guys come get you."

"Come get us? Jesus Christ, you drugged and kidnapped us?"

"Well, yeah, but we ..."

"I don't give a fuck about you or your shitty explanations. Alison, we're getting out of here."

She puts a gentle hand on my shoulder. "Hold up, Jon. I've been awake for a while longer than you and had a chance to hear some of what they had to say. You need to hear them out, too."

Enzo adds, "We had to give you a bigger dose than her to make sure we could handle you, big guy."

"Dose of what?"

"Animal tranquilizer. Horse, to be exact. Works nicely and it's fast."

"Lovely. Alright, I'm listening."

"You're gonna have a ton of questions, we know, but let us explain this, and then we'll answer anything you want." My mother says, offering me a glass of water. "Here honey, drink this, you'll feel better."

I decline the water and begin rubbing my arms and moving my legs to get my body going again.

"First off, we feel terrible we had to drug you to bring you here. I've called you and texted countless times, but you must've blocked me on your phone. We tried your apartment, but it looks like you're not there anymore. We've been over to your girlfriend's place and there's no answer there, either. We finally traced you to your uncle's house, but it got too dangerous for us to make contact, what with all the people that were watching you."

"What? Who knew we were there?" I ask. "How did you know about Alison and where her apartment is?"

Enzo cuts in. "Hold on, I'll get to that in a minute."

This is nuts. "So, you doped us? Why didn't you just pick us up if we were in trouble?"

Enzo says with calm precision, "Would you have come quietly with us? I don't think so, and we couldn't take the chance. We knew you were probably in danger, so we had our guys shadow you for a period of time keeping an eye out for anything out of the ordinary. When they saw

Brown and Reyes show up in the parking lot, they got worried and drove their moving van out back behind the restaurant and called me. I asked them to pick you up quickly and without Brown and Reyes spotting you. Before they could come into the restaurant, you exited the back door and my guys simply reacted."

I don't respond. I have nothing to say; he's right.

"Look, we brought you here because your lives are in danger." Enzo stresses. "And I think you know that. The FBI guys were there to do a job. We knew it and we took you out. Plain and simple."

"You know Brown and Reyes? You knew they were there?"

Enzo takes a deep breath and nods. "Of course, I know who they are. They work for me. At least they used to. We've been following you since this whole mess happened at your building. We lost you for a while, then found out you were at Danny's, and we've had our people following you ever since."

"And the FBI guys have been following you, too." My mother adds.

"I know, I figured out about the box truck. We just didn't know who was in it." I respond. "We knew someone at Portland PD who didn't trust them." I exchange a look with Alison.

"And now he's dead, right? Brown took out Bond." Enzo states in response without emotion. "Reyes was there, but Brown squeezed the trigger. With Bond's firearm by the way. Set up to look like a suicide."

"Really? We knew it wasn't a suicide! Alison, right?"

"Right. We called it."

Enzo appears to have an inside track at the police station. "The police are calling it a suicide. Saying he was despondent over potentially losing his career and pension and he killed himself in the garage for dramatic effect."

"Jesus Christ." I say in disbelief.

"We have dishonest cops in Portland." Alison speculates.

Enzo lets out a laugh. "Of course, they do! Every police department does. Only a few in Portland, though, and none of them are on the take on this job. This is only Brown and Reyes. Brown works for the FBI and used to work for me, and Reyes only worked for me."

"Reyes isn't FBI?" I ask.

"Nah. He's a thug from Brooklyn. We put him in a tailored suit, sent him in with some solid fake credentials and had him shadow Brown. No one asks questions."

"They don't work for you anymore? Why not?" Alison inquires delicately.

"Because I turned." Enzo says. "I turned, and now if I show my face in the wrong place, I'm a dead man."

"What does that mean, turned?" Alison asks.

Enzo shifts his attention to Alison. "It means after we found out your ex-lover Bob mailed you a package, and what the nature of the contents of that package was, I was ordered to take you out as well."

Alison visibly stiffens.

Enzo continues casually. "Which wasn't that big of an issue to me, honestly. No offense young lady; but when Jon came into the picture, I turned. I became a marked man."

I can hardly process what I'm hearing. Enzo knows about Bob. He knows Brown and Reyes. He at least knows who Bond is. He knows about the letter, and the son-of-a-bitch was going to kill Alison.

I have more questions now than when we started.

32

The hotel suite is actually quite nice. It has two bedrooms, a living area, and a well-appointed kitchen. From its appearance, it seems my mother and Enzo have been living here for some time. They have personal effects, snacks, drinks, and the like laying around. I don't know where we are, nor will they disclose the location, 'out of an abundance of caution.' I've looked out the window; we're on the rear of the property, fairly high up, and I don't see any recognizable landmarks.

I'm still a little groggy, but it's minor; just enough to make me grumpy. Alison sits with my mother on the couch. I can't imagine she's comfortable talking to her, but if she isn't, it doesn't show. Sabrina holds up well for a newly-minted fifty-year-old woman. She doesn't have any gray in her strawberry-blond hair, and I believe it's natural. I can't ever recall her featuring a different color. She's wearing it in a high ponytail which causes her to appear even younger. Coupled with the track suit she has on, her look reminds me of Sporty Spice from the Spice Girls.

Enzo, on the other hand, looks his age. He sports salt and pepper-speckled hair and displays a middle-aged paunch, leading me to believe he must be around fifty-five or so. He's still as well-adorned in gold jewelry as I remember.

"You know all about Bob?" I direct to Enzo.

"Know about him? I recruited him. Guy made a lot of money. We all did."

Alison joins the conversation. "You're the person he met at the fish pier with the bag full of money, aren't you?"

"Bob told you about me?" Enzo seems surprised. "I never told him my name."

"Indirectly. It was in his letter he sent me. He didn't refer to you by name. He only described you as his 'Handler,' someone who solicited his service. You haven't seen his letter?"

"No. I'm aware he sent you a letter and the confessional nature of it, but I don't know its specific contents."

"Who told you about the letter?" I ask.

"The guy I hustled for. He's the chief financial officer for General Defense."

"You were working for the CFO of General Defense? No one else? The CEO?" I probe further.

"No. Only the CFO. It wouldn't have worked any other way. He was able to recruit some underlings and hire some crooks to collude with. We engaged Bob from the outside auditors; your firm, to corroborate internal control procedures, results, valuations – whatever was necessary. The chief executive officer and chief operating officer were in the dark, as was the board of directors. It wasn't until the government came snooping around that it all went sideways."

"That all makes more sense to me than you could know." Alison chimes in. "Did you kill him and make it look like a suicide like Brown did with Bond?"

Her temperature rises.

Enzo isn't fazed one bit. "No. I would have though, but he beat us to it." He says matter-of-factly.

"You're a sick fuck, Enzo." I say.

"You have no idea."

"I need to know where my phone is." I demand. "I need to call Danny. He was supposed to meet us at the police station this afternoon. It's not in my pants pocket. He must be going nuts right now."

"Me too, please." Alison follows up. "I can't find my phone either."

My mother interjects on this one. "We're holding your phones. We had to disable them for your own safety. That's how they're tracking you. You're pinging cell towers wherever you go."

"I need to call Danny." I repeat.

"We have disposable burner phones you can use. We swap them out frequently, so they're not traceable. Here." Enzo hands me an old flip phone. "What are you going to tell him?"

"The truth! He knows about everything happening anyway! He was meeting us at the police station so we could spill what we know."

He's scrutinizing me intently. "Tell him not to say anything. Tell him to sit tight and let me handle it."

"Why would I do that?" I bark.

"His uncle's a loose cannon, E. We need to tell him something." My mother says.

"Don't say a fucking word about him, Ma."

"JK!"

"Don't call me JK, goddammit!"

Alison steps in. "Okay, okay, let's all calm down."

Enzo raises both hands as though motioning for silence. "You can't go to police. You're fortunate we found you before they did. Agent Brown has both you and her," he gestures to Alison, "set up as significant players on the fraud. General Defense is working with him as well. Your asses will be thrown in the state penitentiary faster than you can blink. I wouldn't be surprised if they were working on pinning you to Bond as well. They knew you'd find him. I'm guessing they were watching you as well – maybe video recording."

"So how do we get out of this mess?" Alison asks politely.

"Your best bet is to lay low in the hotel for the short-term." Enzo answers. "Then you have a few choices. One, you can tell the cops what you know and hopefully successfully shield yourself from involvement in it. My opinion is you won't be able to do it. Two, you could wait this whole thing out. Bob's dead; he can't squeal to anyone. Bond's dead; he won't be snooping around. General Defense has a lot of horsepower to fight a government review of its business practices, and they might pull through this relatively unscathed, who knows? What I do know is they most likely won't allow either of you to pull through unscathed. Three, you can change your identities, relocate, and start your lives over. I think you ought to go with option three, and I can help you with that."

"I need to call Danny." I say while standing up. "Alison, want to come with me?"

She rises from the couch and we walk into one of the bedrooms.

Alison speaks first. "What are we going to do?"

"See what Danny says we should do. He's got to be going crazy right now."

It takes me three tries to punch in Danny's number; this is an older phone and the buttons are small and sticky. After the fifth ring, the call goes to voicemail – 'This is Danny, leave a message.'

"Hey Danny, it's Jon. We're okay. We got in a mess with Brown and Reyes after we left work this morning, but we're safe. It's best to call me back at this number you see on your cellphone. We had to shut our phones down. Talk soon."

"I wonder where he is." Alison says.

"Yeah, me too."

"What should we tell them when we go back out?"

"Pretty much the truth, I suppose. Danny didn't answer, and we want to talk to him."

"What about the three options … uh … Enzo talked about? It's awkward for me to say the name 'Enzo'."

"I know. It's a strange name, but you get used to it. As far as the options, I don't want to change my identity and I'm guessing you don't either." I surmise.

"No, and I think option two is out. We won't survive doing nothing."

"Right. That leaves us with option one, defending ourselves, but we need access to our audit work papers and the engagement plans."

"Yes." Alison states. "In every engagement I had, I noted in the files that my responsibility consisted of reviewing staff-prepared work papers for all of the General Defense and subsidiaries' balance sheet accounts excluding inventory and the cost of goods sold associated with it. Bob actually insisted I include that statement every year and he certified it."

Alison has a bit of an epiphany.

"At the time, I thought it was weird he certified my statements although it had nothing to do with generally accepted accounting principles or best practices, but it all makes sense now! He was giving me some protection in case something like this happened!"

"Then that's the resolution! The letter along with the year-over-year demonstration of the segregation of responsibility could remove any culpability on our parts!"

"We hope." Alison says cautiously. "Should we tell your mom and … Enzo?"

"Let's tell them number two is out, but one and three are on the table."

I switch up the subject. "Man, Danny not answering his phone has me worried now. He won't be able to sit still until he connects with us. Something's going on if he hasn't gotten back to us yet."

33

To no one's surprise, they believe we're making a mistake in not changing identities and running. I don't care one bit, and I don't trust Enzo. We haven't shared our plan with them yet, either. If Danny agrees with them, then maybe I'll reconsider. Not a moment sooner.

"Can we get some food? I'm frigging starving." There is no nicety in my voice.

"Yes, sure, what would you like?" My mother replies. "We can get room service here, or we have a bunch of menus from nearby places."

"Menus, please." I drone.

We figure out what we want and compile an order for Enzo to chase down. Interestingly, I note that he places the order under 'Smith.'

"I'm guessing the hotel is booked under 'Smith' as well." I remark sarcastically.

"No. 'Jones,' actually." Enzo responds nonchalantly, putting on his coat.

As he gets to the hotel door, he looks back at us somberly. "Jon, you're not a prisoner here. No one will stop you if you choose to leave; however, I don't recommend it. You and Alison are marked. They will find you and they will kill you."

There's no condescension in his voice; he's simply stating what he believes to be fact. He disappears through the hotel door, leaving just the three of us and the ghost of our past.

I check out the contents of the refrigerator. To my relief, I see a solid supply of beer and I help myself.

"Want one?" I offer to Alison, extending a beer.

"Sure. Thanks."

"Would you rather have some wine?" My mother asks.

Alison reconsiders. "Yes, actually. Thank you."

Perfect. Now I have a back-up brew. My first one won't make it through the commercial playing on the flat screen anyway. I look at the cell phone sitting on the table. I've called Danny close to a dozen times with no answer.

"Ma, I need my phone. I'm sure Danny has tried to contact me on it. I need to get his messages. For some reason, he's not calling me back on this phone."

"He's not calling back because a number won't show up on his caller ID. This is a blocked phone."

"Damn it. Where's my phone?"

"Honey, Enzo has them both. We're in trouble here as well. We can't risk a trace back to the hotel."

"Why the hell are you with this douchebag? Is this really you? What happened to you?" I'm completely exasperated.

She exhales deeply. "That's a pretty powerful question, honey. And I don't have an easy answer."

"I have time." I make no attempt to hide my frustration.

"I presume you're asking a much deeper question than why am I with Enzo. You want to know more about me and your father."

I'm sitting on the couch glaring at her. I crack my second beer.

"Your father and I drifted apart over the course of our marriage. We were headed in different directions; we wanted different things. He wanted to become complacent, and in my mind, irrelevant. I wanted adventure; I wanted romance. That just wasn't him."

"Then why did you marry him, for God's sake?"

"He wasn't as introverted when I met him. Sure, he was quiet, but after we got married, it's like the façade came down and his true self emerged. I tried to be more like him, but ... I ... I just couldn't adapt. I loved him; I really did – for a while."

"He was your polar opposite from the start. You knew he wasn't like you."

"And that was part of the appeal. I come from a family of outgoing people. Most of them are deadbeats though; interested only in instant gratification, as you know. Some would argue I am as well."

Alison and I make eye contact.

"Case in point." She says, noticing our glance. "Your father was stable for me. He was a good influence and a good provider. He allowed me to grow and see a new world; a new way out."

"And that's how you repaid him. Walking out."

"God, I never wanted to hurt him, believe me. I didn't know or expect the toll it would take. Leaving him and leaving you was the most painful decision in my life. Look, you don't want to hear this, and I understand, but Enzo is my soul mate. I can't explain it."

"I can. He takes you back to your white trash roots. You guys are meant for each other."

"I can't tell you how much that hurts to hear you say that." She responds with a truly pained expression. "Look, I'm not going to try and defend Enzo and what he does. There really isn't a defense. But, I made my choices and I have to live with them."

I feel a brief pang of remorse for hurling negativity and insults, but I don't really have control over it right now. These feelings have been suppressed for so long, I decide to cut myself a break. This is an incredibly stressful situation for all of us.

"Why did you leave me? Why didn't you fight for me?"

"I couldn't. I couldn't." She's looking at the floor and shaking her head; tears streaming down her face. "I couldn't. It wasn't safe." Her head rises up as she collects herself. "There was no stable life for you. Your dad was the best influence you could ever have had. Look at you! Look what a wonderful young man you've become and this tremendous woman by your side! The best thing I could have done for you then – in my mind – was to stay as far away from you as possible and not drag you down with me. And I failed at that, too. I'm sorry, Jon. I'm so sorry for all of it." She whimpers.

"Well, that's one way to look at it. You vanished from my life because it was in my best interest. Hmm."

To my surprise, Alison approaches my mother and puts her arm around her. My mother readily accepts it, and the two fall into an all-out embrace for an extended period of time.

I get up to go pee. Damned if I don't have the smallest bladder on the planet.

34

I return from the bathroom in time to hear Enzo's room key swipe the access pad on the door. A light buzz indicates success, but he's denied entry when he attempts to swing it open and it hits the internal security latch. My mother rushes over to release it, but she doesn't make it in time and the door rebounds into Enzo and closes again, forcing him to re-swipe his card.

"Thanks, babe." He says, walking into the room with way too many pizzas and a brown takeout bag. "I'm glad you're using the inside lock."

I thought he would be irritated with having to re-scan his card while juggling an armful of stuff, but quite the opposite. He was relieved.

I'm so hungry, I'm into a pepperoni pizza faster than a buttered bullet. After eating my second slice, my receptivity to brainstorming our situation and devising a solution increases considerably. But first, I need questions answered.

"Tell me about the bombing." I say to Enzo, tempering my tone with more of an 'ask' and less of a 'demand.'

"What do you want to know?"

"Everything. All of it. We need all the background we can get. Obviously, we know the bank wasn't the target."

I share with them exactly how my morning unfolded that day, beginning with my exit from the bank and interaction with Reyes, to approaching the plaza and witnessing the explosion.

Enzo says nothing; his face expressionless. After a moment or two, he serenely looks at my mother.

"We know, Jon." She says.

Alison and I shift our attention over to her.

"We were there, and we were watching you to make sure you weren't in the building."

The surprises never end.

"Let me fill in the holes." Enzo states.

"When the government came snooping around," he begins, "we knew we had to make a move. We pulled the plug on the weapons diversions immediately – I assume you know how the operation worked – and set to covering our tracks. That meant discussing the situation with Bob. From his standpoint, we determined we needed to destroy all of the records connected to General Defense. The difficulty was in crafting a plan by which we could accomplish that, but not appear we specifically targeted one client, thereby drawing attention to that one client. To that end, we constructed a plan that would include destroying the entire building; with the damage concentrated to the side the file room was on, but make it look as though the principal target was the bank."

"Bob was part of this?" Alison asks, dumbfounded.

"He didn't have much of a choice, young lady, but yes. He was a big part of it. Building layout, personnel location; all inside information we needed. I suspect the guilt of what was going to take place broke him, and he off'ed himself over it."

"I could have been killed." Alison murmurs.

"Yes, unfortunately." Enzo replies. "Having said that, we knew about the office meeting on the other side of the building and the majority – the great majority – of employees would be there. Even so, we weren't sure we would go through with it just then until we saw Jon leaving the building. We had an alternate plan to ensure you would have had to exit," he directs to me, "but we didn't need to employ it. Then the race was on. Jon, you would have been interrupted coming from the coffee shop on your way back to work if you'd been any quicker."

"You were there." I say distantly, my mind swirling.

"Yes. Reyes nearly blew it when he bumped into you as you left the bank. He was distracted because I was talking to him through an ear-piece he was wearing, and it startled him when he saw you."

"Ma, you called me after the explosion. It all makes sense now. You said you were thankful I was outside and not in the building. At the time, I couldn't understand how you knew that!"

"Yes. I could see you from my location."

"Jesus Christ. I nearly forgot. I went home that afternoon and turned on the TV. I saw both of you in the background on the Channel 12 news coverage!"

Enzo replies, "That, we didn't know."

I switch the subject back to the bank. "So, what was in the black briefcase Reyes was carrying? Brown told me it was some sort of 'EMF' device."

"When did you speak to Brown?" Enzo annoyingly answers my question with a question.

"At the police station the following day. I went in at my sched-uled time like everyone else, but instead of interviewing with uniformed cops, I was on a list to be segregated. They sent me to a separate area and

Brown fed me some bullshit story about a bank fraud they were trying to prevent that went bad."

Enzo turns to my mother. "Those sneaky bastards. That would have been right around the time when we had to disappear."

Turning back to me Enzo continues, "The black case contained a device that was part of a detonation system bridging the transmission between a portable ignition unit and the explosives within the building."

"And you had the portable device." Alison contends.

Almost robotically, he responds. "Yes. I wouldn't have typically been this close to the action, but I needed to insure this didn't get screwed up. I needed to make sure Jon was far enough away from the detonation."

"Well, thanks ... I guess." I offer. "So, you attempt to destroy the file room and any paper evidence. What about electronic files? HW has been transferring everything to the cloud for as long as I can remember. Did you go after the electronic files? I met with our IT guy who was trying to retrieve them, and General Defense's were missing. He wasn't sure if they were lost or if they're still hanging out somewhere in cyberspace."

"I can't answer that." Enzo replies. "I've known about the file conversions, and Bob was supposed to address it; but I've lost the thread on where everything stands. I'm effectively out of the loop and in protection mode."

"You're not part of this anymore?" I probe.

"Not since I've committed to protecting you, no."

"Where are you in the organized crime hierarchy?"

"It's better if you don't know too much."

"Do you think it really matters now?" I can't hide my frustration or impatience.

Enzo considers my question. "Well, I'm the number two guy in my group; at least I was number two. I was responsible for running this region. I'll leave it at that."

"Fair enough. Man, I can't imagine the odds of working at the same company where my mother's husband masterminds a criminal operation."

Enzo half-laughs. "The odds are pretty damn good. Who do you think got you the job?"

His comment drills me square in the face.

"And by the way," he adds, "I wasn't the architect of the operation. That was the CFO of General Defense. I was merely an operations facilitator. More akin to a general contractor supervising a construction project on behalf of an owner."

Everyone pretty much finishes with dinner. Clean-up is next to nothing; it consists of throwing away paper plates and utensils and putting leftover pizza in the refrigerator.

"Does anyone have a laptop or device I can use to at least check email? I'm expecting to hear from Peabo ... uh ... our IT guy at work on locating those electronic files."

"Your work email is functional, and you have remote access?" My mother inquires.

"Yes. That was one of the first issues the firm addressed." Alison answers politely. "I would be most appreciative to use it as well."

Enzo leaves the room and subsequently returns, passing his tablet to me. "Here. We're connected to hotel wi-fi. Please be vigilant in not revealing anything sensitive that could compromise our safety."

I hand the tablet over to Alison. "Here baby, go ahead and check yours first."

Alison goes to work on the tablet and I go to work chasing down another beer.

"Anything worthwhile?" I set a fresh glass of wine next to her on the coffee table and pop the top on my beer.

"Doesn't look like it. Mostly garbage. I just have the daily firm status update that I don't really want to look at. I'll log out, so you can check yours."

Enzo doesn't hawk over us, per se, but he's in our vicinity, observing with a casual eye.

I log in to my account. Alison watches the screen with me and we're both instantly drawn to an email entitled, **'PBowen@hwcpa.com.'** It's Peabo.

"There he is. Open it." Alison sounds like a child on Christmas morning wanting you to open a present.

"Should I?" I say with exaggerated delight, mildly poking fun.

"Sorry." She says sheepishly. "I'm just excited."

"Ha, ha. I'm just playing with you."

I double-click on the email, revealing Peabo's expectedly short and concise message:

> *Jon,*
>
> *I've been unable to locate any electronic files for General Defense. No idea what's happened to them. Staff tells me that a storage records index file preserved in the basement of our old building indicates paper files exist for GD. If they do exist, they most likely would be here in an adjacent warehouse with all the others.*
>
> *Peabo.*

"That sucks." I say.

"At least paper files exist." Alison counters optimistically.

"Maybe. But it sounds to me like Peabo is pessimistic. Wouldn't surprise me if there's nothing."

I address Enzo and my mother. "Can you sneak us out of here and bring us to our temporary office at the convention center, so we can look for these files? We think the contents could exonerate us."

"How?" Enzo asks.

"Bob always had me include a letter in every audit file that he certified indicating he was solely responsible for the inventory and related accounts attestation." Alison offers.

"Amazing." Enzo responds. "If ever someone had a conscience …"

"Well? Can you do it?" I press him.

"Yes. On one condition – you listen to and follow everything I instruct you to do. Without question. Can you do it?"

"I can do it."

"We can do it." Alison modifies.

Alison and I have both had enough of this discussion and retreat to our bedroom.

"I haven't had this much interaction with my mother in a dozen years. I'm so sorry for dragging you into this."

"It's not your fault."

"C'mon! My mother's married to this clown! This guy's a fucking murderer."

"Yes, but you need to look at it differently."

"How, for God's sake?"

"Look, this scheme, this fraud, or whatever you want to call it, would have taken place with or without Enzo in charge. If he wasn't part of it, then another mobster would be, and you and I would likely be dead right now. It was only because Enzo was running it that we're here and have a shot at getting out of this. On top of that, thank God your mom married him. He, or anyone else for that matter, wouldn't have given a rat's ass about us otherwise if it weren't for her."

"I can't argue with your point. You're absolutely right."

Alison has an innate sense as to how to bring me back when I'm spinning out of control. I've never felt that type of connection with any-one before. It's a foreign experience for me, one I never knew could ex-ist, and one I don't want to be without.

"Jon?" Alison says as we lay in the dark.

"Yeah?"

She goes quiet for a moment and without seeing her face, I can't get a read on what she's thinking.

"Bob never warned me not to go to work that day."

"Huh?"

"The bombing. That morning. He never warned me or tried to get me not to go into work." She begins to breakdown. "I don't think it was by accident, either."

"Oh, baby." I reposition myself to squeeze her in tightly.

35

S he's right about Bob, but at the same time, why would he leave her the money if he wanted her gone? Maybe he was simply crossing his fingers she would make it out okay. We'll never know. We laid in bed for a long time talking about it and everything else under the sun until sleep finally captured us. All things considered, we slept reasonably well, but morning is upon us and we're ready to get going.

"I can't wait to get out of here." Alison declares with her towel-turban wrapped around her damp hair in its full majesty.

"Same." I'm already dressed and ready to go. "I'm gonna wolf down some cold pizza. You want something?"

She's in front of the mirror putting on makeup my mother gave to her. "No. Thanks. Not hungry. I'll be out in ten minutes."

"Perfect. See you in a few." I shut the bedroom door behind me and walk out to the kitchen.

Enzo looks ready to go. "Your mother's almost ready."

"Yeah, same with Alison." I say while getting pizza out of the refrigerator. "Hey, she and I were talking last night. Is there any possibility I can reconnect my phone somewhere for only a minute or so, just to check for messages from Danny? Maybe drive somewhere not close to here and then afterward disassemble it again?"

"Uh … Let me think about that for a minute."

"Sure. Take your time." Now isn't the time to make demands.

My mother comes out of her room and over to us. "Good morning, Jon." She says with a cheery tone.

"Morning. Hey, I've noticed you've stopped calling me JK."

"Yes. That's what you wanted, right?"

"Yes. Thanks."

Enzo joins the conversation. "Yeah, we can activate your phone and Alison's too; but only for a very short time."

"Great. Thanks, Enzo." I'm relieved to hear that.

"We can do it after we leave the convention center. There's really no good place to stop in between. Actually, it would be best for us to drive even further out."

Alison joins us looking fresh-faced, but in yesterday's clothes. "We ready?"

We're driving in an old, beat-up Mercury Cougar painted a 'vintage' burnt-orange accented with patches of rust. The smell of exhaust and smoldering oil leaks into the interior. Even so, it's nice to finally see the light of day. According to Enzo, we're in Greenfield, about fifty miles outside of Portland. Though we've heard of it, neither Alison nor I have any familiarity with Greenfield. It's farmers' country.

"Hey Enzo, seems kind of strange, the route we're taking. We're going west, right? Don't we want to go southeast?" I point out.

"Yes, eventually. We're triangulating. We have another car that we'll swap out with to lessen the chance of being recognized."

Alison and I look at each other, and she mouths 'wow' to me.

We pretty much spend the remainder of the ride in silence and it goes by relatively quickly. To my surprise, there is no car waiting for us when we get to our destination. Enzo parks the Cougar in a bus station park and ride.

"We're taking a bus?" I ask.

"Yes. Less traceability." Enzo responds. "I'll go in and buy the tickets."

"I know this is frustrating." My mother says glumly after Enzo leaves. "Lately, I'm feeling like a prisoner."

"Christ, I wonder why?" I say sarcastically.

We all get out of the car and head toward the bus ports. Enzo comes out of the terminal and motions for us to follow. When we make it over to him, he hands each one of us a ticket. Mine has the name 'Jack Wallace' on it. Alison's has 'Amanda Wallace.'

"Hey Amanda, do you think we're married," I ask her, "or just brother and sister?"

"Hmmm … Let's go with married; otherwise we'll have to stop sleeping together."

"Right."

The ride is short – maybe forty minutes or so. Enzo's thorough if nothing else regarding safety and covering his tracks. We arrive at the bus station and walk across the street to a small, three-floor covered parking garage.

"Where did we park?" My mother asks. "I forgot the last time we were here."

"We're second floor. Middle area."

The garage appears run down. The interior decking has leftover wet, winter sand from a harsh season of snow and ice spread around that grits when you walk on it. We skip the elevator and opt to take the stairs. I'm not confident the elevator operates, actually. The trash container on the ground level overflows with garbage. Paint peels from the handrails, exposing assorted layers of unappealing color painted over the years. The garage clearly hasn't seen much attention lately and that's probably why Enzo uses it.

We file out of the narrow stairwell landing one at a time. As we round the corner, we see virtually no cars; except squarely in the middle of the parking deck sits a shiny, black Mercedes SUV.

"That car looks very familiar." I say.

"Does it?" My mother replies.

"Yes, we've seen it. First at the police station. A few other times as well."

"That was a smart tactic – leaving Alison's car in the garage that night." Enzo says as he removes some sort of over-sized wand from his duffel bag.

"Thanks. What's that for?"

"It's an amplification signal detector. Detects GPS trackers and listening and recording devices."

Enzo passes the wand around the perimeter of the vehicle, and appearing satisfied, proceeds to do the same with the interior.

"Alright, let's go." He says optimistically.

This last leg of the trip passes quickly and uneventfully courtesy of our upgraded ride. To no one's surprise, Enzo doesn't take us directly to the convention center entrance. He parks strategically; with an unobstructed visual pathway from the vehicle to the office entrance.

"We'll stay right here. Call when you're ready to leave." Enzo instructs.

"Will do. Thanks." I reply.

"Hi guys! It's so good to see you!" Sharon gushes when Alison and I walk in. "Boy, if I didn't know better, I'd think you two were an item, walking in together again!"

"Hi Sharon!" I say cheerily. "Great to see you, too!"

Alison greets her as well, and we both disregard the comment about being 'an item.' Discovery of our romance is the least of our concerns right now.

"You ready, Amanda?"

"Ready, Jack." She smiles at me.

"Let's do this."

Peabo hunkers down in his work space with even more empty Coke cans than when I saw him last. He's using them to build a pyramid. He sees Alison with me, so I know he'll be less abrasive in our conversation.

"Hey, Peabo." I say. "I got your email."

He looks at me with confusion.

"Your email to me about not being able to find General Defense files electronically." I clarify.

"Oh, right. Yes. I can't find anything. Pretty strange, too. Usually I'm able to find something; digital data or some other marker indicating something was there, anyway. But this one's ghosted. Totally disappeared."

I share in his disappointment. "That sucks."

"What about paper files?" Alison asks. "You mentioned something about paper files in a nearby warehouse."

"Yeah, look outside. Behind us there's a storage building. I was told that's where all the remaining paper files are that were recoverable from our basement. We'll be working on converting those once we finish with the existing file recovery and rebuild."

"Thanks, Peabo." I say.

"Sure. No problem. See you guys later."

"Talking to him is like talking to a wall unless you're around." I grouse as we leave.

"Mmhmm." She agrees, winking at me.

We open an exit door, exposing a surprisingly sizeable building situated behind us; maybe twenty to thirty yards away. Remarkably, we hadn't known of its existence, nor would we have, had we not been told about it.

We tentatively peer inside the front entrance and discover a fair amount of activity going on. Maybe a half-dozen people – some with dollies and others with flat-bed hand-trucks, move boxes around and log information. The space resembles a small airplane hangar, only with no airplanes; just boxes stacked everywhere. From what I understand, this represents only about a quarter of our remaining paper files. No wonder Peabo's going crazy.

"We need to find someone in charge to help find our way around here." Alison declares. She asks the nearest worker, whom neither of us recognizes, who's in charge of the warehouse.

"Mr. Osterman. Over there." He points out our chief operating officer.

"Oh great, thanks." Alison responds, and then turns to me.

"Why don't you go talk to Harold?" I say. "I don't really know him that well."

"No problem. He's a decent guy. I'll be right back."

Alison leaves and I begin to have a closer look around. I'm reminded of our old file room – pre-tragedy. Sarah's gone now; there's no sign of her anywhere. She was meticulous in 'her domain,' in the sense she was super-organized and always knew where a file folder was located. If it wasn't in the file room, she knew who had it, when they got it, and usually how long it would be out for. Now everything's changed.

As I wander around, my thoughts shift to Danny. I'm hoping we can find what we need quickly and get out of here to check messages and make calls. It also occurs to me I should probably see if Santa's around. I'm sure he's wondering what's going on, too.

"Hey."

I spin around to face Alison.

"Jeez, you jumped me. I didn't expect you back so quickly."

"Ya. Well, I talked to Harold briefly. I think we're looking for the proverbial needle in a haystack. Very little here," she gestures to the massive mountain of file boxes behind us, "is catalogued yet. It's only just been removed from our building and brought here. And to add another dynamic, out back behind this wall of boxes in front of us, sits a butt-ton of wet boxes damaged by the building's sprinkler system. That sound you hear? Industrial fans. Big industrial drying fans, blowing on them. We're not gonna be able to get at them until they're dried out."

"Whoa, this is gonna be a nightmare." I say, stating the obvious. "Even the dry boxes will cause us trouble. We can't even reach the top of any of them. How the heck are we supposed to check those and then get into the boxes under them?"

"We're not. Harold said we could look as long as we wanted to, but we're probably better off letting his guys go through and log them."

As if reading our minds, Harold comes over to us.

"Hello, Jon." He says to me and then addresses Alison before I can respond. "Listen, you never told me who you're looking for. I can keep an eye out for it and let you know."

"Oh great, thanks. It's General Defense. Peabo hasn't found any electronic files on them, yet. We only need audit files; we don't need any tax work papers."

"Sure thing. Let me have your cell number and I'll get back to you if I find anything."

Alison gives him the number for her phone Enzo deactivated, and he logs it into his phone.

"Thanks." She says.

"No problem." He responds while walking away.

Alison sucks in air, exhaling audibly. "Holy, I didn't know what to say. I have no idea what the number is on the phone Enzo gave us. I had to give him something. It looks pretty stupid if I can't remember my own number."

"No worries. He'll call your phone and it'll go straight to voice-mail. We'll figure out how to get the message."

"Ya, I guess." She sighs and looks up at me with her stunningly beautiful eyes. "Want to get out of here? I actually would like to check my messages."

"Yeah, same. I'll call Enzo and let him know we'll be out in five minutes. Can we stop in and see Santa for a check-in?"

"Of course."

36

I'm like the little boy fidgeting in the back seat of his parent's car on his way to Grandma's house wondering, *are we there yet?*

"How much further do we need to go?" I ask impatiently.

"Ahh … I don't know; until it feels comfortable." Enzo replies languidly. "I'm not sure of the distance between cell towers, and better to be safe than sorry."

We travel another twenty minutes or so talking about nothing really, and it feels kind of good. My mother chats away with Alison, reminding me somewhat of earlier, happier days. The sun streams through the passenger-side window, highlighting her hair. She really is quite attractive; she still has a girlish laugh and coupled with her animated hand gestures and bouncing ponytail, it reminds me of a specific event in what seems like ages ago.

Every summer after the little league baseball season ended, the coaches hosted a team picnic. All of the parents and kids, including siblings, gathered and celebrated. It was a time when the kids could eat as

much junk and drink as much soda as they wanted to without any paren-
tal repercussion. This particular summer – I can't remember if it was the
same year Dad waved me around third base and I was tagged out at home
plate, or if it was the year before – we held the picnic at a lakeside camp-
ground. I remember it so well because we had a parents-versus-children
softball game, and my mother meaningfully participated. In those days,
she was usually too busy with food preparation or some other task to join
in the events, but this time she did. When she was up to bat, I remember
pausing to look at her. I'm not sure what I was thinking at the time. She
managed to hit the ball – a solid connection; and began running to first
base. She was laughing the entire way and her ponytail bounced as she
ran, much like it is now. I hadn't thought of that moment, perhaps ever,
until now. Her joy was short-lived, though. When she crossed first base,
she twisted her ankle on the uneven surface, suffering a mild sprain. A
bunch of middle-aged men quickly made their way over to her to offer
support. Truth be told, I think that was about the end of her participation
in anything I was involved in.

Enzo interrupts the girls' gab session. "This looks like as good a
place as any to stop." He says more to himself than anyone else.

Enzo exits the highway, entering a rest area some fifty minutes
away from our temporary office. He drives to the furthest end of the lot
and backs in to a parking spot so as to see any approaching vehicles.

He leans in toward my mother, reaching for his duffel bag resting on the floor of the passenger seat near her feet. After fumbling with
the hand straps, he pulls it up and rests it on his lap. He unzips the bag,
carefully rifles through it, and methodically removes components of each
of our phones. As near as I can tell, they need only the battery and SIM
card inserted to be functional.

Enzo turns back to face Alison and me. "Here." He passes our
phones to us. "Ten minutes or so?" He requests.

"Thanks." Alison says, turning it on.

"No problem. Thanks." I add.

It takes a minute or so for the phones to cycle through their internal functions and recalibrate. When the progression concludes, a wave of emails and texts begin to come through. I scan through mine, skipping a bunch of texts from Santa – they came in before I checked in with him earlier at work – and come to the one from my contacts list I was hoping to find:

UD – Uncle Danny

I open the text message and read: **763-2299**. A phone number. The message is simply a phone number. I'm not certain when it was sent due to our phone interruption; the time stamp shows today, but it's positioned lower down on my text list, so it must have been sent sometime yesterday morning.

"I got a message from Danny!" I exclaim. "It's just a number."

"What?" Alison asks confusedly. All eyes are on me.

"It's a phone number. He only texted a phone number for a message. Seven-six-three, two-two-nine-nine." I recite. I press the number in the text box and a message activates asking me if I would like to call 763-2299.

"Don't call that number." Enzo interrupts with a tone of urgency before I can connect. "Use the burner phone." Before I ask why, he explains. "No trace. To you or maybe more importantly, the person on the other end."

Damn. He's right.

"Hello?" A woman's voice answers hesitantly. "Who is this?"

"I'm trying to reach Danny." I counter, ignoring the request for identification. "He left me this number in a text."

"Oh God, who is this?! I don't know where Danny is! I haven't seen or heard from him since yesterday. I'm so worried." She laments, clearly in distress.

"Is this Jennifer?"

"Yes, yes, it is. Who is this? Please, who is this?"

"Jennifer, it's Jon. I got a text from Danny. All it had was this number, so I called it."

I leave out any mention the text had to have come in yesterday and I didn't check it until today. Nor do I mention any danger Danny or she may be in. No sense adding either dimension to the conversation.

"Jon, I'm going crazy over here. He's never not in contact with me. He's not answering his phone or responding to any of the messages I've sent. I've gone over to his house and he's not there. No sign of him. I'm about to call in a missing persons report."

I don't get it. I'm truly bewildered.

"Jennifer, don't do that yet. Let me check a few things out first and I'll get back to you real soon."

"Oh, thank you Jon, thank you so much."

"No problem. Hey, was everything okay at his house?"

"Yes. Everything was fine. Only thing missing was him and his Jeep. He told me he let you borrow it a few days ago."

"Yes, I have it." I say, realizing it's still in the brewery parking lot, or at least it was last I knew.

"Okay, thanks again. Let me know what you find as soon as you can."

"Will do. And Jennifer –" I pause to purposefully construct my sentence.

"Yes?"

"No need to go back and check his house. My girlfriend and I are staying there tonight. We've got that base covered."

No sense in her risking any more danger, I reason.

"Okay, thanks."

"Your uncle is missing, but his house appears normal. He managed to send you a message with his girlfriend's cell number and nothing else. His girlfriend has no idea where he is, so the directive from him to call her is puzzling." Enzo summarizes. "Have I got that about right?"

"Seems about right." I reply.

"If he was under duress," Alison posits, "he would only be able to quickly send out an abbreviated message."

"Correct." Enzo agrees.

"But it's pointless. Jennifer has no knowledge as to where he is or what's happening." I counter.

"Maybe not." My mother joins in.

We're surprised by her addition to the conversation. We pause, waiting for her to explain.

"If he was under duress like you speculate Alison, having only enough time to send a quick message like the one you received, he may have purposely been vague so as not to put Jennifer in danger. Or at least try and not put her in any danger."

Seems logical but unlikely. "So, I get a cryptic message for the sake of protecting Jennifer? Why send it at all if it's of no help to me?"

"But it is." Sabrina Garibaldi says, channeling her inner Enzo. "You know if Jennifer has no idea where he is and she's upset and nervous on top of it, Danny's in trouble. He knows you'll figure that out."

That feels like a hot knife into my stomach. She's right. Alison's right. Enzo knows they're both right. And I know it, too.

"We need to find him. I'm going back." I demand.

"It's not safe." Enzo says.

"I don't care. I'm going back."

"Jon, let Enzo handle it." My mother pleads.

"How?" My voice begins to rise.

Enzo interrupts with a calm, calculated demeanor as he always does. "I will eliminate the CFO of General Defense, Agent Brown, and Reyes. After that, this will be over. The trail ends with them."

"We need to eliminate them." I say. I feel Alison stiffen next to me.

"I work alone." Enzo says. I believe him.

"Then work alone. I'm gonna find Danny."

Alison and I hand our phones back to Enzo and watch him nimbly disable them.

The drive back to the bus station feels twice as long as the drive from it. Enzo hasn't responded to my declaration of finding Danny; undoubtedly, he's processing multiple scenarios as to how this could play out. One is certain. My first order of business will be going to Danny's house. I need to have a look around for myself. I know what should be there and what shouldn't. I'll detect if anything is out of place.

Enzo pulls the Mercedes over just before we get to the bus station, letting it idle. He stares at his hands for a full minute before letting out a deep breath.

"We'll go tonight." He says with a tone of resignation. "The sun will have set by the time we get back, and it's the practical, safe move to check out his house under cover of darkness."

"I appreciate it, Enzo."

Enzo doesn't acknowledge my response, but I don't get the feeling he isn't grateful. He puts the vehicle in gear and accelerates, driving past the bus station. After a brief moment or two, he begins verbalizing his plan.

"You all need to follow my instructions, or this is off."

No argument from me.

"We'll go directly to his house, monitoring it in stages. First, we watch the neighborhood. Then I move to the beach; Jon, you can come if you want. Third, I do a perimeter walk-around of the property and in-spection of the exterior of the house. I'll be using my detection wand to scan for bugs and the like. I assume you have a key to the house?" He directs to me.

"Yes."

"Good. I'll go in – alone," he emphasizes, "and do a check. As-suming it's clear, we can all go in. Any questions?"

Even if I had one, I don't think I would ask it.

Without having to take a roundabout route between bus stations, we make pretty good time in getting back. The problem I'm having now is with the three 'stages' Enzo referred to in the surveillance plan. The neighborhood watch consists of an agonizing forty-five-minute wait in the car looking for any suspicious activity. I opt to go with Enzo on stage two at the beach, and we're essentially doing the same thing. Hopefully, Alison is taking a nap back at the car.

I'm going bat-shit crazy; silently of course, when Enzo finally whispers, "All right. I'm going up to do the perimeter walk-around. This won't take as long. Let me have the house key."

I pass him the key and he pockets it.

"Wait here. I'll be back for you."

"Okay."

Enzo disappears into the darkness with his duffel bag in tow. I sit down on a nearby driftwood log under a clear, crisp moonlit night.

Roughly twenty minutes pass, and Enzo reappears through the dunes scanning the area for me. I rise, which draws his attention, and he glides over to me like a hockey puck on ice.

"All clear. Let's get the girls."

"He's not there? No sign?"

"No sign of him. It looks completely normal as far as I can tell. Clean and neat."

It takes us under ten minutes to get back to the SUV, update the girls, and drive down Danny's driveway. I can't jump out of the car fast enough and fly into the house. I hit the light switches as soon as I enter, illuminating the kitchen and living room. I move methodically room to room performing a quick overview, finding nothing out of the ordinary. In the basement, I find more of the same. When I come upstairs, I see my mother and Enzo poking around, looking for anything suspicious or out of place.

"On my first pass-through, I'm not seeing anything out of place, either." I announce to the room.

Alison comes out of my old bedroom. She's changed her clothes and has her bags packed with her stuff.

"That's a good idea." I say.

"Ya. I figured while we're here …"

Enzo goes over to the answering machine and hits the playback button, immediately grabbing our attention.

"This message is for Jon Williams."

The voice seems to be from a man, but it is hugely distorted like you hear on crime shows coming from a darkened image of a witness on a couch in anonymity. "Call three-four-three-one-five-seven-nine."

My heart jumps in my throat.

"Jon, look at me." Enzo commands.

"We'll call, but not here. On the burner phone out of range. Take two minutes and gather what you need."

I do as instructed with no objection. I'm back in the kitchen in less than two minutes with my gear; including the firearms and ammunition Danny gave to me. I choose not to inform Enzo out of fear he may try and confiscate them. My head is fuzzy and I'm not thinking clearly. I'm truly scared.

Enzo pulls his magic wand out of his duffel bag and passes it over my and Alison's bags that we've stacked on the kitchen floor, checking for tracking devices. The wand remains silent and he seems satisfied. He places it back in the bag, pauses; then removes another device. This guy's like a frigging magician pulling rabbits out of his hat.

"Hey Jon, catch those lights, will you?" He motions me to shut the lights off.

"Sure. Why? What's that?" I ask while walking to the front door where the wall switches are.

"It's a black light. It's used in testing for blood residue."

The hair stands up on my neck. "I thought Luminol is used for that. I've seen that on TV."

"Luminol fluoresces blue in the presence of blood residue pretty much no matter how well someone tries to clean it up. I have that in my bag as well. Blood residue in the presence of a black light shows up as darker than its surroundings because it absorbs light. It looks like a black hole."

I kill the lights and Enzo puts the black light on. Alison's sneakers instantly illuminate super-bright, as does my mother's white t-shirt. It reminds me of midnight glow-bowling on Saturday nights at the local alley when I was a kid. Enzo walks around the kitchen and hallway, bent over and holding the light outward like he's warding off evil spirits. He returns to the kitchen with no discernible change in his affect.

"Can you move your bags?" He asks. "Just push them out of the kitchen."

We do as we're told, relocating our clothes to the other side of the kitchen bar next to the dining room table.

Enzo waves the black light around then holds it steady over the center of the kitchen floor for a minute or so, and then turns to me.

"Jon, switch the lights back on, will you?"

I catch the lights while Enzo rummages through his bag again. He removes a spray bottle and I know without asking that it's the Luminol. He liberally sprays it all over the kitchen floor and looks up at me and nods. No verbal instruction necessary. I shut the lights off again and come over to the kitchen.

The Luminol reveals a blue amorphous-shaped hue spread over most of the floor. Enzo continues to spray in wider swaths, revealing dots of deep blue, seemingly everywhere. I know what it is without having to ask – blood spatter.

My heart sinks.

"Grab your stuff. Let's go." Enzo says softly.

37

A s soon as we get to the Mercedes, I jump in shotgun. The burner phone sits in the cup holder; I grab it and dial the number messaged to me on the answering machine. After the third ring I'm tempted to hang up, but on the fourth, that same filthy, altered voice from the answering machine picks up.

"I'm glad you called. I've been waiting. You have something I want. I have something you want."

I hit the speaker command on the phone so everyone in the car can hear us.

"What do you want?" I demand.

"I want two things. One – I want a letter you have, or possibly Ms. Brigham has, from Mr. Robert Roberts."

I look at Alison. She's frozen in terror. I reach back and squeeze her hand to give her support, and I mouth 'don't worry' to her.

"Two – I'd like an in-person conversation with Enzo Garibaldi, whom I know you know, and are likely with."

"Where's Danny?" I'm seething. "Let me talk to him."

"He's with me, but I can't let you talk to him right now."

"You fucking prick. Put him on."

Enzo gently clasps my wrist, slowly shaking his head from side-to-side in a 'no' gesture. He follows with a hand motion indicating I need to take it down a notch and keep it cool.

The devil's voice responds. "I'm afraid I can't do that. He's had a slight accident, but it's nothing to worry about. Now, back to my kind request. Garibaldi and the letter. Bring them both to the Maine Mall parking lot behind Sears; ten am tomorrow. We will be in a gray sedan. Understand?"

He hangs up before I can answer.

"What do you think?" I ask Enzo.

"Undoubtedly, it's got to be Brown. Most certainly Reyes, too. Particularly in a gray sedan. I think they don't really care about the letter. You could have photocopied it any number of times and they know that. Bob's dead; that's all they care about. What I am certain of, is they want me dead. And you." He says, eyeballing me. "And you, too." He directs to Alison. "Let's get back to the hotel and figure out our next move."

"I'll have to go." I declare.

"Let's get back to the hotel and figure this out." Enzo repeats.

We arrive at the bus station nearest our hotel to pick up the Cougar. We skipped the first bus station to go directly to Danny's. Enzo wants to take both vehicles back to the hotel; he isn't sure if our planning design for tomorrow will include the need for two cars. Alison offers to drive with my mother and we assure them we'll follow closely behind.

Enzo and I drive mostly in silence for the remainder of the ride. I have a million thoughts rolling through my head and none of them cogent.

"Okay, I have a number of questions." Enzo opens with, as we prepare food at the hotel. "First, is there anyone else you can recall dealing with or coming into contact with besides Reyes and Brown?"

We think for a moment. "No." I respond.

"Just Bond, and he's gone." Alison clarifies.

"Right." I agree.

"How many vehicles have you seen following you and what do they look like?"

"Two that I can think of. We've seen that stupid box truck with the penguin in the chef's hat a couple of times, including at the brewery when you had us picked up."

"And a gray sedan with it at the brewery." Alison adds. "Probably the one the guy referred to."

I breathe an audible sigh. "We've seen others that have looked suspicious, but nothing we can directly link to them."

"I know that box truck. It's theirs. You haven't seen this guy?" Enzo shows us a picture from his phone. He looks remarkably like Ned Flanders, a neighbor of Homer Simpson in *The Simpson's* animated series.

"Not in real life. Maybe in a cartoon, though." I lamely joke.

Enzo lets out a stifled laugh, the first time I've seen him come close to a full one. "I know what you're referring to."

We sit down to eat, putting the planning session on hold while we banter about mindless things. We stay away from anything too personal and emotional. We need clear heads and clear thinking.

When we finish with dinner, we clean up quickly and move to the living room. I've cracked open another beer and Alison's having wine with my mother. Enzo isn't drinking anything.

"Well, this is where I stand on tomorrow." Enzo begins. "I know how these guys operate. They've learned it from me. I recommend that Jon, Alison, and I go to the mall and we take the Mercedes. Sabrina, you stay here at 'home base' with the Cougar. Alison, I would suggest you stay with Sabrina as well, but we may need you nearby in case a request for your presence is made. You won't be with Jon and me; you'll be in the mall, safe and surrounded by shoppers. You'll have the Mercedes to pick us up."

We're riveted on Enzo.

"Jon – Alison will drop me off at the Fairfield. If you've seen the hotel, you will remember it sits up somewhat on a bluff and should afford me a clear visual corridor to watch everything from."

"Then I think you and Alison should park by the food court and have Alison go inside and wait for a call from us for pickup when we're ready. Jon, you head over to the spot and meet whoever this jackass is; most likely Brown, at a gray sedan outside of Sears."

"Um. I'm a sitting duck?" I question.

"No, but you'll need nerves of steel. Most likely you will have a firearm trained on you. However, they will instantly know that when you show up alone, I am somewhere nearby with them as my target. In fact, I believe they will expect it."

"What if they balk at you not being there and don't let Danny go or tell me where he is?"

"I don't think Danny will be in the car. Then it would only be a shootout. No one wins. Keep in mind, they want me as well as you, and it's for a lot more than just General Defense."

"Okay. Now, what if they try and snatch me as well to force you to come out?"

"I'll rifle a bullet through his head before he can flinch. That's where your nerves of steel come into play."

Enzo surveys the room, looking for questions and reading our faces and body language.

"Are we good?" He finally asks.

"I guess." I say.

"Yes." Alison follows up.

"Alright, get some good rest." Enzo says and retreats to his bedroom. My mother goes with him and we do the same.

"Jon, I really like your mother." Alison says while undressing. "I know the past and I know your pain. You have every right to harbor anger and resentment. But today, I like her."

"Yeah. I hear you."

Alison crawls into bed and pats the blankets softly, motioning for me to join.

"One sec. Just need to use the bathroom."

Once inside, I zip up my Glock nine-millimeter pistol into my coat pocket along with an ample supply of loaded magazines. I flush the clean toilet, run the tap for effect, then come back into the bedroom and climb into bed.

I wake to the smell of coffee emanating from the kitchen. In my former life, that is 'Before Bob,' I would have simply set an alarm on my smartphone to wake up. I softly kiss Alison's sweet forehead. She rolls over, spills out of bed, and stumbles to the bathroom. I throw on sweatpants and go out to the kitchen. Enzo is there drinking coffee and putting some clothing into his duffel bag.

"Thirty minutes?" He queries. "I need time to scope out the area and get settled."

"Sure thing." I reply, pouring a cup of coffee.

I go back to the room and relay the schedule to Alison. She puts it into gear and we're ready to go in the allotted time.

My mother lingers in the entryway, embracing Enzo and whispering into his ear.

"I love you, too." He says tenderly.

She goes to Alison and gives her a hug. "Be careful, hon."

"I will."

Finally, she faces me. "I'm sorry you're going through this. Be safe. I love you, Jon."

I can't say it. I just can't say it back. "I'll be careful. Thanks."

We're out the door and on our way. We make good time, arriving at the mall around a quarter past nine. We park at the Fairfield early enough to give Enzo about a half-hour to find his perch. There's a thick wood line at the edge of the bluff, providing Enzo natural cover between the parking lot about seventy-five yards away, and the hotel. At about a quarter of ten, Alison and I head out for the food court parking section. When we arrive, she shuts the car off and we sit for a moment.

"So, you're going into the mall and sit at the food court, right? Get some breakfast or something?" I say to lighten the mood.

"I can't eat."

"You have the burner phone with you?" I ask, knowing full-well she does.

She holds it up for me to see.

"Good. We'll call you on Enzo's phone to come and get us when we're done."

It's almost ten, according to the car's clock. I unbuckle my seat belt as does Alison and we get ready to move.

"Jon?"

"Yes?"

"I love you."

My eyes instantly glisten. "I love you, too."

It takes no effort to find him. Agent Brown stands outside of his gray sedan making a big production of looking at his watch. I'd like to shoot him where he stands.

"Mr. Williams." He hollers to me as I cautiously approach. "You seem to be missing at least one of the two items I asked you to bring. Oh, and it's good to see you again. I'm sorry to have missed you at the brewery."

"I brought them both." I respond, wondering if he can hear my heart thundering in my chest. "One of them is in my back pocket and the other is nearby."

Saying this out loud boosts my confidence in dealing with him. Brown appears to be alone, near as I can tell; Reyes is nowhere in sight. "I don't see the item you were responsible for bringing."

"Oh, I brought it. He's over there." He says while yanking his thumb in a hitchhiker's motion to an area some thirty yards away.

I take a closer look and spot a sizeable truck fairly well-hidden next to a large industrial trash dumpster. Son-of-a-bitch, it's the penguin box truck. I didn't see it when I was approaching because I was focused totally on Brown.

Without prompting, Brown turns and walks toward the truck. I could shoot him right now. I could shoot him right into the back of his fucking FBI head. Enzo's words ring in my mind though; *most likely you will have a firearm trained on you.*

I choose to follow him to the truck, reaching the back door moments after him.

"Open it." I demand, confident Enzo has his scope trained on him and he's ready to shoot. I position myself such that I am fairly certain there's an open line from Enzo to Brown.

He flips the latch and rolls up the door revealing a body slumped over in the far end of the truck bed nearest the cab. Blood pools thickly around the body and streams through the grooved channels of the floor, nearly reaching the door where we stand. I see daylight shining through what must be fifteen bullet holes in the back wall.

"What the fuuu…?" Brown shrieks, jumping into the truck.

"Danny!" I yell. I'm right behind him.

I'm up and at the body just as Brown flips it over. Brown spins and leaps over me, sprinting for the door. He hits the pavement full speed running toward the sedan. I look back at the body, fearing the worst.

It's Reyes. He's dead. I can't readily see how, though it doesn't take a forensics expert to surmise the array of visible bullet holes in the wall played a role. Squealing tires in the background pull my attention back to Brown and I spin back in time to see him speeding off. I jump down from the truck, adrenalin racing through me, and promptly collide with Enzo who's just coming around the corner.

The collision knocks me off balance and I bounce to the ground. Enzo extends a hand to help me up as he removes his cell phone from his pocket.

"Alison? Enzo. Come get us. We're in the lot." He hangs up.

"You okay?" He says to me.

"Yeah. What the hell just happened?"

"When I was watching you and Brown, I didn't see Reyes but I saw the truck tucked behind the dumpster and it hit me what he was try-ing to do. Brown knew I wouldn't be openly visible and would likely be watching him, so his plan was to stuff you into the truck and use you as live bait to draw me out."

I'm in awe as to how this man's mind works.

He continues. "It was then I realized Reyes was probably in the back of the truck waiting for Brown to force you in. It would have been quite easy for them. Reyes only had to flash his firearm and you would have had no choice but to get in. An instant hostage situation – and you would not have made it out alive."

I continue to focus on him.

"I snuck down while you engaged with him at the car, nice work stalling by the way, and quietly entered the cab. I heard some rustling in the back, confirming my suspicions he was there. I then fired two magazines through the wall until I heard a body thump."

"That could have been Danny! You could have killed him!" I stammer.

"I was confident it wouldn't be."

"I didn't hear any shots fired from where I was."

"Silencer." He states unassumingly.

Enzo jumps up into the truck to inspect Reyes and I follow him.

"Yeah, it's Reyes." Enzo observes. He takes a pocket flashlight out of his coat and surveys the space. There are mover's blankets, push brooms, and other miscellaneous stuff stacked about. Enzo moves in for a closer inspection. He moves a stack of blankets, revealing a large black bag with a zipper running the full length.

"Jon." He turns to me after unzipping it partway and steps aside. I move to his spot and look in. It's Danny.

"Ahhhhh …. Oh no …. NO … NOOOOO!" The strength evaporates from my body and I drop to my knees. I look at Danny with tunnel vision, virtually unable to process what I see.

His face is bloated; he's obviously been dead for a while. A giant gash extends the span of his neck with no visible fresh blood present. He was slaughtered, plain and simple. Enzo was right. I didn't get what he meant when he said he was confident it wasn't Danny he was shooting at and now I see why. I didn't want to believe it could be true, but Enzo knew he was dead before those bastards took him from his house.

"Follow me. We need to move right now and get far away from here. We're taking the truck."

Enzo picks me up from my underarms, helping me down from the truck. After closing the door, he walks me to the passenger side of the cab and I get in. Alison pulls up in the SUV and Enzo quickly gives her instruction and gets back into the truck.

I look around numbly, noticing a collection of spent bullet casings strewn about the seat and floor.

Just another day at the office.

38

The sting of tears and pure unadulterated anger and hate blind me. I'm hunched over the glove box struggling to focus on the road ahead while Enzo drives the truck. Danny's in the back and he's dead. *God damn it, he's dead and it's my fault!* I am resolute in my mission to kill FBI Agent Scott Brown. There won't be any law enforcement involved. Periodically, I look in my side-view mirror to eyeball the Mercedes behind us. I should be driving it and not Alison, but right now I'm unable to. She appears calm, though Enzo says she doesn't know Danny died. She only knows about Reyes decomposing in the back and that we need to dispose of him.

Enzo faces me intermittently as he drives. "You're somewhat in a state of shock, so just listen to me. We're going back to the bus station and we'll leave the Mercedes there. Alison can join us in the truck, and then we'll head back to the hotel. When we get near, I'll call your mother and she can take the Cougar and follow us. We'll dispose of Reyes at the waterfront under cover of darkness and then we ditch the catering truck. I'm sure it's untraceable anyway. No one will be looking for it."

"What about Danny?" I moan. "He should be laid to rest in the water as well. That was his second home. Somewhere far from that son-of-bitch Reyes, though."

"This is going to be hard for you to process," Enzo begins, "but hear me out."

I'm on the edge of throwing up.

He continues, "If we bury your uncle at sea, no one is going to know."

"So?" I reply, defeated and confused.

"Jon, I'm going to go out on a limb here. If I had to guess, I'd say you're Danny's sole heir."

I'm staring at him.

"Your life, and his estate, will be much less complicated if he's found. You need to heal. You don't want to undergo the prolonged, gut-wrenching process of waiting out the period to declare him dead before having closure. In most instances, that period is at least seven years."

In my present state of mind, I don't have the capability to process or protest his suggestion. I simply answer 'yes.'

"Yes, what? You're his heir, or 'yes' he should be found?"

"Both."

"An unbelievably hard decision you just made. I'm so sorry you had to do it."

"Do you have a thought for a method of discovery? How do we make sure he's found without anyone finding out the truth?" I can barely get the words out.

"I've been thinking about it during the ride. If you're agreeable, we can move Danny to his master bedroom and place him in his bed with dignity and respect. I have some experience staging houses and generating fires without utilizing accelerants by crafting faulty electrical outlets, running frayed extension cords under rugs for more fuel; stuff like that. I didn't notice if he had curtains, but those work well for spreading fire. There are some other things I can do as well. It will appear the fire started in the bedroom and he died in his sleep in a tragic house fire. You'll receive the insurance proceeds. You don't want the house anyway. I think we both know he was likely gone before those assholes left his house."

I can't believe I'm sitting in this truck with this guy.

"It will also allow you, and Jennifer too, to have a proper service and burial for him instead of living with a secret no one else knows. That can be a hugely difficult burden." He adds.

I'll have a secret no matter what.

"I need help. Can you help me?" I plead. "I won't be able to do it. I can't. He's all I had."

"I'll take care of everything."

Enzo puts his directional signal on in plenty of time for Alison to respond in kind and drive up beside him at the bus station. She rolls her window down and Enzo points her in the general direction of where he would like her to park.

"Pick any spot in the middle of the second floor, please. We'll be waiting for you here."

Alison pulled up on Enzo's side of the box truck, so she didn't see my face and that I've been crying. I try to collect myself, but it's a waste of time. She'll see right through me.

In a minute or two, she comes bounding from the garage toward us. I slip out of the front seat and let her slide into the middle, then climb back in.

She leans in to give me a kiss. "Baby, are you okay?"

"No. No, I'm not."

"What's wrong, besides all the crazy crap we're dealing with?"

I turn to her, my voice shaky. "Danny's gone. Oh God, Danny's gone."

"Oh no! What happened? How did you find out?" She rockets a few more questions at me. "Who did it? Where is he?"

"He's out back in a body bag." I croak. "Enzo found him when he went to put Reyes' dead body in a bag. His throat was slit. It was slit ear to ear."

I feel the blood beginning to boil in my body. "He was probably killed at his house on the kitchen floor where we saw the blood residue." I'm moaning my way through the dialogue.

Uncharacteristically, Alison spits nails. "Those fuckers." Tears start flowing.

I spend the better chunk of the drive recounting my and Enzo's conversation and subsequent plan for dumping Reyes and dealing with Danny. Enzo fills in the specifics on how we'll carry out what essentially amounts to Danny's cremation.

"I'm so sorry." Alison whispers, shaking her head. She hugs me tight and I hug her back tighter. I don't want to let her go.

"Hey babe." Enzo says into his cell phone. "We're about fifteen minutes out. I'm afraid we're going to have a long night. I wanted to give you a heads-up to dress comfortably and bring anything you need for an extended period of time."

We can only hear one side of his conversation.

"He's doing alright. We have a situation here that I'll fill you in on. We're going to show up in a box truck with a big penguin on the side. I'll explain that later as well. We'll park in the loading area visible from the west-side entrance and then I'll call you. Take the Cougar and follow us."

A minute passes with Enzo listening to my mother.

"I love you, too. Bye." He disconnects.

She waves to us as she leaves the hotel and heads straight to the car. Enzo puts the truck in gear and rolls slowly to the exit, then waits. My mother tucks in behind him and both vehicles exit the parking lot.

The ride is excruciating. I can't stand being inside my own skin right now. I can't stand the loudness of my own thoughts. I turn the shitty radio on to listen to anything that can distract me. Enzo's on the phone with my mother relaying to her what's happened. He spares her the most violent aspects; I can tell this is standard operating procedure between them.

As we approach Portland, city lights begin opening up before us. Hadlock Field stadium lights, the Time & Temperature building, and the medical center all contribute to the visual.

Enzo snakes his way through city streets on a path to the waterfront. He's silent now. Calculating. We end up by a small building adjacent to the fish piers. Clearly, he's done this before.

"Is this where you hired Bob?" Alison asks, with no discernible tone to her question. It was as neutral as it possibly could be.

"Yes." Enzo replies while shutting the truck off.

"Jon, will you be able to give me a hand with him?" Enzo asks.

"God damn right."

Enzo exits the truck and I follow. He says to Alison, "You may want to wait with Sabrina in the car."

"Okay." She agrees and exits with us.

Enzo has the back door to the truck rolled open; he's climbed in and placed a mover's blanket over the bag containing Danny's body. He proceeds to drag Reyes' bag to the edge of the truck.

"Grab that handle. We're going to move him inside."

Enzo jumps down and opens the door with a code on a keypad. He returns and takes the opposite handle and we pick up Reyes and bring him into the building.

Inside it looks like a small, nondescript commercial packing facility. Enzo moves about swiftly; walking to the far end of the building and returning quickly with a blue fifty-five-gallon plastic drum. He lays the drum on its side, closest to one end of the body bag and unzips it. He begins peeling the bag down around Reyes with significant effort.

"Give me a hand, will you? When I lift his shoulders, strip the bag as far as you can; I'll move down and we'll keep doing that until he's out."

I move into position and Enzo lifts his shoulders. I begin to peel the bag as instructed while looking at his cold, ugly, Rocky Balboa face. When we finish, Enzo positions the drum at his head in preparation for stuffing him in.

"Hold on a second before we put him in."

I take one final look at him and spit in his face. "Alright. Let's do this."

I lift his head and Enzo proceeds to slide the barrel down. I lift his shoulders; Enzo slides the barrel down a little further. I lift his waist and then half of his body is in. At this point, I lift his legs while Enzo tips the barrel upright and we're almost there. His legs protrude, but Enzo appears to have a method for addressing it. He crosses Reyes' legs, casually mentioning it's good we're doing this before rigor mortis sets in any further. Enzo retrieves a sledgehammer and proceeds to mash Reyes' legs down just below the rim of the barrel creating a particular crunching sound I've never heard before. I'm not remotely troubled by it.

"Now what?" I ask.

"We're almost done in here." He says. "Just a few more steps."

He proceeds to weave large, lead sinkers into the barrel. "This will keep the body gases from causing the barrel to float to the surface."

Following that step, he unseals a five-gallon white bucket and carefully pours its contents into the barrel. I hear a low sizzling sound as it begins to eat into Reyes' flesh. After pouring in another bucket, Enzo finishes the project by capping the drum with a matching blue cover and sealing it shut with an industrial heat gun and glue.

"Now what?" I ask again, sounding like a broken record.

"We get a hand dolly and move him to the commercial winch out on the dock used for loading and unloading gear and seafood from the boats. Instead of loading him into a boat, we're going to unload him into the channel. It's dredged, so he'll go very deep. If he's ever found, which I highly doubt, the acid and Father Time will have removed all DNA traces. No one will look for this asshole, anyway."

We head out to the dock and do our business. It felt so satisfying when Enzo let me hit the release button, dropping the son-of-a-bitch into the channel. As we head back to the girls, I can't help but wonder how many blue barrels lie down there.

"Now we need to get rid of the truck." Enzo notes as if checking off a box on his mental mobster list. Reyes dead? Check. Box truck discarded? On deck.

"Are we moving Danny into the car?"

"Yes, I think that's best. We'll move him into the trunk of the car and then dispose of the truck on the north side of the bay. We can drive it off of the breakwater jetty surrounding the crude oil tankers and it won't be discovered. There will be no one looking for it, anyway. Any GPS or other trackers that may be imbedded in the truck will be useless."

"Sounds like you've done this before."

He doesn't acknowledge my comment. "This may sound weird, but try and be as efficient and as casual as you can when we're working around the girls. It will be hugely beneficial to us to keep them as calm as possible, believe me."

Christ, are you kidding me? Be casual? Be efficient? Let's get this over with you fucking sociopath.

"Will do." I reply.

We move Danny swiftly. Enzo then gives my mother direction as to where to meet us and we all leave the wharf.

We drive up to the north side of the bay, stopping the truck at the end of the landing pier at the oil depot. I get out of the truck and wait and watch. Enzo leaves the vehicle running while he examines the surrounding area. He eventually finds what he's searching for – a medium-sized slab of cement or something that looks close to it. He returns to the truck and places it on the accelerator, causing the engine to roar. He slips the truck into gear and off it goes to its watery grave; most likely adding to the underwater automotive cemetery below us.

Enzo shifts his attention to me. "We're through here. Nice work. Let's go."

Nice work … I want to throw up in my mouth.

39

We drive in silence. I'm numb from head to toe, barely feeling Alison's soft caress on the back of my neck. When we arrive at Danny's neighborhood, Enzo parks in the municipal beach access lot instead of a side road closer to the house. The Cougar would be too out of place and could draw attention from neighbors. This 'watch and wait' method of reconnaissance is entirely maddening. Enzo sits in silence; therefore, we sit in silence. After a forty-five-minute wait – that seems to be the customary time block for waiting – he quietly exits the vehicle, beckoning for me to follow. I exit the car and immediately hear the doors lock behind me. Probably standard protocol for my mother.

We track the beachhead and push through the dunes, appearing in front of Danny's house. It looks exactly as we left it. Enzo goes first, pausing on the front stoop to run his fingers up and down the door. He finds what he's looking for, tugs hard and removes a small piece of cloth from the frame.

"I placed this here when we left to see if the door's been opened prior to us coming back. I think we're fine; Brown will probably lay low for a while anyway."

We move through the house methodically clearing one room at a time. I have my pistol locked and loaded, though Enzo isn't aware I have it. After we conclude our search, Enzo calls my mother and tells her it's safe to drive up.

I plop down onto the couch, close my eyes and try to regroup.

"Let's go." Enzo says.

So much for regrouping. I silently follow him to the car.

Enzo catches the girls before they exit the vehicle. "Hey guys, stay in the car for just a moment until we go back in, okay? Then come inside in a minute or two."

They both follow his request to remain inside the car. Enzo pops the trunk and in a very soft, hushed voice explains he'd like us to move Danny into the bedroom together and then have me leave after we place him on the bed.

"It's better if you leave the room and I get him prepared for you and the girls to view." He rationalizes.

It's late and Enzo and I are not much more than shadows moving about as we maneuver Danny into the house. When we place his body onto the bed, I hear the girls come in and the front door shut behind them. I'm struggling to leave the room.

"Take your time." Enzo says.

"Yeah. Let me know when I can come back in."

After a short period, Enzo joins us in the living room. We're all on the same page as to what's going to take place, and we're ready to say our final goodbyes. I enter first to see Danny lying in his bed, eyes closed with the blankets pulled up to his chin. The body bag he was brought in with is nowhere in sight. I sit down on the bed next to him and place my hand on his forehead, brushing his hair back.

"Danny, I'm so sorry." I sob. "I'm so sorry." I lean over and kiss his forehead. Alison stands behind me with her hand on my back. She's crying, too. I stand up and we embrace each other tightly while the others look on. I take a step back. My mother takes my place.

"Rest easy, Danny." She says. "Thank you for all you've done for my boy. I can never repay you." She kisses her hand and places it on his forehead and steps away.

"Are we ready?" Enzo says thoughtfully. "I don't want to rush anyone."

"I'm ready." I say. "I'll stay in the room with you."

"That's fine. You girls may want to wait in the other room."

They leave, and Enzo gets to work. I sit back down on the bed with Danny and watch. He pulls out a multi-tool, akin to a Swiss Army knife, and removes the plate cover to an electrical outlet. Using the tool, he frays the wires by removing the insulated sleeving to leave them exposed. He takes a lamp off of the nightstand and begins to disassemble the base, I'm guessing for further fuel.

My mind drifts to Danny and what he must have gone through. I picture him restrained on the kitchen floor, tied up and unable to move. Was he ambushed? He probably had just a very short time to react; only enough time to send me a phone number. Did they try to get my location from him? He didn't know where I was. He wouldn't have known Enzo and my mother had me. Did they slit his throat; murder him in cold blood as a punishment? He had nothing to do with this.

No ... they did it as a message. A message to me, a message to Alison, and a message to Enzo. And they set all of us up to find him and do the same. Well – we killed one messenger and I'm going to kill the other.

"We're ready, Jon. It's time to say your final goodbye."

I inspect his work. "This will set the room on fire?"

"It will when I reconnect the wires. Then I'll need to screw the outlet cover back on quickly before it gets out of control or fire inspectors will catch that and know it's been tampered with. I shorted the lamp out and that will help with the process. He has plenty of blankets, curtains, throw rugs and the like to turn at least this part of the house into an inferno. I'm reasonably confident investigators won't be able to determine if there's smoke in his lungs or not or be able to see any evidence of a gash on his neck. It will simply look like a tragic accident."

I take one last look at him. "Bye, Danny." My partially audible voice cracks.

I step back, and Enzo sets his final stage of the plan in motion. He attempts to connect the wires, resulting in low popping noises. It takes him a few tries as he receives small electrical burns each time he attempts to attach them to one another and needs to pause.

His efforts pay off when he produces a solid connection and the sound morphs from popping noise to steady-state hissing. Enzo quickly grabs the outlet cover, places it over the receptacle, then rapidly inserts the screws. The outlet almost immediately catches fire and I can smell electricity in the air. It reminds me of the old electric car racetrack I had growing up. If you held a car down and squeezed the hand trigger, you could produce an electric smell while the wheels peeled out on the track. This was just like it, only more powerful; more concentrated.

"Oh shit!" Enzo howls, flapping his arm. He has the cover plate on and retreats, flailing his shirtsleeve, which has caught on fire. I step forward and wrap it up in my arms, smothering the flame.

"Thanks." He says.

"Yeah."

"Okay, we need to go." Enzo lightly urges.

I take one last look at him as I move away. I go into his closet, retrieve all of the old photo albums and then leave the room. Very calmly, we all file out of the house making sure to lock the front door behind us. We drive away from Danny's with almost all of us in a state of shock and sadness.

After a few minutes on the road, the silence is broken.

"Jon!" Alison shrieks in a panic, grabbing my arm and causing me to jump out of my seat. Startled, Enzo and my mother whirl around.

"The money!"

40

There's no chance of us returning for any reason, including for the money. Danny's house is undoubtedly in flames; we wouldn't be able to get through the front door, let alone access the basement. Fire and rescue will be on site shortly if they're not already there, anyway.

Enzo thinks there's a good chance the money won't burn in the gun vault as long as it's appropriately fire-rated. I recall Danny mentioning it had fire protection, but I forget the rating. I don't care either way. If it burns, let it burn.

"Jon, you'll need to think about a way to connect with Danny's girlfriend. She'll be notified of the fire and won't have a way to contact you." Enzo says. "You'll have to find a way without it appearing odd or out of place."

"How will the police know who to call?" I wonder.

My mother answers. "Jennifer will see it on the news and call in or go straight to his house."

"Then that's my opportunity." I reason. "I'll call her; extremely distraught, which I am, and say I saw Danny's house on the news. She'll tell me about him then."

"Fair plan." Enzo asserts.

The drive back to the hotel isn't as comfortable in the exhaust-laden Cougar. I'm thankful we complete it in silence.

We arrive at the hotel and I flop down on the couch, tired both mentally and physically. My mother sits down with me, probably equally as tired.

"I'm going to bed." Enzo says. "We have a lot to talk about in the morning. We need to game plan for Brown. I have some ideas, but I want to sleep on it."

"Include me in anything you come up with." I say in a guttural growl.

Alison exhales deeply. "I'm going to bed, too."

She gives me a kiss on my cheek, hugs my mother, then disappears into our bedroom leaving me alone with her.

"You want to watch TV?" She asks.

"Not really. I'm probably going to go to bed."

"Are you okay?"

"No. Not really."

"I understand." She pauses, fiddling with her fingernails.

"Jon," she waits for me to look at her, "Danny was a good man. I always liked him."

I can feel the hot tears start to flow.

"I want to tell you something. Something you don't know … or at least I don't think you know."

I'm not sure I can deal with any more surprises, secrets, or clandestine stuff. Regardless, I give her my attention.

"Danny stayed a friend to me even after the split with your father. He didn't know it, but Danny would let me know where you were and what you were doing pretty much all the time. Even when he was on the water he would get emails to me with schedules. There were many situations where I could attend your events without being noticed, especially after your father passed."

I'm dumbfounded.

"But sometimes I couldn't go because you would have discovered me, and I didn't want to hurt you or your dad."

"What? Why are you telling me this? And why now?"

"Danny wanted me not to. With the huge responsibility he took on with you, I respected his wish."

"I'm not sure I believe you."

"I've kept the emails from Danny and me that I could show you, if you'd like."

"Tell me some of the things I've done that you've seen." I ask skeptically.

My mom smiles warmly. She doesn't skip a beat in recounting some of her most cherished moments. "Oh, there are so many. Seventh grade basketball against Greenwich, you were down by a point; you took the last shot as time was running out and missed it."

I break a small smile. I know how this story goes. How could I forget?

"But you were fouled." She continues. "You made the first free throw to tie the game and then the other team's coach called a time out to try and ice you. I nearly jumped out of my seat when you hit the game winner."

I laugh a little. "Yeah, I peaked in seventh grade."

"Hardly. What about in tenth grade? You were one of only a few sophomores that made varsity football. That in and of itself was impressive. I was surprised you didn't play after that season."

"Yeah, I was tired of getting my head bashed in."

"I cried like a baby at the convention center when you accepted your high school diploma. Same for college."

"Well, God damn. How weird is this?" I say with a chuckle; but then I get serious. "I'd like to know about the custody hearing and your involvement, or lack thereof, after Dad died."

She gets up silently and goes to the bedroom, returning in a few moments with a manila folder. She spreads the contents out on the living room floor for me to sift through.

"Danny and I were in contact for the entire proceeding."

She shifts specific papers toward me for examination. They're emails between her and Danny. They delineate exactly how they would both like the proceeding to go. The decision for Danny to have full custody was determined by both of them, amicably, in advance of the application process. She indicates she will provide for my support, whatever is necessary, and understands and agrees she and Danny will keep this from me until the time is right, if ever.

"You've been financially supporting me all these years?"

"Yes. We both have. Enzo included. We supported you through Danny."

"The car Danny bought me at sixteen? You?"

She nods, blinking through tears welling in her eyes. "I really liked that Mustang."

"College?" I probe.

"A lot of it. The financial aid package you received was legit. We weren't disclosing any income for them to consider. It was all based upon Danny's financial situation."

"Enzo said he got me the job at Harding-Williams."

"Yes. He had Bob hire you. Not that you wouldn't have made it on your own, but it doesn't hurt to have an inside track." She says smiling.

"Yeah." I say with a laugh.

"So, you and Danny agreed together that he would have custody of me to protect me from the environment you were in. Along with that, you provided the financial support I needed?"

"Yes, essentially. We agreed I would try to be a visible part of your life when you were older and independent. Problem is, when that happened, you didn't want me in your life." She says dejectedly.

"Can you blame me?"

We sit in silence. This is a lot for me to process, especially with all that's happened. Probably a lot for her as well.

"Hey, here's a question for you." I say lightheartedly. "Were you there when I was the emcee of the school talent show in eleventh grade? It was opening night."

"Ha, ha, ha, yes!" She laughs. "You tripped on the mic cord and fell, and when you got up you announced you were the opening act. You earned an Honorable Mention award! You did a terrific job pulling that off!"

As tired as we were, we spent the better part of the night talking and reminiscing of events I had no idea she had been a part of. When finally we were all talked out, we decided to call it a night.

"Good night, Jon. I love you." She says, giving me a hug.

"Good night, Mom." I hug her back and then break away toward the bedroom.

"Hey."

"Yeah?" I look back at her.

"You called me 'Mom'."

"Well, you are, aren't you?" I reply smiling.

41

I feel a soft fingernail trailing the length of my back. I was starting to wake up anyway, so it's not unpleasant or intrusive. Sleep was fitful; I dreamt about Uncle Danny and the events of yesterday throughout the night. My t-shirt is soaked with sweat, as is my pillow.

"Good morning." Alison breathes softly. "How're you feeling?"

I look at the clock. It reads: 11:17 am.

"I feel tired." I groan. "I can't believe it's already after eleven."

"You needed it. I just woke up myself."

The reality of the day smacks me in the face. News outlets must be reporting on the fire and Jennifer will be trying to contact me. I'll need to figure out a game plan on that quickly. I roll out of bed and shuffle off to the bathroom sporting morning wood without any intention of making use of it. After I finish with my toiletries and come out to get dressed, I see Alison noticed it as well, and has every intention of making use of it.

The idea of trying to be quiet during sex is somewhat foreign to me. I think it is for Alison, too. We find ourselves taking turns 'shushing' each other lightheartedly when we get a little too loud. Eventually we get the hang of it and find our groove. She must be as worked up and on edge as I am; it doesn't take long for her to orgasm and I'm right behind her.

I leave the bedroom while Alison stays behind to get ready for the day. I notice right away Mom and Enzo in the living room with all of their bags packed. I see four suitcases and about eight duffel bags.

"Morning everyone." I say with a scratchy throat. "What's with the bags? Are we leaving?"

"Well, well … he rises. Almost good afternoon to you. There're doughnuts on the counter." Mom says with a smile.

Nice, I'm starving.

"Yes, we're leaving when you're ready. We need to periodically switch hotels, and in light of the interaction with Brown and the fact that we've circumvented our safety protocols a number of times, now seems to be the right time." Enzo responds.

"Where are we going?" I ask as Alison enters the room.

"Coincidently, the Fairfield Inn by the mall where we set up for our meeting with the assholes."

"Is that safe?" Alison asks.

"Depends on what you consider safe. Brown's the last loose end we need to tie up. My plan is to bait him into a trap, so we ought to be a little more 'accessible'." He explains.

Enzo relates his plan to us for entrapping Brown. He intends to move all of our belongings to the hotel by the mall. Then he'd like Alison and me to go back to her apartment and act as bait for Brown to discover. Enzo keeps surveillance, and when Brown makes his move, Enzo takes him out.

"How are you going to eliminate Brown?" I ask.

"I haven't gotten that far yet." He answers. "But I will."

I have no doubt. "What about the CFO of General Defense? You said Brown was the last loose end."

"Yeah, I know what I said about taking him out, but he's nothing. He's a business guy with big ideas and no muscle. That's why he got me involved. We can deal with him on our own timeline after Brown is gone. You and Alison will be able to move on without worry from him."

I'm starting to feel there may be a light at the end of the tunnel of this mess. Enzo's assertion visibly brightens Alison.

"Now," he continues, "before we do anything, we need to focus on your uncle. The fire's been plastered all over the news; Danny's girlfriend must be trying to reach out to you."

"I suspect as much. I need to contact her, but I'm really not sure how to go about it."

"Well, I've got that worked out as well. We're trying to attract Brown. The two primary methods are one – reassembling your phones; permanently, to allow Brown to continue his probable cell tower trace, and two – both of you hanging out at the apartment, assuming there's a listening device planted, and he knows you're there."

"Excellent, we'll get our phones back. That'll be good." I say.

"I thought that might be the case. She will have left you a voice message, so you can call her from the car when we're on our way."

Alison turns to the bedroom. "I'll start packing our stuff."

"Perfect. Thank you." Enzo says.

I grab another doughnut while surveying the bags laid out in the living room.

"Christ, you guys don't travel light. What's in all of those duffel bags?"

"Roughly two and a half million dollars." Enzo says with barely any emotion.

"No shit?"

"No shit."

"You keep all of your money with you?"

"No. Only about a tenth of it."

We load up the Mercedes with the money and Mom and Enzo's stuff. The Cougar has mine and Alison's. She opts to travel with my mom and I'm with Enzo. He assembled both of our cell phones and gave them to us, so we're fully connected with the outside world again. I have a ton of email and text messages, but just one voicemail. It's from the number Danny texted to me in his final message. I activate it and hit 'speaker' so Enzo can hear the message:

> *Jon, it's Jennifer. Call me as soon as you*
> *get this. You must have seen the news.*
> *Danny's house burned down.*

Jennifer's voice is barely comprehendible. She cries throughout the entirety of the message.

> *Jon, he didn't make it. He was in the*
> *house. They're saying it started in the*
> *bedroom and the electrical in the house*
> *was faulty. Please call me.*

"Well, under the conditions, that's the best we could hope for." Enzo offers.

"Yeah."

"You should call back."

"Yeah."

I dial her number on speaker-phone and she answers on the first ring. "Hello?"

"Jennifer, it's Jon."

"Jon, oh Jon." She wails.

"Jennifer, what happened?? It can't be true, tell me it's not true. I saw the TV, I saw the house …" I ramble on tearfully. "I'm on my way. I just saw it. I'm on my way to his house."

"I'm here now. There's nothing left of his house! It's completely burned! Danny's been taken away by the coroner's office." She's falling apart.

"I'll see you shortly." I look at Enzo to make sure what I say is true. He nods to me.

I don't know what else I can say to her, so I just say 'bye' then disconnect.

"I wasn't sure if you would be on board with us driving over to the house."

"Just the two of us. Sabrina and Alison can go to the hotel. We don't want the Cougar anywhere near the house, just in case."

"Right. Do you think it's a good idea for them to be at the hotel by themselves?"

"I do. Sabrina is very good at setting us up in the hotel according to our set plan."

"I meant from a safety standpoint."

"Actually, yes. I fully expect Brown to be at your uncle's house or somewhere nearby. He would have seen the news as well and know we're behind it. It leads him right to us."

"Okay, so will we be safe?"

"There will be a lot of activity around. He can't make a move."

I text Alison about what's happening, filling her in on Jennifer. Enzo's on the phone talking to my mom and updating her as well.

I filter through my email messages, scanning for anything important. I see a message from Peabo and open it up. It was two days ago.

> *Jon, we found some files on General Defense. All of them are paper files. Some have water-damage, but some are OK. Give me a call.*
>
> *Peabo*

"Thank Christ, some General Defense files were found. Alison and I are hoping there's information in them to get us off the hook."

"Just make sure we handle Brown first before you both go back to work, please."

"Yeah. Good advice."

I send Peabo a return email indicating we'll get back to him on it. Following that, I call Alison on her cell; there's too much to talk about for a text.

"Hey babe." She says, answering on the first ring.

"Hey. I got an email from Peabo. They've found some General Defense files. Some are damaged, but some aren't. I'm supposed to call him when we can."

"Ya, I know. I got a voice message from Harold saying they've found some of them. I'll forward the message to you."

"Sounds good. Alright, I'll see you back at the hotel after we go to Danny's."

"Call me when you're on your way back, okay?"

"Will do. Love you."

"Love you, too."

Alison's forwarded message comes in and I play it on speaker-phone for Enzo to hear as well.

> *Hello Alison, it's Harold Osterman call-*
> *ing. I found some General Defense files.*
> *Some are water damaged and of little use.*
> *Some of them look pretty good. Call when*
> *you want to come in for them. I'll have*
> *our guys pull them out for you.*
>
> *Take care.*

I experience tunnel vision driving down Danny's private road. It's swirling before me like a cartoon spiral spinning in an endless loop. Police barricaded the last thirty yards, so we have to stop and give my name before we're let through. Jennifer told them to expect us.

When the house, or the spot where the house stood, comes into view, we see yellowish 'caution' tape strung around the perimeter. A few stray, charred pieces of wood jut skyward, still smoldering. I get out of the car and spot Jennifer at the same time she sees me.

"Jon." She moans, completely distraught. Her eyes are so puffy, they're nearly shut. She comes to me with her arms open and I hug her tightly. She's barely five feet tall, so her head buries into my chest. She's gorgeous and petite, of Asian descent; and even though she's distraught, she's as beautiful as ever.

"I'm so sorry, Jennifer. This was bad electrical? He couldn't get out?" I ask, trying not to break down.

"They're saying the fire was super-fast moving and because he was asleep, he was most likely overcome with smoke. He didn't have a chance. He may have had some inoperable smoke detectors."

"Oh God." I whisper. I don't remember Enzo disconnecting any smoke detectors, but he may have before I came into the bedroom.

I begin walking with Jennifer arm-in-arm along the edge of the basement foundation. Peering down reveals nothing but ash and burnt wood. In the spot where I expect the gun vaults should be, I can just make out the top of each one. It's impossible to tell if the contents of either one are intact.

We stand and stare somberly. She audibly weeps, and I cry silently amidst stray smoke tendrils drifting in the light wind.

"I don't understand where he was before this and why he came back here to sleep and didn't call me." She laments. "I don't know if he was mad at me or if I did something to make him mad ..." She trails off.

Jennifer's tormented by the thought she may have driven Danny away. I need to disabuse her of the notion and of laying responsibility on herself. It also reminds me she thought I was supposed to stay here with Alison last night.

"He may have only been here because he thought Alison and I would be here, but at the last minute, we decided to stay at her place." I say, trying to avert further questions.

After a pause, I offer lamely, "We'll need to plan for a service."

"Yes. You're his closest relative; the only relative I'm aware of. I was told by police you need to deal with the release of his body." Her voice cracks painfully.

"I am, and I have an original of his will. I'm the executor of his estate and I'll figure out what we need to do."

"If you handle the authorizations, I'll handle the service and funeral arrangements – if that's okay with you."

"Yes. I think that would be good. Especially if it helps for closure."

I'm somewhat relieved she offered to handle the arrangements. It will allow me to concentrate on Brown and the General Defense files, knowing Danny's final arrangements are in good, loving hands.

I give Jennifer another long, affectionate hug as an indicator I'm going to leave.

"I'll go talk to the fire inspector or whoever's in charge here to find out what I need to do for Danny." And what I need to do to retrieve the safes. "I'll call you as soon as I know."

"Thanks. I'll check with you on what I come up with for Danny to make sure it's okay."

"I'm sure it will be. Thanks." I kiss her cheek and break away.

After meeting with the lead investigator and figuring out what I need to do for Danny and for removing salvageable contents, I go back to the SUV. Enzo watches and waits patiently.

"Are you all set with affairs here?"

"Yes." I quickly recap my discussions with Jennifer and the fire inspector.

"What about Brown?" I follow up.

"No sign of him. I'm surprised, actually. I thought for sure he'd be here."

"Hmm. Well … should we go to the hotel and regroup? Figure out the game plan for Alison's apartment?"

"Yes. I checked in with Sabrina and Alison. They're set up in a suite, waiting for us."

42

"**A**lright, thank you. Yes, I'll have arrangements ready by to-morrow. Very good." I disconnect the call.

"Was that the coroner?" Alison asks.

"It was the medical examiner's office." I reply as I sit down on the hotel couch. "Probably the same division, but a different department. I'm authorized to remove Danny's body. The examiner's death certificate will list the cause of death as thermal burns – accidental. You were right Enzo; as hard as this is, it was a good move to have had him found. I'm thinking more for Jennifer than for me. She'll have some level of closure with the process of planning his funeral."

Mom spread lunch out on the kitchen counter. Italian subs with potato chips and Diet Coke. I couldn't ask for anything more. Alison relaxes in an athletic-style outfit extraordinarily resembling my mother's, and her hair is pulled back in a strikingly similar ponytail. It's a little odd how much they look alike. I glance over to Enzo. Yeah, we still couldn't look any more different.

"I assume he'll be cremated?" Mom asks softly, understandably treading lightly.

"Yes … I would expect so. I don't mean to seem insensitive, but he's part-way there."

"No, I understand. You'll need to call Jennifer to figure out who she's using for the funeral home. They'll be the ones to go after him and make arrangements with the crematorium." Mom points out.

"Yeah. Makes sense. I'll call her to confirm. I'll have to be there too, to sign paperwork. But first," I say, patting my belly, "I need to eat."

I left Jennifer a voice message detailing the process for bringing Danny home. In the meantime, while waiting for a return call, Alison and I take a quick nap. I may have set a new Guinness World Record for the least amount of time needed to fall asleep. I hadn't had an opportunity to tell Alison about my discussion with my mother after she and Enzo went to bed, so when we wake up I recount the conversation to her. She's not as surprised as I thought she would be. Apparently during the course of their 'girl talk,' little snippets of my past spilled out, leaving Alison wondering as to how Mom knew some of these things about me.

"How do you feel about all of this?" She asks me.

"Better. Not perfect."

"Nothing's perfect."

"You said it."

We get cleaned up and come out of our room to find Mom and Enzo lounging on the couch. It's early evening and they're unwinding in front of the television, eerily resembling an ordinary, middle-aged couple watching the news. They're anything but standard issue, though.

"Hey." I say.

"Hey yourself." Mom says playfully.

"Any word from Jennifer?" Enzo asks.

"No. Nothing yet." I reply. "Are we going to talk about Brown? Just wondering if you thought of how we should go after him."

I feel awkward saying this. I imagine I sound much like the look of a teenager attempting to smoke a cigarette for the first time but act as though he's been doing it for years. I take a puff, and my statement comes out like a cough.

"We're not going after him." Enzo replies.

"No way are you keeping me out of this." I insist.

"Easy there, tiger. I mean, we're not going after him; he's going to come to us."

Now we're getting somewhere.

"This is what I propose." Enzo begins. "This doesn't need to be too complicated. First, I take you and Alison back to Alison's apartment. Then we'll safely clear the rooms and sweep the apartment for listening devices. I expect to find one or more, and after I do, both of you simply engage in a scripted conversation we work on in advance. Nothing specific; just general banter. Odds are he'll eventually show up and I'll intercept him."

"That sounds easy." Alison says.

"Sometimes that's the case." Enzo points out.

"What if there aren't any listening devices?" I ask.

"We'll cross that bridge when we get to it. But I don't think we will get to it. I'm fairly confident that's how they tracked down Bond."

That comment would have hurt a lot more a few days ago.

Mom chooses to come with us much to Enzo's objection. He's a tough guy, but not when it comes to her. I sort of appreciate that in him. For as violent as he is, he's equally as gentle for her and her concerns.

When we get to Alison's apartment, Enzo modifies his 'wait and watch' method somewhat. Alison and I are instructed to be as visible as possible when we enter, and at the same time Enzo and Mom will sneak into the garage and come up through the elevator. The idea is to slip those two into the apartment undetected. Brown should only expect Alison and me inside.

Enzo parks the car in a similar spot Alison and I parked in when we made our last trip in Danny's Jeep. Then she and I emerge from the tree line and walk to the front lobby, hand-in-hand, chatting mindlessly. About the time we enter the building, Mom and Enzo should be entering the garage. Alison gave them the elevator code, so we ought to get to the front door around the same time.

We take the stairs and come out onto the landing at the fourth floor directly across from Alison's door. I use her key and jiggle it into the damaged lock and crack the door open. I hear the 'ding' of the elevator stopping on the fourth floor, and we wait for Enzo and Mom to come out. After they do, we all go in. I immediately flick the light switch and Enzo silently sweeps the apartment with his firearm drawn. It is actually impressive, though I wouldn't say it out loud to him.

He quickly returns and gives us a 'thumbs up' indicating a clear apartment then directs my mother over to the couch. He spins it so the seat portion faces the wall, and the back of it acts as a direct barrier to the front door. Mom kneels down on it.

Enzo retrieves his bag and sets it behind the couch. He removes his magic wand and begins his task of investigating for a bug, starting in the kitchen. It makes no noise, but I see on the wand it contains a line of lights; all presently glowing green. The scan of the kitchen proves uneventful. The lights never change from green. He approaches the living room, where Mom waits, and we see a blink of yellow appear. He stops to home in, but all lights revert back to green. False alarm. He joins Alison and me in the dining room. He scans the table and then the fruit bowl; complete with fake fruit, getting another yellow hit. He moves away, and it goes green. Back to the bowl; yellow. He seems puzzled, until he looks up. Slowly he raises the wand up to the hanging light positioned directly above the bowl. The wand lights instantly turn a bright red. He moves it away; they go back to green. Back to the light; red.

Enzo shuts the wand off and makes deliberate eye contact with both of us and nods upward. The listening device is somewhere in or on the hanging light. He removes a flashlight from his bag and shines it on the light, examining closely for the device. When he spots it, he gives us a 'come here' finger gesture and points right to it. It looks like a small, round, black magnet. It's roughly the size of a dime and attached to the inside of the shade.

He walks over to the couch and starts arranging stuff from his bag. The back of the couch blocks our view, so we cannot see what he's doing. He gets our attention by standing up and spinning his index finger in the air. I'm assuming it's a sign to start a benign conversation.

"Do you want to check out a movie?" I ask. I figure it's a good question because it would appear as if we'd be here for awhile and unguarded.

"Sure. What do you have in mind?"

"No chick flicks."

"Excuse me?" She says testily.

I shrug my shoulders hoping to communicate a silent message I'm only doing it for our audience and I don't mean it. She's entirely on board and winks to me with a smile. Whew. Dodged that bullet.

"Uh, I mean do you want to watch a romantic comedy or action film or something else?"

"Mmhmm. That's better." She jokes, silently laughing. "So how about a comedy?"

"Sure. Let's see what we have On Demand." We move closer to the couch, but not all the way. We're not certain if the device will be able to pick us up that far away and we want to make certain we're heard.

"Hey, Jon."

"What?"

"I have a question for you."

"Hang on. Let me get this frigging remote control programmed right." I didn't have the remote control; I said it only for the effect.

"Okay, what's up?" I reply after a moment.

"Would you move in with me?"

I look at her. She's not making any indication she's kidding. My heart jumps in my chest.

"Really?" I ask earnestly.

"Really." She responds sincerely.

She walks over and puts her arms around me, whispering in my ear. "Really. I love you."

I'm mouth-breathing and nodding my head. "Yes, I will absolutely move in with you."

We spend the next two hours or so doing nothing really; merely pretending we're doing stuff simply to make noise for whoever's listening – if anybody. The time passes quickly for me; I'm incredibly excited Alison asked if we could move in together.

My phone vibrates in my pocket and I check to see who it is.

Alison asks, "Who's calling?"

"Uh … It's Jennifer." I look to Enzo and shrug my shoulders in an effort to find out what he wants me to do.

He's nodding his head and giving me a thumbs-up.

I answer it. "Hello? Hey Jennifer. How are you doing?"

Enzo quickly comes to the table with a handwritten note.

Put her on speaker-phone.

"Jennifer? Hang on a second. I'm going to put you on speaker-phone, so Alison can hear you as well. Okay, go ahead."

"Hi Alison."

"Hi Jennifer, how are you doing, hon?" She asks concernedly.

"Not good."

Her nose is stuffy, causing her nasally voice.

Alison consoles her. "I'm so sorry, honey."

"Jon, I just wanted to let you know I have Burton Funeral Home picking up Danny tomorrow at four pm."

"Where?"

"At the state morgue, where he was brought."

"Jennifer. I know this is hard. God knows it's hard for me, too … I think we should have him entirely cremated, given what's happened. What do you think?"

"I think that's absolutely what he would have wanted. No question. I was thinking we ought to spread his ashes out to sea, too."

"Thank God. I couldn't agree more."

Enzo's visibly excited and he's urging me to go on. I'm not quite sure what else he wants, so I simply keep the dialogue going.

"So where will Burton take him for cremation?"

"I asked that same question. After you sign for him, they'll take him to their crematorium. It's in the Haverford Industrial Park; about two miles from Burton's. They told me it's pretty camouflaged. No signage. They pick him up so late in the day because they only operate at night."

"I can see why. Definitely. I'll be there before four tomorrow to sign the papers."

"Okay. After they take care of him, I'll come up with a day and time for the service."

"Perfect. Let me know. Thanks Jennifer."

"Bye, Jon."

Enzo passes another note in front of us.

>*Let's get out of here. Find a reason to leave.*

"Hey," I say to Alison, "want to go out for pizza?"

"I'll race you." She says.

We leave the apartment in the exact opposite fashion as we arrived. I'm hesitant to say anything until we're well underway and out of the area.

"So, what just happened?" I say somewhat cryptically.

"How so?" Enzo replies.

"Well, I'm not sure I was reading you correctly and I'm not certain I got it right."

Enzo says emphatically, "You nailed it. You did exactly what I wanted."

"Okay, great. Help me understand what I nailed." I reply half-laughing.

"Yeah, I can understand your need for more clarification. After two or three hours go by, I realize Brown isn't coming. He's too careful; too wary. What I am certain of is he was listening, and listening closely. That's a hot mic in the dining room light. My wand would not have gone red if it weren't. When Jennifer called, it hit me like a heart attack that we can use the morgue situation to our advantage."

"I see where you're going with this. Brown knows we'll be at the morgue at four tomorrow."

"Exactly. Tell you what. Let's go get that pizza. We can relax some, and then you and I can talk about how to approach tomorrow when we get back to the hotel. I have some solid ideas. No offense to the two of you." He says to Mom and Alison.

"None taken. I think we'd much rather be out of this, anyway." Mom says with a laugh.

43

W hen we get to the pizza shop parking lot, Enzo waits for a car to vacate a specific spot despite having multiple spaces open reasonably close to the entrance.

I'm beginning to notice these little things with him; things most people wouldn't ever think about. I know why he's waiting for this spot. It's situated directly in front of the restaurant's picture window. He wants an unobstructed view of the Mercedes at all times. I'd bet a hundred dollars that when we go in, he'll request a table with a clear sight line to the window and then take the seat facing toward the parking lot.

"I'm ready to eat!" I announce to no one in particular.

"Same here." Alison says. "I may have a glass of wine, too – or two." She says, holding up two fingers.

"Perfect. I hope they have PBR on tap."

"Ugh." Mom teases lightheartedly. "Haven't broken away from your college beer, yet?"

"Heeeeeeyy. That hurts."

"Oh, poor baby." Alison piles on.

"I actually like it." Enzo says, holding the restaurant door open for us.

"Welcome to Anthony's. Four?" The hostess smiles, gathering menus.

"Yes, and can we sit at a high top over there ... like that one?" Enzo's pointing to his table of choice.

"Sure, no problem. Follow me, please."

As we walk by the bar, I spot the draft beers on tap. Outstanding – they have PBR. Now we're speaking my language. Enzo arrives at the table first and pulls out a chair for Mom, then sits exactly where I thought he would. Alison wiggles her adorable bum over her seat, waiting for me to push it in.

"Ah, quite inviting. May I push your stool in, m'lady?" I offer with exaggerated British gallantry.

"Yes, please and thank you."

My somewhat suggestive joke passes completely over her head undetected and I think the better of drawing attention to it.

"Hey, let's order." I propose, mainly to change the subject.

Enzo smiles and shakes his head like, 'you idiot.'

It doesn't take long after we place our order for drinks to arrive. Conversation buzzes all around us and I can't help but think back to our night at Asbury's with Santa and Merri. Alison dropped the bomb about her and Bob and his misdeeds, and I told everyone about my interactions with the double douchebags and Bond at the police station. In some ways it feels like that was a thousand years ago; and in others, yesterday. This place has much the same feel as A's. Wide-screens dot the walls, broadcasting all manner of sporting events. Sports memorabilia; much of it autographed, hang on the walls paying homage to the golden age of Boston sports.

I believe I'm going to get along wonderfully with our server. I make quick work of my first PBR and she's delivered another one sans me asking.

"I'll need to find a contractor to dig the safes out for me tomorrow." I'd been thinking about this for some time.

"They'll likely be charred and maybe somewhat melted. We can contract for a backhoe to lift them out and then you can check them and dump them back into the hole." Enzo says.

"I'm not sure I want anyone around to see the contents."

"Understood. I'll run a screen for you with the SUV. We'll make sure no one's around. How much money did you put in the gun vaults? Or how much *was* in them?" Enzo asks.

Alison looks at me with some concern. I covertly pat her thigh as a signal it's okay. He has more money than we'll ever have.

"Not nearly as much as what's in your duffel bags. Half a million. And only in one vault. The other's packed with firearms."

"Bob gave you five hundred grand? Good for you." Enzo says to Alison.

"Yay. Lucky me."

"Smart move on both of your parts to remove it from his self-storage unit."

His statement catches Alison and me by surprise. "Bob told you about that?" She asks.

"No, but I knew he was keeping his money over there. I knew everything Bob was up to."

Our dinner arrives, and I waste no time getting into the pizza. Enzo scratches his head in bewilderment.

"I've never seen anyone go at a meal quite like you, Jon … anyway, back on the vaults, I hope they did their job and protected it."

"We'll see." Alison interjects.

"Enzo," I say, changing the subject with a mouth full of pizza, "who were the guys that intercepted Alison and me at the brewery?"

"Jon, c'mon. Finish chewing, please. Sheesh." Alison chides.

"Sorry, my bad." I swallow hard. "Those two guys who smuggled us out. Who were they?"

"Just a couple of guys that owed me a favor. They're long gone now."

Enzo's keeping in peak form with not disclosing anything that needn't be disclosed. He operates on a 'need to know' basis only; I know not to press too hard when he gives an answer like that.

The remainder of the meal consists of pretty low-key conversation. We have a couple more drinks, finish eating, and clear the bill. Time for us to head back to the hotel for Enzo and me to plan out tomorrow's activities.

I find myself scanning the greater area around me as I enter the Mercedes. I'm acutely aware of my surroundings now; I've never been like that before. I wouldn't call it paranoia; just elevated awareness.

The night gets long and traffic scarce heading back toward the mall. I'm sitting in the backseat behind Enzo and I notice him periodically looking into his rear-view mirror. He's checking more so than usual in the normal course of driving, and in my view it's become excessive.

"What's going on?" I ask. "Do you see someone or something behind us?"

"I'm not sure. They're close, but not quite tailgating. The headlights are brighter than usual, so I can't make out the vehicle."

That puts all of us immediately on edge. We travel the next minute or so in silence with Enzo continuing to work his rear-view mirror.

"Hand me my bag, please." Enzo requests from my mother.

She willingly obliges, keeping it low and out of sight. Enzo removes a firearm from the bag and slips it underneath his right leg.

"Here. Thanks." He hands the bag back. "Can you fit that under your seat?"

"Yes, I think so."

I'm not certain Alison caught on to what was happening, but I sure did.

"What do you think?" I ask while reaching into my coat pocket for a firearm check.

Before Enzo can answer, the interior of the Mercedes lights up with bright, almost blinding, blue lights. I take my hand out of my coat and sit stone-faced.

"Relax everyone. I'll handle this."

A police officer places a powerful spotlight onto the SUV and approaches the driver-side window incredibly quickly. Enzo rolls down the window.

"License, registration, and proof of insurance, please."

Enzo doesn't miss a beat. "I'll need to reach into my glovebox for the registration and insurance card, and also into my vest pocket for my driver's license."

"Very good. Thank you."

Enzo gathers the requested items and hands them to the officer. In the meantime, he shines his flashlight into the vehicle, inspecting the rest of us.

He takes a quick scan of Enzo's credentials. "Sir, do you know why I stopped you tonight?"

"Can't say that I do, officer."

"You have a defective license plate light. Sit tight while I check your license and registration, please."

The cop walks back to his vehicle and I have to pee. Seriously. "Hey, are we coming out of this or do we have trouble? I have to take a wicked piss."

"I don't know, and you're gonna have to hold it." Enzo says.

After what seems like an eternity, the cop comes back over.

"Okay Mr. Callahan, here's your license, registration, and insurance card." He passes Enzo's items through the window. "And this is a probative ticket for the burnt-out light. If you take this to a state inspection-authorized service station, have the light replaced and signed off on within five days; simply mail it in and the ticket is voided. If not, the fine becomes active."

"Okay, thank you officer. I'll have it addressed right away."

"Have a good evening."

We stay long enough for the police car to take off ahead of us. No need to have him following us again.

"See, there's nothing to worry about until there's something to worry about." Enzo pontificates.

"Uh, Mr. Callahan? I need to pee before we leave."

44

Back at the hotel, Enzo and I sit at the kitchen table. The girls relax on the couch watching television looking adorable in their sweatshirts and yoga pants. It's almost normal.

"Where do we start?" I ask.

"Let's get your uncle's house figured out and then cover the trip up to the morgue."

"Fine."

"There're a bunch of local contractors that can handle this job. We'll hire someone to come in tomorrow; we can pay a kicker for them to come in quickly – they'll want the work. We'll have them pull the gun vaults out right off, say noontime, and then let them have the rest of the job clearing everything out. We can get into them …", he pauses with a puzzled expression, "… you know the combinations, right?"

I nod.

"Good. We can get into them and pack up the SUV and get out. Shouldn't be a problem. Then we'll head straight up to Westfield and the state morgue. It's about an hour away, so that will give us a solid buffer before your four o'clock appointment."

"What are we doing during the buffer time?"

"Well, that's what we need to figure out."

"I assume it will involve waiting and watching. That seems to be the common denominator for a lot of this stuff."

"Undoubtedly play a role, yes. The way I see it though, the drive up to the morgue is less of a concern. The morgue's a state government building; Brown may be credentialed to move about inside as he pleases. That gives him the advantage, but there will be people around. We need to stay visible."

"So, you don't plan on contending with Brown in Westfield?" I probe.

"Not if I can help it. I have a better idea. I just thought of what we should do with our buffer time."

"Hold that thought. I need to pee."

"Christ, you're like a sieve."

I have to pee, that's not a lie, but I also need a break and I want to make a stop after my bathroom duty in the living room with the girls.

After I finish my business, I pause at the couch, poised over the two beauties below me.

"So, what are you watching?" The girls seem pretty interested in the show.

"NCIS. Love this show." Mom says, not taking her eyes off of the screen.

"You're basically living the show."

"Hardly. Who invited you, anyway?" Mom jabs teasingly.

"Ya. Go away." Alison backs her up. They're all sisters.

"I'm going. Man, tough crowd."

"Alright, I'm back." I say enthusiastically.

"Can your microscopic bladder tolerate fifteen more minutes of discussion?"

"Don't be a hater. Where were we?"

"We were talking about what we were going to do in between the time we go to Danny's until the time we leave for Westfield."

"Visit the funeral home?"

"Even better – I'll go to the crematorium in advance and have a talk with their guy who runs the ovens. I have some experience working with him."

Oh man. I don't want to ask how, and I hope he doesn't go into detail.

"I'll pay the operator a certain sum to disappear for a few hours, allowing the grieving family to conduct the cremation among themselves with no one else around. It won't be a hard sell. An actual deceased person is coming in with proper credentials. He'll be fine with it."

"I'm confused. I sort of see where you're going with this but fill in the blanks for me."

"I'll visit the crematorium early in the day like I said. When we pull in at the state morgue sometime later, Brown will likely be there or show up somewhere when we're on our way back."

"What if Brown just disappeared?" I reason.

"It's possible." He contemplates. "If this doesn't draw him out, we'll have to consider that scenario. But if he's there, I'll take Brown out and we'll have a two-for-one back at the crematorium."

"Christ, man."

"Sorry, a little callous."

"Are we done here?"

"For now. I may come up with some more ideas after I sleep on it."

I get up from the table, move over to the living room, and plop my ass down between the girls to watch the show.

It's almost normal.

45

It's an overcast, damp morning with the outside temperature hovering at about fifty degrees. The kind of morning annoyingly cold in September; a prelude to the upcoming winter season, but in late March, it feels quite warm.

I've been on the phone with the Portland police department securing authorization to begin clean-up on Danny's property – my property now – and Enzo's been on his phone for the better part of the morning talking with excavation contractors. On his third try, he finds a 'father and sons' outfit that can get over there by eleven. I overheard him saying he would 'take care of you' for being so accommodating.

We're gathering our gear; Enzo has his MacGyver bag loaded with Lord only knows what, and he's busily rearranging its contents. I only have a jacket to put on. He's already informed my mother what the game plan is for the day, including a detailed outline of how he sees the trip going from Westfield back to the crematorium. I've only given Alison a general synopsis.

"You and Mom need to be careful." I feel stupid just saying that. No shit, they need to be careful.

"We will. We're not going anywhere. By the way, I think your mom knows how to use a gun." She whispers this conspiratorially, like she's an accomplice to America's Most Wanted female. "I think she has one, too."

I'm sure she does. I rethink the idea of revealing to her I brought my own firearm and I'm keeping it in a coat pocket along with a cache of loaded magazines.

"We're going to leave here shortly, and we won't be back until around ten – best guess. I'll call to let you know what I find at Danny's."

"Okay. Be careful."

"I will. I love you." I kiss her on the cheek and break away to meet Enzo at the door.

The contractors are already setting up when we get to Danny's. Enzo removes a brown bag from his duffel and walks over to the dump truck. There's a fat guy with a clipboard jotting down notes on a piece of paper. He looks to be the 'father' of the 'father and sons.' Two other guys circle the perimeter of the foundation eyeing the mess and talking about where they're going to begin. I head over to them.

"There are two safes down there." I point them out. "If you look closely, you can just see the tops of them near where the floor collapsed over there. We need those two out first so I can go through them and then everything else can be hauled out."

"Yeah, I think I got it. We'll have them out quickly."

They fire up the backhoe, assaulting the peaceful tranquility of the community. Black smoke belches out of exhaust stacks, filling the air with diesel fumes. The backhoe is modified like a lumber tractor with a picker unit to grasp heavy items. This thing is impressive.

The operator shimmies the machine into the proper location and swings the picker arm out over the pit. He's moving at breakneck speed until he reaches the area where the safes are. Then, he slows down to a snail's pace and gently positions the pincers at the top of one unit.

I have an immediate flashback to the commercial for the child's board game, Operation. 'It takes a steady hand ... don't touch the sides. There goes his funny bone! That's four hundred dollars for me!'

With a surgeon's precision, our guy grasps one of the units and gently lifts it out of its place. Charred bits of wood and black ash stain the exterior, but when he places it nearby and swings the arm away, it appears intact.

Enzo finishes with the fat guy, then moves the SUV over to me and waits for the next safe to come out so he can block the view. I watch the backhoe's swing arm as it gently grasps the next safe. With the shift in debris, I can only just recognize a remnant of Danny's pool table. The other safe is up and out in just as short of a time as the first. Pretty damn impressive. These guys will make short work of the rest of this project.

Enzo positions the SUV into place, shuts it down, and joins me. I reach into my breast pocket and remove two items: The first is the picture of my dad and Danny that I took from his house; and the second, a piece of paper with the two safe combinations. I don't know which combination belongs to which safe and there's only one way to find out.

I focus in on the safe closest to me. The spin dial grinds, but it's functional. I follow the instructions Danny gave me: *spin two times, stop on the first number, back to the next number, back to final number, but you have to go one full turn past it.*

I've used the combination I identified as the 'money safe.' We'll see if I got it right, and even if I did, if it still functions. I rotate the three-spoke handle until it can't turn anymore. Grasping the handle, I pull on it. It moves slightly. I pull as hard as I can but it doesn't move anymore. Enzo jogs to the SUV and returns with a tire iron, wedges it into the door, and pries it open with little difficulty. Inside, we're looking at $500,000 in perfectly preserved bills.

"There it is. All in good shape." I say.

"Perfect. Hang on one second, I'll be right back." Enzo leaves and then returns with two duffel bags. "I emptied these out at the hotel. The money ought to fit into these."

We shift the money systematically; I remove it, and then hand to Enzo to arrange in the bags. We make quick work of it and pack it into the Mercedes.

The next safe works pretty much in the same fashion with the exception of prying the door open. It takes quite a bit more effort to get it open; but we manage, and the small arms and shotguns come with us as well. In light of the exposure to heat and other external forces, Enzo says it's better to leave the ammo behind. He's concerned it's unreliable and I'm fine with that decision.

Before Enzo and I exit, I address the crew. "These can go now." I gesture to the safes. "Thanks for pulling them out first. Everything else can go to junk or salvage or whatever else you want to do with it."

"So, who's this guy we're supposed to meet?" I ask on the ride over to the crematorium. I check out my phone; we're making great time and moving exactly as scheduled.

"We're meeting Bernie."

"Does Bernie have a last name?"

"I don't know. I don't even know his first name."

"Uh ... it's not Bernie?" Dude, don't make me think too hard.

"No, Bernie's his nickname. It sounds like 'Burnie' with a 'u,' not 'Bernie' with an 'e.' He runs the ovens."

"Oh Christ, that's sick."

"I didn't come up with it."

That's some pretty disturbing shit right there. Switching gears, I pull out my phone and send a text to Alison to let her know we were successful with the safes.

Hey, $$ intact. All of it

She's right back at me:

Yay! Nice work!

"Well, Alison's happy we got the money."

"Glad to hear that, you both have certainly earned it."

"That's exactly what I said to her about it a while ago, when she didn't want anything to do with it. I said, 'illegal or not, Bob worked hard for it, essentially paid for it with his life, and he wanted you to have it'."

"Now you and she have worked equally as hard."

Enzo pulls into the main entrance at Haverford Industrial Park. There's a large directory sign-board we pass by without so much as slowing down.

"Looks like you know exactly where it is. You didn't so much as glance at the directory."

"Yes. Wouldn't have mattered to stop anyway. It's not listed. I think that's pretty standard in the industry. Have you ever heard of the location of any crematorium?"

"Come to think of it, no."

"Exactly. There are three parallel roads off of this main strip. The facility's located at the end of the middle road, secluded from every other building in the park. You'd have to know it's there to discover it."

We turn on to the middle road – the street sign indicates 'Eternal Rest Way.' There's nothing of interest around us – it's largely vacant and thickly wooded on either side. It takes us at least a half-mile, if not longer to get to the end. We pull into the small parking lot with the SUV facing an unremarkable building. It's a one-story, pillbox-shaped config-uration; maybe twenty-five hundred square feet, colored a drab brown. The only distinguishing feature is a large chimney stack jutting through the center section of the roof.

We enter the building, triggering some type of electric security eye announcing us with a 'ding.' We find ourselves in a cramped waiting area, facing an administrative office segregated by a wall with a sliding window. After a moment, an expressionless man enters the office from a back entrance and shuffles to the window. He's slight; maybe a hun-dred and twenty pounds and appears to be about fifty-five years old. He wears a white smock with three-quarter sleeves that recede to half-sleeve length when he reaches out to slide the glass window open.

"Can I help you?" He leans in to overdramatize his inspection, scrutinizing me up and down from head to toe.

I don't respond to him. He switches his attention to Enzo.

"Can I help you … Tony!" He says, brightening up considerably. "It's good to see you!"

"Hey Bernie. How've you been?"

"Good, good, what can I do for you?"

"Bernie, I need a favor."

Bernie's excitement instantly deflates, and he looks directly at me.

"It's okay, Bernie. He's good. This is actually an easy one."

Bi-polar Bernie's emotional state smooths out, and his attention returns to Enzo.

"This is Jon Williams. Check your docket, you should have his uncle, Daniel Williams coming in tonight from Westfield by the Burton Funeral Home."

Bernie checks a clipboard sitting out of sight.

"Yep, I have him right here. Oh, I'm sorry. It says here he's the guy in that terrible house fire in Portland."

"Yes. Thank you." I say.

"Bernie, we'd like to have just close family in here; only three, maybe four of us, and I'd like to handle the cremation process if that's okay with you."

"Would you like me to be around or absent?"

"Absent, please."

"Very good. The standard fee will apply."

"As I expected. I have it here with me."

"Excellent. You two go around back and I'll let you in through the rear door. We've done some upgrades since you were here last, Tony, and I'll need to walk you through them."

"Perfect. Thank you so much."

Enzo and I leave and go back to the car.

"What's the standard fee?" I ask.

"Ten grand. I've already got it ready."

"We can get this one if you'd like."

Enzo smiles. "I got this. But thanks – it's the least I can do for your uncle."

He drives us around to the back. A small loading dock extends outward from the building and it's the perfect height to accommodate a hearse.

The door slightly cracks open and Bernie pops his head out. His mannerisms remind me of Beaker from *The Muppet Show*. My dad used to show me all of the old episodes on video when I was growing up.

We move quickly into the building and shut the door behind us. Bernie briskly marches into the oven room, pointing out what's new and what's not. Judging by Enzo's conversation with him, he feels at home around the cremation process. He takes us into a storage closet pointing out where the containers are for storing ashes. We finish with a rundown of the oven shut down procedure and closing checklist.

"What time is he coming in?" Bernie asks.

"Burton's got him at four; so, five? Five-fifteen?"

"Fine, I'll check him in and place him in the prep room. I should be out by five forty-five. I'll leave the back door open and you come in at six sharp. Sound good?"

"Yeah, sounds good, Bernie. Thanks a lot." Enzo says, handing him a small bag.

"Thank you, too." He replies. "Sorry about your uncle."

"Thanks, much appreciated."

46

Enzo's becoming consistently more open with me, seemingly in an attempt to let me 'see behind the curtain' into his thought process. I don't know if it's subconscious or not; it may simply be that he's more comfortable with me now. He's beginning to verbalize his thoughts and actions real-time as they occur. For example, when we left the crematorium, he directed me to where secondary routes of egress are located. When we drove away, he expressed his dislike of the road system within the industrial park – one way in, one way out. Now we're zipping down the highway on our way to Westfield chattering about his analytical process relative to before, during, and after our business at the morgue. He's delivering a stream of consciousness and it's somewhat fascinating to see inside the mind of a criminal. I feel some remorse in thinking of him like that, but if I'm being honest with myself I have to admit he's a criminal.

We're clocking excellent time and right on schedule. By my estimation, we should arrive between two-thirty and three o'clock, and according to Enzo, the ideal time to allow for us to scout out a location and inspect the surroundings prior to conducting our affairs inside – my affairs inside.

"So, I'm thinking we should go over how we're going to handle Brown if we see him. I assume it will change depending upon when we see him?" I postulate.

"Correct. I have a general course of action for three scenarios: One – if we see him early. I'll follow him, hopefully unnoticed, modifying my behavior depending upon surroundings, situations, et cetera. Two – if we see him inside. There's not much either of us can do in that case."

"What if he pulls the FBI tough-guy card and tries to arrest us or something like that?"

"You make a good point. A really good point." He looks at me appreciatively. "You need to go in by yourself, then. Under any scenario. It would be a waste of his time and effort to arrest you alone. Risk does exist though; you're right. However, if you go in alone, he'll know I'm nearby and he'll have to contend with me outside. It's a risk, but a calculated one."

Despite my contention Enzo is a criminal, his acknowledgment of the significance of my observation buoys my spirits. I sit up straighter and puff my chest out confidently.

"It will be up to you to contact me and tell me if he's inside."

"Got it."

"The third scenario is if we find him after you've handled your business. To me, that's the most desirable."

"Alright, if we see him after I sign for Danny, walk me through what the plan is from the time we spot him to what we do about it."

"We need to bait him into a set-up. If he knows we've seen him, then it will be impossible to surprise him. If he believes he hasn't been identified, then it's to our advantage. I have a number of driving tactics I can employ depending upon what the situation calls for. Some of them are subtle; some not so much. When we leave Westfield and he follows;

assuming he follows, which I can't imagine he won't, I'll know what we need to do to handle the situation."

He said 'we' and not 'I.' I welcome that. I have a job to do and I'll damn well do it.

"And our end game will conclude at Haverford." I say this as a declaration and not a question.

"Correct."

Two forty-five, right on time. Built partly into the side of a massive hill, the building looks like a modern medical center. The drive up the access road proves disadvantageous to us. Anyone up there can easily see those approaching from below.

"I don't remember feeling so exposed the last time I was here." Enzo says. "Granted, it's been a long time."

"This place is huge. There's got to be more going on besides the state morgue."

"Yeah, there's a bunch of government buildings, the biggest being the VA hospital."

"Now that makes sense. The complex looks clinical."

Enzo slowly drives a full revolution around the property before settling on a location that allows us to see the main entrance on one side and the access road on the other. He reaches into his duffel bag and removes a pair of military-grade binoculars.

"This looks like some serious ground to cover." I say. "It won't be hard to miss him."

"You're right. They've significantly expanded this place since I was here last."

Periodically over the next hour, we change our parking spots for safety in case we're being watched and also to establish different vantage points. None of Enzo's ideas and methods prove productive. At a quarter to four, I unbuckle my seat belt and get ready to go in.

"Should I wait for the Burton guy to get here before I go in?" I ask.

"No. The hearse will go out back to get him. I'm guessing you'll be signing papers somewhere in an office out front. After you take care of the paperwork, we can drive out back and watch for them."

"Sounds good. I'll send you a text if I see him."

I walk briskly toward the main entrance. It feels like I'm being examined like a scientist observing a slide under a microscope.

The signage inside the lobby directs me through a maze of corridors, eventually guiding me to the medical examiner's office. The waiting area reminds me of the motor vehicle registry. It has a 'take a ticket' numbering system like you find at the supermarket deli. I take a number and sit down. There's no one here but me. A pleasant-looking woman in nurse's scrubs advances the number on the waiting room screen.

"Sixty-two, please," she broadcasts over a crackly loudspeaker, "number sixty-two."

Well, what do you know? I'm number sixty-two.

"Can I help you?"

I'm tempted to ask her for a pound of honey ham, thinly sliced with a pound of American cheese ... but I think the better of it.

"Yes. Hello, my name is Jon Williams. I'm here to authorize the release of Daniel Williams to the Burton Funeral Home. They're scheduled to pick up at four o'clock."

She looks down, flips a page on her scheduling book, traces her finger down the page and pauses. She looks up at me.

"Identification, please?"

I reach into my coat pocket for my wallet. Nope, not that pocket. Nine-millimeter pistol in that one. Ah, there it is. I remove my driver's license from my wallet and hand it over. She takes a moment to study it, then hands it back.

"Sign here, please." She hands me a form and points to the signature line.

I execute the document and she pulls the form back.

"Thank you." She says.

"That's it? Anything else?" I'm surprised how little there is for me to do.

"No. That's all. The funeral home will handle everything from here."

"Okay, thanks."

I snake my way out using the same route I came in. When I get to the front vestibule, the doors automatically open prompting me to feel overwhelmingly exposed and vulnerable.

The sun is getting low in the sky, and I use my hand as a visor to aid my inspection of the parking lot. I don't see Enzo anywhere. I'm instantly alarmed and shoot him a message as fast as I can get my phone out. He immediately responds that he drove around back and he's coming out front now.

I hop in as soon as he pulls up, and before he can ask, I let him know I didn't see anything out of the ordinary. He has a similar story.

"The hearse arrived out back." He says.

"So what now?"

"Well, we keep our eyes open on the way home."

"And if we don't see him?"

Enzo shrugs. "Maybe he did disappear." He turns to me slightly, shaking his head. "That's not a loose end I want dangling."

"What do we do about Danny?"

"I'll cremate him as I was planning on doing and then we'll go home."

"Can we stop at a drive-thru on the way back? We'll have a few minutes for Bernie to get set up anyway before we can go in."

"Yeah sure, but we need to be quick about it. I want to be back in time to see if anyone else shows up."

The drive back proves uneventful. No trace of Brown; nothing unusual. I send a text to Jennifer to let her know what's happening. She replies that she's scheduled the service for Saturday at noon at the funeral home. I call Alison and give her a rundown of the day. She seems quite content with Mom; they've had a marathon 'On Demand' movie day. I'm glad she had some down time without having to think about this stuff.

When we finally arrive at the industrial park, we pass the hearse on its way out of Eternal Rest Way. There's one lone vehicle in the parking lot. I think I recall it being here when we came earlier, but I can't be certain.

"Is that Bernie's car?" I ask.

"Probably. He'll be the only one here, but I'm not one hundred percent on that. Let's sit and wait. We're in no hurry."

Enzo has an extraordinary level of patience. I go stir-crazy after only five minutes. We make it to six-thirty and still no activity.

"Hand me that duffel bag, will you?" He asks.

I pass the bag over and he unzips it, pokes around, then removes a pistol. He reaches in again and removes a device I recognize when he attaches it to the pistol. It's a silencer.

"Let's go." He tucks the pistol into his waistband. "We'll go in the rear door; maybe Bernie needs to talk to us. Actually, maybe Bernie can just do the job and we can go home."

That would be great I think to myself.

The back door is cracked open as we anticipated; as Bernie said it would be. Enzo steps in first and I'm following behind. It seems much brighter inside at dusk than it does in daylight.

'Pop .... pop .. pop.' I register three shots. One shot followed by a short pause; and then two successive shots. Even though they sound like firecrackers, I know right away it's gunfire. Enzo is driven back into me with tremendous force, arms flailing, jarring me out of the doorway before I can completely enter the building. Searing pain rips through my forearm. It feels like it's on fire. I don't know if I'm hit directly, or if it's from a bullet passing through Enzo. He's crumpled to the ground, lying prone on the concrete decking of the stairs. I'm launched into the metal handrail and then ricocheted down the steps to the pavement below. Lying on my back, adrenaline coursing through me, I see a figure stepping over Enzo on the stair landing above with a firearm drawn.

"Hello, Jon. It's been a while." Agent Scott Brown says.

I roll onto my side and hear a bullet ping off of the ground from the spot I just vacated. I'm up and running, wholly governed by survival instinct. My best chance is to get out front and find cover. I race around to the front of the building, wildly scanning the lot and thick trees lining Eternal Rest Way. I'll never make it to the woods. Brown will pick me off before I can get halfway there. I dart over to the Mercedes for cover while squeezing my injured forearm, applying pressure to the wound. I shimmy out of my jacket and it falls to the pavement, my left arm useless. One-handed, I tear into my coat pocket to retrieve my Glock. Time begins moving in slow-motion … I manage to free my pistol … Awkwardly, I slide a loaded magazine into the chamber using my good arm and positioning the firearm against my leg for leverage …. cock the hammer and …… God, no …. Noooooooo!

Brown's gun locks on me.

"Goodbye, Jon."

I close my eyes and … *'ffffttttt'* … *'ffffttttt.'*

I open my eyes in time to see Brown collapse into a heap at my feet. Enzo stands behind him, arm extended, smoke tendrils curling from his pistol's silencer.

47

"What …? How did you …?" I say groggily; kicking Brown away from me.

"Kevlar vest." Enzo draws his jacket open, revealing two shredded sections where the bullets hit. "I have at least three broken ribs and I'm bleeding, but overall not badly."

He steps over Brown and kneels down in front of me.

"Let me look." He says while tearing off a section of his under-shirt.

As the adrenaline diminishes, searing pain radiates into my arm, shooting up through my shoulder and into my back. Enzo tears my shirt sleeve open, quickly assessing the situation.

"Perfect. The bullet's gone straight through. That's much better; no bouncing around doing more damage."

He encircles my forearm with his t-shirt section and ties it very tightly, knotting it over the entrance site tourniquet-style.

"It doesn't seem to be bleeding terribly, at least anymore. I need to know – do I take you to the hospital now, or can we finish our business here and go afterward?"

"No. Let's get this done. I'll let you know if I need to leave."

"Perfect. Let me help you up."

I experience a dizzy spell but after a moment, it passes. Enzo's struggling to pull Brown through the parking lot and I see he's wincing in pain. With my good arm, I reach down and grab one ankle; Enzo holds the other and together we drag him out back, up the stairs, and into the oven room. The oven is fired up and ready to cook. No doubt Brown was in here preparing for us.

Enzo lowers the motorized adjustable table and we drag Brown on to it. After raising it back up to oven-height, Enzo guides Brown in, then slides him off of the table with a gigantic paddle resembling an over-sized pizza spatula you see in brick-oven pizza shops. The doors close with a hugely satisfying 'click.'

In bright-red LED lights, the temperature gauge reads a balmy 1600° F.

"I think this is about a three-hour process; maybe a little less, I forget." Enzo says. "How're you holding up?"

"If I don't move and breathe very shallow, I'm okay. If the wind blows at all, I'm in agony."

"Sounds about right." Enzo smiles. "Good to see you still have your sense of humor."

He's walking around the prep floor addressing stuff needing to be done. "You know, in my line of work – my former line of work –" he corrects himself, "this would have been a cause for celebration. Your first gunshot wound."

"Yay for me."

"Alright, I'm going to check for Danny in the storage room. Do you think you can check for bleach in the supply closet? We need to wash down the parking lot and the path we dragged Brown along, then work our way inside. It should be in the same closet as the ash containers."

"Yeah, sure."

Enzo disappears into the storage room while I gradually shuffle across the floor and open the supply closet.

"Danny's in there." Enzo says, returning to the prep floor.

"Hey, you're gonna want to see this." I say.

Enzo peers into the closet. Bernie stares back at us with lifeless eyes and a neat bullet hole into his forehead.

"Ah, shit. Another one to cook. And a lot more clean-up. We're gonna be here all night. Can you start pulling the bleach out?"

My arm has stopped bleeding for the most part; it aches like a son-of-a-bitch, though. Enzo says there's a one hundred percent chance at least one forearm bone is broken, if not shattered. Lovely.

We're done with Brown. It takes a good hour after shutting the oven down before we can open it up to get him out. Even then it's still hotter than hell's acre inside. Enzo utilizes a long pole with a wide blade attached at one end to push the remains into a collection bin. The process is one-way only; in through the front, out through the back. The collection bin has a drop-trap underneath it for funneling ashes into a smaller receptacle, reminiscent of a gumball machine. Place the container under the bin, open it up, and gravity handles the rest. After we sift Brown into a container, Enzo asks me what I want to do with him.

"Flush the asshole down the toilet."

"Good idea. Don't pour him in all at once. Three times, maybe four, so you don't clog it up."

I wonder if he has experience disposing human remains in toilets, too.

I pick up what's left of Brown with my good arm and go to the restroom. I pour a third of him into the bowl, place the container on the sink, unzip, and then piss on him. Too bad I didn't have to take a dump. Oddly satisfied, I finish him off with two more flushes.

We scrubbed the parking lot while Brown was cooking. It made for quick work; there wasn't much to it. Enzo brought out a mop bucket to 'swab the deck' and I followed up with a generous amount of bleach. Inside will be much more involved. Brown left a bloody mess and Bernie drained out in the supply closet. 'Ex-sanguinated' as Enzo puts it.

When I return from the bathroom, I see Enzo has Bernie out of the supply closet and dragged over to the prep table. Although I'm struggling with the bloody smell, Enzo appears to be totally unaffected. I give him a hand pulling Bernie onto the table, and he's up and at oven-level quickly. We can't load him in until the oven gets back up to temperature, which thankfully doesn't take as long as cooling down. After we place him in the oven, we set about to clean-up. It's tedious work, but we grind through it. Enzo is only satisfied after all the bleach is gone and the room resembles a hospital operating room. At about the same time, Bernie finishes his physical conversion. We undertake a similar exercise as Brown, only this time with respect and dignity. Enzo scatters Bernie's ashes outside wide and far, allowing the wind to do the remainder of the spreading. That leaves us with Danny. It's one o'clock in the morning, and I'm exhausted and in pain.

"Jon, let me take care of Danny – at least the first part. You don't want this to be your last memory of him."

"Yeah, thanks. I'll connect with Alison and let her know everything's okay."

"Fine. Tell her Brown has exited, and everything has unfolded exactly as we've wanted. Leave it at that. After we go, I'll call your mom and let her know what's going on."

"I need to get fixed after we leave."

"Yes. I'm going to take you to the hospital and drop you off at the emergency department. Then I'll go back to the hotel and fill in the girls – it will be morning by then. You'll need surgery; and we'll come in to see you when you're done."

"What the hell am I supposed to tell them?"

"Simply that you were cleaning your firearm and it accidentally went off. They won't believe you, but it doesn't matter. There's nothing they can do about it. Just stick to the story."

"Will do. I'm going to text Alison."

Alison was irritated it took us so long to text, but it comes from a place of concern. I told her we'd check back in a few hours on our way home. Just a little white lie. Danny's body is almost finished converting and then we'll have to wait until the oven cools down. That leaves Enzo and me with some time on our hands.

"I had a good talk with Mom the other night."

"I heard some of it. She was pretty excited when she came into the bedroom."

"Yeah, me too, actually. Talk about taking me by surprise. I'm not sure she handled it exactly the way she should have after Dad died, but I can appreciate the effort."

"That's understandable. There was no instruction manual for us to look at."

A small laugh escapes me. "Hey, I wanted to thank you for the support – the financial support all these years. I had no idea."

"Yeah, I know. It's all good; don't think anything of it. Happy to do it."

I'm not sure if I made him uncomfortable, but he changes the direction of the conversation. "I'm concerned we're running out of time before the morning shift gets in. We need to be out of here before anyone gets here."

I don't have anything to say to that.

"Also, we can put Danny's ashes in a storage container, but we can't take him with us."

"Why not?"

"Because the funeral home will be here to pick him up. If he's not here, they'll know something's wrong."

"What about Bernie?"

"It will be a mystery. They'll think he skipped out. We'll leave a prominent label on Danny's ashes and put the container in a conspicuous place, so he'll be found tomorrow."

After a short time, we shut the oven down and wait for it to cool. I look at my phone to pass the time and after an hour or so, we empty the ashes.

"I'd like to do this part." I say to Enzo.

He helps me situate the ash pole, but after that I take over. Carefully, I remove every speck of ash from the oven. Sweat and tears drip down my face and fall to the floor. After transferring everything from the container bin to a storage box, I collapse into a chair. I'm cried out, worn out, and ready to go. Enzo crafts the note, attaches it to the box and places it on the administrator's desk out front.

He shuts the lights off and joins me in the administrative office. I'm staring at Danny's remains. Enzo puts his arm around me and after a moment, gently guides me out back and through the preparation area, until finally, we reach the back door. He's wiping door knobs and light switches along the way. After we get into the SUV, I remember nothing until we arrive at the hospital emergency department entrance.

48

The staff sees me lumber into the emergency department, dead arm hanging by my side. I'm placed on a gurney and quickly brought into the trauma unit, then loaded into a large, doughnut hole-type machine head-first, up to my neck.

I've been administered a mild sedative which has taken the pain edge off and has me feeling kind of groovy.

"Sir, may I have some information from you?" A voice requests through a speaker in the machine.

"Yeah, sure thing. What can I do for you?"

"I need your personal information; name, address, that type of stuff."

"If you reach into my jacket pocket, you can get all of that from my driver's license. My health insurance card should be in there, too. I'm not sure where my jacket is, though."

"That would be very helpful, thanks. It's right on the chair over here."

She pats down both of my front pockets. "Which side? They're both full."

Shit, I forgot I left a full clip for my pistol in one of the pockets, but I can't remember which side. I can only hope she picks the right one.

She reaches into the correct pocket. "Found it, first try. Thanks."

"No worries." Phew, dodged a bullet on that one, so to speak.

Another clinician asks me what happened.

"I was cleaning my pistol and it discharged."

"Into your forearm?" She asks skeptically. "I haven't seen that before."

"Yes. Into my forearm."

She doesn't believe me, not by a long shot, nonetheless she disappears, leaving me with the technicians. At this point, I don't give a shit if they believe me. I just want my arm fixed and then to sleep for a week and finally put this whole mess in the rear-view mirror.

After I've finished with imaging, I'm ferried back to the trauma bay, I'm guessing to wait for the results of the scan. In the meantime, a fairly attractive nurse helps me out of my street clothes and into hospital surgical garb. I wonder what Alison will say when she finds out what's happened. On the one hand she'll likely be worried sick, but on the other, I hope relieved I'm okay and we may be able to return to some sense of normalcy. I expect Enzo to be as adept at generating an optimistic story for her as he is at crafting just about everything else.

The trauma surgeon enters the bay.

"Mr. Williams, I'm Dr. Reed."

"Hello. I'd shake your hand, but … you know." I gesture to my arm with a nod, trying to be funny.

He's not amused. "I understand you had an accident handling a firearm?"

"Yes sir, that's right."

"Okay, let me have a look."

He lifts up the bed sheet to inspect my arm. He's sporting those goofy surgeon's glasses with the built-in light to magnify his vision. He's not moving my arm much, thankfully; he's moving his head around my prone arm. After a thorough inspection, he pulls the sheet back over my arm and lifts his glasses up to his forehead.

"Well, the human forearm is made up of two significant bones – the radius and the ulna. The MRI, the machine you were in, shows me you have a shattered ulna and a cleanly broken radius. A cleanly broken bone poses no real issue, but the shattered bone requires a more in-depth procedure. The standard course of action involves screws inserted in the cleanly broken bone, in your case the radius, and a titanium plate to repair the shattered ulna. It's not a difficult surgery and I expect you to regain full use of your arm."

"That's fantastic news!" I exclaim.

"Yes, it is. Just one more thing." He adds. "Your stage of blood coagulation suggests this wound wasn't sustained recently. In fact, as far back as sometime yesterday." He leaves the statement hanging as an open door for me to explain more.

"Honestly, I did it late last night. I don't know why I waited so long to come in."

"Ah … I see. And you got here how? I don't see an ambulance transfer on the intake log."

"I had a friend bring me and drop me off out front."

"Right … well, shall we get started?" Before I can answer him, he launches into the surgery process. "We're going to wheel you into the operating room, whereupon you will be transferred to the operating table – with your help if you're capable. Our anesthesiologist will administer a mild anesthetic to relax you, followed by general anesthesia. When you wake up you will either be in our surgical recovery room or already into an inpatient room. Any questions?"

"No, I'm good. Thanks."

"See you when you wake up."

In the operating room, the anesthesiologist comes in and a sense of relief floods through me. God, put me out already.

She's wearing a surgical mask and cap, so I can't see what she looks like, but she's very friendly.

"Alright, I'm going to inject this," she says while holding up a syringe filled with clear liquid, "into your I.V. tube. After it takes effect, I'll use this mask to cover your mouth and nose to put you under. Okay?"

"Yup."

She injects the liquid and I immediately feel a light burning sensation morphing into painlessness.

"How do you feel?" She asks.

"In beer terms, I feel like about five in."

"Ha, ha, perfect." She turns a dial on a portable tank placed next to her and then places the mask over my nose and mouth. "Nighty-night."

"Here he is."

I feel like I'm going to be sick. My eyes start to come into focus in time to see a nurse backing away and replaced by Alison.

"Jon, can you see me?" She asks worriedly.

"Uh … yes. Hey baby, how are you? Careful with my stomach, I might throw up. Umm … where am I?"

"Oh baby, thank God you're okay! You're in an inpatient room in the hospital. The surgery's over. It went very well."

"Yes, it did," the nurse adds, "and the nausea is perfectly normal until the anesthesia completely wears off."

I look at my arm. It's immobilized and wrapped up in so much gauze and bandage it's the thickness of my leg.

"My arm looks like the Michelin man."

"The what?" Alison asks.

"Never mind. Not important. Where's Mom?"

My mother pops up from the other side of the bed like an eager Whack-A-Mole. "Here I am! How are you feeling, honey?" She lightly strokes my hair.

"Religious."

"Religious? What?"

"You know, hole-y." I smile while nodding at my arm. "Is Enzo here?"

She laughs. "No, he's back at the hotel. He didn't think it was a good idea to show up here. He should be sleeping right about now."

My mother lowers her voice considerably. "He told us all about yesterday, start to finish. You had quite an experience."

"You could say that."

"Thank God you're okay." Alison says. She leans in close to me and whispers into my ear. "You are such a badass; I can't wait to get you home. You have no idea."

"Okay? I'm great! When I get home, we have to celebrate!"

"Yes!" Mom says excitedly. "To a new start!"

"Yeah, definitely to a new start; but I'm talking about celebrating my first gunshot wound!"

"Whaaaat?!?" Alison groans.

Mom cuts in. "I've heard this one before." She winks at Alison. "Don't ask, I'll tell you later. Tough guy stuff."

"Oh. I get it. Can you flex your good arm for me, pleeeaaase?" She says with amused sarcasm, hands clasped together in prayer.

Two sharp knocks abruptly ring out from the doorway, followed by a male voice.

"Mr. Williams?"

A uniformed police officer enters the room followed by a floor nurse. The nurse explains to the officer she is to be present at all times to ensure the health and welfare of the patient. The police officer indicates he fully understands, and he need only ask a few questions.

"Mr. Williams?" He repeats.

"Yes. I'm Jon Williams."

"I'm Officer Alan Danton with the Portland police department. May I ask you a few questions?"

"Why?"

"It's standard operating procedure with firearm incidents. We're required to investigate."

"Fine."

"Can you tell me how this happened?"

"I was cleaning my firearm."

"Where were you? At home?"

He's trying to back me into a corner. If I say 'yes,' he'll want to see where the bullet lodged.

"No. I was in my backyard. Sitting on the patio."

"I see. Which hand is your dominant hand?"

"My right."

"So, you were gripping your firearm with your left hand, while cleaning it with your right?"

My left arm took the bullet. My story wouldn't make sense if I was holding the pistol with my left hand.

"The firearm discharged before I actually started cleaning it. I was about to check the chamber when it accidently went off."

"That would make sense," he says, "though I find it odd that the bullet's entry point was the front of your forearm and not the inside."

"Sometimes the craziest things happen."

"They sure do, Mr. Williams."

"Are we done here?"

"Just one more question. The diameter of the entry wound indicates the firearm muzzle was at least five feet away from you when it discharged. Can you explain that?"

This guy knows I'm covering up for something. "Nope. I don't claim to understand the physics behind force and velocity, sir."

"Hmm. Right. Well, I appreciate your time Mr. Williams. We'll let you know if we have any more questions or follow up."

"Okay. Thanks."

Officer Danton leaves and I breathe a deep sigh of relief.

"Jon, that was brilliant." Mom says. "Just like a pro."

"Pro what?" I mumble. "Guys, I think I'm going to take a page out of Enzo's book and try and get some sleep."

"Okay. Sleep well, angel. We'll come back later tonight." Alison gives me a big kiss.

296 | P a g e

49

I checked in with Jennifer during my hospital stay. The funeral home picked up Danny's ashes the next morning, the morning of my surgery, and we've heard nothing from the crematorium about Bernie. Danny's service is tomorrow. It will be simple; Danny didn't have many friends locally. Most of them are shipmates scattered far and wide. Jennifer's been flooded with condolences, and although she's sad, I get the sense she will recover.

My stay in the hospital lasts three agonizingly long days. I was ready to leave the next morning, but hospital protocol requires a three-day observation period. No clotting or infection materializes, so according to the medical staff, I'm 'in the clear.' I need only keep the surgical site sterile, dry, and elevated. I'm in an arm sling, and will be for a couple of weeks, but other than that I'm no worse for the wear. I'll follow up to have the staples removed and be on my own for physical therapy.

Enzo sits out front in the SUV with Mom. Alison came into the hospital to keep me company during the ridiculously long discharge process and to walk me out.

She opens the car door for me, and I gingerly slide into the back seat. Next to me sits an ornately-wrapped present.

"Hey! It's good to see you, my man. How're you feeling?" Enzo says excitedly.

I haven't set eyes on him since he dropped me off at the hospital, and I'd be lying if I said I wasn't happy to see him.

"Good, now that I'm out of there. I'm a little sore, but all-in-all, not bad. What's in the box?"

"That's your 'Initiation into the Club' gift!" Enzo says.

"Ha, ha, you're kidding me."

"Not in the least. Open it."

"Uh, maybe you could help me?" I ask Alison.

She tears off the wrapping on her side while I pick at my side.

"What's in it?" I ask her.

"I have no idea."

Alison seems quite content. It's been a while since I've seen her this positive. Mom glances back at me with anticipation and she's smiling from ear to ear. The gift wrap is gone and we're staring at a box.

"Well, open it." Alison chides good-naturedly.

The cover comes off easily and we peer inside. It's completely jam-packed with cash. A lot of cash.

"Wow. How much is in here?"

"A hundred grand." Enzo replies proudly.

"Holy. You don't need to do that."

"It's the least I can do for someone who saved my life."

"C'mon. I didn't save your life. Please."

"You surely did."

Enzo must have told them one hell of a story. I can't wait to hear about my heroics later on.

"Can we go out to celebrate?" Mom asks. "We can find a place with the finest PBR on tap!"

"Now you're speaking my language."

We drove back to the hotel so I could clean up and change my clothes. It's going to be a challenge for me to do anything by myself for a while. Luckily, I have a willing partner in Alison to help me in and out of my clothes.

The celebration location is my preference, so what better place to celebrate than Asbury's? The place is hopping tonight, and although it's not an ideal fit for Mom and Enzo, they seem to be having a good time. Alison's having a blast and I feel good. Really good. The beers go down easily and even though I've had five of them and have to pee every ten minutes, it's not an issue. I'm adept at unzipping with one hand – my dominant hand.

Alison and Mom leave the table to use the ladies' room. This is the first time they've left the table together since we got here. This gives Enzo and me the opportunity to recap the night at the crematorium.

"Hey, I appreciate you embellishing to the girls about me 'saving your life'." I say, gesturing one-handed with air quotes.

"I wasn't embellishing."

"C'mon. I didn't save your life, you saved mine."

"Jon," he says with no trace of amusement, "when I got hit and was thrown into you, I watched you crash down those stairs and onto the pavement. Brown stepped over me, started down those same stairs, and fired a round at you. You could have frozen in pain and fear; many men would have, and died right there. Instead, you rolled out and took off for the front of the building. Had you not done that, Brown would have shot you dead then returned and emptied his clip into me. God damn right you saved my life. That gave me enough time to gather my senses, catch my wind, and get around that building to eliminate him before he could eliminate you."

I don't know what to say, so I say nothing.

"By the way, your mom told me exactly how you handled the Portland police in your hospital room as well. First-rate. Couldn't have done it better myself."

I see the girls walking back from across the room and they're chatting cheerfully. I feel my phone vibrate in my pocket. It's a text from Santa that I'm reading as the girls rejoin us. Alison texted Merri from the restroom and invited them both to come down to A's. What a great idea.

"Is that Ben?" Alison asks. "I sent Merri a text inviting them to join us."

"Yeah. He just sent it and said you invited them. Great idea."

"We old people need to get back to the hotel before we turn into pumpkins." Mom says.

"No problem. They'll give us a ride back." I reply.

"And speaking of rides," Alison says, "I'm so anxious to get my car back."

"Yeah, I've missed the Tic-Tac." I say smiling.

"Where is it?" Enzo asks.

"Oh, it's at my apartment. We thought it would be smart to leave it there in case it was tracked."

"Solid move. That also reminds me, we ought to work out what we're doing after Danny's service tomorrow. Your mother and I want to take a little vacation, so we're planning on leaving the hotel."

"Well, I'd like to go back to my apartment if I can and bring Jon with me." Alison says.

Enzo reflects on the notion. "That's reasonable. Tell you what, let Jon and me go to the apartment first. He and I will scan your car and clear it, then remove the bug from the hanging lamp and make sure the rest of the apartment is clear as well."

"I can drive your car back here to the hotel." I add.

"Right. We can move your gear plus your money in advance so you're move-in ready."

"Thanks. Sounds perfect!" Alison delights.

I need to pee again, so we give hugs all around beforehand, so Mom and Enzo don't have to wait for me to get back before they leave A's.

When I return to the booth, Alison is very affectionate and I'm loving it.

"At some point, we'll have to figure out how to move your stuff out of your apartment and either into mine or get rid of what you don't want."

"Yeah. You know, I was thinking about what Enzo said about him and Mom taking a vacation ..."

"I know where you're going with this and I think it's an awesome idea! We have some disposable income we can use!"

"Yes, we do!"

Before long, Santa and Merri arrive at our table and we have a spirited reunion complete with group hugs and kisses.

"Dude, how are you?" Santa asks.

"Pretty damn good, actually. Seriously unbelievable; these past two weeks."

We spend the next two hours or so filling in some of the holes for them, trying to be as generic as possible. I'm wary of being too detailed. I think they recognize that and appreciate my boundary. Despite the seriousness of the story, we're still having a great time. Eventually, we move away from this whole mess and on to more mundane, inconsequential yet interesting topics. I probably pee about three more times before we decide to call it a night.

"Listen, Merri and I need to tell you something." Santa has our full attention. "We're getting married."

"Oh my God, that's fantastic!" I say. "You're going to be Merri Kris Crindle!" I direct to Merri.

Merri shows her engagement ring to Alison. She's been hiding her hand all night, so we wouldn't see it.

"Dude, when?" I ask.

"This summer. And I have a question for you. Will you be my best man?"

"Hell yes! It'd be my honor!" I reach out to him with my good arm for a sort of bro squeeze. We laugh and enjoy ourselves for a period of time before Santa drops another bomb on us.

"The second part to this is not so happy, though." His statement brings us back down to Earth. Again, he has our full attention.

"Merri and I are moving back to Nebraska. Well, I'm moving back to Nebraska and Merri's coming with me."

"Wow, I didn't see that coming." I say.

"I've been thinking about it for some time now. My family's all there, and I haven't been enjoying the work here. Now that the firm's in a state of flux, I thought this would be the time to do it."

"No … yeah, I can see that. Well, I'm happy for you. For both of you."

"Thanks, Jon. Thank you too, Alison. *We are so gonna miss you guys!*" Merri says in a drawn-out, happy-whine voice.

"Oh my God, we're gonna miss you, too! When are you leaving?" Alison asks.

"Well, that's the thing." Santa says. "I landed a job at the University of Nebraska in their accounting department, and I start on Monday. This has all happened so quickly and I didn't want to bother either of you about it until Jon got home."

"When do you leave?" I ask.

"Tomorrow morning. We've had stuff moved out there in advance and we're all packed and ready to go."

I stand up and Santa stands up with me. "Man, am I gonna miss you." I give him a big hug. "I love you, bro."

"Love you too, man."

50

The bed in our hotel room never looked so inviting. Mom and Enzo have long been asleep and we're just getting back from A's. I detour for a pit stop into the bathroom and come out to find Alison sitting on the side of the bed – naked.

"Come over here, big fella. Let me help you get undressed."

I do as I'm told. I'm standing in front of her and she looks up at me with those eyes, those sexy almond-shaped eyes.

"I don't want you to do a thing. I'll take care of you."

She slowly unbuttons my jeans and lets them slide to the floor, never breaking eye contact with me. She follows by slipping my underwear down and I step out of both. Alison stands up to unbutton my shirt with my rock-hard erection pressing against her. She kisses my chest after each button comes undone until she reaches my stomach, then takes me in orally. Very quickly I'm nearing orgasm and Alison knows this, so she backs off. Standing again, she removes my shirt from my uninjured arm and carefully strips it down over the other. Finally, I'm totally naked save for the bandages wrapped around my arm.

Alison turns around, bends over the side of the bed and looks back at me.

"See anything you like?"

I place one hand on her fine bottom and enter her with a groan. She lets out a low moan, pushing back against me as hard as I'm pushing into her. After a while, she guides me onto the bed and then on my back.

"You relax," she says, climbing on top of me, "I got this."

At ten o'clock, Mom wakes us up with a soft knock at the door. Danny's service starts at eleven, so we need to get ready. I'm a little hung over, but frankly it takes my mind off of the dull, persistent ache in my arm. The injury affords me the opportunity to skip the formal dress and wear something more comfortable. Danny would want it that way, anyhow. He wasn't big on fancy dress.

I come out of the room and see doughnuts sitting on the kitchen table. I really could get used to this.

"So, what's the game plan?" I ask while choking down a glazed doughnut.

"Well," Enzo replies, "I thought we could all go to the service and then you and I could bring the girls back here. We'll pack your and Alison's clothes and money, then take it over to her apartment. I'll do the sweep of the apartment and car, and then we come back here for the girls. You drive Alison's car back."

"Sounds like a plan. Alison and I can go back to the apartment afterward. What are you guys doing?"

"Nothing set in stone yet. We'll check out of this hotel and go to another one adjacent to the airport. Either we're going to fly out somewhere or we're going to take a road trip. In either case, we need to ditch the Cougar."

"Amen. Ugliest car I've ever seen. Rest in pieces."

Enzo laughs. "Yeah. She's ugly as sin, bless her heart. But she's a workhorse."

"Maybe you ought to dump it with Reyes and the box truck."

"Not a bad idea, but she's untraceable. We'll bring her with us to the airport parking lot and leave her there with the keys in it. Somebody will grab her eventually."

"Good idea. If it's free, it's for me. Right?"

Burton's Funeral Home looks like every other funeral home in the country. The outside of the property doesn't readily divulge the business operating inside. It's nondescript, with a well-manicured lawn and an interior design like a 1940's parlor of an affluent family's manor. Various awards and recognitions hang from flowery wall-papered walls. If I concentrate hard enough, I can almost smell the mothballs.

Jennifer's done a magnificent job of celebrating and remembering Danny. She has pictures of him on a board propped up on an easel; some with family, some without, and a lot of them with her in the many places they've traveled to. As expected, attendance is light, but the quantity of flowers and messages of support sent by friends from around the world paying their respects overwhelms the room.

I had no expectation of discussing Danny's estate with Jennifer today out of respect; however, she brought it up by acknowledging he essentially left everything to me – primarily his Jeep and beach property. Included in that will be the insurance proceeds from the fire. I asked if there was anything I could do to help her, and she said 'no.' To Danny's credit, God love him, he had a five hundred-thousand-dollar life insurance policy with Jennifer as the beneficiary.

She also informed me the Nolan County Sheriff's Department tracked her down and said they had Danny's Jeep towed from the brewery parking lot because it had been parked there for a couple of days. She picked it up and it's at her house whenever I want to come get it. Good to know. I haven't had a moment to think about it.

"Just curious, why did you leave it there?" She asks.

"Uh … I had too much to drink, so I took an Uber home. They towed it before I went back to get it." Not a bad story off the cuff.

"Why didn't you ask them where it was towed to?"

She's got me there. "I just got wrapped up in work and I'm distraught about Danny. It got away from me, plus I had my arm accident." I pathetically flap my sling.

"Yeah, I can understand that. Changing subjects, when do you want to spread his ashes?"

"What do you think? It might be nice to plan something in the summer, so we can go out on the water and celebrate his life."

"I think I'd like that. I think he'd like that, too." She says softly, tears rolling down her cheeks.

I give her a one-armed hug. "Would you like to keep his ashes until then?"

"Yes … yes, I'd like that. Thank you, Jon. Danny loved you so much. Like the son he didn't have."

"I loved him, too." I can't hold it back anymore. The floodgates open and every last bit of raw emotion I've bottled up comes roaring out. Danny … my father … Mom … Alison. All of it.

51

We stop for a light lunch following the service and head back to the hotel. Alison does virtually all of the packing for us, which admittedly isn't much. She makes fast work of it, and we take our stuff out to the SUV in just two trips. I'm somewhat recovered from the emotional roller coaster of the service. I feel much better. There was a catharsis of sorts that came from that experience.

"Are you positive you don't want me to come with you?" Alison asks.

"And come between you and my mother having a spa day?" I say, smiling. "Not. A. Chance." I slowly over-enunciate each word.

"Yay!" Alison claps her hands together like a child about to be handed an ice cream cone. "Mani-pedi. I can't wait!"

I can't wait to experience those sharp fingernails later. I snatch a Diet Coke from the fridge and chase down Enzo. He's checking in with Mom and probably hearing a similarly excited spa-day story.

"Yo, LoZo. Let's roll."

"Yeah, I'm coming." Enzo says, exiting the bedroom. "C'mon, LoZo? Really?"

"I thought about just going with 'Zo,' but 'LoZo' has a stronger flow."

"Whatever. Let's go."

He's putting up a good-natured affront, but I think he might secretly like it – or maybe not-so-secretly.

"You know, I bet if I say that to my mother, she'll roll with it."

"I heard that!" Mom calls out from the bedroom. "I love it! See you soon, LoZo!"

Enzo rolls his eyes and walks out the door.

As we pull up to Alison's apartment complex, Enzo asks where he should park.

"There's a visitor's lot out back. Can't say I've used it, though. This is the first time I'm coming here without sneaking around."

"Fine. Let's deal with her car first while we're down here at the garage." He grabs his duffel bag, no doubt containing his detection wand. "Do you know where it's parked?"

"Yeah. It's the white Fiat. Right there." I point to the car.

"Hmm. I see why you call it a Tic-Tac."

We walk over, and I hand him the keys. He unlocks the car and awkwardly slides into the tiny front seat.

"Ahh ... my ribs are still bothering me."

He adjusts the driver's seat back as far as it will go and begins his scanning process. I like watching this segment of Enzo's skill set – the James Bond espionage spy stuff. He completes a general inside scan and progresses to a more comprehensive inspection. The steering wheel column gets a wand pass; as does the glove box interior, underneath the seats, door frames – you name it.

"I break spaces down into quadrants to ensure I don't miss anything." Enzo says, unsolicited. "I cover every surface, similar to painting a wall, or in this case, a tight space." I imagine a forensics analyst works in much the same fashion.

Enzo completes his interior review and moves on to the exterior. He plunks down to his knees to work on the underbody and immediately receives a positive indicator beneath the driver-side door. He reaches under, pinpoints the source, and after a brief effort pops a hockey puck-sized device from the frame.

"We got a hit."

"What is it?"

"GPS tracking device. The user on the other end will know exactly where this vehicle is at all times. When's the last time you used it?"

"Not since before I had Danny's Jeep. We fully expected there to be something on Alison's car."

Enzo walks over to a Fed Ex delivery truck parked some forty yards away and tucks it into a wheel well.

"Are you trying to throw someone off of our trail? I thought you said no one's monitoring us anymore?"

"That's what I said, and I stand by it. I just think it's funny for when the Fed Ex fleet maintenance workers find it and get all worked up that someone might be tracking them."

Gangster humor. Enzo concludes his inspection with the underside, exterior panels, and engine compartment.

"We're good to go." He says.

"Great, so I should maybe bring a load of stuff up with us from your car."

It only takes two trips to get everything inside. I make a mental note to purchase a fireproof safe and have it delivered, and also deal with the property managers on replacing the damaged front lock.

Enzo removes the listening bug from the hanging light right off and squashes it between two spoons. He begins his sweep of the rest of the apartment while I start to unpack our gear. It's slow going for me – one arm to carry, one arm to open drawers, one hand to put stuff away. I don't mind, though. I'm just happy we're here. For the short-term, I place all of the money in the closet.

When I'm done, I go to the refrigerator, crack open a beer, and plunk down onto the couch with the remote control. Enzo's finished with the living room and kitchen and has moved on to the bathroom. I'm flipping through channels, looking for sports recaps when Enzo comes into the kitchen.

"Hey, come over here."

I drag myself off of the couch and back to the kitchen. "What?"

"I found another one." He holds up another bug, slightly bigger than the first one he's crushed, but similar in all other respects.

"Is it new?"

"I can't be absolutely sure, but I don't think so. I found it on the bed frame. I thought I checked that room pretty thoroughly the first time, but it's entirely possible I could have missed it."

"So ... what does it mean? What do we do?"

"Not much we can do. I'm inclined not to worry about it."

It's slightly unnerving, but Enzo doesn't seem concerned. Since he's my barometer for intuiting all things hazardous, I opt to not be worried either.

Enzo methodically finishes his sweep and we head out.

Alison's car has some zip to it. I can see why she's anxious to get it back. It's late in the afternoon when we get back to the hotel with the Fiat and Mercedes. Alison left me a text saying she and Mom are all done with their treatments and are waiting for us back at the room. Apparently, Mom's all packed up; we need only load up their stuff and they can check out of the hotel.

Enzo opens the door to the hotel suite, thumping into suitcases and bags. Mom and Alison placed the gear too close to the door, blocking us from getting in. Mom hustles over to the door, pulling bags out of the way.

"Oops, sorry about that." She apologizes. "Didn't see that one coming."

"No problem, babe." Again, I'm struck by how warm and caring this tough guy is to my mother.

"Are we all set?" Alison asks excitedly. "With the apartment?"

"Yup. We're good." I opt not to inform her of the second bug.

"Great! And my car's here?"

"Sure is. Drove her myself!"

"Fantastic!" Alison's giddy.

Enzo chimes in. "Jon, what say you and I load our stuff into the SUV?"

"Sure thing."

I'm not much help, but it's not the reason why Enzo asked me to go with him. He wants to talk to me about Mom.

"So, we told you we're going to go away for a while." He says as we take the first load across the parking lot. "Part vacation, part just plain ol' disappearing."

He opens the Mercedes trunk hatch and deposits one suitcase in, then the next. I hand him an airplane carryon-sized bag I'm holding and a backpack that was slung over my uninjured arm.

"Your mother's desperately wanting to rekindle a relationship with you and I thought maybe after this past week, that could begin to happen. I just wanted to check in on how you feel about that."

"I'm feeling good about it, honestly. It won't be an instant thing, but I see it developing into a close friendship."

"I'm glad to hear it. For Sabrina and for you."

"Yeah, me too. Have you figured out what your plan is?" We're walking back to the hotel lobby.

"We're still mulling over some ideas, but we'll nail down a trip tonight when we get to the airport hotel. Probably a week or two away. When we get back, I think we'll move a little further south, but not too far. Easily within visiting distance."

"Okay. Let me know when you get back and where you're dropping anchor."

We arrive at the door and everyone's ready to leave. I decide to take a proactive role in addressing Mom's concerns.

"Hey, I was talking with Enzo. He mentioned you may take a week or two for vacation. Let us know where you're going and when you get back. We can connect then."

"That would be fantastic! So, you'll take me off of your phone's 'blocked' list?"

"Ha, ha, yes. You're already off. Have an awesome time."

I give her a one-armed hug and she squeezes back tightly – for a long time.

"I love you, Jon."

"I love you too, Mom." Eventually, I break away. "LoZo – take care of this one, she's a keeper."

"I say the same back to you." He smiles at Alison. She steps up and hugs both of them.

We gather the array of moneyed duffel bags and head out the door. Enzo's driving the Mercedes, so all bags go with him. Mom goes to the front desk; presumably to check out, and Alison and I head outside with Enzo. Alison spots the Fiat parked next to the SUV and hustles over, dropping her duffel bags at the SUV's rear hatch.

"Yay! I have my car back! I'm so excited."

I help Enzo load up the duffel bags full of money into the back. Alison jumps behind the wheel of her car and fires it up. Mom leaves the hotel and heads over to the Cougar parked across the lot. She drew the short straw on choice of vehicles. I'm guessing Enzo wants to be the one close to the money and firearms.

I extend my arm to Enzo. "Safe travels, man."

He reciprocates, and it transforms into a meaningful handshake. "You too, buddy. We'll connect when we get back."

Mom's waving at me as she gets into the Cougar. I return the wave and hop in shotgun into the Fiat.

"Hey." I say, leaning in for a kiss. "Let's get out of …"

A flash of light blinds me followed immediately by a deafening boom. The Fiat rocks on its wheels and I spin around to see a fireball of orange mayhem blasting skyward. The Cougar spun one hundred eighty degrees and it's scarcely recognizable. As quickly as the ball of fire discharged upward, it disappeared into the sky, replaced by acrid, caustic, black smoke spewing from the car's shell.

There's nothing left. Nothing. The tires are gone, and all of the windows are blown out. One door has traveled thirty yards or more and the other hangs from the frame. Stray pieces of rubber and metal smolder in the parking lot. There's a side-view mirror right below my window; it looks completely intact. I distantly wonder how it made it over here without shattering. Another explosion, this one smaller, bounces the back end a foot or two off of the pavement, causing us to reel back in our seats. Numbingly, I presume that was the gas tank igniting.

I feel like my soul left my body and I'm floating on air. Mom? There's no sign of her. Mom?

Very slowly, at less than walking speed, Enzo begins to drive away. Traumatized, undoubtedly in shock, Alison and I follow.

52

I figured out some time ago where Enzo's going. The waterfront. To the building where we handled and disposed of Reyes. Alison had to switch seats with me, she couldn't drive any longer and I'm not much better. We swapped out at a traffic light; we didn't want to lose sight of Enzo. I had to physically shake her at the light to break through her stupefied state. She's sobbing overwhelmingly now, more so than I've ever seen, and that includes what happened with Bob. Maybe it's because of Bob? Maybe it's because she felt a genuine connection with my mother? Maybe she feels the heavy weight of all of it? I don't feel a thing. I don't feel anything physically or mentally. My mind is blank. It's like I'm looking at a plain white wall. An extraordinarily plain white wall. There's no ceiling, there's no floor. Just white. Blinding white.

I drive down the short entryway to the fish piers. I see his Mercedes parked at the end, roughly in the same spot as when we had recent business here. He's already inside when we get out of the car, and fortunately, the door to the building's not entirely shut. Slowly we open it and peer inside. It's almost completely dark, but we can hear his voice. With deadened souls, we follow the sound of his voice and trace him to a small office in the back. He rests on a four-legged stool, head facing the floor. We just watch and listen.

"How did I not check the car? It's my fault." His voice is harsh, cracking, and filled with anguish. It transforms into abrasive, unsteady, and unforgiving. He travels through an emotional spectrum, tormented by his decisions or lack thereof.

"How will I live? I don't want to live. I can't live without her."

I'm not certain he's aware we're here.

"Oh baby, what have I done … baby … You fucking animals! I'll piss down your dead throats! *It should be me, God damn it!!*"

He buries his face into his hands and weeps voraciously.

I put my hand on his shoulder. I don't want to startle him; I'm unsure of what this man is capable of at this stage of his mental state. He reaches up and rests his hand on mine.

"I'm sorry. I'm so sorry, Jon." He wails. "It's my fault. I never meant for this to happen. I'm so sorry."

I've never seen such torment come from someone. Tears stream down my face. Alison's crying openly. She joins us for comfort and we huddle together for support.

She's gone. There's nothing for us to do. Mom's gone. There's nothing left of her for investigators to attempt to identify. There aren't any records at the hotel of any use to anyone; Mom and Enzo use aliases wherever they go. The hotel won't know the victim is, or was, a current or former guest. No record of the car exists. There're no personal belongings left behind. She's a ghost.

I'm sure it destroyed Enzo and filled him with a massive sense of betrayal to leave my mother behind, but it was the appropriate course of action. I can see this in hindsight, as I'm sure Enzo will too, someday. I hope he can someday.

Late into the night, I help Enzo up and guide him outside to his car. I place him into the passenger seat and get behind the wheel. He's only one level above catatonic. Alison assures me she's capable of driving her car, so we exit the pier and head back to the apartment. She leads the way and I follow.

At the apartment complex, we guide him upstairs and lay him on the couch. I head back out to unload the SUV and bring his stuff up. It takes me about six trips.

"Enzo. Take a couple of these." I hand him two of my pain pills, opioid epidemic be damned. The prescribed dose is only one, but under the circumstances, it's warranted. I haven't been taking them, anyway.

He doesn't object. In fact, he's doing everything we ask without question. We sit with him for roughly an hour or so until he falls asleep, then Alison and I go to the bedroom. Sleep will not come tonight.

"Jon, are we safe here?"

"Yes. Enzo says we are." I'm not sure I believe what I'm saying, and I don't think she does, either. "Brown knew we were at the hotel and he knew what cars we were driving in. He rigged that car before we got to him. We just hadn't used it in a long time."

"I don't want to go back to working at Harding-Williams." She says.

"I don't either, truth be told. We don't have to." I posit to her as a consideration. "We have some breathing room with our finances until we figure out what we want to do."

"We can move away. We have no close connections here anymore. We can move someplace else. Start over."

"What about your mom?"

"She can visit us. We can visit her."

"I like that idea."

"Do you think we're done with General Defense?"

"Ah, I don't really know. We should sit down with Enzo and go through that when he's able to. He had said to me the CFO of General Defense was the last person involved in the scheme and he was only the brains behind it. Enzo was the leader of the muscle. He wasn't worried about him, but we ought to make sure."

"Edgar Jacob. I've met him a number of times. I can hardly believe he was running it. He's just a pipsqueak. He would be in the right position to pull it off, but I can't believe he did. Can we turn him in?"

"Probably not without him exposing Enzo, and through extension, us. We risk a domino effect of everyone else in the pathway."

I don't feel as though I slept, but I must have. It's eleven o'clock in the morning and Alison's still asleep, thankfully. I walk out into the living room and see Enzo still out cold on the couch. I flop into an armchair with a Diet Coke and turn the television on with low volume so as not to wake him. After flipping through nearly all of the sports channels, I settle on ESPN. Last night's Celtics game is on replay and I welcome the mindless banter. It was short-lived though. At halftime, a commercial airs from a local news station describing a 'shocking car fire,' with details coming up after the break. My stomach turns and a sour taste permeates my mouth. I don't know if I'm ready to see this, but I have to.

After the next series of commercials, the news anchor appears onscreen:

> "The Fairfield Inn on Piedmont Avenue was the scene of a grisly car fire yesterday. Police and fire personnel arrived on site to find a vehicle completely engulfed in flames following what's been reported by eyewitnesses as an intense explosion. Police confirm there was one occupant in the vehicle who died at the scene. As of now, the victim

hasn't been identified and police indicate the body
is so badly damaged that they've so far been unable to determine if it was male or female. Police
are asking for the public's help. If you saw anything ..."

I change the channel. I don't want to see any more. I can't see
any more. The camera crew shot close-ups of the wreckage as well as
the rescue personnel removing Mom's remains from the scene. There
wasn't enough to warrant using a stretcher.

"I heard that." Enzo mumbles from the couch. He's not facing
the television.

"Hey. Can I get you anything?"

"No. Thanks. Just want to lay here and rest."

"As long as you'd like."

"Hi." Alison says softly. She's standing in her pajamas on the
threshold of the living room, her hair pulled back in a ponytail. Her face
is puffy and her eyes bloodshot from crying the better part of the night.
I imagine mine are as well.

"I don't know what to think, but I'm scared. I'm not sure what
I'm scared of; I'm just scared."

"Come here, babe."

She squeezes into the armchair, nuzzling into my good arm and
I stroke her hair gently. Enzo rolls over to face us, lying quite close to a
fetal position. His eyes are open, but he's not looking at us, nor does he
say anything. He blinks occasionally, though.

We sit in silence for some time. In my mind, I revisit my tumul-
tuous relationship with Mom. It felt so good to connect with her and learn
so much of what was kept from me all of these years. I still believe she
could have found a better way to handle it, but we all have our human

failings. I think in her mind it was the best course for her to take to give me the best outcome.

"You don't need to be scared." Enzo says to Alison, shattering the silence.

He has our full attention. He still isn't looking at us; he's more just staring at the wall.

"Jacob's the only other person from the company and my crew left. He only dealt with finances. Never got physical."

He gets up. "Could I have another painkiller?"

"Of course. On the bathroom counter. Can't miss them."

Enzo leaves for the bathroom.

"My heart aches for him." Alison says.

"Yeah. Mine, too."

I get up right after him to get another Diet Coke and bring one back for Alison as well.

Enzo reappears from the bathroom and lies down on the couch again.

"What are we gonna do about Mom? What can we do?" I ask.

"I don't really know. I don't think there's anything we can do." He replies solemnly. "She'll be taken to the medical examiner's office." His voice cracks. "What's left of her."

"What will happen to her?" I struggle to get the words out.

"I think they'll take a DNA sample, provided they find any usable; then finish cremating her and put her remains in storage. Like in an unsolved crime evidence lock-up." He has the greatest of difficulties expressing this to us.

"I make this promise to you." He affirms. "I will find a way to get her remains, so we can have a right and proper service with the dignity she deserves."

"What do we do now, Enzo?" I ask.

"There's nothing left. It's over. What do you do?" He eventually looks at us. "You both live your lives and love each other fiercely. That's all you can do."

53

Enzo's been with us for a little over three weeks. He hasn't left the apartment, but at least these past few days he's been sitting up on the couch and has begun to eat again. He's quiet; nothing really to say and we respect that. Alison and I have only gone out for groceries. The three of us sit in our sweatpants, eat when we feel like it, and watch mindless TV. The news stopped reporting publicly about the car explosion – they haven't referred to it as a car bomb, which is exactly what it was.

I ordered two safes, similar to Danny's, and they were delivered and installed this morning. I stocked one of them with cash and the other with Danny's firearms. I opt to leave my pistol out now. Alison knows I have it, and although she doesn't say as much, I think she may be reassured somewhat by it. She called the property manager a few days back and had our front lock replaced. I installed a new interior chain lock and security doorstop. She also spoke with the owner and made arrangements for me to be added to the lease. Our plan to move away will need to be put on hold at least until the lease expires in nine months.

On the personal front, I need to finalize Danny's estate. I'm not all that concerned about it; we have an Estates and Trusts department at HW that can help me through that process. I submitted the claim to the insurance company for the fire. The proceeds amounted to one hundred fifty-thousand for the value of the house. Now I need to decide what to do with the land. For now, I'm going to keep it.

My arm's coming along. I don't have constant aching pain anymore, only sharp jolts on occasion if I move it too quickly or bump up against something. The docs say it's perfectly normal. My sling is gone, and I had the staples removed yesterday. I have a bandage and support wrap for my arm that's easily covered with a long-sleeve shirt. As far as I can tell, I don't have any issues with mobility. I am having trouble with sensation in some of my forearm areas due to nerve damage. That will be a longer recovery process; they tell me it takes about a month per inch of nerve to heal.

Alison and I lie on the couch watching an old rerun of *Friends* when Enzo comes out of the bathroom. He'd been showering, and he's now fully dressed and sits down in the armchair.

"Alison. Jon." He says, making deliberate eye contact with us both. "It's time for me to go. I'm not sure where yet, but it's time. I can't express to you how much I appreciate what you've done for me. I love you both."

"What? Where are you going? You can stay here for as long as you'd like." Alison quickly replies.

"You sweet child. I can't tell you how appreciative I am." He's looking at her lovingly.

"Hey. You're not telling us a permanent goodbye." I counter as a statement and not as asking a question.

"No. God knows I thought about it, though. I've thought about it every day. I'll probably think about it some more too, but no. Sabrina would be very angry with me."

He gets up and piles his things by the door.

"Can I leave your mother's belongings with you? I can't bring them with me and I can't bear to throw anything away. I would feel much better if they were with you."

"Of course. We'll take care of it. You really don't know where you're going?" I ask.

"No, I really don't. I'm gonna disappear – at least for a while."

Alison asks, "Will we ever see you again?"

"Eventually. I couldn't walk away from either of you." He says with a slight smile.

I can see why my mom fell in love with him. He's good to those he cares for.

"I want you guys to have these." He places two duffel bags in front of us on the couch, walks back to his belongings, and returns with two more. "There's a million here."

"Are you fucking kidding me?" I'm blown away.

"Nope. No fucking kidding here."

"We can't take this." Alison replies with absolute amazement.

"Don't worry about it. I have another million with me roughly, and a lot more than that in different places. By the way, I suggest you do the same. Bank safety deposit boxes work well."

"Yeah. I don't know what to say, Enzo. Thank you doesn't seem to cut it, but thank you."

"You'd be surprised what a plain old 'thank you' means to me. The way you opened up to your mother and the way you both provided for me these past three weeks means the world. Alison, your friendship to Sabrina, though short, was exactly what she'd been missing. With the two of you, she was happier than I'd ever seen. This is my 'thank you' to you."

Alison and I stand up and we each give Enzo a hug. A great, big hug.

"Bye, Enzo. Thank you." Alison kisses his cheek.

"Take it easy, LoZo. Don't be a stranger, okay?"

"Got it. And by the way, I don't need to tell you this I'm sure, but be careful with the money and how you feather it into use. If you can wash it – do it. No large deposits into a bank account."

"Understood. Hey, one other thing – Alison and I are both going to leave the accounting firm. Too much baggage there for us to go back. I'm not sure they'll be back in business anyway, if I'm being honest. You think we need those records from General Defense in case anyone comes snooping around; namely government or law? They're the files Bob said he placed certified letters in, clearing Alison and me."

He ponders the question. "You know … it can't hurt. You might as well get what you can, when you can. Offhand, I can't see why you'd need them, but why not, right? Probably a good idea to hold off quitting until you get what you need."

"Right. Kind of what we were thinking, thanks. Let me give you a hand down to your car."

I grab two of the duffels in one arm and follow him out the door. When we get to his car, I'm surprised at myself for how emotional I'm feeling with him leaving. It wasn't that long ago I thought this guy was a crazy son-of-a-bitch married to my psycho mother.

"You know, I didn't think I'd ever catch myself saying this, but I'm gonna miss you."

"Heh – thanks. I'll miss you, too. Take care of the girl; she's a beauty."

"I will. Check in with me sometime, alright?"

"Yeah, I will."

"What a crazy-ass world we live in." I say to Alison when I get back up.

"Jon, we have over a million and a half dollars here! What. The. Fuck."

"You can say that again. And I have another one hundred fifty-thousand coming from the insurance and Danny's Jeep is in the parking lot, as well. Not to mention I have his parcel of land."

"With this comes a lot of tragedy, though."

"Oh babe … I'd trade it all in to have them back. Even Bob." I say with a half-hearted chuckle.

"Me too. Even Bob … but I'd still be with you."

With that, we walk arm-in-arm into the bedroom and make love until every last ounce of energy has left our bodies.

54

I t's late Friday morning and the sun shines brightly. The mercury rises steadily day-by-day and the warmth feels good. It's healing. Alison and I eat breakfast in the dining room mostly in silence, simply enjoying each other's company. Absentmindedly, I stare at the spot on the hanging light where the listening bug used to be.

"I wonder where Enzo is." I say somewhat ethereally.

"I know! I was wondering the same thing! I think about him a lot. Sabrina, too."

My stomach roils at hearing my mother's name. I miss her, too. I miss what could have been but will never be. That's almost as much a tragedy as her death.

"Do you think he's going to be okay?"

"Honestly? I don't know. He's a tough guy – a violent guy; but vulnerable at the same time."

"Sounds like someone I know."

She switches up the conversation before I respond. She senses where we're headed and knows we shouldn't go down the Dark Road. Sometimes it's one-way.

"What do you want to do today?"

"I wouldn't mind getting our trip to work over with and resigning. What do you think?"

"I think that's a great idea."

"Good. I'll check in with Peabo to see if we can come in and go through the GD stuff. He sent me an email way back that I never followed through on."

I pull out my phone and craft an email to him:

Peabo –

Sorry I haven't gotten back to your email. Any chance the GD files are still around for Alison and me to go through?

Jon

I drop Alison's name in the email to make sure I get a response. I hit send, and put my phone away.

"Well, that's that. Just need to wait for a response."

"So, what now?" Alison asks, then contemplates for a moment. "Hey, I have an idea. Why don't we start getting your stuff out of your apartment and bring it over here?"

"Great idea. Some of it I think I'll leave, though."

We take the Jeep, mostly because we can't fit much more than a toaster in her car. When we arrive at the house, I look at it in a different light. It seems a lifetime ago I lived here. The mailbox is largely full, but not overflowing. I suppose the mailman stopped delivering and the post office stockpiles hordes of my junk mail and bills. It's funny, I haven't thought nor cared about it since before we met with Bond. We walk up the rickety back stairs and enter the apartment. It's stuffy inside; the air is dead. In some respects, it's reminiscent of a time capsule – frozen in time 'before Mom and Enzo,' while now is 'after Mom and Enzo.' Everything I own radiates of my dad and to a lesser degree, Danny. Nothing in here reminds me of my mother.

There isn't much I want to bring with me. My personal items; clothes and pictures. I can't leave the Snoopy phone behind. I don't care about dishes, I can leave those. I should probably part with Danny's old waterbed. It would be as much symbolic as hygienic to leave that thing behind. I'd like a couple pieces of furniture – an end table and some other small items, but other than that, I'm good with walking away.

It takes us until early afternoon to finish packing and move back to the apartment. We're tired and hungry when we finish unloading, so we decide to go out for a bite to eat.

"I'll call my landlord tomorrow and let him know I'm out. I'll probably lose my security deposit with all the stuff I left behind, but oh well."

"Sounds like a plan. Have you heard from Peabo?"

"Oh crap, I forgot all about him."

I check my phone and see he sent me an email.

"Yeah, he got back to me. He says the place is crazy overloaded with workers moving the last of the boxes out of the back warehouse area and into our permanent space."

"We have a permanent space?"

"Man, we've been out of the loop for a while. We're leaving the convention center for a new office building. Down on the waterfront. He goes on to say that he talked to the guys and they asked if we could come in tomorrow morning to find what we need instead of today. They'll set the boxes aside."

"That's okay with me. Are you okay with that?"

"Yeah. I guess. Doesn't really matter to me."

I send an email back to Peabo saying it's no problem and we'll be in around ten.

"Cool. Email sent."

"Hey." Alison changes the subject. "Want to venture out to A's tonight?"

"Yeah, definitely. Friday night; it'll be jamming."

"Let's go home and chill for a while and then we can head out. I'll even drive."

"Oh baby, you spoil me."

Asbury's is rocking, just as I predicted. Music's pumping, taps are flowing, and it feels good to be a twenty-something hanging out on the weekend. Alison looks hotter than a pistol and she's on my arm – my uninjured arm. She wears a tight shirt and body-hugging jeans; hair and makeup flawless. I'm down with this crowd. Everyone appears outgoing and friendly, making for an enjoyable, energetic atmosphere. But I know better now. We're not the only ones with a story. It's been said to be kind, for everyone you meet is fighting a harder battle. Man, if anyone here is fighting a battle harder than ours ...

I send a text message to Santa letting him know we're at A's and wishing he and Merri were here. Tonight's one of the semi-final college basketball games and we usually watch the Final Four together. I never ended up doing picks for the tournament brackets; I can't imagine many from our firm did. Virtually every wide-screen in this place has the game on, so everywhere you look, you don't miss a thing.

I order my third PBR and contemplate my first pee break. Alison's chatting it up with some people she knows from somewhere at the high top next to us. I'm more interested in the game and simply relaxing. I like to check out Alison occasionally to watch her in an animated and seemingly carefree way. She's been through so much and it's good to see her enjoying herself.

Try as I might to ignore, nature calls for me, so I excuse myself and head to the restroom. On my way back, I see some dudes from HW across the room; I know them, but not well, so I choose not to go over. I'd be lying if I said I didn't want them to see me with Alison. I sit down and take a long slug from my glass and continue to watch the game.

Without warning, Alison repeatedly taps me on the shoulder in an agitated way.

"What …?" I turn around and find her gawking wide-eyed at a nearby television.

We can't really hear it. It's just noise intermingling with the surroundings, but we see a news video camera still image of a vehicle on a bridge with a subtitle, 'Chief Financial Officer – General Defense.'

Quickly, I get up to move closer, but before I can get there, one of the bartenders changes the channel to a hockey game.

"We need to find out what that was about." I say to Alison when I get back to the table. "I didn't catch anything before it was changed."

I square up the bill and we hustle outside.

"When we get to your car, I'll go online to the news website. If it's on TV, then it's posted to the site."

Inside the Fiat, I fumble with my phone attempting to check the report. I see Santa sent me a text back saying they missed us and wished they were here with us, too. I'm not so sure that'd be the case if they had the full story.

"It's posted." I announce to Alison. I click on the video and turn the volume up all the way. She leans in to watch with me.

> "A man is dead after passersby discovered a body washed up on the shores of North Bay near the fish piers Friday evening, according to Portland chief of police Douglas Morelli. Morelli said passersby reported the body at six-thirty this evening. Officers attempted to revive the man, but efforts were unsuccessful. Although the body has not been identified, a vehicle was found abandoned on Veteran's Bridge near where the body was discovered. News12 has learned the car is registered to Edgar Jacob, fifty-seven years old, of Southborough. Jacob is the recently departed, former chief financial officer for Maine-based General Defense, one of the state's principal employers. His abrupt departure came as the Portland Times was preparing a story about financial malfeasance alleged from a former worker. Jacob was aware he was under police investigation and News12 learned Jacob has a sealed indictment pending, the specifics of which are not public. News12 will be following this breaking story closely and updating you accordingly."

"Ho – Lee – Shit! Jacob's dead!" Alison exclaims.

"Enzo?" Right away, I think about him and his potential for involvement.

"You think? Jacob's under indictment, he has a whistle blower, and his car is on the bridge. Maybe he jumped?"

"Maybe. But if anyone could dump him off the bridge and make it look like a suicide, it would be Enzo."

"Ya, no doubt. Damn, I didn't even think of that. But Enzo did call him the last link and that he was harmless. Did he have a change of heart?"

"After what happened to my mother? I wouldn't bet against it. He thinks she's gone because he got complacent; didn't tie up loose ends. This may be him tying up that loose end."

"This is going to be a huge story." Alison anticipates. "I would think HW's gonna be circling the wagons. Should we even bother going in tomorrow?"

"I think so. If we get shut down, then we get shut down. We'll call it a day on this bullshit one way or the other."

55

The news of Jacob cuts our night off early. Neither of us feels like going back inside once we make it to the car. It's just as well; we have a relatively early morning tomorrow. A weather front moved in while we were inside and now a steady rain falls. We're silent on the ride home; the only sound is of the windshield wipers slapping in rhythm against the windshield. I run any number of scenarios through my mind as to Enzo's potential involvement with Jacob. I suspect Alison's doing the same.

When we arrive at our apartment, I fully appreciate the benefit of underground parking during inclement weather. Sheeting rain pelts the side of the building, yet thankfully we're sheltered.

Alison makes a beeline to the bedroom to change into comfortable clothes. I turn the television on in anticipation of the eleven o'clock news and then go to the fridge to grab a beer.

"I think I'll have some wine with you." Alison considers when she comes out. She's wearing my favorite Dalmatian pajamas.

"Great, I'll get it for you."

I pour a glass and bring it over to the couch. "I'll be right back; I want to put on some sweats and get comfortable, too."

It takes me all of one minute and I'm back.

"Hey, I was thinking about the news website video we watched in the car. Did you see that they reported Jacob as the *former* chief financial officer of GD?" I ask.

"Ya, that's right, it had slipped my mind. It makes sense though, if he's under investigation."

It's quarter of eleven; fifteen minutes until the news comes on. Santa texted again asking if I saw the end of the game. I text back, 'yeah, what a game,' even though I didn't. I don't have it in me to explain why I wasn't watching. He'll be super-interested to hear about General Defense, and I'll tell him, but I don't want to deal with it right now. I check online to see what went down with the game. Apparently, it was a barn-burner with a game-winning three-pointer at the buzzer in overtime. A's must have erupted when the shot was hit.

"Hey babe," Alison says, "I think I'm just gonna go to bed. I'm so tired."

"No problem, I'll be in soon. Right after the news update. Love you."

"Love you, too." She gives me a kiss on the cheek and disappears.

I flip through the channels while I finish my beer. ESPN shows the highlights of the game and Santa was right. What an awesome finish. I would have liked to enjoy it at A's. The eleven o'clock news is coming on and I have just enough time to get another beer.

I change channels as I sit down to find the commercials winding up. The newscaster comes on and predictably, the body washed up on the shoreline leads off.

"Good evening, I'm Janice Houlton. News12 is reporting tonight on a body discovered in North Bay, directly underneath the Veteran's Bridge. The body has been positively identified as Edgar Jacob, fifty-seven years old, of Southborough. Jacob was the former chief financial officer of General Defense, one of the state's largest employers. Jacob's vehicle was found shortly thereafter abandoned on Veteran's Bridge, and police crime scene investigators are still on site. News12 has recently learned that Jacob has been the subject of an ongoing federal investigation for financial improprieties. A sealed indictment was filed in Federal District Court Wednesday, the substance of which is not available at this time. Our reporter, Kelsey Carter, stands by live at the scene. Kelsey?"

The camera cuts to Veteran's Bridge where Jacob's car still sits. Lights flash from the police crime scene van. It seems like an unusually long time to process an apparent suicide, so to me it means police may have found something. Then again, it may only be due to the legal implications surrounding him that they're taking a closer look.

The cub reporter doesn't add anything of substance to the story. The eleven o'clock update itself doesn't really add anything to the story. The chief of police comments on location with the usual rundown – the investigation's ongoing, it would be premature for police to comment on this or that, and the public's not in danger.

I drain my beer in one slug and kill the TV. Off to do my toiletries and jump into bed. Hopefully, I won't have to get up more than two times tonight to pee.

The rain moved out sometime overnight replaced by blue skies and a few scattered, wispy clouds. The morning air is crisp; winter still holds us hostage, but its harsh grip slowly loosens. We decide to go out to breakfast this morning, as neither of us feels like cooking or cleaning up afterwards. We drive to the mall area and hit up Eggscellent Choice along with what appears to be the rest of southern Maine on a Saturday morning. It's about a half-hour wait for a table, and we have the time, so we stick it out. I'm a people-watcher by make-up, so in an absurd way I enjoy the wait. I pass the time dissecting everyone within sight, conjecturing their life's story.

In one booth, four guys sit hungover from last night's pub crawl. One of them looks much worse than the rest. Every few minutes or so, he gets up and goes to the men's room. Probably just some toast for him this morning. The church-going elderly couple just finished paying their bill. They're dressed in their best church clothes and more than likely got here at seven, so they can have the senior breakfast and still make nine o'clock mass. There's a young mother with three kids, all under six years old, and she constantly corrals the gang, trying to bribe them into behaving with Dum-Dum lollipops. She hasn't slept through the night in recent memory. She carries an over-sized 'mom bag' taking up the space of a small human. A cursory inspection reveals diapers, bibs, wipes, lotions, and a fleet of snacks.

There's a middle-age couple whose children are out of the house and they have nothing to talk about anymore. And rounding out my observational profiling, we have the NASCAR fans, high school kids, and the loner who likes to dine out by himself. Then there's us. A young couple in the throes of love and passion. Oh yeah, and on the fringes of murder and mayhem.

Our buzzer vibrates and lights up, indicating our table is ready. The hostess seats us and our server arrives at the table almost instantly, handing us menus. She's one of many staffers wearing a Boston-themed sports shirt; and in her case, the New England Patriots. Good choice.

Our server takes our drink order and disappears, leaving us with our menus.

"I think I know what I'm going to do later today." Alison states.

"And what might that be?" I reply, while perusing the breakfast choices.

"I am going to research cruise ships and find a Caribbean cruise for us to take." She says matter-of-factly.

"That sounds like something I can get onboard with." I say, using some clever word-play.

"Oh, har, har." She responds sarcastically. "Did that blow wind in your sails?"

"Yeah, nice try. Not that funny."

She reaches out for a single-serve container of jelly nearby that didn't get put back into the jelly holder. She takes aim and flicks it at me, bouncing it off of my forehead.

"Oops. Sorry." She giggles adorably.

"Hey! You'll get a spanking for that later."

"Promise?"

Our server comes back to the table, then promptly leaves, taking our food order with her.

"Seriously though," she says, "I'm worried we won't find anything from Bob today."

"I hear you." I breathe a deep sigh. "Well … look. We've done nothing wrong. We knew nothing of what was happening. We ought to have faith the investigative process will discover that and exonerate us. We may not even come into the investigative picture. Who knows?"

"If Bob's letter goes public; which we'll probably have to make public if we're accused, then it will become known about the money."

"Maybe not. The money was described on the last page, right? We could exclude it. Besides, even if we had to give back the money, we still have the money Enzo gave us."

"True."

Breakfast arrives and I'm not shy. I'm about a third of the way through several plates arranged in front of me, while Alison still works on preparing hers.

"Will you pass me a strawberry jelly?" She asks.

"Sure." I take aim and flick it at her.

Her Wonder Woman reflexes activate, and she deflects the jelly before it reaches its intended target.

"Yeah, nice try."

56

W e pull into the parking lot at the convention center. It's empty save for an old street sweeper and some miscellaneous beat-up snow plowing equipment piled in the back corner.

"Man, there's no one here." I complain.

"Well … it's Saturday. I wouldn't be here either, except for this. Plus, HW's supposed to be moved out of here, right?"

"I guess. At least we get front row parking."

"You're right, though. I hope it's been left open and they didn't forget about us."

We exit the car and walk to the door. I have one of Enzo's empty duffel bags in case we want to smuggle any files out with us. Thanks to the advent of the smartphone though, we can take photos of everything we need, anyway.

We find the door to the rear warehouse unlocked and enter the building. Alison's right; we are moved out of here. The space looks massive with all of our boxes gone.

"No one's here?" Alison asks rhetorically.

"Doesn't look like it. There's gotta be a light switch around here somewhere. Let me see if I can find it."

There are no obvious light switches, but I see a gray panel box nearby. I swing the panel door open to find circuit breakers stacked in a breaker box.

Systematically, I flip each breaker and banks of lights come on with each switch until they're all triggered. They don't illuminate very well; they're the type of lights needing some warm-up time before they achieve their full brightness. They buzz slightly while in the process of warming up.

"Okay. Now we're in business." I say while examining our surroundings. "Looks like there's a bunch of junk leftover in that back corner."

Boxes sit stacked in the corner; maybe a dozen, maybe more. A few work tables sit nearby, as well as some movable shelving. The building floor itself has been swept clean and tidy. The lighting gets progressively stronger, and we no longer have difficulty seeing where we're going.

"All right." I mutter. "Let's get this shit-show started."

As we approach the stacks, I spot 'General Defense' hand-written on many of them.

Alison catches this at the same time. "I see at least a few marked 'General Defense.' Good. Peabo took care of us."

"Yeah. He took care of *you*."

She flashes me her million-dollar smile. "Don't be a hater."

We open some of the boxes. Inside a couple of them, we can see the water damage Peabo spoke about. Many of the documents are dried up and crinkly, resembling paper-maché, and won't be of much, if any, use to us. Finally, we locate an undamaged box. The files are from 2011, a rebound year in terms of financial performance for the company. I back away and let Alison take the lead in going through it.

"There's so much superfluous junk in here. Bank confirmations … government contracts … accounts payable and receivable cutoffs. I think we only need inventory work papers, government requisitions, deferred revenue, and purchase orders. Anything else you can think of?"

"Uh … Probably Bob's certifications of his sole responsibility for inventory?"

"Yes! Exactly, thank you."

Phew. I didn't follow half of what she was talking about.

"Do you want to thumb through other boxes and see if you can find one? I assume he did one for every year."

"Sure."

It takes me three or four boxes to find another one undamaged – this one from 2008. The sheer volume of paper is dumbfounding. There are at least three boxes for every year. I spend a half-hour or so skimming through them to find nothing. Alison comes up empty as well.

"This is like pissing in the ocean." I complain.

"What the hell does that mean?"

"Needle in a haystack. Same thing."

"Oh. Rude."

I refocus on examining more boxes and find one with no dates written on it. I open it up to discover it's not damaged and it contains file folders. The first folder is an index entitled, 'Permanent File.'

"Hey, I found the perm file." I announce to Alison.

Permanent files, or perm files as they're sometimes referred to, contain documents kept indefinitely. Generally, documents are destroyed in accordance with prescribed IRS guidance, but some records are permanently retained. Typically retained documents include board minutes, company charters, formation documents, and a whole host of other stuff.

"Cool, maybe he put them in there. That way no one would get rid of them."

"Or look for them." I posit. "No one goes back to the perm file unless they're specifically looking for something."

I briefly scan the index page for anything noteworthy. Nothing stands out to me. Nothing catches my eye ... except for ... the last entry on the index reads, 'Miscellaneous – MISC.' I sift through the box, locate a file folder entitled 'Miscellaneous – MISC,' and remove it.

"Alison, come look at this."

I walk with the folder over to a work table and Alison joins me. The only items within are five virtually identical documents, each from a different audit year, spanning 2014 – 2018. In each document, Robert C. Roberts, CPA, Partner-in-Charge of General Defense, certifies that he and he alone, is and has been solely responsible for all issues of inventory, inventory valuation, and inventory requisition attestation for General Defense. At no time was staff involved in that portion of the engagement.

Alison's reading as quickly as I am. We finish at the same time and look at each other wide-eyed.

"Here they are. You found them! Every one of them!" She says in disbelief. "Bob's counterparty letters to my own certifications!"

"And he's signed and dated each one." I add. "I'm stealing this entire file." I say as I drop it into the duffel bag.

"Should we take anything else?" Alison asks.

Before I can answer, the door we came in slams shut with a loud crack, startling us.

It's Harold Osterman, our chief operating officer.

"Oh hey, Harold." Alison calls out to him. "You scared us with the door. Peabo gave us the heads up to come in today."

"Sorry about the door. It got away from me." He says as he approaches. "Yeah, Peabo checked in with me and I actually instructed him to ask if you could wait until this morning to come in. It was a madhouse in here yesterday. But now we're out."

His already booming voice amplifies in the now-vacant building. This guy should be in radio, not business management.

"Have you guys found what you're looking for?" He asks.

"Ya, I think so." Alison replies.

"That's good … that's good." He repeats, but much softer.

He's looking down at his shoes. "You know," he picks his head up again, "I'm looking for something, too."

"Um. Okay. What?" Alison asks.

"Oh, nothing you can give me, Alison."

He looks at me. "I'm trying to locate Enzo Garibaldi. Jon, perhaps you can direct me to him?"

I feel an instant adrenaline-rushed panic and I instinctively step in front of Alison. Harold removes a firearm from his jacket and runs his fingers over the barrel. He's trying to intimidate me, and he's succeeding immensely. I recognize the device attached to the muzzle. It's a silencer.

God damn it. I have my nine-millimeter in my coat pocket; I've been carrying it with me everywhere I go. I can't reach for it without him finishing me first.

"Mr. Osterman, what's going on here?" I ask, trying to buy time to process my next move.

"What's going on Jon, is … I want to know where Garibaldi is. You know, your stepfather? The one that's married to – or was married to your blown-up mother? You shouldn't have spent so much time in the

Cougar, by the way. Regrettably, Mommy was the only casualty, though she wasn't who I was going for."

You fucker. You were in on it. You are in on it.

"I see the confusion on your faces. Let me help you. Have you heard the news?" Harold asks solemnly. "Of course, you have. But you don't need to hear it from me to know what's going on, do you? You have Bob's letter."

I feel Alison shaking uncontrollably behind me.

"I had Peabo recover Bob's work file directory from the cloud after I burned his house down. I read the love-letter he sent to you, Alison. Hellooooo ... yoo-hoo, the one behind Jon." He says in a sing-song voice to Alison. "I knew you were fucking him."

My blood boils. Today I may die, but not her. I've got to squeeze off a round before he ends my life, and it's got to count.

"Yes, that's right, I burned Bob's house down. I intended to kill him, but guess what? He beat me to it. And before you regard yourselves as super-sleuths; yes, I knew you were all in the house, too. My mistake was I thought there was no chance you'd get out alive. I won't make that mistake again."

"I don't know where Enzo is." I growl.

"That's unfortunate. Perhaps if I put a bullet into Ms. Brigham's head, it will spark your memory?"

"He's gone!" I maintain. "He disappeared after my mom died! I don't know where he is!"

"He hasn't disappeared, Jon! He's here!"

His face turns a shade of purple and spittle flies when he roars. "That fucker killed my brother last night!"

"I don't ... I'm not following ..." I stammer.

"Edgar Jacob is my brother! My half-brother God damn it! That son-of-a-bitch killed him, I know it. He wouldn't have jumped. That bastard threw him off the bridge or made him jump!"

"What?? The CFO of General Defense was your brother?" I react in shock.

"Yes!" He moans in anguish, his thundering voice rebounding off of the building walls. "Do you think that fat fuck Bob Roberts could make this happen on his own? My brother and I were the leaders! We ran the show!"

By God, it was Osterman and Jacob masterminding this. Each flanking a side of the criminal bookend of Harding-Williams and General Defense.

"Give him up, Jon. It's his fault your mom's dead. He got complacent and content. He should have checked that car long before your mom got inside."

"You knew! Noooooooo!"

I reach for my pistol. "I'll fucking kill you!" I scream.

As I grasp the gun stock, Harold slowly raises his arm and takes aim at me. I'll never make it. Not a chance. Just as I free my pistol, and without warning, Enzo silently rises up from a waist-high wall of boxes stacked directly behind Harold, injects a syringe deep into his jugular, and completely depresses its contents. Harold collapses unconscious to the freshly swept floor.

57

"**B**aby ... baby, are you okay?" My hands cup her cheeks as I try to get her to focus in on me. Her face contorts in a soundless cry. "Hey ... look at me. You're okay. We're okay."

"I wet myself." She bawls.

"It's okay. Everything's okay, don't worry about it. We're fine."

"Is this ever going to end?" She sobs.

Man, I hope so.

Enzo's hard at work dragging Harold to the back door. He must have pocketed his firearm as well; I don't see it lying anywhere.

"Can I have some help?" Enzo says calmly.

I help Alison to her feet, snatch the duffel bag, and support her as we stagger over to him. She did indeed wet herself.

"Is ... is he dead?" She asks.

Not yet.

"No." I reply. "He's unconscious. Same stuff that knocked us out."

"But twice as much." Enzo adds. "Jon, grab an arm and a leg."

I do as I'm told and Enzo does the same. He kicks the back door open, revealing his Mercedes SUV with the rear hatch propped open. We toss him in like a sack of potatoes and Enzo covers him with a blanket.

"I'll take care of this from here." Enzo says.

"I'm going with you."

"Me, too." Alison adds.

He looks at us long and hard, turns to his driver-side door, and gets in. We interpret his silence as approval, and Alison and I spin around the side of the warehouse and head for her car.

He passes by us while we walk. When he gets to the parking lot exit, his brake lights come on.

He's waiting for us.

We rode to the convention center in Alison's car with her driving, but I'm behind the wheel now. Enzo's obeying every rule of the road, with good reason, and I'm following suit. I suspect he's going to the fish piers again, and thus far our route indicates as much. Alison climbs into the back seat and retrieves a workout gym bag that has been sitting in her Fiat for months. She trades her damp jeans for stretchy yoga pants and a sweatshirt and hops back into the front seat.

"Jon, I don't know what to say. You were willing to give up your life trying to save mine."

A hot tear forms on my eye and begins its trek down my cheek. There's nothing I can do to make it stop. She raises a finger and catches the droplet, and at the same time gently caresses my face.

"Thank you. Thank you so much."

"I would do it again." I whisper.

After fifteen minutes or so, we arrive at the fish piers, as I suspected, and drive down the access road alongside his building. This feels like the Reyes show all over again. I pull up close to the SUV to provide cover for hauling Harold out of the back. I would much rather have Alison go home, but I know there's no way she's going to let me out of her sight. Enzo unlocks the building and goes inside. After roughly a minute, he comes back out, leaving the door propped open.

"Ready?" He says to me.

"Babe, why don't you go inside first, and we'll be right behind you."

Alison does as instructed while Enzo and I arrange ourselves on either side of the rear of the SUV.

"As soon as we remove him from the back, we need to move as quickly as possible inside. How's your arm?"

"Never better."

Enzo counts to three and we have him up, out of the car, inside, and on the building floor in less than fifteen seconds. Enzo locks the door behind us.

It's at this moment I feel as though I can take a deep breath and begin calming down somewhat. Enzo flops down on a stool, bends over and wraps his arms around himself in some type of pathetic self-hug. He looks terrible. Probably hasn't slept – or showered – in days.

"I don't know what to say, Enzo. We'd be dead if it wasn't for you."

"I saw what you did back there. You're one of the bravest men I've ever met. Ever."

"I have so many questions …" I trail off.

"I'm sure, and I have a lot to tell you. But first, we need to process him." He looks over to Harold, still wrapped up in the blanket lying on the floor. "What I do want to tell you before we start is that I learned he was the one who controlled everything. Nothing went down without his direction."

"We got a feel for that at the warehouse."

"Alison, honey," Enzo says, "could you go into the office for a little while? Jon and I need to deal with this."

"Yes. Of course."

I think she's relieved to be excused. After she leaves the room, Enzo addresses me:

"I'll get the drum. We'll shimmy him in like Reyes, weight him down, and then drench him."

'Drench him.' He crudely refers to the technique of dousing the body in corrosive acid to dissolve his flesh. Oddly, I'm not affected one iota by this progression. Enzo rolls the bright blue drum over to Harold and positions the opening at his head. I lift it, and Enzo slides the drum. I lift his shoulders, Enzo slides more. I lift his waist, Enzo finishes sliding. Each of us takes a side and we tip the barrel up so Harold's legs are the only body parts protruding. We've got this process down pat. Harold is much easier than Reyes. He's shorter and lighter, so there's less effort; and he's still alive so no rigor mortis is present. It makes for stuffing his legs below the rim of the drum quite easy.

Enzo drags a bag of weights over to the barrel and strategically places them into the drum. He repeats the process, only this time with a five-gallon plastic bucket containing the acid. Damn, we're gonna do this with him alive. Fuck 'em.

"Enzo, let me do it. Please."

He pauses and exhales deeply. "Are you sure? Once you do this, you can never go back." He warns.

"Yes. I'm sure ... wait ... do you have another full bucket?"

"Yes."

"Let's do it together."

He smiles a wan smile and retrieves another bucket.

Enzo unscrews the cap on his bucket. "Okay. You stay on your side, I'll stay on mine. I don't have to tell you to be careful. This stuff is nasty. On three. Ready? One ... two ... three."

We both begin pouring the acid and it sizzles and smokes almost immediately. Harold's body twitches and convulses sporadically.

"Can he feel that?" I ask.

"No. It's reflexive. I wish he could feel it."

Me too. I picture his face melting and perhaps his lungs filling with acid until it chews through his innards.

After we drain both of our buckets, Enzo places the blue cover on the drum and begins his process of sealing it shut with the heated glue gun.

"Now what?" I ask. "We can't move him, yet."

"Nope. We have to wait for nightfall. Now we just sit."

Alison comes out from the back office and pulls up a stool to sit with us. She's quiet; I think she knows Harold's in the drum by the door but she's not asking. I'm not offering.

"So ... first off ..." I begin. "Thank you for saving our lives – again. This is getting to be a habit for you."

Enzo half-smiles.

"Man, I have so many questions ... how did you know?"

He undertakes a long, tired pause. "Probably makes sense to let you know what I've been up to."

"Sure. We've been wondering."

"As you might imagine, I've spent a great deal of time reflecting upon the last few weeks, particularly the events leading up to your mom's passing."

Enzo stops to compose himself and regroup. "I skipped steps. I skipped safety steps when we were traveling." He's looking at the floor and almost-imperceptibly shaking his head side-to-side.

"I've walked through it countless times. We must have been discovered when we drove to the convention center with you that one day. I never knew anything about Osterman or his role – at least then. He had to have been watching us."

"How did you find out about Osterman? He said you killed his brother. Did you know Osterman and Jacob were brothers, or half-brothers?" I'm peppering him with questions and he gives me a 'slow down' hand gesture.

"No. Not right away. Like I said, I didn't know anything about Osterman, and I thought Jacob was harmless. I was partially ... or mostly right. He was harmless; but his brother wasn't."

Christ, I'm on the edge of my seat.

Enzo continues. "I thought a lot about Brown and of him being a 'loose end' we needed to contend with. I didn't want to make the same mistake with Jacob, so I went to his house to have a talk with him yesterday late afternoon. I intended to only have a discussion with him and if it progressed into something more, then so be it."

Alison fidgets on her stool but says nothing, appearing to detach herself from the conversation. Maybe it's a function of her survival instinct. Conversely, I'm completely mesmerized by Enzo's recollection.

"Over the years, I've learned Jacob's habits. He wasn't home at the time I went over, and I didn't expect him to be. He would have panicked if he was there when I showed up. I let myself inside intending to simply wait for him."

'I let myself inside.' Enzo-code for breaking and entering.

"In the meantime, I walked around his house inspecting his stuff and when I got to the living room, I saw a bunch of framed pictures dispersed throughout. In many of the photos, Jacob and Osterman were in them together as kids and adults, and although I didn't know who Osterman was, I knew I had seen him before."

"Where?" I'm nearly standing now.

"I definitely saw him go into the warehouse when we were waiting for you that day, and I think I may have seen him on news coverage about the building explosion."

"That got you suspicious?"

"No, not right away, but it made me curious. After a short time, Jacob came home and I was sitting on his couch waiting for him. As you might imagine, he was very upset and nervous. We had a fairly pleasant conversation; as pleasant as could be under the circumstances. He knew he had an indictment pending and his goose was cooked."

"The news reported that last night as well." I add.

"Yeah, I caught that. So," he says, redirecting the conversation, "Jacob was convinced I was there to kill him in his house. He apologized for Sabrina. He said he never wanted that to happen and he was sorry he lost control over Brown to his brother. That's when I found out."

"He told you Osterman was his brother?" I ask incredulously.

"Yeah, indirectly. I think he either thought I already knew about him or maybe he just forgot I didn't know about him. Either way, I played it off like I knew what he was talking about. I pointed to pictures of him and his brother, asking if they were close growing up. He said they used to be, but they've drifted apart over these last years as his brother started to spin out of control with the scheme. That's all the acknowledgment I needed to piece this together."

"Did you kill Jacob?"

"Actually, no."

"He jumped? I can't believe it."

"Yes, he did. He asked me if I was going to take his life. I was vague. I said, 'Should I?' Truth be told, I likely would have. He begged me not to, saying he needed to do it himself. I never said a word."

"Well, God damn."

"Right? He said he would jump off of Veteran's Bridge at sundown; which was only an hour or so away from happening. I said, 'Okay, when it's time to go, I'll follow you.' I was very in tune to him trying to escape, but he didn't break. An hour later, he drove to the bridge, hopped out of his car, and over he went. No fanfare, no display."

"Wow. Unbelievable; and yet, not so much."

"I am certain of one thing."

"What's that?"

"This truly is over. There's no one left … except him." He nods to Harold in the corner.

Alison visibly straightens up on her stool. That's a positive sign.

Enzo explains further. "In that final hour before we left, I went through every detail with Jacob. Bond's murder – we suspected Brown, but it was on Osterman's order. Danny's death – the same. Harold would have been the only loose end left had we not addressed it."

"So you left Jacob at the bridge. You then turned your attention to Osterman?"

"Yes. I found his home easily through an internet search, but I couldn't access him. There were too many people around him within a crowded neighborhood. I was in no rush anyway, as long as I could watch him. Predictably, the call about his brother came around dinner time and he raced out of the neighborhood. I followed."

"Where did he go? The bridge?"

"Yeah. The bridge. The police station. Then he went to each of your apartments and sat in his car. Then he went to the warehouse." He's ticking off Harold's locations.

"By this time, the sun was beginning to rise. He went inside the building for the better chunk of the morning. I just sat watching. Around nine o'clock or so, he drove next door to get food. I flew around back to wait. I thought it would be the perfect opportunity to take care of business, until I saw the two of you show up. His objective became crystal-clear to me at that moment. I went in through the back door. Boxes were stacked up providing me with some good cover. I knew I needed to wait for the right moment where he was positioned close enough to me to drug him. I had my pistol trained on him the entire time, though I didn't want to shoot him there if I could have helped it. I wanted him to disappear – no body, no mess, no evidence."

"Damn, you cut it close."

"I didn't tell you I was there because I didn't want you to have to try and act casual. It was a good situation for me to take him out. He would be distracted and taken completely off-guard."

"What if he just shot us?"

"Eh. You did fine. I had my gun set on him the entire time. He didn't stand a chance."

I think back to the moment, walking through the chain of events in my mind. "Osterman must've walked back to the warehouse from the restaurant. I didn't see any cars when we left."

"Now that you mention it, you're right. His car's probably still there."

The three of us spend some more time discussing Osterman and Jacob and the trail of misery they left behind. We had a purging of sorts; a catharsis whereby we tried to expel their evil from our souls. The remainder of our afternoon consists of passing time until nightfall, relating stories of Mom, Danny, and even a little bit of my father.

At half-past six, we're more than ready to finish what we came here for. Harold's already fastened to the hand dolly. We need only wheel him out to the end of the wharf, hook him up to the winch, and drop him into the channel.

"Alison, are you good with going to the car by yourself?" I ask.

"I'd like to come with you, if that's okay."

"Yeah, no problem."

Enzo gets behind the dolly's hand rails and I help tilt the drum back. I can hear Harold sloshing around inside. Carefully, we wheel him out of the building, down the transition ramp, and onto the wharf. As we walk its length, the uneven surface causes the dolly to jostle and rattle.

Comfy Harold?

At the end of the wharf, Enzo swings the winch arm over to us using the mechanical control buttons and connects the steel hook to the drum. He raises the drum and positions it in approximately the same spot as he did with Reyes.

He presents the control device to us where his thumb is poised over a big green button.

"All together now?" Enzo inquires.

Alison and I place our thumbs next to his on the green button.

"On three." Enzo instructs. "One … two … three."

58

L ife goes by so fast. Everything can change in the blink of an eye. Believe me on that, I'm the living proof. Alison, too. It's amazing; one moment you're headed down a path certain, or so you think, and the next, you've veered in a completely new direction. One year has gone by since Mom passed. It feels more like a day. I have a new recurring dream about her to go along with the home run dream I have of my dad. It's of when we left the hotel that terrible day and Mom was walking out to the Cougar. Before she gets in the car, she stops and waves. I wave back to her, but then in my dream, instead of getting into Alison's car, I walk over and ask if I can ride with her. She's thrilled with the offer and we both get in. I know right away something isn't right – I can feel it and I instruct her not to start the car, but to slowly and carefully open the door and get out. I do the same. Enzo sees us and drives over to find out what the issue is. I tell him I'm not certain, but something doesn't feel right to me with the car, I just know it. He performs his check of the vehicle and discovers it's wired to blow. Mom gets in the Mercedes with Enzo and we all pull out together, leaving the Cougar behind. Enzo and Mom happily go on the vacation they were planning to take. Like my other dream, I inevitably wake up realizing there is no fairy-tale ending.

Alison and I have settled into a pretty awesome routine. She's the peanut butter to my jelly. I just left her at the apartment, actually; I'm on my way into work. In fact, I'm just pulling into the parking lot. We did finally take that cruise; we only got back a couple of weeks ago. She and I have become completely intertwined, emotionally and physically.

I lock Danny's Jeep (it will forever be Danny's Jeep) and walk through the front door where I see Sharon answering the telephone. She waves excitedly to me as she greets whoever's on the other end.

"J.K. Williams, P.A., how may I direct your call? Oh, hi Alison, how are you?!" She gushes effusively. "Yes, he just got here. Give us a minute so he can get over to his office and I'll put you right through. It's so nice talking to you, too! Alright, hang on, Alison."

Hmm. Why didn't she call me on my cell? I step into my office and answer the phone on the first ring. "Well, hello there stranger, can't get enough of me?"

"I absolutely can't get enough of you! I know you're super-busy right now, but I hope you always have time for me."

I look around my newly-appointed office. I have practically no clients and no files to speak of. Only a couple of pictures and a new CPA certificate hanging on an otherwise bare wall.

"Yeah, well, I am over my head with client deadlines, but I can squeeze you in. What's up?"

"Nothing really. I wanted to let you know you left your phone at home, and I'm also trying to plan out my day and wondered what you felt like for dinner tonight. I meant to ask you before you left."

That explains why she called me on the office line. "I have an idea ... let's get wild and go to A's tonight."

"You don't have to twist my arm! I'm in."

"Perfect. See you after work. And I'll even drive."

"Oh baby, you spoil me!"

My day is slow, but that's to be expected. It takes more than I realized and expected to get the firm off the ground and up and running, but I'm up for it. When it came time to name the firm, Alison suggested I go with 'J.K.' in tribute to Mom. I rather like the nickname now and I think it lends an air of professionalism and panache to the business.

I'm looking through my old client list to see who I could potentially pick off, when Sharon appears at the door.

"There's someone out here to see you. He says his name is Jack Wallace." She whispers conspiratorially.

Jack Wallace. Jack Wallace. Where do I know a Jack Wallace? Ahhh ... yes. Jack Wallace. My bus ticket.

"Oh, great! Send him in, please. He's an old friend of mine. One I haven't seen in a long time."

When Sharon sees my confusion transform into enthusiasm, she brightens back to her old self. She disappears through the door and in a moment Enzo walks in.

"Hey, catch that door." I say, getting up. When he turns around I give him a big bear hug.

"Jack Wallace? Wasn't that my alias?" I ask jokingly. "How the hell are you, man?"

"Good Jon, I'm doing okay."

"Whew, you look a lot better since the last time I saw you." I'm not just saying that, he really does. He looks like the old Enzo; stylishly dressed and gold jewelry adorned in his customary places.

"Well, the last time you saw me I hadn't slept in a long time."

"Or showered, either." I joke.

"True."

"What the heck have you been up to? Is everything okay? How did you find me?"

"Whoa, slow it down. You ramble on when you're excited. I've discovered that about you. Nothing's wrong. I only went away for a while like I said I would, and I wanted to come back and see how you're doing. Alison, too. I found you by following you this morning when you left the apartment. I was driving up just as you left."

"Awesome! Are you local tonight? We can get dinner. We were gonna go to A's, but we can switch it up."

"Sounds good. I'd like that. And I love the name of your company. Sabrina would be so proud of you."

"Thanks, Enzo. The name was Alison's idea and it's a tribute to Mom for sure. As far as what's been going on here, obviously you see I got a new place. Alison helped me pull all of this together and she's been working behind the scenes, but she doesn't want to jump in full steam."

"Cool. Why the change?"

"Harding-Williams went belly-up. They closed the doors. You knew Alison and I were quitting anyway, right? Funny thing is; it folded before we quit, so we each ended up getting a pretty nice severance payment out of it."

"Was it because of General Defense?"

"Pretty much. The old building was gone. Their reputation was shattered when the cover was blown off of the GD scam, and they were hemorrhaging personnel. I don't know if you've followed the story, but the Feds pieced together Osterman and Jacob. We gave them Bob's certifications of his responsibility on the audits and no one's ever questioned our involvement or lack thereof."

"Amazing. I'm glad it's worked out."

"Totally. We never shared Bob's letter with anyone. We didn't want to give up the money. Everyone thinks Bob was working for Osterman. I don't think Bob had a clue about Osterman."

"I don't either. So, you decide to go into the accounting business yourself?"

"Yeah. I figured I could pick off some of the smaller clients and build a little practice. Who knows? Honestly, I'm not much interested in getting big. I just want a modest, manageable practice for other reasons beyond being a business owner."

"Oh? What reasons?"

"Well … Only one really."

He's waiting for me to go on.

"A wise man once told me to be careful how I put my money to work. I believe the phrase he used was, 'If you can wash it – do it'."

Enzo's eyebrows rise up high on his forehead. "Is that so?" He replies with drawn-out intrigue. "Well J.K. Williams, you have learned a thing or two over this past year."

"You could say that."

"Perhaps you might help me with my laundry?" He asks inquisitively.

The one-time laundromat owner requesting my laundering services. What a bizarre turn of events.

"Perhaps I might."

ACKNOWLEDGMENTS

Every story has its roots in truth, and this story is no different. Everyday events, as they happen, may seem inconsequential and perhaps a bit boring. But we draw on those experiences and they shape our behaviors, our relationships, and how we perceive this awesome world we live in. From those seeds of experience can come the most wonderful tales.

My wife, Jennifer, has been by my side for a lifetime. We've grown up together and I thank her immensely and without reservation for her consistent support and encouragement. My two children, Ian and Sydney – IanSydious – have inspired me more than they could ever know. Guys, you've taught me so much more than I've ever taught you.

Owen Wells, you've opened my eyes to the world and provided me with opportunities I could never have predicted in my wildest dreams. You took a chance on me, and I'm forever grateful to have you not just as my mentor, but as a part of my family.

As a child, I got into my fair share of hi-jinx. Usually, my brother Eric was by my side; most often as the instigator, though he would likely argue that! There are nuggets of our shared adventures liberally sprinkled within these pages.

This book would not exist without the encouragement of Chris Emmons. When I told him about this crazy idea for a novel, he pushed me to put pen to paper – so I did. After finishing a handful of chapters, his enthusiastic review gave me the confidence and energy to go for it, and I'm not sure this would have happened otherwise.

To Aaron Baltes, one of my oldest and closest friends, a sincere thank you for your considerable and measured copy edit and review. You let me know whenever my shoes came untied and didn't press me when I insisted upon walking around with my laces purposefully undone.

And lastly, thank you dear Reader, for without you I would have no one to confide in and unburden my soul of the weight of this Deadly Account.